Grandmother's House

Also by Janet LaPierre

The Cruel Mother
Children's Games
Unquiet Grave

■

Grandmother's House

A Port Silva Mystery

■

Janet LaPierre

Charles Scribner's Sons
New York

Maxwell Macmillan Canada
Toronto

Maxwell Macmillan International
New York Oxford Singapore Sydney

M
LAPIERRE

Charles Scribner's Sons   Maxwell Macmillan Canada, Inc.
Macmillan Publishing Company   1200 Eglinton Avenue East
866 Third Avenue   Suite 200
New York, NY 10022   Don Mills, Ontario M3C 3N1

Macmillan Publishing Company is part of the Maxwell Communication Group of Companies.

Library of Congress Cataloging-in-Publication Data

LaPierre, Janet.
    Grandmother's house : a Port Silva mystery / Janet Lapierre.
        p.   cm.
    ISBN 0-684-19382-5
    I. Title.
    PS3562.A624G7   1992   91-27596
    813'.54—dc20   CIP

10 9 8 7 6 5 4 3 2 1

Printed in the United States of America

Book Design by Diane Stevenson, SNAP•HAUS GRAPHICS

This book is dedicated to the town of Fort Bragg, California, from whose atmosphere and landscape I have borrowed so liberally in furnishing my own town of Port Silva.

Author's
Note

There were Finnish communes on the west coast in the early 1900s, but the one I refer to in this novel is entirely fictitious. Finn Hall, however, is quite real, borrowed in all its blue and white splendor from Berkeley, California.

■

■

C h a p t e r
O n e

■

T he house was made of wood: sturdy siding painted a soft
gray-green, frames, roof brackets, the cornice above the
doorway and the door itself a darker green. It was really a cottage raised above a basement, not large but airy and full of
light; inside, it had the slight springiness of a healthy old tree.
It had stood on its lot for nearly a hundred years, and Charlotte
Birdsong thought it could probably stand for another hundred
if given the chance.

They had lived in it almost four years, the longest time she
had spent in any one house in her whole life. She could be here
in the kitchen chopping celery and know without lifting her
head just what lay around her. Former dining room now music
room at the front, home to her grand piano; living room across
from that, with its slanted bay window and clinker brick fireplace; her bedroom and the bathroom behind the living room.
And along the back the old sleeping porch now split into a sunny
breakfast room and Petey's big bedroom, his sanctuary. Every
now and then such familiarity sent Charlotte off to a flea market
in search of a ladder-backed chair or a bright afghan to jar
things loose a little.

As she scooped the celery into the skillet where onion and
leeks were simmering with bacon pieces, the clock in the music
room struck a single note. Three-thirty, said the part of her
mind that worried and kept track of things; which made it likely
that Petey had chosen not to come directly home from school
today.

Charlotte twisted the tops off a bunch of carrots with more force than was necessary. If they should lose the house, she knew that any sadness on her part would be quickly dispelled in the pleasure of a new road, to a different place. Her son, however, lacked her nomad's heart. From babyhood a keeper, a holder-on, Petey had planted himself here like an oak tree and was likely to resist being uprooted with all his considerable strength. And as much of hers as she could muster, she thought with a sigh.

She had a row of scraped carrots lined up like little soldiers on the cutting board when footsteps sounded on the back stairs. The figure outside the steam-clouded panes was tall, and familiar; Charlotte called "Come in," as he rapped.

"Charlotte, you shouldn't just yell 'Come in.'" Val Kuisma pushed the door shut behind him and set a paper bag on the floor so he could remove his down vest. "In fact, with so many strangers in the neighborhood you really ought to keep your doors locked."

"Whenever I do that I lock myself out."

Val rolled his eyes at her and picked up the bag to carry it to the refrigerator. He opened a bottle of Sierra Nevada ale for himself, offered her one and then poured her a glass of white wine instead, this last arranged via a series of glances and nods that reminded her comfortably of what good friends they had become during the three months he had been renting the studio apartment in her basement.

Now he settled into the high-backed wooden rocker with his beer, the fingers of his free hand stroking the satiny wood of the chair's arm. "I was headed for my place to sulk, and I noticed you were cooking instead of teaching. Music lessons generally don't steam up the windows," he added in explanation. "I hope you don't mind, Charlotte. Thing is, you're the only person I like these days, or at least the only one who likes me."

She gave him a quick smile, to assure him that she was glad of his company. "I guess Chief Gutierrez wasn't willing to override the doctor and let you return to work?"

"Hah!" said Val, in what Charlotte, wincing, suspected was a direct quote. "Chief Vince Gutierrez does not second-guess doctors. Chief Vince Gutierrez says that if I'd followed the doctor's advice *and* the department rules in the first place, my leg would no doubt be completely healed by now."

"I see." Still working his way back from the effects of a bad motorcycle smash, Val had been told to take things easy. Then two weeks ago a celebration planned to mark the second anniversary of demonstrations against oil drilling on the California north coast had developed into a major display of muscle and opinion by environmentalists. As representatives of every group from Abalone Alliance through Earth First! to the Wilderness Society converged on Port Silva, Val had insisted on hitting the street with his colleagues and had hit it harder than he meant to. Charlotte thought his frustration was compounded by the fact that he'd been felled by people whose politics he approved.

Wind slapped the house, rattling the panes in the breakfast room and sending a chilly draft through the kitchen. Charlotte tossed a quick glance at her visitor and noted that his olive skin was flushed above the curly black beard, his green eyes glittering; pushing off with his good foot, he was rocking the big chair as fast and hard as he could.

Maybe Val was catching cold, like half the people in town, including several of her piano students. She added diced carrots to the simmering vegetables, gave the lot a good stir, then touched a finger to the fat flank of the teakettle and found it still hot.

"Anyway, I can stay on medical leave and go crazy. I can hang around the cop shop and help the clerks. I can probably put in some unofficial time looking for that guy who disappeared. What I can't do is go back on patrol." He rocked on in glum silence for a minute or two, then brought the chair to a sudden halt and said suspiciously, "What's that?"

"Hot whiskey," she said, and handed him a steaming glass with a cinnamon stick for stirrer. "Lemon, cloves, lots of good stuff. Much nicer on a cold day than beer."

He frowned, lifted the glass to sniff, sniffed again. Took a cautious sip. "Mm. Thanks."

"You're welcome. Has nothing turned up on the missing Mr. Boylan? There was a story in the paper this morning," she explained in response to his raised eyebrows. "An interview with his wife, poor woman."

Val shook his head, his expression changing from personal irritation to a somber concern. "Not a whisper. It's been almost a week, and the guy might have stepped off the edge of the earth for all we can find out."

Here on the precipitous north coast, thought Charlotte, such a fate was not metaphor but real possibility. "His wife clearly feels that she, or he, is not being taken seriously."

"Off the record, Charlotte, you don't start an immediate dogs and helicopters search for a competent adult with no known medical problem when there's no evidence of foul play. And this particular guy has a history of drinking and playing hard after work; he's a developer and I understand he'd just brought off a big deal."

The warmth of the drink, and of the kitchen with its good smells, was smoothing the jagged edges of his temper, loosening the knots in his muscles. Val settled himself against the chair's high back, took another deep lemony inhalation, another sip. "Hey, this stuff is terrific, it's going to turn me back into a human being. Anyway, I can understand Mrs. Boylan's feelings, but I assure you that we're doing everything we can to find her husband." The pendulum clock in the music room interrupted with its mellow bong; counting the four strokes, he looked up to see Charlotte doing the same.

"What's the matter, Charlotte?" Worry, he thought, sat oddly on that round face with its wide brown eyes and high color. Charlotte was no more than five feet two, and beneath an apron wore her usual garb: sneakers, jeans, and a man's white shirt with the sleeves rolled over her forearms. Only the flecks of silver in her short black curls testified to the fact that she was in her mid-thirties and mother of a thirteen-year-old son.

And there was the surest source of worry for this balanced and savvy lady. "Pete not home yet?"

She shook her head without looking at him. "He took his good bike today. I suppose he's out on the back roads with his friends."

"You *suppose?*"

"Petey is very good about . . . about not doing the things I ask him not to do." There was a hint of defensiveness in her voice. "So I try to keep the list short."

"Okay. So why are you so upset now?"

"Oh, because *he* was upset this morning. He's worried about the house, and I couldn't promise . . . but we'll find out more about it tonight, I think. At the meeting at the Bluejay Café. And I need to get this soup together so I can take it along. For tomorrow, they do a big lunch business on Saturday."

From Charlotte, who sang or whistled or hummed a lot but was spare with words, such a disjointed string of phrases was astonishing. "Meeting? Is this something Chief Gutierrez should know about?"

"Not unless Port Silva has suddenly become a police state," she said so sharply that Val snapped to attention right there in the rocker. "So far it involves only the people here on Finn Lane. I think. Just a minute, Val." She tipped the contents of the skillet into a big stockpot, set the flame under the pot as low as it would go, then untied her apron and tossed it at a chair before picking up her nearly full wineglass.

"Maybe you should have a hot whiskey, too," he suggested uneasily.

"No, I'm not a very good drinker. The man who owned much of the Finn Lane property died recently, in San Diego. Apparently no one here knew about it until the tenants in number 22 learned their lease wouldn't be renewed. Then on Monday those of us on the Lane who own our houses got letters from the lawyer representing the widow, saying we could expect substantial offers. We're to meet with him at the Bluejay tonight at eight." She gave a small, helpless shrug, and moved into the music room, past the big piano to the window where she stood gazing out. Val got to his feet and limped after her.

"It's so . . . not pretty. Cheerful," she decided. "Cheerful and unusual. What do you suppose will happen to it?"

Following her glance, Val saw that "it" was Finn Hall, a three-story wooden building with many windows, a broad, pillared entryway, and decoratively railed balconies echoing the entry at the upper stories. The building itself was painted a gleaming white, the rails and window frames and any other elements distinct from the siding a bright and glossy blue.

"What do you mean, happen to it?" Val had gone to Boy Scout meetings in the Hall's echoing rooms, to Luther League, to dances and songfests, even, briefly, to Finnish lessons. With a long history of being useful as well as cheerful, the Hall was presently a temporary refuge for about two dozen homeless people. "It belongs to the town. Or maybe to the church."

"I'm afraid not. The city only leases it, and the park too. They belong to the San Diego widow."

"Well, shit." Swallowing the last of his now-lukewarm whiskey, Val stared out the window. Finn Hall sat on its own small headland, a grassy, tree-fringed plot larger than a city block with the Pacific as its north and west boundaries, the curving dead-end street called Finn Lane marking south and east. The whole area had belonged communally to a group of Finns sometime around the turn of the century; they had built the dozen or so houses on the Lane, they had built their Hall. At some point the communal scheme was set aside, and individual families took title to houses. Although several of the little wooden houses were now in poor repair, local Finns regularly spruced up the Hall, and Val had assumed, without really thinking about it, that they owned it. "God damn."

"That's more or less what Petey said."

"Maybe there's something we can do," he said, not very hopefully. On his way to the kitchen with his empty glass, he found his eye caught by something familiar atop a stack of papers on a side table. "Charlotte, where did you get this?"

"I guess it was with the junk mail today; I didn't really look at it."

The letter-sized sheet of paper was a copy of a very simple line drawing. At the top of the page was a house, with a peaked roof, a gabled doorway, a not-very-plumb chimney issuing a curl of smoke, and a sun beaming down from above. Below the house was a larger building, with arches and crenellated towers: a castle. The artist had drawn a heavy circle around the castle, and then a slashing line top left to bottom right. Four words were printed beneath: Real Places/Real People. At bottom, like a signature, was a small tilted tombstone bearing the letters R.I.P.

"It looks like something a six-year-old might draw," she remarked, peering around him to inspect it.

"Haven't you seen flyers like this around town?"

"I don't think so."

"Then you haven't been paying attention. The last one was about sheep."

"Oh. Wait a minute." Charlotte hurried out of the room, to return with another sheet of paper. "This was on Petey's bulletin board, between a no-oil-drilling poster and a Friends of the Sea Otter poster."

It was tattered at the edges and appeared to have been rained on. Big letters S O S perched like a tiara above the head of a sad-faced sheep. "Save Our Sheep!" said the block-printed words beneath. "Or you might have to wear Chardonnay to keep warm."

"Save our sheep. And I suppose this latest one means 'no castles.' In other words, no developers?"

"That would be my reading," said Val.

Charlotte touched a finger to the bottom of the tattered page, where the little tombstone tilted again. "Now that I think about it, I find this a rather ominous logo. Val, I saw the big anniversary parade, or most of it, and I didn't see anyone carrying a sign like this. What is this group?"

"I don't know. Truly, Charlotte," he added in response to her skeptical look. "I don't, and so far as I've heard we, the police, don't. Might be a large number of concerned but quiet people, might be just a few who are radically committed to a cause. Officially they don't exist; even Earth First! is more up-front than these Rip guys."

"Rip? I assumed the letters stood for 'Rest in Peace.' "

"They probably do, or did. I think the logo is a reference to their first big battle, to stop a developer from moving an old graveyard from a ridge site so he could build townhouses there. They won."

"*Did* they. How, Val?"

"Well. There was the usual stuff: surveyors' stakes torn up, fences cut, equipment damaged, even a creek diverted to flood the site. Then they dug up personal info on the developers and some county officials . . . bankruptcies, foreclosures, penalties, arrest records, delinquency in child support. And publicized it." He brandished the flyer and then dropped it on the piano.

"Oh, my. And have they successfully stopped developments besides the graveyard?"

"I think they've stopped a couple and slowed down others."

"Have they hurt anyone? I mean a person, not property."

"Not so far as I know, but I haven't been on any of the investigations. I did hear that they may have, um, burned down a house. That is, they were suspected of setting fire to some building material, and the fire spread to a house." Val paused, aware that he was coming close to indiscretion with police information. "Charlotte, how many people on the Lane own their houses?"

"Buck and Billy, Joe James. The Duartes; Harry has been stamping and snorting since the letters came and Lucy looks excited. The Lees own, of course. Jennifer Mardian, I think. And me, or rather Petey. Those are the only ones I know for sure."

"Petey?" A cheerful face and a frank curiosity about his fellow man won Val, usually, a satisfying flood of information. But not with Charlotte; during the three months he'd known her,

Charlotte had heard the whole boring story of his life while revealing almost nothing about her own. "How come . . . ?"

But Charlotte had had enough of personal questions. "I'll ask you to excuse me, Val. I have a student coming in just a few minutes."

Chapter
Two

■

T he bike came around the curve at a sharp lean, studded
tires throwing up gouts of mud. The rider crouched low
over the handlebars, pedaling furiously; tree-filtered winter sunlight drew sparks from wild red curls and made the clenched
white face whiter still.

"Hannah!" Taking advantage of a brief downhill stretch, the
closer of the two following bikers used his greater weight and
longer legs to make up the twenty yards or so separating him
from the girl. "Look," Petey Birdsong gasped, releasing his right
handlebar to gesture at a sign on a fencepost: Mendo Dairy
Cooperative.

"Johanson's place," he said, and straightened to gulp big
drafts of air as Hannah slowed her pace and allowed him to pull
even with her. "There's a little side road along here someplace.
Off to the right. Okay?"

She didn't look at him but jerked her head in a quick down-
up nod. He stood on his pedals, glanced over his shoulder and
made a "follow me" wave to their friend, Eddie Duarte, still
trailing.

The side road, really a pair of muddy ruts with patchy grass
between, wound through high brush and skirted a small hill
before turning left to meander along the face of another, longer
up-slope. Petey braked at this last turn, stepped free of his bike
to let it fall and flung himself down on the grass of the hillside,
eyes skyward. "Wow," he said, softly and to himself.

Hannah dropped to the ground beside him, tucking herself into a tight bundle of drawn-up knees and wrapped-around arms. Eddie tossed his bike atop the others with a clatter. His olive skin was shiny with sweat, his dark eyes ringed in white.

"Whoo-ee," he said on a long outgust of breath. "Hey, Hannah, you look kinda green. Pretty scared, huh?"

"No, I . . ." She lifted her chin and scowled at him. "You'd have to be totally stupid not to be scared when somebody shoots at you."

"I don't think he was shooting *at* us, exactly," said Petey. "More like just one barrel over our heads, to scare us."

"Listen, man, I heard stuff whistle right past me," said Eddie.

Hannah, who had turned her gaze on Petey, now reached out and touched his down jacket, where the puffy garment lay loose around his skinny hips. "Petey. There's a hole there. A little round hole."

He sat up and tugged at the jacket, pulling it around for a closer look. "Um, yeah. Look at that, there's two of them."

"Petey, what's your mom going to say?" asked Hannah.

"She won't even notice."

"Here's what I think, Petey." Hannah rested her chin on her knees and stared straight ahead. "You better not do this stuff anymore."

"What're you talking about?"

"Eddie and I are small for our age. Anybody that sees us would think we're just kids messing around. But you're so tall, from a distance you probably look like a man."

"You guys!" Speaking in a harsh whisper, Eddie waved them to silence. "There's somebody over there. Get down!"

All three threw themselves flat, faces buried between outstretched arms. After some moments Hannah lifted her head, listened, then inched up the slope to part the thin screen of brush at the top. "Nothing to do with us, just some people camping," she reported in a low voice.

The other side of their grassy slope fell steeply away to a creek. Beyond the creek the land stretched flat for perhaps fifty yards, populated by scattered rocks, old Douglas firs and valley oaks, and today by a big green tent as well.

"Hey, a bunch of hippies!" said Eddie. "Camping on Mr. Johanson's land, he'll be really pissed."

"He never puts his cows down here, why would he care?" said Petey.

"Your property is your property, man!" Eddie, twitching with suppressed energy, pounded a fist on the ground for emphasis.

"Bullshit," said Hannah, and lurched sideways to give Eddie a nudge that made him grab at a bush for purchase. "Land shouldn't be owned; it should just be used with respect, by whoever needs it. And it's not a couple of campers in a tent that mess up a watershed. Hey, Petey," she added, rolling onto her belly again to observe the trespassers, "didn't we see those guys before, the day of the demonstration march?"

The three people moving about before the tent were just ordinary no-particular-age adults to the thirteen-year-olds watching them. Denim- and down-clad, like anybody out in the woods on a chilly winter day. The two men were tall, the dark-haired one sipping from a steaming mug of something while the other, blond hair tied in a ponytail, warmed his hands at the campfire. The woman splitting kindling with a hatchet was short, her head crowned by an explosion of curly bright hair.

"I dunno," said Petey.

Hannah gave an impatient wriggle that took her closer to the edge of the bank. "That woman, anyway. She was hanging out with some Earth First! guys, all of them smoking pot right there on the street. My mom says that kind of hippie behavior is counterproductive."

"These guys don't look any *kind* of productive to me." Eddie slid backward and rolled to his feet. "Let's tell Mr. Johanson. Then let's go home and get something to eat. I'm starved."

Petey said "Unh-hunh," but stayed where he was. In the clearing below, the woman added a small log to the fire, set her hatchet against a tree, and disappeared into the tent. The dark-haired man filled his mug from a pot set by the fire before following her.

A second woman came from the tent. She set a basin on a table, tossed aside down vest and sweatshirt, peeled off a turtleneck and began to wash. Her long straight hair shimmered, now red, now gold; her skin was so white that even from this far away Petey could see her large pink nipples.

"Hey, Petey, are you coming?"

He thought he caught a pause, like a brief freeze-frame; then she went on soaping her breasts, must not have heard Hannah's voice after all.

"Oh, wow!" Hannah breathed the words softly as she squatted beside him. "I'm going to have boobs like that pretty soon; my mom says hers were awesome before she had three kids."

Sounds from two directions now: rustles and a muttered "What's up?" as Eddie came back, and from across the stream a low murmur, words not distinguishable, as the pony-tailed man approached the woman and said something to her.

Her lips moved in a brief, inaudible reply, one long white arm sweeping the glowing hair high and to the side to bare her neck to the washcloth. The man bent closer, spoke again. When she ignored him he grabbed her arm, spun her around and slapped her, flesh meeting flesh with a mean sharp sound that hung in the air like something visible.

"Petey, come on right now." Hannah grabbed his jacket and yanked hard. "We should be getting home."

"Bastard," said Petey under his breath. His skin, faintly tanned even in midwinter, was stretched tight over his jaw, and a patch of angry red marked each cheekbone.

"Hey, she was practically asking for it," said Eddie. "I mean, standing around outdoors naked and all."

"Eddie Duarte," Hannah snapped, "you are such a jackass they ought to keep you chained in the backyard."

The three bikes lay in a tangle at the foot of the slope. Eddie yanked one free and set it in motion, leaping aboard as it gathered speed. Hannah got hers upright, propped it against a bush and was swinging her backpack on when Eddie returned in a spray of muddy water.

"Eddie, you . . . are you crazy or what?" She pointed an accusing finger at the wooden stick that jutted from his handlebar, the ribbon of orange plastic at its tip fluttering flaglike in the breeze of his motion. "You get rid of that right now!"

He simply grinned more broadly as he wove a tight figure eight around his two stationary companions.

"Okay," Hannah said through clenched teeth, "let's vote. How many people think Eddie Duarte should ride into town waving a surveyor's stake?"

"Hey, come on! I wasn't going into town with it, you think I'm nuts?" Eddie pulled the stake free, broke it over his knee and tossed the pieces to Petey. "Here, you got bigger pockets."

"The other thing," said Petey slowly, as he shoved the stick into his side pocket, "is, what do we do about what happened today?"

"Put it on the net," said Eddie.

"Well, I guess we could."

"Oh no," said Hannah. As the two of them eyed her, she shifted her stance and the angle of her body, composed her face and became someone else, someone looking down on them in a dark-browed judging fashion underlined by an impatient twitch of broad solid shoulders and a head-toss to send long heavy hair swinging.

"Boy, I hate it when you do that," muttered Eddie.

"So okay, we have to go by Gaia and tell Sarah we found out there's a watchman on the Tri-Star site now but he, uh, saw us," Petey said glumly, and Hannah nodded as she settled onto her bike.

"Look, you guys do it, okay? I haven't paid my dues this month, and I don't have any money with me." Without waiting for an answer, Eddie set off down the rutted path toward the road.

"I can't hang around at Gaia very long," Petey told Hannah as he let her precede him. "I need to get home and keep an eye on my mom, or she'll forget all about the neighborhood meeting tonight."

"Your mom is a wonderful person," said Hannah with some

asperity. "I'm probably the worst piano student of her whole life, but she never gets mad about it. I love your mom."

"Me, too. But sometimes I wish she was more . . . ordinary. If she had her piano and maybe her tape player, she'd probably be happy to live in that tent down there. Never mind, let's get going."

Hannah stood up on the pedals to propel her bike along the rough path. Petey followed, through low shafts of late-day sunlight that gave his passage a dark-and-light jerkiness. A ray fell across his eyes, briefly short-circuiting vision and leaving him with a picture that had somehow painted itself in his head: a pale woman washing herself in sunshine.

"Hey, Petey. Come on!"

In front of him, Hannah's bright head and small frame moved from sun into shadow, and he saw again or anyway remembered her transposing herself into Sarah Stonemountain, broad and heavy and full of dark disapproval; and the prospect of the rest of the day washed over him like cold rain.

Chapter
Three

T he back halls of the police station were surprisingly quiet
on this Friday evening. The chief's door was closed, but the
light was on in there. Val listened for a moment, heard no
voices, rapped gently.

"Yeah?"

As Val stepped into the room, Chief of Police Vincent Gutierrez took off the half-glasses he used for reading and dropped
them on the papers spread out before him. Val saw several crime
reports, two green-binder casebooks, a copy of the duty roster,
and on the corner of the desk, today's *Sentinel* with its photo of
the missing Edward Boylan.

"Kuisma, I told you . . ." Gutierrez rubbed his eyes with
thumb and forefinger and sighed. "Sorry. You know what I told
you. What's up, Val?"

"Probably no big deal, Chief, but I'm living on Finn Lane now,
and this turned up out there this morning." Val laid a copy of
the R.I.P. flyer atop the other papers. Unwilling to worry Charlotte further by asking for hers, he had instead rifled the mailbox of her neighbor, a UC-Port Silva professor who was teaching
in Berkeley this semester.

"Well, shit, that's all we need." Gutierrez rolled his chair back
to stretch and yawn. He wore a plaid wool shirt and Levi's
rather than a uniform, and his lean face was weary. "Did you
talk to anybody about it?"

"Only my landlady, Charlotte Birdsong; she'd brought it in

with a handful of junk mail and hadn't paid any attention to it. She'd never heard of Rip. But she did tell me someone's trying to buy up the property around Finn Park, so I guess there's some kind of development plan in the works."

"Whoever's behind the plan probably doesn't know it's open season on developers around here. Never mind, forget I said that. What we'll do," he said as he got to his feet, "is give this to Johnny Hebert; the Rip thing is his baby."

"I haven't heard anything about them for quite a while," Val remarked.

"It's been too wet, for building *or* for sabotage," said Gutierrez. "But that will change, eventually. I think. Listen around out there in the neighborhood, Val, and if you come across anything interesting, bring it to Johnny or to me."

"Yessir."

At eight-fifteen on a cold night in February, Finn Park was simply a vacant expanse of wet grass, muddy paths, and dripping trees, all only faintly illuminated by a light pole near Finn Hall and another at the south end, across from the Bluejay Café. Charlotte noted that the front doors of the Hall were shut tight, confining at least ten small children inside. "*If* the homeless people are still there," she said aloud. "Do you suppose the owner might have closed the Hall already?"

"She can't, yet," Petey informed her. "The city has a lease with almost two years to go, I asked Mr. Benjamin after social studies today. He's on the city council."

"Oh. That's good."

"Yeah, except he says the city will probably let the owner buy the lease out. The city could use the money and anyway, people can usually find ways to break leases."

She looked at her son, looked *up* at him as she'd been doing for more than a year. In the spill of light from a neighbor's porch, his expression was tight and angry, eyes narrowed and lips curled back from big teeth his face had not yet grown to fit. Charlotte had always understood that boys on the threshold of puberty were obsessed by sex, but Petey's juvenile passion was directed at his adopted home, from his grandmother's house to the Hall his great-grandfather had helped build, and on to the forests and coastlines of this damp northern place.

"Petey," she began, and then couldn't think of anything hopeful to say. Without asking direct questions, she had attempted over the past few days to gauge the attitudes of her neighbors and had picked up no spirit of unity, no sense that people were preparing to band together in defense of home and neighborhood. Curiosity was there, and excitement, everybody wondering what the lawyer meant by "a substantial offer." No organizer herself, and certainly no fighter, Charlotte suspected that the little green house would not be theirs much longer.

"Well, here we are," she said lamely, and squared her shoulders. "Let's go see what's happening."

Inside the Bluejay, tables had been stacked against the end wall; white plastic chairs were ranged in a double semicircle facing the counter, on one end of which a double hotplate kept two glass pots steaming.

"Charlotte, I'm so glad you finally got here. And Petey, too, how nice." Buck Watson bent from his willowy height to take Charlotte's hand between his own. "I think everyone else is here. The lawyer just arrived, he's gone in the back for a quick pee."

Charlotte looked past him: perhaps fifteen people, quite enough to make a room seem crowded. Although several of the faces were unfamiliar, most belonged to people she knew in casual, neighborly fashion. "Oh, Val Kuisma brought down your beautiful black bean soup," Buck said into her ear.

Yes, the soup. "Before you heat it tomorrow," she said, "take out the hamhock bones and the bouquet garni. And keep an eye on it; once the rice has been added, it's inclined to stick."

"Even Buck knows how to stir soup." Billy Kaplan, Buck's partner in life as well as in business, was a short man, round but not soft, with a circlet of steel-wool hair around a bald dome. "Good stuff, Charlotte. I'll pay you first of the week, okay?"

Under beetling gray brows, Billy's eyes were the blue of a clean gas flame, but cold. "Well, no," she said after a moment's hesitation. "I did the work, and I'll need to be paid for it. Several of my piano students canceled this week because of illness."

Billy blinked in astonishment. "Well. Okay, I'll give you a check, for . . . what was it last time, thirty-five dollars?"

"In fact, it was forty," said Charlotte, feeling that everyone in the room was looking at her. "But I see from your chalkboard that you've raised your price to three-fifty a cup. At nearly twelve quarts, call it forty-four cups, you'll take in a hundred fifty-four dollars for my soup. The cost of the ingredients plus two hours of my time comes to seventy dollars. And I'd like it in cash, please."

"Pushy, *pushy*," said Billy. He caught Petey's movement and said quickly, "Sorry, Pete, merely jesting," as he pulled a roll of bills from his pocket. "Twenty, forty, sixty and ten, done."

Charlotte still felt warm as she marched to a chair and sat down. Petey settled next to her, with a sidelong glance that she thought combined pride and embarrassment. "Would you get me a cup of coffee, please?" she asked him, and he got up again quickly.

"Hello, Jennifer," Charlotte said to the sturdy, russet-haired young woman in the chair to her right. "Hi, sweetie," she whispered to three-year-old Cybelle, who was dozing on her mother's lap.

Don and Marlene Cummings nodded from beyond Jennifer; retired schoolteachers now busy with painting and bird-watching, they were tenants of several years' standing and the people whose lease renewal had been refused. There was Joe James, Charlotte's neighbor to the west, a former lumberman, mill worker, and old radical who was a good friend of Petey's. And the O'Malleys, a young couple whose first names escaped her because she always thought of them as Ken and Barbie. Mr. and Mrs. Lee, who met her glance with matching polite nods of their smooth graying heads. And black-browed Harry Duarte, uncle of Petey's friend Eddie, looking as if he'd like to wrap his hard fisherman's hands around somebody's throat. Harry was alone; probably Lucy had stayed home with their little boys.

"What's the matter with Harry?" Charlotte asked Jennifer in a low voice.

"He still objects to having poor folks, or anyway *official* poor folks, quartered in his neighborhood. The kids are trained thieves and vandals, the women will be turning tricks on the picnic tables. And the tall skinny black guy probably has lice in his dreadlocks, which you and I will catch along with lots of other stuff when he rapes us."

"He's a mechanic whose wife abandoned him and their little boy," said Charlotte. "And he's very nice, except I suppose he would be wise to change his hairstyle." As a young woman from Social Services had explained to Finn Lane residents, the people being placed temporarily in the Hall were not derelicts or wandering psychotics, but ordinary working people tipped over the economic edge by bad luck, a weak job market, and a long, wet winter.

"Harry Duarte is a bigoted bastard," said Jennifer in normal speaking tones; Harry glared in her direction, and she gave him a tooth-baring smile.

"Well. Jennifer, who are those people?" Charlotte whispered.

Jennifer followed Charlotte's glance toward a rear corner of the room. "The hunky blond guy and the dark-haired girl? Grad students. Chris is a writer, had a poem in the last *North-Coast Review*; and Lisa's in environmental studies, sometimes baby-sits for me. They've been renting number twenty for several months.

"The other two I don't know by name." The young women sat side by side against the back wall, faces blank and closed, hands buried in their jacket pockets. "Students too, I think, renting either number four or number eight. Oh, oh. Here we go," she added, and settled squarely into her chair, face front.

"Hello, friends."

Now *there* was an inauspicious beginning. Charlotte stared at the smooth-faced young man with dark hair clipped close, at his gleaming tasseled loafers and gray three-piece suit and dark red tie with a paisley pattern. He did not look like a friend of hers.

"I'm Hal Michaelson, of Michaelson, Michaelson, and Purdue, in San Diego." He set a expensive-looking leather folder on the counter at his back and picked up a mug of coffee. "I came up here to let you folks know just what's happening with your new landlady, or your neighbor as the case may be. And to tell you what our tentative plans are."

The "landlady" was a Mrs. Cynthia Leino, widow of the recently deceased John Leino. The Leino family went all the way back to the old commune, and had clearly been smarter or more acquisitive than most: Cynthia Leino now owned six houses of the fourteen on Finn Lane, plus the park and Finn Hall.

"Well, she don't own number twelve," said Harry Duarte. "My dad bought the place right after the war, sold it to me when I got married. And I've put a lot of time and money into it."

"And she doesn't own number sixteen," Petey said loudly, and flushed as everyone looked at him. "It's mine, from my grandmother."

"Let me explain some of the possibilities here," said Michaelson smoothly. "As you all must know, Finn Lane and Finn Park make up an unusual parcel. The park has been maintained in private ownership for nearly a hundred years. The Lane has dwellings in place and in use, so renovating or replacing them would probably not be in violation of the land-use restrictions in your Local Coastal Plan. This means that although no single house is worth big money, adding the remaining ones to those she already owns will give Mrs. Leino a very attractive package. Which is why she is willing to pay you well above the market price for your houses."

"With what purpose?" asked Charlotte, to get the facts right out on the table.

"What is envisioned is an exclusive residential development. A central unit, clubhouse or small hotel, would replace the Hall. That little cove below the headland? Somebody told me the locals call that kind of thing a dog-hole port; we might be able to put a small private marina down there. As for the houses, some of them might be retained and improved; more likely they would all be replaced by architect-designed residences. Take out most of those old trees in the park, and every residence would have a whitewater view."

"Those trees are redwoods over a hundred years old." The taller of the two as yet unidentified young women took her hands from her pockets and made an open-palmed gesture. "It would be indecent to destroy them just so some city asshole can come up here on weekends and look at the ocean from the comfort of his sofa."

"I sympathize with your feelings, Miss, um, Harding, is it?"

"Clark. Ms."

"And you and Ms. Harding rent number eight Finn Lane on a month-to-month basis. Well, Ms. Clark, they are lovely trees, but as any landscape architect will tell you, redwoods make very poor city trees."

"And weekenders make very poor citizens," said Ms. Clark's companion.

"Damn right they do, and they send property values so high that ordinary working people get forced out. And pretty soon what used to be a real town is nothing but a dressed-up tart waiting to have her picture taken. Christ, just look at Mendocino Village." Chris the poet's deep voice vibrated with anger.

"And you are Mr. Jones, tenant in number twenty," purred Michaelson.

"Right. And I, we, have a lease."

"I think you will find that your lease can be canceled upon specified notice should the lessor, in this case a Mrs. Thelma Ridgeway, decide to sell her property." Michaelson gave a shrug and a sad smile.

"Mr. Michaelson?" Marlene Cummings raised her hand and introduced herself. "I volunteer at the Senior Center, and Don and I both attend city council meetings regularly; and we think it would be a real shame to remove small affordable units like those on Finn Lane from the very limited supply of such housing in Port Silva. Seniors need places to live, Mr. Michaelson, and so do young adults who grew up here and don't want to move away from their families."

"But these people don't have to live on prime coastal property, Mrs. Cummings. And property owners are entitled to the best return on their investment; that's the American way."

Nasty little hypocrite, thought Charlotte, turning slightly for a covert inspection of faces. Polite attention, alert interest. Craft and greed, that was Harry Duarte. Jennifer looked mildly sad, Joe James's leathery skin was flushed. And beside her, Petey was shifting in his chair and cracking his knuckles. She put her hand over his and cleared her throat to catch Michaelson's attention. "If Mrs. Leino's plans are carried out, what will happen to the Hall?"

"First, let me assure you that I object on my client's behalf to the unacceptable use to which her property is currently being put, and I intend to pursue the removal of those people." He paused for breath. "But if the building survives, and if there should be sufficient interest, Mrs. Leino might agree to share the cost of moving it to another site."

"No!" Petey stood up, eluding Charlotte's belated grab. "The Hall belongs where it is right, where it's been for a hundred years. And so does my house. I won't sell my house, not for a million dollars."

"Fellow," said Michaelson, "I'm afraid you're too young to have much say in the matter. And I'm sure your mother has her priorities in better order. Not that we're talking any million dollars here, you understand," he added hastily.

Charlotte stood up in her turn, and wrapped both her hands around Petey's right arm. He was trembling, and sweating, and she realized that if he should really try, he could shake her off. "My priorities are in excellent order," she said, "as are those of my son. If you will excuse us, please." She moved toward the door, pulling Petey with her, and was greatly relieved when he made no resistance.

■　　■　　■

There was no rain yet, just cold heavy air and a bitter wind from the northwest that intensified the sound of the ocean into a steady low hum not much different from the noise of freeway traffic. Parked cars had misted-over windshields; a low-slung red machine bearing the vanity plate HRM 1 blocked the driveway at number 24, the house next to the Bluejay. Charlotte pulled her jacket close around her shoulders and contemplated the cost of her display of family solidarity, or maybe it was just temper. Later tonight, or tomorrow, she would have to hunt up her neighbors to learn what had happened after her departure. To find out how they all felt about the situation, what they intended to do, what they might expect from her.

". . . who that asshole thinks he is! Drives up here in his lousy 'jag-you-are' and thinks he owns the north country."

Clearly he owns a nice little piece of it, or at least his client does. Charlotte kept these thoughts to herself and said, merely, "Um." She missed her footing on a broken bit of sidewalk and caught at Petey's arm, second time she'd done that tonight. But for different reasons. A thirteen-year-old boy was just too many people at once, particularly to himself. Add homeowner and caretaker of ethnic legacy to the more usual roles, and he could wear himself right out.

"All this damp gray weather makes me remember how wonderful New Mexico was," she said in reminiscent tones. "I went to, let's see, fifth and sixth grade in Santa Fe. Incredible shapes and colors, and hot summer days that always cooled at night because it was high in the mountains. And rainstorms that would come fast and practically drown you and then go away and leave the sky blue again."

"I don't want to hear!" His voice was high. "I won't move again and you can't make me!"

"Petey, I was only . . ."

"Leave me alone!" He jerked away from her grasp. "I gotta go, there's some guys I want to see." He turned and set off across the park, jogging toward the Hall and then around to the south side of it, toward a shadowy group of two or three people, or perhaps around them, too.

Sometimes Petey stayed out after dark, with his friends; he nearly always respected his ten-o'clock curfew, and she believed he was safe, or as safe as anybody could be and still have a modicum of personal freedom. She sighed, and thought of a pot of tea, and of the Bach partita that lay on her piano and in the back of her mind. About to turn into her own yard, she stopped to stare after another figure hurrying from the Lane into the park; something about the way it, he, moved set off alarm bells. Then he was gone, and she wasn't sure.

She climbed the fourteen steps to her door, which it turned out she had not remembered to lock. Half an hour later, with a cup of tea in her hands and the Bach open before her on the music rack, Charlotte stared at the flurry of black notes and saw, behind them, that almost-familiar figure. No word of the man for more than three years and now she had seen—she *thought* she had seen—Martin Lindberg twice this week.

She set down the cup to flex her fingers and felt for a moment like crossing them, to ward off trouble. There was no real doubt in her mind, nor hope, either; she knew too well Martin's genius for turning up just in time to make any problem infinitely worse. And how would Petey react?

Chapter
Four

J oe James's pale blue eyes narrowed in anticipation as he guided a bit of butter-drenched muffin toward his mouth. Charlotte filled his mug with hot coffee, filled her own, and nudged the control of the electric heater with the toe of her sneaker, from half on to full. The windows of the breakfast room were gray today, looking out on a thin mist that seemed to hang in the air rather than fall. She made her usual rainy-day vow to put curtains out here, a vow she knew she would forget as soon as the sun reappeared.

"You're a helluva cook, Charlotte," said Joe as he broke open another muffin. "Ought to start your own restaurant, you'd put those fags down the street out of business in a week."

Charlotte had cooked in restaurants, she had worked as an accountant. But here in Port Silva, with no mortgage to meet or rent to pay, she could support herself and Petey in less strenuous, more pleasant fashion. "I'd much rather give music lessons," she said, then sipped from her mug and smiled across the table at him, her morning's catch fortunate for both of them. At least seventy-five years old (the exact number of Joe's years was a secret between the old man and his maker), he no longer drove a car, and his ingrained dislike of homosexuals kept him out of the street's only eating place. For the price of a few homemade muffins he should be willing to deliver his acute if faintly malicious observations about last night's meeting.

"Where's the boy?" he asked as he eyed the muffin plate. "Ought to save some for him."

"He had three with his oatmeal, and then he went off on his bike. He's angry about what's happening on the Lane."

"Ah." Joe wiped his mouth and then his fingers on a napkin. Although his big bones were now only sparsely fleshed, he still held himself square-shouldered and erect. "The bastards always win, you know. Time the boy learned that."

"Petey's only thirteen years old."

"Shit, that's plenty old enough. I'd had my first job and my first woman by the time I was fourteen." Joe met her eyes, and splotches of pink stained his stubbled cheeks. "Sorry, Charlotte. Old fart has to get his digs in, only power he's got left."

Charlotte shook her head. "I don't disagree with you, if by 'the bastards' you mean people with money and influence. But I have a son who believes in heroes; perhaps I read him the wrong books. Joe, what happened after we left last night? Did the meeting go on for long?"

"I always found lawyers to be sonsabitches. Five minutes with one of them is about four too long." The old man looked down at his hands, swollen and twisted with arthritis, and pulled them off the table and onto his lap, out of sight. "Fella played Harry Duarte off against that young guy rents Thelma's house, Harry wound up taking a swing at the kid. Course, it don't take a whole lot to light Harry's fuse."

"Did Harry connect?"

Joe shook his head. "One of the fags, the fat one, sat Harry right down, hard. Said he didn't want his restaurant broke up. After that, there was a whole bunch of snapping and snarling, and I went home pretty soon."

"I wonder who *will* sell," she said, half to herself. The Lees probably would; their daughter had recently finished medical school, Mrs. Lee had a heart condition and Mr. Lee was opening his market later and later on cold mornings. Harry Duarte would, after what he judged the right amount of macho posturing and chest-thumping. Harry had a big mortgage on his fishing boat and a wife who yearned for better things.

"But Jennifer loves it here," Charlotte noted. "She says it's the perfect place for her little girl." Jennifer, a weaver and maker of coats and capes, ran a shop from her house.

"Jenny plain can't afford to turn down a good offer," said Joe flatly. "The s.o.b. she used to be married to told her he'd go to jail before he'd pay child support. But the ones that won't sell, that'll make a real fight of it, is the fags. That little fat one is tougher than a boiled owl, and smart. If you're gonna hold out, better join up with him."

"I don't want to hold out. This is a nice little house, but it's still just a house to me," Charlotte said, and sighed. "I hate fighting. I'm not good at it and it frightens me."

"Yeah."

"What about you, Joe? You're a fighter."

His gaze met hers and slid away. "Like the lawyer said last night, a man of eighty-three is gonna need to be took care of before long, stands to reason. Had my druthers, I'd stay in my house till I die, been there fifteen years now. But there's plenty of other places'll keep me warm and dry. I'll probably turn down the first couple offers, just for the hell of it, and then sell."

Like the lawyer said. So Mr. Michaelson had come equipped with the secret of Joe's age, and had used it in public. Charlotte rose and went to get the coffeepot. "Yes, I see. But they cannot *make* us sell. I suppose Petey and I could just go on as we are, in our nice little hundred-year-old house in the middle of their development."

"Young prick lawyer had an answer for that," Joe told her. "Seems the university would like to have the whole place for a conference center. They'd save the Hall, and use it. Take down some of the houses, or turn 'em into apartments. If this development plan don't work out, the lady owner will sell what she already owns to the university. Lawyer said the state could claim the rest of the property, pay fair market value and just take it."

"Oh. So if I hold out, I'll eventually lose my house anyway and everyone will lose money."

"Looks that way."

"Shit," said Charlotte.

The old man blinked in surprise, and then smiled grimly. "Yes, ma'am, I'd say that's what you're about to be knee-deep in." He drank the last of his coffee and set his cup down; Charlotte reached across the table to touch his hand.

"Wait, Joe. There's something I forgot." She pulled the R.I.P. "No Castles" leaflet from under the sugar bowl, unfolded it and set it before him. "This was in my mailbox yesterday. I wondered whether anyone else got one."

He squinted down at the sheet of paper. "Oh. Oh yeah." He ran the knuckles of his right hand along his jawbone, tight dry skin rasping against stubble. The eyes he turned up to her a moment later were bright. "Sure, everybody got one, far as I know."

"But what does it mean? Who made this?"

"Well, could be anybody. Every now and then, ordinary folks get fed up with being pushed around. I remember in 1927 . . . Never mind, you don't want to hear an old man run on."

"Joe, I'd feel better if I knew who was behind this."

"Maybe you would, maybe not." He edged his chair back from the table, set his feet squarely on the floor, and levered himself upright. "You feel like talking personal to the lawyer, he's at Tidepools Lodge, one of the garden cottages, for the next couple days. Wants to get everything settled real quick, says he'll be glad to answer any questions, give us lots of high-priced legal advice for free."

"My own lawyer tells me free legal advice is worth about what you pay for it." Charlotte stood up and stretched, and looked at her watch. "Besides, weekends are my busiest teaching time."

"Well, you just be sure to watch your back and your wallet if you do decide to visit the little shit."

The morning mist had changed to a steady, straight-down fall of rain. Although his two-piece rain suit kept the water out, it also kept sweat in, and Petey was beginning to feel uncomfortably damp. Besides, the rain made it hard to see, probably not safe to ride. And he had left his helmet, that his mother had asked him never to ride without, at home under the front steps. Charlotte never nagged or yelled, as his friends' mothers did; it was an ongoing mystery to Petey how her soft-voiced requests played themselves back inside his head like some kind of tape.

He swung onto Frontage Road, pumped hard and pulled back and got himself and the bike briefly airborne at the humped little bridge over the creek. Came down with a jar and a splash and nearly lost it as gluey mud grabbed at his front tire. "Well, shit," he said aloud; he brushed water from his face, sat up straight and pedaled in good-driver fashion around the corner and onto Finn Lane. Home.

The Lane looked dreary today, just a curving row of old wooden houses like a faded picture in a schoolbook: California small town a hundred years ago. Approaching his own driveway, Petey noticed lights on in the Hall and changed mind and direction. Maybe he'd find somebody inside to shoot baskets with.

In the sheltered entryway he had pulled off his boots and was shucking himself out of the rain suit when he heard running footsteps inside the building, and voices, the shrieks of little kids playing. The basketball hoops were upstairs in the big room, which was where people were living right now and like a dumb jerk he'd forgotten. He'd go home and call Eddie, and maybe they'd go to the rec hall at St. Joseph's.

"Got any spare change, mister?"

"Huh?" Petey blinked at a shrouded figure that had suddenly sprung out of the gloom, saw an outstretched white hand and looked into eyes green as grapes. "Uh, I've only got . . ."

"Oh, hey. No, it's okay, I don't hit on kids." The girl, or woman, pushed back the hood of her slicker. "You fooled me for a minute, you're real big for a kid."

In a faint wash of light from the door Petey saw long smooth hair that looked to him to be pink, and a narrow face so pale it seemed to glow, like the inside of an abalone shell. "Say, I think I've seen you someplace, like maybe . . ." He caught his breath as he suddenly remembered, and a wave of heat enveloped his whole body. He'd seen her standing in the sunshine naked and gleaming.

"Probably at the Anniversary Demonstrations," she said with a shrug. "That's why we, my friends and I, came here. We read about it in the paper and thought it would be a blast."

"Oh, yeah." Petey swallowed and tried to grin. "Yeah, that must be where it was."

"The four of us were camped outside of town until yesterday," she told him. "but then this redneck farmer came and chased us off. Say, kid," she said, leaning closer, "do you think the people who run that little restaurant down the street might have a soft spot for the hungry homeless?"

"No way, not if Billy's there," he told her. "But my mom does, she's always feeding people. Come on, I just live across the street." He stepped off the porch into a puddle, looked down at his stockinged feet and felt his face burn. "Wait, I better put my boots on."

When he set off again, she followed, but several steps back. "Look, kid," she muttered as they gained the opposite sidewalk, "moms are not usually thrilled when their kids bring home strays."

"Charlotte won't mind." He wheeled his bike to the garage, which was open and empty. "Anyway, she's not here; I forgot that Saturday mornings she goes to the Senior Center and gives a group lesson. Come on, I can find you something to eat." He led her around the side of the house and up the back steps, turned the doorknob with a flourish and stepped aside to let her precede him into the back hall.

"You just sit here at the table," he instructed. He turned the breakfast room heater on and hurried into the kitchen, where Charlotte's double muffin pan sat on the griddle with a towel draped over it. "Hey, good, there's some muffins left. It'll only take a few minutes to heat them up."

"Never mind!" she said sharply. "No, really, I'd just as soon have them cold."

Petey dumped the four muffins onto a plate and carried them

quickly to the table. "Here you go, and there's the butter. Um, can I get you some milk, or what, Miss . . . ?"

"Just call me Annie. Sure, milk would be good, or maybe some coffee?"

Petey turned on a flame under the teakettle before pouring a tall glass full of milk. Annie looked up briefly at his approach, then turned her attention back to the food. She had shed her slicker, to reveal a stained, unbuttoned down vest over a man's tee-shirt with a stretched-out neck. Her bare arms were skinny, pale, and not very clean. Even the incredible hair, somewhere between red and gold but pink still seemed to him the best word for it—even that looked stringy and slightly greasy in full light.

Maybe she'd like to take a shower. This idea brought yesterday's scene instantly to mind again, and he fled in red-faced relief to silence the whistle of the teakettle. Boy, he was turning out to be a worse sex fiend than Eddie even, really disgusting and he didn't know what to do about it.

He made a mug of filter coffee and carried it carefully into the breakfast room to set it before his guest. The milk glass was nearly empty, and a single muffin remained on the plate.

She nudged the plate in his direction, and he shook his head as he sat down. "I had lots for breakfast."

She shrugged, took a sip of coffee, poured the last of the milk into the mug, grinned at him and then frowned. "No coffee, either? How old are you, kid?"

"Uh, fourteen. And my name's Peter, Peter Birdsong."

"Hey, great name." She took a big swallow of coffee, tipping her head back in pleasure. Petey, watching her, realized that what he had taken for dirty marks on her face were actually bruises: an ugly bluish smear just below one eye, another along the line of her jaw. Now he recalled unhappily the rest of yesterday's scene, the tall man slapping her; and another horrible possibility occurred to him. Eddie had said he was going to report the campers to Mr. Johanson, a huge silent man who always looked angry. "Did he, that farmer, hurt you?" he asked, and cringed inwardly at the squeak of his own voice.

"Who?" She caught the direction of his gaze, and gave a sharp bark of laughter. "That redneck? Hell, no, he wouldn't dirty his hands on somebody like me. Just came roaring up, he and another guy, with shotguns and this big dog, ordered us off his land and took most of our money. Said some meat we had was one of his calves, which it seems to me would be pretty hard to prove.

"No, what happens to me is, I've got a mean temper and so has my old man, but he's bigger."

"Your father?"

"My father?" She drawled the word, mocking him or herself. "Listen, my father was a drunk and my mother was a slut, and I haven't seen either of them since I was about your age, okay?"

"Oh."

"Jesse is my old man, my . . . boyfriend. He's downtown trying to do a deal with this garage to get our van fixed. We figure for tonight we can pitch our tent in that park across the street."

"Finn Park? Well, I guess you could. Mostly the people who don't have a place to go sort of camp in a vacant lot next to the Lutheran church, on Albion Street."

"We were down there last night, but Jesse got into it with this black dude about something, probably me. Then somebody mentioned Finn Hall, and that sounded familiar, or I guess I mean friendly. But it turns out the place is full, or at least that's what they say.

"It's a nice neighborhood, though, and this is a nice house," she went on in a lighter tone. She pushed her chair back and got up, to move into the kitchen, where she eyed the gleaming old Wedgewood stove, and from there into the music room, to trail a hand along the curve of the piano. In the living room she inspected the pictures on the mantel, ran a thumbnail across the backs of a row of books, and went to look out the front window.

Petey had followed silently behind her. "It's my house," he

told her now. "My grandmother's family built it, and she left it to me. Because she liked me, and I needed a house."

"Everybody needs a house," she said, and turned to smile over her shoulder at him. "I guess you had a nice grandmother. I hope you live here practically forever, and leave it to *your* grandchildren."

"Me, too," he muttered, and thrust his fisted hands into his jeans pockets. "I hope."

"Hey, Peter Birdsong, what's the problem?"

"There's this asshole lawyer, from San Diego," he said through his teeth. "Drives around in a big red Jaguar. He's trying to make us sell our house to this Mrs. Leino, so she can wipe out the neighborhood and make a fancy development here."

"Tear down all these nice little houses? Just the sort of thing some rich bitch from San Diego would do. Oh, hey," she said as the clock in the music room began a series of strikes that continued to eleven. "Listen, I gotta go. Jesse will be expecting some income here and I better get to work."

"Annie, I don't have any money but this." He dug two quarters from his pocket and offered them. "But my mom will be home pretty soon, and she'll . . ."

Annie shook her head, then changed her mind and reached for the quarters. "That's plenty, that's what anybody on the street would give me." She dropped the coins into her own pocket. "And look, Pete. Better not tell your mother you brought a stranger in here while she was away, okay? No point in upsetting her." She laid her hand on his forearm, trailed her fingers down and encircled his wrist in a fleeting clasp; then she picked up her slicker, shrugged it on, and slipped out the back door.

Saturday's final student was late arriving, as usual, and late finishing, because Charlotte insisted. A fritatta, she thought, as the door closed on him at six-fifteen. She could make some salsa to go with it, and there were black beans vinaigrette, by-product of yesterday's soup. No busy and sensible person, in Charlotte's view, made one dish of anything at a time.

She poured herself a glass of wine and was washing spinach leaves when Petey came into the kitchen. "Onion," she told him over her shoulder. "One large one, sliced thin, not chopped."

He sighed dramatically but plucked an onion from a hanging basket and began to peel it. "Hey," he remarked as he looked more closely at what she was doing, "is this another no-meat night?"

"Yes, it is, poor baby. Do you suppose you'll survive?"

"Probably not. Coach says . . ."

"A growing boy needs red meat!" they said in unison, and grinned at each other.

"Well, I just hope there's lots of beans," he said.

"A whole pot, all yours. This is a chamber music Saturday."

"Oh, boy, I forgot. Mom, I don't know why you want to have anything to do with that dweeb, Gil."

"Dweeb" was a word that didn't seem to need definition. "He's a friend, Petey, and an excellent musician."

"Not as good as you."

"He's very good," she said firmly. "And the others aren't bad. We make a nice quintet, and I love it. Besides, he has a harpsichord."

"Oh wow. I know somebody that could build you one."

"Do you really? Who?"

"This guy at school's brother. Mom, you aren't interested in ol' Gilbert, um, you know, sexually?"

"No," said Charlotte, suppressing a sigh. After the failure of the committed (on her part) relationship that produced her son, she had ventured once, and then a second time, into what was supposed to be a no-strings affair, friendship and shared interests including sex, which after all was natural and necessary and made everybody feel better. Perhaps such arrangements even worked for some, and she wished those lucky persons well. But Gil Feder, while a nice enough man, was not someone to tempt her into that minefield again.

Nor, in fact, had he given any indication that he wanted to. "Gil has a girlfriend," she told Petey. "She's an associate professor in the English department at the university, divorced, with a little girl. A nice woman."

Petey's answer was lost in the chime of the doorbell. "You watch this," she told him, gesturing to the skillet and handing him her wooden spoon.

She flipped the porch light on against the winter evening, peered through curtained glass panes, recognized the nearest of two shadowy figures and opened the door. "Mr. Michaelson. I'm sorry, but I'm busy now, and I haven't come to a decision."

"We'll need to come in, if you don't mind." Michaelson stepped past her, followed by . . . a policeman, for heaven's sake! Tall, with muscular shoulders straining his uniform shirt, a freckled face under sandy hair.

"Officer Boatwright, ma'am." He was young, and uncomfortable. "Mr. Michaelson had this complaint, and we should clear it up."

Complaint. That she had rudely walked out on his meeting? Failed to visit him as asked?

"Mom?" Petey was behind her, his hand on her shoulder.

"That's the young man, Officer. He's the one I want you to question."

"Question . . . Oh, I think not," said Charlotte. "No. Whatever it is, you may ask me, if you're quick about it."

Boatwright flushed red and looked as if he wanted to draw circles in the rug with the toe of his big boot. "Mr. Michaelson here says . . ."

"When I returned to my car last night, after a brief social time with Mr. and Mrs. O'Malley, I found a tire flat." Michaelson stood stiff-shouldered, chin out. "I was too tired to worry about it; I simply called a cab for myself and a tow truck for the Jaguar.

"But this afternoon, when the car was delivered to me, I learned that all four tires had been slashed. A classic juvenile act, Mrs. Birdsong, and given the animosity your son demonstrated toward me last night, I asked Officer Boatwright to accompany me here to make inquiries."

"I never touched your dumb tires!" said Petey.

"Where were you last night after you left the meeting?" demanded Michaelson. "And what kind of knife do you have? I want the police to examine it."

"Sir, maybe you should let me ask the questions," said Boatwright.

"The only pertinent question has been answered," Charlotte stated. "My son did not slash your tires. My son does not own a knife. I have many knives, but if you want to see them, you'll need a warrant. Have you a warrant?" she asked the policeman.

"No, ma'am."

"Then I'll ask you both to leave."

"Yes, ma'am," said Boatwright, and a moment later he ushered a still-sputtering Michaelson down the front steps. Charlotte closed the door, locked it, and turned to find her son staring at her, round astonished eyes making him look about six years old.

"I don't like to fight. But that doesn't mean I will let someone push me around," she said in a voice that shook only slightly. "Now, let's get the fritatta in the oven; I still need to shower and find something to wear."

In the kitchen Petey stirred the vegetables while she beat eggs and milk and cheese together. He was out until ten last night, she remembered, looking at her son's bent head. He was very angry. Some of his friends carry pocket knives.

"Petey?"

He turned and met her glance, eyes still wide and a half-smile curving his mouth. "Yeah?"

Charlotte picked up her glass and drowned that particular question in a mouthful of wine. He'd answered it once, she would not ask again. "Are you going to Hannah's tonight?"

"Yeah, if that's okay."

"I'll pick you up there on my way home."

Chapter

Five

Advancing age was only part of the problem, twenty-eight-year-old Val Kuisma decided as he levered his sweaty body off the weight bench and limped over to the exercise bike. He never had been much good at blind dates; a slow goer by nature, he was still getting acquainted about the time today's woman started expecting real moves. Last night's girl, Carrie something, a friend of his friend Al's present lady, had after all been nice enough. Maybe he'd look her up again when he was in shape for dancing.

The news section of the San Francisco Sunday paper was propped on the reading rack of his bike. Legs pumping steadily, he flipped the paper to look at the bottom half of the front page, and the vague blond image from the night before vanished from his mind for good. There in front of him was a lengthy story on the bereft Boylan family, with a photo: a gaunt, wild-eyed woman with four little kids clustered around her like hungry baby birds. Really made you want to find their daddy; or at least, he thought grimly, find out what had happened to the poor guy.

The radio weatherman was predicting a real storm by tonight; but what Val found when he poked his head out the door half an hour later was no more than a drizzle, no serious obstacle to a Jeep four by four. And if Chief Gutierrez had refused to put him back on patrol, there was no reason he shouldn't drive his own vehicle up and down back roads he'd known all his life and maybe pick up a trail. Wearing a rain poncho over his down vest, he headed for his Jeep and then moved beyond it, to cross the street for a long, sad look at Finn Hall. Cheerful, as Charlotte had said, even in the gray rain. Damn it, the building *belonged* here; the thought of its demise made him remember how he had felt when his grandmother died.

His gloomy thoughts of families bereaved and histories disturbed were interrupted by the sound of voices, angry voices. Off to his right, near the northern edge of the park, someone had pitched a big tent; it was dark green in a wet green setting, which was probably why he'd failed to notice it earlier.

He was looking at the backs of two men, one of them unknown to him and the other immediately identifiable by his height and his shock of almost-white hair as Officer Bob Englund. Facing this pair were four people who apparently belonged to the tent. Tall blond guy wearing an eye patch, Val noted as he quietly moved closer; head forward, jaw out, mad. Big fellow behind the first guy's left shoulder, for backup. The two others were tight together and off to one side, both in rain gear with hoods up and from size and stance Val figured these were women.

"... tough shit, fellow," said Englund's companion, a medium-sized man in a tan raincoat bristling with buckles and straps. He held a big black umbrella high above his head, and looked as though he might bring it down on somebody else's head any minute. "This is private property, not some open-air facility for the voluntary poor. The owner wants you out of here, now!"

"Man, you and your owner can just go fuck yourselves! I said we'll leave when we get our wheels working."

The umbrella came lower, the tent-dweller got his fists up; Val rolled his shoulders loose and prepared to move but Englund moved first, plucking the umbrella from its owner's grip and interposing his lanky frame between the two men. "Now, Mr. Michaelson, why not ... ?" The rest of it was a rumble, too low for Val to catch the words; but Michaelson grabbed his umbrella back, shook it, and set off for the street.

"The parts man told me Monday, so I should have the van

back by Tuesday and we'll haul ass out of this chicken-shit town." The blond man's voice was sullen now rather than aggressive; Englund's answering rumble had a soothing tone. Val grinned to himself, turned to head for his Jeep and crashed chest to shoulder into Petey Birdsong.

"Hey, whoa. Sorry, Pete, didn't see you coming." He held on to the boy for a moment, to be sure they were both solidly on their feet.

"What's happening?" demanded Petey. "What was that ass-hole lawyer doing here?"

"What he had in mind was evicting squatters," Val told him, with a nod toward the tent.

"They're not hurting anything. They couldn't stay in the Hall because it was full."

"Friends of yours, are they?"

Petey's face went pink and shut down. "I know one of them, a little bit."

Which one? Val wondered. In his brief observation of them, the quartet had struck him as mildly unsavory, not the kind of people you'd expect a kid of Charlotte's to know. "They're okay for the time being, Pete. Officer Englund calmed things down."

"Yeah, okay." Petey hunched his shoulders under his yellow slicker as he eyed the now closed and silent tent, then sighed and turned away, to head in the general direction of his own house. "Thanks, Val," he called back over his shoulder. "See you."

"Right. See you, Pete." Val crossed the street and climbed into his vehicle, a vague uneasiness about the boy deepening his already gloomy mood. Charlotte Birdsong was a wonder, a warm, thoughtful, soft-spoken person who could also be breath-takingly direct. She was a loving mother. But Val had a notion that successfully guiding a boy into and through adolescence was best managed the way his uncle raised his Labradors: lots of affection and an occasional kick in the butt. He suspected that kicking butt might be beyond Charlotte's capabilities.

Not really any of your business, he told himself as he headed north on the coast highway. The missing Ed Boylan is your business; if you're not yet in top fighting shape, at least you're one hell of a snoop.

"Is this a bad time, Charlotte?" the tall woman asked as Charlotte, having first peered carefully through the curtains, opened her front door. "Katy asked me to pick up some music."

"No, of course not; please come in. It's just that I've had some strange visitors recently." Meg Halloran was a friend, Charlotte reminded herself. She was also the mother of Katy, Petey's classmate and one of Charlotte's favorite piano students; Katy, who had the flu. The fact that Meg had recently married Port Silva's dark-visaged and rather intimidating chief of police was irrelevant.

"Actually, your timing is perfect," Charlotte went on. "Both my afternoon students had to cancel, and I've finished marking some fingering and dynamics on the Schubert Impromptus for Katy. Is she still very sick?"

"The body is on the mend, but the temper is absolutely vile."

"Then give me your coat, and stay for a visit. I just this minute made a pot of tea." Charlotte thought Meg looked weary; the greenish eyes were heavy-lidded, the thick mane of gray-streaked dark hair loose and frizzle-edged in the damp.

"I will, thanks." Meg followed Charlotte to the kitchen and settled with a sigh into the high-backed rocker. "Oh, this is one of Val Kuisma's chairs, isn't it? He made one for me, too."

"I didn't have any tall-people's chairs, so he brought this up here in self-defense," said Charlotte. "And I can't understand why anyone who can make a chair like that would be . . . doing anything else," she finished lamely.

"You mean something really strange like being a policeman? Vince does it because he has the kind of in-the-bone authority that people pay attention to, and crime, especially violent crime, makes him angry. And Val I think because he's curious, and very much interested in and protective of his fellow man. And maybe a bit of a puritan. Don't tell either of them what I've just said."

"I won't."

"Good." Meg sighed and stretched her legs out. "What I've been meaning to tell *you* is that the piano you found for us has been a blessing; and the thing Katy hates most about having the flu is missing a lesson. I wish you'd let me pay for it."

"No." Charlotte set a plate of lemon wedges and another of cookies on the table beside the cups in their saucers. "That's the whole point of being free-lance: flexibility, for me as well as for my students."

"Sounds absolutely wonderful, says a poor schoolteacher who sees Christmas vacation long past and spring break way out there ahead. Anyway, Katy will be back next week. She says your playing just blisses her out, her words; she thinks you should be giving concerts."

Charlotte shook her head. "I hate competition, and that's what professional performers do, compete. With others, with themselves. And I realized a long time ago that my talent was real, but not large. Sugar?"

"No, thanks, lemon's fine. Is Petey musical?"

"When he wants to be. He has perfect pitch, and he's been playing the piano since he was five; but lately he seems to have lost interest." Charlotte made a wry face as she rose to pour more tea. "These days, whenever he's not riding his mountain bike, he's in the back room of that nature-ecology-new wave or whatever store called Gaia, with the other computer club kids."

"Oh?" Meg's eyebrows arched high. "Katy tried that for a while, but she didn't last long. She took a serious dislike to the woman who runs the club."

Charlotte had met the woman three or four times. Sarah Stonemountain, who owned both the Gaia shop and the computer store next to it, was about fifty years old, with coarse black hair and a tall, broad-shouldered frame that probably carried a hundred seventy pounds and none of it fat. "She's unusual," Charlotte admitted. "Or maybe what I mean is overpowering. I'm not usually conscious of being small, but she somehow reminds me that I am. Small and frivolous. But Petey seems to like her."

"Katy felt Sarah was manipulating the kids. Jerking them around, was the way she put it. But being resistant to any kind of management is part of Katy's attitude these days," said Meg with a grimace.

"Actually, she's been very nice to us. She had her son bring over a computer this morning, for Petey. It's a used Mac they took as a trade-in on a more powerful model. The young man said there's not much market for this one right now, so Petey might as well use it. Of course Petey was ecstatic," Charlotte added with an open-palmed gesture of helplessness. "And I couldn't think of a way to refuse."

"No, I can see that." Meg's face was thoughtful. "Well, I'd better be going; Katy's alone at home. Thanks for the tea, Charlotte."

Charlotte ushered her guest to the door, watched her down the stairs, then glanced for some reason in the direction of the park where a big tent had sprouted mushroomlike at the northern edge.

As Meg's van, lights on, pulled away from the curb, a young woman stepped out of the tent and moved some distance from it, to stand gazing at the houses on the Lane. She wore a rain slicker but her head was bare to the drizzle, long red hair clinging wetly around her pale face. She lifted her head, and it seemed to Charlotte that their eyes would meet; and then a man, very tall, came from the tent, put a hand—affectionately? Charlotte wasn't sure—on the back of the girl's neck. Possessively, anyway. And the two of them returned to the tent.

Quelling a sense of unease, Charlotte in her turn surveyed the street. On this wet, quiet Sunday afternoon, most of the houses showed lights, and most had cars in driveways. Instead of retreating to the refuge of her music room, she should gird her loins or at least put on a raincoat, visit her neighbors and try to find out what was happening.

About an hour later Charlotte approached number 26, the westernmost house on Finn Lane. The basement café was dark; Buck and Billy took Sundays off in the wintertime. She trudged up the stairs to the front door, rang the bell, and winced at the resulting explosion of shrill yapping.

"Alfred! Amanda! You hush now, hear me?" Buck Watson pulled the door open and two mop-shaped whirlwinds flew at Charlotte's ankles. "They won't bite, Charlotte, I promise."

"I know," she said, and waited until the pair of Yorkshire terriers had tired of the game. They dropped back and sat, tiny pink tongues lolling; she stepped inside and Buck closed the door.

"They're looking for your monster dog; I imagine they still smell him on your shoes."

"I look for him sometimes myself." Fenris, Petey's huge wolf-hound cross, stiff and slightly deaf at age nine, had been struck and killed by a car three months earlier.

"You know, we're planning a litter this spring," said Buck, bending to scoop up a dog in each hand. "Perhaps you and Petey would like . . . no, I don't suppose so."

"Buck, that's sweet of you." Charlotte reached out to run two fingers over a small warm skull. "But Petey says he won't have another dog."

"Well, I can certainly understand that. I was depressed for months after we had to have Amanda's mother put to sleep. Come on back, Charlotte; Billy is working on the books and I'm sure he'll welcome the chance to take a break."

This house was near-twin to Charlotte's, but Buck and Billy had made the whole sleeping porch into a long office/sitting room. As the other two entered the room, Billy looked up from his computer monitor and muttered, "Just a minute."

"Here, Charlotte, you sit down and relax," said Buck, pulling a cushioned rocking chair up for her. "Can I get you some tea?"

Charlotte sat back in the chair and thought she could hear her stomach slosh: tea, coffee, mineral water. "I think I'll turn to alcohol; what have you to offer?"

When a bottle of sauvignon blanc had been poured, tasted, and pronounced tolerable, Charlotte settled her glass in her lap and fixed her eyes on Billy Kaplan's ruddy face. "How much has Mr. Michaelson offered you for this place?"

Billy's bristling eyebrows nearly met in a fierce scowl. "What the hell business is that of yours?"

"None at all and thank you for the wine." Charlotte prepared to rise and Buck waved her back.

"Mind your manners," he said to Billy and then, to Charlotte, "Nothing, yet. We told him Friday night that we don't plan to sell. What about you?"

"We haven't discussed it yet." She sipped at the wine and found that it had soured slightly, or perhaps her mouth had. "But I have talked to nearly everyone else on the Lane who's involved."

"Well?" snapped Billy.

"And what approach do you take, Mr. Kaplan, when you find charm ineffective?"

Billy's face grew several shades more ruddy, and he brushed a hand across his bald dome. "I whine. Sorry, Charlotte. Please, is Michaelson making specific offers to people?"

"Yes, and I don't understand the pattern, which is one reason I'm here. He's offered one hundred eighty thousand to Jennifer, which is an even hundred thousand more than she paid three years ago."

"No shit!" said Billy.

"She says she hates the idea of wimping out on her friends," Charlotte told them, remembering the sad and slightly embarrassed expression on Jennifer's freckled, usually cheerful face. "But she says the money would mean she could buy another house and continue to work at home until Cybelle goes to school, instead of having to put her in day-care somewhere."

"Oh, dear." Buck hunched his shoulders in a guilty gesture that exactly mirrored Charlotte's own feelings. If she, and they, won this battle, nice people like Jennifer would lose.

"Yes. Anyway, Joe James says Thelma Ridgeway has been offered the same amount, one eighty. Thelma owns number 20," she added in response to Billy's questioning look. "She lives with her daughter in Oakland, and Joe says she has always intended to come back to Port Silva after her grandchildren were older and her daughter could manage on her own."

"But presently she's renting her house to that blond young man who was so eloquent about saving Port Silva," remarked Buck.

"Yes, I remember." Charlotte had a fleeting image of the young poet who looked more like an angry lumberman. "But here's the strange thing. The offer to the O'Malleys was two hundred; to the Duartes, two ten. What do you think that slimy man is up to?"

"Easy," replied Billy, leaning back in his chair and resting his wineglass on his belly. "He figures the low end folks, who don't really want to sell, will get all upset and bust their asses to get as much as the other guys, pretty much the same houses after all and why should Harry Duarte be the one to get rich?

"And then . . . well, if I were doing this," said Billy with a shrug, "I'd let myself be nudged and persuaded up to oh, as much as two fifty all round, have everybody floating on clouds. About the time they've all put down payments on their yachts, I'd tell them the whole deal is off unless everybody sells. Meaning us."

"Did you know that Michaelson had his tires slashed here Friday night?" Charlotte asked.

"No shit!" said Billy once more, and "Goody!" said Buck.

"He came to my house on Saturday, with a policeman, and accused Petey of having done it. Then this morning he called and apologized. He had leapt to a flawed conclusion and sincerely hoped it wouldn't affect our future relationship."

"Tricky little bastard is working to keep you off balance," said Billy, reluctant admiration in his voice.

"Did he say what changed his mind?" asked Buck.

"It seems the people who repaired the tires found a flyer in the car, the same one that was distributed here on the Lane Friday. The one with the tombstone logo, marked R.I.P. Didn't you receive it?"

Buck and Billy looked at each other. "I showed it to you, remember? A very primitive drawing of a house and a castle, with a buster-bar through the castle," said Buck.

"Oh. Yeah, but I didn't remember the logo."

"You don't know anything about these people? Rip?"

Buck shook his head and Billy said, "Nope. Why?"

Charlotte hesitated, aware that she had not quite worked out her stance regarding this group. "I'd like to know who they are. They're opposed to development, which is good. I think. But they've done some illegal things, destroyed property. This makes me nervous, either because I'm deeply law-abiding or because I'm a coward."

"First the woods fairies, now the town fairies," growled Billy. "Excuse the expression. You can play call-a-hippie if you want to, Charlotte; me, I think I'll buy a shotgun."

Chapter

Six

■

V al Kuisma, having fortified himself with a large chili-
burger at the Hungry Wheels truckstop, climbed into his
Jeep and headed north. The slow swush-thump of his windshield
wipers made a rhythmic background as he thought over what
he knew about the man the whole Port Silva police force was
seeking.

Ed Boylan, a contractor and builder specializing in second-
home and vacation developments, ran a small Santa Rosa–based
firm that he intended to make one of the big boys. Skilled at
spying out promising properties—farms or ranches whose owners had grown old or tired, pieces of logged-out land not suitable
for farming—Ed had become a familiar if not particularly welcome visitor to Port Silva over the past six months. Val had
even met him once, when he came to the police station to complain about a parking ticket.

Wednesday before last, Ed had arrived in town with a younger
man, one of his employees. The two stayed in separate rooms at
the SandDollar Motel on Highway 1 and completed their business early Saturday. On Ed's instructions, his employee made
arrangements for the pair of them to fly to San Francisco the
following morning. Departure time arrived, Ed failed to turn
up, and so far as anyone could tell he had not slept in his room
Saturday night. Ed Boylan was missing, along with his rental car.

More irritated than worried, the other man had reported the
disappearance to the police. Edward Boylan, he told Captain

Hank Svoboda, was an irascible man who had begun his career as a construction laborer; away from home and his family, he liked to spend his free evenings in bars and not classy bars, either. Chances were Ed had gotten drunk, insulted some local fellow's politics or tried to pick up his woman, and would trail in soon nursing a hangover and a collection of bruises.

Val turned off onto a county road. About three miles in, just before it turned into a lumber road, was a little country bar, your basic beer joint like the dozen or so others he had checked out over the last couple of days. Be nice if these places would get in something better than Bud, he thought as he spotted the narrow, false-fronted wooden building set in a muddy parking lot. But he was willing to suffer for the pleasure of having useful work to do. According to the newspaper story, and to Chief Gutierrez, Mrs. Boylan thought a week was a very long time for even her Ed to be laid up with a hangover.

The man behind the bar in John's Place glanced at the photograph Val laid on the bar, scratched his hairy chest through a buttonless gap in his shirt, and shook his head. "We get just regulars in here, specially this time of year. And if this fella was huntin' for pussy, this ain't the place, no single women let to hang around here and I don't hold with guys messing with each others' wives, neither."

Forty-five minutes later Val got much the same answer, in a slightly smoother delivery, at Ernie's. He also got a Carta Blanca, a big step up in his opinion. Probably should switch to Coke next time, so he didn't get careless and bury his Jeep in the mud; some of these roads were graveled, some were merely graded and pretty soggy by now.

At 4 P.M., after a pointless run down a road that finally petered out against a hillside, he decided to make one more stop, at a place on the coast highway a mile or so after that road begins its swing east to join 101. Old country tavern with cabins, he could visualize the place from having passed it often but couldn't remember whether it was still in business. He'd look in, and then sign off for the day and head home for supper. He had no formal boarding arrangement with Charlotte, but she'd made it clear that he was welcome whenever she had a meal on, which was most days; he kept careful track and added a suitable amount to his next rent check.

The rain was heavier now, beginning to blow hard against his windshield; he turned up the wiper speed and kept his eyes on alert while his mind loped back to Port Silva and Charlotte, and her son. The kid was big to start with, misleadingly so; and he was growing about an inch a week, heading for an early physical maturity that Val for one didn't think he was ready for. One of those shitty tricks nature seemed to enjoy playing now and then. Maybe he'd have a talk with Charlotte, in a noninterfering kind of way; and as soon as the weather cleared he'd set up a not-too-strenuous backpacking trip, himself and Pete and maybe one of Pete's buddies.

There it was, the Rainbow Tavern, a slope-roofed place with a porch across the front and the whole affair looking rickety, a worn wooden shell draped over a roof beam. Several pickup trucks were nosed in against the porch, though, and lights were on inside. Bud sign, Hamm's sign, terrific. He could just make out, through the rain, a row of pointy-roofed little buildings behind the main structure; none of these showed any light, and the "Cabins" sign he'd remembered no longer hung from the porch rail.

The man behind the bar, probably a one-time lumberman, would have dwarfed John or Ernie or anyone else Val had seen today. "Sorry, can't help you," he said. "We get real busy in here weekend nights, see there?"

"Live music Fri and Sat," proclaimed glittery letters on a piece of posterboard over the bar. "Hank and the Hooters." Val eyed the sagging, splintery floor on which, presumably, people danced. Then he reminded himself that he was in the county rather than in Port Silva, and anyway code violations were not his problem.

"But I can tell you for damn sure, the new ownership, that's me, Marv Whatley . . . I and my brother cut off any fellow gets drunk and mean, show him the door and make sure he uses it. And I don't rent no cabins to whores neither, way the other fellow did. Fact is, I'm going to have them old cabins took down, soon as I got the money or the time. Just a terrible problem, that's what they are, drunks or horny kids getting in no matter what kind of lock I put on."

"Would you mind if I took a look out there?" asked Val. As the big man hesitated, Val shrugged and spread his hands. "Like I told you, I've got no jurisdiction here. But if I have to call Sheriff Roncalli and then wait around for a deputy to show up, I'm going to be real late for my supper."

"Well, what the hell. Just let me tell the old lady to keep an eye on the bar for a couple minutes."

Val stopped at his Jeep to pick up a flashlight; then the two of them trudged through mud and rain to what turned out to be a double row of small wooden buildings, five in front and four behind. Each had three steps up to a two foot by three foot scrap of porch, one front window, a wooden door. Each door had a hasp and padlock, and each padlock was firmly in place except the last one, that on cabin number nine.

"Well, shit," muttered Whatley. "Some bastard just popped that sucker right off, must of had a crowbar."

Val pushed the door open and looked into a single dank, musty room, empty except for a wooden straight chair and a bare double-bed-sized mattress. The filthy floor was crisscrossed with tracks, how recent it was impossible to say in a brief, flash-lit survey. He hooked the toe of his boot around the door to pull it shut, then stepped off the porch to circle the building. With rain nearly every day for the past week, the ground was just beaten mud and standing water; but this cabin, the last in line, had a road or at least a trail leading past it into the woods.

"Where does that go?" he asked, pointing with his flashlight.

"There's a crick back there a ways, more like a river this time of year. And just a lot of woods and brush."

Val crouched and squinted along the trail. In the pounding rain it was impossible to tell whether the twin ruts leading into the woods had been used recently. And so what if they had? You're chasing butterflies here, Kuisma, he told himself but didn't believe it. It was like being deep in the winter woods, staring ahead through bare branches and trunks, seeing nothing move but knowing a deer was there.

Thing to do was call the sheriff, get a deputy out here. Be dumb to slog down that muddy trail in fading light, slip and slide in the mud and probably blow out his leg again. "How far to the creek?" he asked Whatley.

"Oh, maybe three, four hundred yards. Look, I got a business to run and I'm getting drownded besides."

Val waved the other man away and set off down the trail, needing the flash because trees met overhead and cut off most of what remained of daylight. Didn't seem to deflect the rain, though. He slipped and grabbed at a branch, falling to one knee; fell again later, harder, and swore. Head down and watching his feet, he nearly tumbled down a steep bank into a creek he could finally see but not hear because of the noise of the rain.

He could see something else, too: a squarish shape too big and too symmetrical to be a rock or a log. He crouched at the top of the slope and stared down at the back end of a pickup truck with its nose buried in the stream. A clutter of sticks and branches and dead leaves moved sluggishly against the vehicle's upstream side, suggesting it had been there for a while.

Just somebody's idea of how to get rid of an old truck, probably; but he played the flash around some and it looked to him like a nice old truck, a late-sixties Ford half-ton with pretty good paint. Nobody dumped a truck like that, not in the country.

Should go down there, he told himself; might be somebody in the cab. Yeah, but not somebody alive. He stood up and rubbed his leg for a moment before turning to retrace his path.

Stunned by his good fortune, Petey Birdsong had spent most of Sunday afternoon with his computer—looking at it, working with it, shaping up his wish-list of games and programs. Some he could borrow from the club, or from Hannah; and maybe he could convince Charlotte to let him borrow some money from himself, from his own savings from yard work and occasional odd jobs, to buy others.

Now and then the figures on the monitor were obscured by his memory of Sarah's face, when he and Hannah reported to her Friday afternoon. Frozen cold, it was, and her voice lashing them, him in particular, like sleety rain. Maybe the computer was her way of apologizing. Maybe it wasn't anything but what her son, Rob, had said, an in-the-way extra. Didn't matter which, Petey was glad to have it.

And now and then something, a chill draft from the old windows or the rattle of the rain in a push of wind, had drawn him to the front of the house to look out at the park. There'd been a few comings and goings at the Hall, but no noisy action that would suggest more trouble, from cops or lawyers. Now, as afternoon was dimming into evening, he stood on the park grass and stared at the big tent. Looked like a pretty good one, and with the rain fly it was probably dry inside. He wondered if Annie had had any luck getting money, if she'd had anything to eat today.

A tent didn't have a door to knock on. He stood there in the rain, shifting from foot to foot and trying to think what he could call out, like hello, or hey you. Something, maybe his movements, brought a man to the opening beneath the flap that was propped up like a little porch roof.

"Hey, kid, you want something?" He was tall, big-boned but skinny, with yellow hair stringing loose over his shoulders, a yellow mustache fringing his mouth. One blue eye blazed down at Petey; the other, a paler blue, pointed off to one side in a way that made Petey want to turn and look over his shoulder.

"Um, no. Well, yeah, I just wanted to say hey to Annie?"

The man shrugged, gave an exaggerated bow and made a sweeping gesture with one arm. "You're a little young, but what the hell. Annie?" he barked. "Company."

Petey ducked his head under the flap and found he could stand easily once inside. A lantern hung from the center support of the tent, and a little propane heater sat on the ground beneath; waves of heat from these blended with the almost visible damp and a hanging haze of smoke to make the whole room shimmery, weird. With each breath, he pulled in a heavy mix of smells that seemed to lie separately on his tongue: hot metal, beer, sweat, something salty-musty, the sweet sickish tang of pot. It was like a cave where something had lived for a long time, trolls maybe. Or giants, he thought as he squinted up at the blond man who loomed against the tent roof, next to another man nearly as large.

Two figures huddled close to the heater, and the nearest turned glowing green eyes up at him. "Hi, Pete. Come in out of the rain and meet everybody," said Annie. "That's Jesse who let you in, you've heard about him. Tiffany over there soaking up the heat, known as Tif." Petey nodded to the other woman he'd seen in the woods two days earlier and noticed that she wasn't pretty like Annie. Her skin was rough, her pale eyes red-rimmed and kind of vague-looking; and her brief grin revealed a couple of gaps where teeth should have been.

"And Bo, Tif's old man." Bo, a very wide man with pale skin and a thick shock of straight black hair, stared down at Petey and blinked and said, "Yo."

"Guys, this is my friend Pete, Peter Birdsong; isn't that a great name? He has a house across the street. Come on and sit down, Pete," she said in softer tones. Her cool thin fingers found his hand and wrapped around it; he followed the pull and settled next to her on a rolled-up sleeping bag. She released his hand, snaked an arm across his shoulders to give him a friendly hug, then let go. Petey thought maybe he was sitting too close, practically right against her, but decided it wouldn't be polite to move away. He shifted position only slightly, to get his feet close and flat on the ground, and draped his hands over his knees. "It's nice to meet you."

With a grunt Jesse hooked a low stool with one foot, nudged it close to the heater and lowered himself to sit. He kept his good eye on Petey as he stretched his left arm up toward Bo and snapped his fingers. Bo took a quick drag on the cigarette he was cupping in his palm before handing it to Jesse, who grimaced and put it to his mouth and pulled until the limp-looking little tube glowed red.

After a long moment Jesse's hollowed cheeks eased, and smoke began to trickle from his nostrils, from the upcurving corners of his mouth. From his ears, it looked like to Petey. "Ah, good shit. Here, kid, want a toke?" He leaned forward and held the stub toward Petey, butt first.

"Uh, no thanks," said Petey, who had tried pot twice and gotten embarrassingly sick each time. Besides, this spitty twist of paper didn't look like anything he wanted to put in his mouth. "I don't feel like it today."

"Jesse, you dickhead!" Annie snatched the joint, dropped it between her feet where a tear in the plastic groundsheet left a patch of grass exposed, and demolished it with one heel.

"Hey hey hey!" Jesse's belated grab for the joint tipped the stool and spilled him to the ground, where he rolled over and lay flat for a moment. Bo stayed still and Tif did, too, but her halo of wiry curls trembled, as if a breeze had passed.

"Fuck it," said Jesse. He came to his feet, shrugged and bent to retrieve his stool. "There's more where that came from, any-way. Relax, kid," he said to Petey, "nobody's mad. Except at that faggot Jew lawyer that's trying to push us around. Guy thinks a five-hundred-dollar raincoat and a big red car give him the right to sic the cops on white folks."

"Michaelson." Petey swallowed and cleared his throat. "His name is Michaelson."

"Yeah? Well the little bastard better stay out of my way or I'll gut him, hang him, and smoke him. What do you think about that, huh?"

"Um, I think . . . I think it sounds great."

"Right, right! The bastard is gonna chase you off your own property, what Annie told me."

"That's what *he* thinks."

"Good kid," said Jesse, his wolfish grin exposing stained teeth.

"See, the white man, the white working man, he's hardly got a place anymore in this country. So sometimes you gotta stand up for yourself and fight, understand?" He planted his feet wide and reached atop his head with a clawed hand to pull a black patch down over his wandering left eye. "You gotta be a warrior."

"Odin," said Petey.

"Huh?"

The northern gods, in the myths and stories, were big yellow-haired men, too, with wide roaring mouths and faces full of anger. They lived in great halls, but sometimes in smoky caves, eating whole oxen and drinking mead or maybe beer. Fighting, with trolls or giants or each other. Waited on by beautiful women.

"Odin was a warrior," Petey said to Jesse, "king of the Aesir gods. The north gods. He had only one eye, because he gave the other one up for wisdom."

"Hey, right. King of the gods." Jesse grinned down at Petey, then turned to point a long finger at Bo. "And the king's faithful companion here, he have a name?"

Bo sucked deeply from the beer can in his huge hand, staring at Petey from eyes like small black marbles.

"I think . . . he's probably Thor, the Thunderer."

"Hey hey, ol' thunderer, thunder god! You the one keeps making it rain, you sonofabitch?"

Bo lowered his head behind a lifted shoulder and the two men lunged together and rebounded, then tossed punches at each other's chests and biceps, grunting hunh-hunh-hunh, heads brushing canvas whenever one or the other moved away from the tent's center. Tif stared up at them without expression, moving only to tuck her legs out of the way; Annie sighed loudly and got to her feet, pulling Petey with her toward the doorway.

"Assholes," she muttered. "Kick the heater over, burn down the tent, what do I care? If they're gods, I must be a virgin."

Petey's face grew warm. "I think you're Freya."

"Me Freya, why not?" She pulled off her knitted stocking cap and shook her piled hair loose. It looked newly washed and glowed in the dim tent like something richer than gold.

"You have a chariot pulled by gray cats," he told her. "And a cloak made of falcon feathers; when you put that on you can fly."

"Oh, I love that part. I love to fly." She giggled and hugged him, both arms this time. Slightly shorter than he was, she felt very soft in spite of her skinny arms and she smelled like flowers.

"Hey hey, kid," said Jesse. "No copping a feel right in front of the old man."

Petey had a sudden need for fresh air, big gulps of fresh rainy air. "I have to go," he said, and took two long steps toward the doorway before remembering his main reason for coming here. "Do you want me to bring you something to eat?" he asked Annie. "I know there's lots of good stuff in the freezer, my mom cooks all the time."

"What we really need here," said Jesse, "is a load of hamburgers and fries, from that truckers' place on the highway, you know?"

"Hungry Wheels."

"Right. And we've got money, everybody did good today, but what we haven't got is wheels. I understand you got a nice bike, kid. How about you let me borrow it, and I'll ride on down to Hungry Wheels and pick up supper?"

Petey glanced at Annie, who responded with a "whatever" shrug. His mother had given him the tough, many-geared mountain bike for Christmas and he knew it had cost her a lot, more than four hundred dollars. "Well. I don't usually let people borrow my bike." He lifted his gaze to meet Jesse's blue glare; it felt funny trying to look a one-eyed guy in the eyes. Eye.

"No, I don't do that. But if you want, you can give me the money and I'll go to Hungry Wheels for you."

"Would you rather come to the concert with me? I have an extra ticket; I was thinking of Val when I got it, but he's not home yet."

Without answering, Petey turned off the hot water and upended a rinsed pan into the dish drainer. Charlotte noted the slump of his bony shoulders, but resisted the impulse to cross the room to him, to hug him or ruffle his hair. Her formerly open-faced and openhearted son was closing himself off from her these days, avoiding her gaze and sliding out from under her touch.

"So, what's it to be," she went on, "Eddie's as usual, or Christopher Parkening? He's awfully good, Petey."

"Well, shit, I don't know." Petey propped his back against the edge of the sink and stared gloomily down at his high-tops. The usual plan on Sunday nights was for him to go to Eddie Duarte's after supper and spend the night; on Monday morning Eddie's father would drop the two of them off early at the high school pool for junior high swim team practice. Formerly indifferent to sports, Charlotte had in the last year come to hold swimming and soccer essential to her survival.

"Please don't swear just as a matter of course, Petey," she said, and he ducked his head and muttered, "Sorry."

"You should call Eddie if you're not going there."

"Well . . . I don't feel that terrific, why don't I just stay home?"

"Fine, and I'll stay, too; I don't have the Bach quite right yet."

"Oh, come on, Mom! I'm not some dumb baby, I can stay home at night by myself."

"I'm sorry, Petey. With the neighborhood stirred up as it is, I'd be uncomfortable leaving you here alone."

"Well, shit. And that's not matter of course, that's mad, okay?"

"Okay." Charlotte stood where she was, pushed her hands into the pockets of her sweater, and met her son's eyes. Avoider of conflict whenever possible, she hated this conflict most of all.

"So I guess I'll go to Eddie's. You ready?"

"Five minutes."

"I'll get my stuff and then back the car out."

"Only as . . ."

". . . far as the sidewalk," he finished, and grinned at her.

Charlotte dropped Petey and his old bike at the Duartes' two-story white frame house, waved to Mrs. Duarte, who came to open the door, and drove off with a sigh of relief. Her Toyota, new and inconspicuously well behaved, purred its way through town and then north toward the university. She would have enjoyed Val's company, but was happy enough that he hadn't turned up, that she could spend the evening responding only to the music. And much as she loved Petey, in his present state he drained her of emotional energy in much the same way he had, as a ravenous baby, drained her of milk. In her next incarnation, Charlotte decided, she would not have children. Motherhood was too hard, in ways she could not have imagined.

Rain had ceased and fog had taken over, white and woolly, billowing at the occasional puff of wind. The bricks of the central plaza of UC-Port Silva were slippery underfoot, and Charlotte was glad she'd worn her ugly fisherman's-style rubber boots instead of the nice little leather Fryes that wrapped the foot so gracefully.

"No problem, Char—uh, Ms. Birdsong," said the young woman at the ticket window, a university junior and a fine violinist. "I'll sell your extra ticket in about thirty seconds. Enjoy the music."

The concert was being held in the large auditorium, a misfortune in Charlotte's view but an artist of Parkening's fame and quality was just too big a draw in a small university town. She smiled at several ushers, music students all; although she had no official connection with the university's music department, she was sought after as an accompanist and got free tickets to nearly everything as a result.

The guitarist managed to fill the big hall with sound as well as with patrons. When Charlotte made her way back to her car two hours later she was replete, like a lover of fine food who had just enjoyed a near-perfect meal. The fog was close around her, but traffic was light and everyone was driving carefully; she paid outward attention to car and road while replaying in her head a Bach chaconne, a Giuliani rondo, a somber little Scarlatti piece.

Her garage door hauled itself politely up, responding to the electronic opener Val had installed as a gift a few weeks earlier. If he couldn't get her to remember to lock her house . . . she had forgotten again tonight, she realized now with a guilty twinge . . . he could at least secure the garage from invaders. She wondered whether one could buy electronic door-openers for houses.

No light in Val's basement apartment, and she'd not seen his Jeep on the street. Maybe he'd made some exciting discovery in his search for the missing Edward Boylan. Maybe he'd found a new girlfriend.

That thought brought a pang that astonished and then dismayed her. Possessiveness—let's be honest, Charlotte, what we're talking about here is lust—had sneaked up on her, and would no doubt spoil the easy friendliness she'd shared with her handsome young tenant. She blinked back tears and noted that she was spending an awful lot of time these days feeling sorry for herself.

The worn wooden treads of the back stairs were slick with moisture. She held to the banister as she climbed, found the door unlocked as she had expected, stepped inside and saw that she had left a lamp burning wastefully in the kitchen. She needed a keeper, or at least a check-off list beside the door.

She hung her raincoat on a hook in the back hallway, pulled off the rubber boots, and padded stocking-footed into the kitchen. A figure rose from the wicker armchair, and she caught at the counter-edge in cold panic. Scream, Charlotte! don't be ridiculous one does not scream besides my mouth is too dry.

She coughed and swallowed hard, said, "Martin," in a raspy croak and coughed again. "Just what the hell do you think you're doing, sneaking into my house while I'm out?"

"I'd hardly call it sneaking, Charlotte, simply coming into the house I grew up in. The house I was born in."

"According to your mother, you were born in a hospital in Ukiah." Her groping fingers found the wall switch for the main light; Martin blinked and put a hand up to shade his face.

"Same old Charlotte, completely literal-minded." He gave a self-conscious little chuckle and thrust his hands into his trousers pockets, jaunty-debonair. The bright overhead light beat down cruelly on his head, glinting off the bald spot, picking up silver roots of dyed brown hair, laying harsh lines of shadow on creased cheek and stringy neck. Time had finally caught up with Martin Lindberg; Charlotte considered for a moment and decided he must be fifty-five and looked ten years older than that.

"Literal-minded enough to know that you have no legal right to enter, uninvited, premises that do not belong to you."

"Charlotte, my dear! You were such a kind, loving girl; that's the way I always remember you. Warm, and forgiving. I can't believe that you're still angry with me."

"I'm not angry, Martin. I simply don't like you."

"And after all," he went on, ignoring her words, "even if you still feel I behaved badly, that was a long, long time ago. Surely it's time to set aside old grievances and declare a truce."

He tilted his head, cocked an eyebrow at her and gave her The Smile, which showed just the edges of his still very good teeth. He'd practiced that eyebrow business before a mirror, he had told her once in a rare moment of candor. And he'd certainly practiced the smile, using it on theater audiences, on his students, on any passing female. Caught between an urge to giggle at his posturing and a twinge of pity for the aging Lothario who didn't know how foolish he appeared, she simply shook her head. "So what do you say, old girl? Let's kiss and make up." The hands that gripped her upper arms were bony and cold through the silk of her blouse; his mouth, too, was cold, brushing her cheek as she turned her head quickly away. Distaste that surprised her by its intensity must have shown on her face, because he stepped back as quickly as if she had pushed him.

"Touch-me-not, Charlotte? At this late date?" He passed both hands over his hair, smoothing its sparse strands gently into place. "I was going to suggest we have a little drink, in honor of, oh, old times? Happier days? And just to warm a fellow up. One of the things I'd forgotten about this miserable outpost of civilization is how goddamned cold and wet it always is."

He abandoned his dapper pose and dropped into the wicker chair with a shiver that was real; and Charlotte looked him over more closely. The tweed jacket was worn napless and thin, the crumpled gray slacks wouldn't have held a crease even when dry; his pointy-toed shoes were cheap imitations of the expensive footgear he preferred for his narrow feet, the sole of one pulling loose from its sodden upper. Martin was clearly broke, probably in debt. It wouldn't hurt her to give him a drink.

She took a small, square glass from a cupboard, and then a wineglass; she pulled open a narrower cupboard door and inspected her supply of liquor, not extensive but of good quality. "Irish, or bourbon?" she asked. "Or perhaps gin?"

"Ah, bourbon. No ice, please."

She poured two inches of Wild Turkey and set it before him, poured her glass full of white wine, and sat down in the rocker, on the opposite side of the long pine table that served as her kitchen work surface.

"Cheers," he said, and sipped and smiled. "Ah, I don't suppose you could fix a weary traveler something to eat? Bacon and eggs, maybe?"

"No, I don't suppose so either," she told him. But she hated to see anyone, any creature even, going hungry. "There might be something in the fridge that you can eat cold."

Times were hard, Martin advised her as he attacked squares of spinach fritatta topped with salsa that she had, after all, heated. His fourth wife had divorced him, perhaps Charlotte had heard about that, and since the frigid bitch had insisted on a prenuptial agreement, the whole experience left him with nothing but bruises and heartache.

So he'd lost his comfortable home and social base in Los Angeles, and was reduced to living in a miserable studio apartment near Long Beach, driving to interviews and auditions in a disreputable little secondhand Chevrolet. "Then there was a chance for this role in a new sit-com, just a one-shot thing but I thought I might make something of the character. Unfortunately, my agent felt it wasn't right for me. The thing is, a serious actor who's pushing fifty has to be very selective." He gave Charlotte a wide-eyed, sincere gaze as he wiped his mouth and reached for the Wild Turkey bottle.

"You're not doing any teaching now?" Martin Lindberg had been an instructor in the drama department at UC-San Diego when Charlotte met him, teaching speech and some introductory acting courses. An uninspired actor, he had been when he bothered to make the effort an excellent teacher.

"Good Christ no! I spent a semester recently on the faculty of a community college, and you cannot imagine, Charlotte, what dregs of humanity attend those institutions. And the administration, looking over your shoulder every minute. Horrible." He gave a shudder, an actor's shudder this time, and pushed his chair back from the table.

Same old Martin. Charlotte was bitterly amused at herself for the hopeful fantasy that had sneaked up on her: Martin Lindberg turning outward and useful, not to her but to Petey.

Well. It was nearly midnight, she had students coming tomorrow and other matters that would demand her serious attention. If she could get rid of her unwanted guest, she might be able to reclaim tonight's concert and take it to bed with her. But she needed to know one thing first, and she was too tired to play games for the information. "Martin, why are you here?"

"My dear, my roots are here!"

"Oh. Of course."

"And I thought it was time for me to pay a visit to my son," he said. "After all, given my age, my circumstances, I'm not likely to have another."

"Martin, you didn't want to have this one. As I recall, you denied having had anything to do with it."

"That was a long time ago, Charlotte, when I was a younger and more foolish man. But those pictures on the old mantel gave me a real *frisson*, an awareness of kinship."

He turned and strode off through the music room and into the living room, Charlotte close on his heels. "Even if I do say so myself, he's a fine-looking boy," Martin said as he picked up the frame that held her most recent picture of Petey. "I can see my father in him and my mother too, but most of all myself."

No, she thought in quiet triumph. Petey had her own father's dark-lashed hazel eyes and high bony forehead, plus a stubborn jaw that had probably come from his grandmother; he'd be a big honest-looking man, not dapper-handsome as Martin had been.

"Good Finnish blood," Martin was saying with relish. "Our inheritance—our heritage."

Oh yes. She'd been thinking along just those lines since last night at least. Inheritance.

"I'm not good about dates, but I hope I've come in time for his birthday," said Martin, eyes still on the photo. "Number thirteen, isn't it?"

There he'd finally hit a nerve. "Fourteen," said Charlotte through clenched teeth. "*Next* month. But we'll manage without you." She took the picture from him and set it back on the mantel. "Your raincoat is in the kitchen, Martin. I'm tired and I want you to leave."

"Just a minute, Charlotte." He had followed her in silence as far as the kitchen table; now he picked up his glass, and poured it half full of whiskey. "Good stuff, you're fortunate indeed to be able to buy this. Now listen to me, while I tell you the way things should be.

"First of all, this house: it was my grandfather's, and then my father's, and now by rights it should be mine. When I'm through with it, maybe it will be here for my son. But he'll have to wait his turn, the way I did."

"Your father left it to your mother."

"And you swindled a crazy old lady, making her think your bastard was her grandchild. I've been talking to people around town, people who will testify and help me break the will."

"You're mixing your roles, Martin; you can't be both the deprived father and the poor fool hung with someone else's bastard."

With a hiss of indrawn breath, Martin lifted his right hand high, then noticed it held his drink and tipped the rest of the whiskey into his mouth. Charlotte turned to the sink and ran a glass full of water, drank it and filled the glass again. She thought the water had a brackish edge, but perhaps it was just her own sour disgust she was tasting.

"Look, Charlotte, be reasonable." He set his empty glass down and spread his hands. "The house is worth over two hundred thousand now, which means your inheritance . . ."

"Petey's inheritance."

"All right, Petey's inheritance. It has more than doubled since you, he, got it. Now I'll do the decent thing and split it down the middle with you, what could be fairer than that?"

Charlotte leaned against the sink's edge and crossed her arms over her breasts. If she were to point out the elasticity of Martin's concept of fairness, he'd be here for another half hour.

His smile took on a nervous edge, and the words came faster. "You and the kid will still have a lot more than you started with, at least a hundred thou. And I'll have a stake too, I'm not getting any younger and like most creative people, I haven't been clever with money. But now there's this little private acting school I have a chance to get a piece of . . . Charlotte, don't shake your head at me."

"No, Martin. It was your mother's to give, this house, and she gave it."

"Stubborn, that's what you always were. Terrible quality in a woman, Charlotte. My son will be more understanding. And where is he, by the way? What kind of mother lets such a young boy stay out till the middle of the night?"

"Your son whom you haven't bothered to see half a dozen times in his life? Toward whose support you have never contributed a single dime? And he's not 'out,' he's spending the night with a friend." Watching Martin's face, Charlotte had an uneasy feeling of circumstances shifting, balances changing. The bottle he had just picked up, nearly full to begin with, looked to be down now by about half. He'd not been a drinker in the days she'd known him . . . a long time ago, she realized.

"So you sit up here on your fat backside, give a piano lesson now and then." He was breathing in short, deep gasps. "Stay warm and dry in the house my grandfather built, drink first-class booze while I buy whatever cheap blend Safeway has on special." He looked at the bottle of Wild Turkey, gave it a little balancing jiggle and flung it at her head.

Chapter
Eight

V al Kuisma gripped the steering wheel more firmly and refused to let himself shiver. He was wet and muddy from his boots to his beard, and the cold night air blowing through the Jeep's windows penetrated to his bones, all of them aching. But when he closed the windows and turned on the heater, a ripe and rotten smell engulfed him, from his clothes or his skin or maybe just from his memory.

When the sheriff's deputies finally arrived at the Rainbow Tavern, one of them turned out to be a guy he'd known at Humboldt State University and the other was best buddy to Val's cousin, Walt Miranda, also a deputy sheriff. Nobody made objection to Val's meddling in county affairs; instead, working in rain and cold water to get into a truck cab half-buried in silt and gravel, the deputies simply drafted him as one more set of hands.

Now he turned his head toward the window, took a deep open-mouthed breath and exhaled hard. The deputies thought it was pretty funny that Officer Val Kuisma had found a body but not the one he was looking for, just some poor anonymous guy who, even though semirefrigerated by flowing water, had clearly been dead for some time.

At least he hadn't thrown up, the way he did the first time he helped to clear a fatal traffic accident. But old Ed Boylan had better turn up breathing, because Officer Kuisma would prefer not to repeat tonight's scene any time soon.

Scattered groups of mist-haloed lights glimmered off to his right, on the headland occupied by the university. Just parking-lot lights, hardly any activity, everybody tucked up studying on a rainy . . . Sunday night! Goddamn! And at—he peered at the digital clock on the dash—at ten fifty-six—the concert was long over. He'd missed Christopher Parkening.

Val let his foot rest more heavily on the accelerator. He'd get home quick, shed his filthy clothes and have a shower. Then, if Charlotte's light was still on, he'd knock on her door and see whether she was up for company and a beer. Maybe even get her to play for him, if she wasn't too tired.

He sped south through empty streets past the center of town, made the jog west to Frontage Road, swung shallow right onto the curve of Finn Lane and noted that the big tent remained in the park but had not been joined by any others. The front of number sixteen was dark, lights only in the rear. Bright lights, though; Charlotte must be cooking. Aches and shivers fading at the prospect of company, music, and maybe even food, Val whipped the Jeep around in a U-turn to park it before the house.

He unlocked his apartment door, reached inside to turn on a light and then crouched to unlace his boots. Sounds from above caught his ear; he pulled the boots off, stepped inside the door and listened. A radio, or television? No, just two voices, one Charlotte's and the other not deep but distinctly male.

And not familiar, he decided as he peeled off jeans and sweatshirt and underwear and socks, to drop them all beside the door. He looked at the wet and filthy pile, then opened the door and shoved the whole mess outside. Let them stink out there, and he'd go see what a shower would do for his aching bones.

Hot water was a definite improvement over what he'd been slogging around in all day; and the enveloping sound of it pro-tected him from the temptation to eavesdrop. He soaped his hair, his beard, his whole body once and then again. Charlotte usually spent Sunday evenings with *him*, but he had not, after all, turned up tonight. Hadn't called to let her know, either.

He rinsed himself free of soap and turned the shower nozzle to massage force. No reason at all Charlotte shouldn't have a boyfriend. She was an attractive woman, small and round and sexy in a basic way that had nothing to do with seductiveness. She could turn him on in a minute if she made the least attempt. Or even if she didn't, he thought glumly, and stifled a yelp as the hot water suddenly ran out.

He squeezed water from hair and beard, then used two towels to get really dry. In the big, chilly space that was both livingroom and bedroom, he eyed the wall heater and decided not to bother; he'd just put on clean sweats and stretch out under the down comforter with a beer and a book.

The sound of a crash from upstairs caught him with a sweatshirt halfway on. Then the scream, and as he fought to get his head and arms clear, another scream. His mind touched and dismissed as unreachable the .38 revolver locked in a metal box in his closet; he flung himself barefooted out the door, cleared the outside stairs in three bounds, hit the upper door and burst into the hall and through to the kitchen where Charlotte stood before the sink drenched in blood.

Small man, white face and lots of shiny teeth, yelling something. Val took him out low with one shoulder, put him down and flipped him onto his belly, planted a knee on his back and braced the other foot wide on the floor and wrenched the bastard's right arm high between his shoulder blades. "Charlotte, can you get to the phone and call downtown?"

The man on the floor flailed about with his legs and his free arm, then got his head up and snarled, "Let me go, goddamn you!"

Val pushed the right arm a notch higher and his captive gave a howl of pain. "Officer Val Kuisma, Port Silva Police. Watch your mouth, buddy, or I'll step on your head." He eased his knee away, got carefully to his feet and hauled the other man upright. "Charlotte?"

Blood like red paint made a wet sweep down the left side of her face, from what Val thought must be a scalp cut. The blouse she clutched closed with both hands was red as well, and wet, but not from blood. From booze, he realized belatedly; the room reeked of it and shards of glass littered the countertop and the floor around her feet.

"This is a domestic matter, Officer, you have no business interfering!" A fine spray of spittle flew from the man's mouth with his words. "I have a right to speak to this . . . to my wife, I have a right to be in this house and to know why my son is not home in his bed at midnight."

"Shut up," said Val, taking another upward hitch in his hold; the man gasped and rose on tiptoe. "Nobody has a right to attack another person with a bottle. Which in case you're interested qualifies as a deadly weapon."

"I didn't, I did *not* . . ."

"Martin. Get out of here." Charlotte's voice was a near-whisper.

"I was provoked! No man should have to . . ."

"Val, make him go away. Please."

"Yes, ma'am," said Val through his teeth. "Out you go, little man. And if you bother Ms. Birdsong again, I will personally pull off all your arms and legs and feed them to you." He propelled his captive into the back hall, toward the door.

"Don't think for a minute we're finished, Charlotte!" Martin yelled over his shoulder.

Val snapped, "Move it!" and half-pushed, half-carried the smaller man out the door and down the stairs, dropped him in the mud and left him there.

Charlotte hadn't moved; the blood on her face was drying, and there seemed to be no fresh flow. "Here, Charlotte, let me look," he said softly and found a shallow, inch-long cut just above her temple, the blood already clotting. "Fine, fine. Shouldn't even need stitches."

Apart from the blood, her face was greenly pale; she was breathing in long, shuddering drafts through clenched teeth. Fumes of liquor rose from her hair and clothing, to bite the nostrils and sting the eyes. "Charlotte, did he hit you anywhere else?"

"No. No, but I'm cold, and the smell is making me sick. And I can't walk through the glass," she pointed out, looking down at her stockinged feet and at his bare ones. "Oh, you can't either. I guess we'll just have to stand here."

"I think I can work something out." He reached past her, plucked a broom from its wall hook, and brushed aside a litter of glass.

"Oh, good. Now I can go wash. Please don't go away, Val," she added in a rush.

"Not a chance."

He swept up the glass, found a mop and swabbed up the whiskey, all with one ear cocked in the direction of the bathroom. Just the sound of water in the shower, no thuds. No singing. He stood facing the sink, his feet where Charlotte's had been but reversed, and saw the dent in the wooden corner post of the cupboard. The son of a bitch threw that bottle at her head and just missed.

He noted the small square glass on the table, finger-smeared and smelling of bourbon. Wineglass there, too, an inch of white wine remaining. Ratty tan raincoat on the back of a chair; he snatched the garment up, carried it to the back door and threw it over the railing to the mud below.

Sounds of water still. He moved to the bathroom door, listened. "Charlotte, are you okay? Can I get you anything?"

"I forgot my robe. The long one, in my closet."

"You got it." He fetched the robe, reached around the edge of the door to hang it on the hook, pulled the door shut.

In the kitchen he opened the liquor cupboard, made a face at his own thickheadedness and turned instead to the pantry. When Charlotte finally came into the kitchen wrapped in her down-filled pink cotton robe, he settled her into the wicker chair and put a cup of steaming cocoa in her hands.

She inhaled the steam in a long breath, smiled faintly and sipped. Val, watching, couldn't think what to say. Maybe, I really think you should press charges against that guy. Or maybe, How in hell did you ever . . . ? No. "Um, Charlotte. You know, there are laws to protect women from spousal battering, no matter what that . . . your . . ."

She lifted her head sharply. "Val, I am not Martin Lindberg's wife, nor have I ever been."

"Oh. Good."

"Yes, good. I did live with him for nearly a year, a long time ago." She took a slow mouthful of cocoa and cradled the mug in her lap. "Martin is, or was, self-centered, manipulative, and a user of people, especially women. But he never hit me before, never even threatened to."

"Tonight was more than a threat, Charlotte. If his aim had been better, you could be dead."

"I don't think . . . It was a spur of the moment thing, Val, not something he had planned to do."

Silence stretched, and then Val said, contemplatively, "Martin *Lindberg*."

Charlotte looked up to meet his gaze, and sighed. "You. You want to know everything, don't you? You are the most . . . do you know about the elephant's child and his 'satiable curtiosity?"

"I guess I missed that one. But my mother did tell me what curiosity was supposed to do to cats. And she pointed out that little Portagee-Finnish boys do not have nine lives."

Val's grin crinkled his green eyes. In spite of the thick black hair and curly black beard, he looked not much older than Petey. Then she remembered his entry into her kitchen tonight; it was not a precise memory, more a recollection of speed, of purposeful and efficient action. Val had heard her scream, she supposed, and had come at once and prevented . . . what? What Martin's next move might have been she had no idea; clearly she needed to give a lot more thought to Martin.

"Val? Thank you."

"Any time. Any time at all."

"Well." Charlotte put her empty mug on the table and sat back in her chair, tucking her hands into the sleeves of her robe. "Here's the way it was, 'satiable policeman. First of all, this is the Lindberg house, from the commune days."

"Okay, sure. A Mrs. Lindberg lived here when I was growing

up, tough old Finnish lady like my grandmother. In fact, I think they were friends."

"Martin was Mrs. Lindberg's only child. He left home to go to college in Los Angeles at age eighteen," Charlotte added, "and he never again lived in this house or in Port Silva."

"And Martin Lindberg is Petey's father?"

"*Was*," said Charlotte. "To be precise, you could say he provided half the original material."

"Ah."

"All right, background. My father was a Jew who came here from Germany in the thirties, the only member of his family to survive. My mother was an orphan, raised by an elderly aunt in West Virginia. They met and married in Chicago; I was their late and only child. That was it, just the three of us."

"And you lived in Southern California?"

She shook her head. "We lived all over the country, mostly looking for a place where my mother's health would be better; her heart had been damaged in childhood by rheumatic fever. And I think they just liked moving. We were happy, at least I was and I really think they were, too. My father taught me mathematics, my mother music; she was a world-class pianist but not strong enough for the concert stage."

Charlotte took a deep breath. "Mother died when I was thirteen, Petey's age. I lived with my father, and went to school and studied piano with other teachers. And then he died, when I was a sophomore in college."

Val made a small sound of sympathy.

"Yes. He was a lovely man and I still miss him. Anyway, when I returned to school for second semester, I met my speech teacher and what I saw was a handsome, thoughtful, sophisticated forty-year-old man who had sorrow in his life, too, poor thing: his second marriage had just broken up. What he must have seen, when he looked at me, was a naive, malleable girl who would adore him blindly, and who happened to have a nice house and a little money as well as potential for a lucrative concert career."

"So the guy was a son of a bitch right from the start."

"Oh, Val, he was selfish. Now he's selfish and scared. But he was an awfully good first lover for someone as totally inexperienced as I was," she added. "I think it was part of being an actor; Martin was always willing to work very hard for applause."

Val cleared his throat. Charlotte pulled her thoughts back to the present, focused on her listener's face and found it pink. "You wanted the story," she reminded him gently, "and I'm much too tired to edit."

If he was embarrassed, he was also determined to hear the rest of it. "So I guess what happened, he got you pregnant and that shot down the career, so he wouldn't marry you."

"*We* got me pregnant," she corrected. "And he wanted to marry me; we'd been waiting for his divorce to be worked out. But he said he was too old to be a father, I'd have to have an abortion."

"Like I said, your basic son of a bitch."

"He certainly lost a lot of his charm in a hurry. So I thought it over. What would I rather have, this suddenly very unromantic middle-aged man, or a nice new baby? It didn't seem a difficult choice at the time."

Twenty years old and sure she could do it; how foolish, how brave, how young. Raising the child with his father's help was not an option, nor would she have chosen to do that once her view of Martin was unclouded by lust. Abortion equally impossible, Martin's child also her father's grandchild. She had thought she could do it. "I beg your pardon?" she said, catching Val's voice but not his words.

"Was that the last you saw of Martin?"

"No. He turned up when Petey was three, and we were in, let's see, San Luis. I'd moved around quite a bit, not to hide but just because that was the way I'd always lived, like a nomad. Martin managed to find me; he could be clever when he wanted something.

"And after that, four or five times, when he was broke or between women. He'd try to get me into bed, sometimes with success; he'd try to get money from me, and at that he always failed. What he wants now is this house, the money from it. He sees this as his last big chance."

"Has he any claim on it?"

She shook her head. "His mother found out about Petey and me, I don't know how. She wrote to my lawyer in San Diego, he's a good friend and we've kept in touch; Mrs. Lindberg asked that I bring Petey to visit her, and I did. When she died, she left Martin one hundred dollars for every time he'd come to see her since he was eighteen, a total of four hundred dollars. She left the rest of her money, not a lot, to the Port Silva Historical Society. She left the house to Petey . . . to 'Peter Birdsong, natural son of Charlotte Vogel known as Birdsong.' And I hold it in trust for him until he's twenty-one."

"Or until somebody runs you down in the street," he muttered. "Charlotte, you have to go downtown and file a complaint, protect yourself by getting his behavior on record."

"What I should probably do is sell and give him half." She stared past Val, as if there were something written in the air or on the wall and she was puzzling the words out. "His claim isn't completely unreasonable. He needs the money. I support myself and Petey well enough. And I hate conflict."

"But," supplied Val.

"But my son needs this place!" she said with sudden fierceness. "I have nothing to leave him: no family silver, no aunts or cousins, no roots he can touch. Nothing but a Steinway piano." Charlotte let her spine slump, lifted a hand to cover a yawn. "Petey's need is more valid than Martin's." The next was too big to cover, a head-back, eyes-closed jawbreaker of a yawn. "I'm sorry. I'm suddenly so tired."

"Go to bed, Charlotte. If you don't mind, I'll stay here a while. I'm not sleepy, and I never got around to turning on the heater downstairs."

"Oh, please stay. And play tapes if you like." This last from the doorway in a voice already foggy with sleep.

Chapter
Nine

"Sorry I'm late, Chief." Val Kuisma slid into a chair, wishing he had not stayed up until two-thirty, wishing he'd slept better after that. Wishing he'd been able to convince Charlotte to file charges against Lindberg. Hoping he wouldn't have to look at the photos on Vince Gutierrez's desk, because he was fairly sure what they were: nighttime Polaroid shots of an extremely dead middle-aged Caucasian male.

"Kuisma," said Gutierrez, with no softening of his lean dark face. Port Silva's police chief was not a cheerful morning man, even on good days; and the nearly empty coffeepot on the side table suggested that Gutierrez's Monday had started long before the present hour of eight.

"I've just been filling people in on your discovery," Gutierrez told him. Val nodded a greeting to his colleagues: Captain Hank Svoboda, propped against a filing cabinet with a coffee mug in his hand; Detective John Hebert, slumped like a bulky question mark at the end of the conference table; and Sergeant Duane Mendenhall, astride a reversed straight chair with his meaty forearms resting along its back. Svoboda nodded in return, Hebert blinked sky-blue eyes that looked sleepy as usual, and Mendenhall grinned.

"Hey, kid," said Mendenhall, "my buddy that's a sergeant with the county, he says they're gonna retire their bloodhounds and keep you on retainer instead. 'Nose' Kuisma, sniffs out bodies wherever they hide 'em."

"I just had a feeling there was something down that road," Val said to the chief. "But I don't know that anybody hid him. It looked like he was drunk or maybe just confused in the dark, drove down there by mistake and ended up in the creek with the steering wheel in his chest. Tell you what, Duane," he added, "next time I come across a body that's nice and ripe, I'll fill a Breathalyzer canister and bring it to you, for training."

Gutierrez's right hand sliced the air in a cut-the-crap gesture; Val sat straighter and sensed Mendenhall doing the same. "The pathologist was at the hospital last night when they got there with the body. He just took a quick look; but he found at least one deep knife wound in the abdomen. And he thinks the guy has been dead maybe a week to ten days."

"But he was the wrong build, wrong hair color." Val cast an unhappy glance toward the packet of photos, gearing himself up for another viewing.

"The dead man is definitely not Edward Boylan," Gutierrez assured him. "The truck is registered to somebody named Gardner at an address in Leggett. The body was found in the county and it looks like he died there. That makes it the business of the sheriff's department, accident or murder. But this poor bastard, Gardner if that's who he is, apparently got killed about the time Boylan disappeared. That fact puts a serious knot in my gut, and I promise you it's going to have an even worse effect on Mrs. Boylan."

"Coincidence?" said Val not very hopefully. "Anyway, I talked to people in back-roads bars all yesterday afternoon and I didn't get a whisper on Boylan."

"From what ever'body says, that fellow worked real hard at bein' an asshole," Hank Svoboda remarked in his slow deep voice. "Saturday night he hit four bars here in town that we know of, drank steady, bragged about the big deal he just pulled off. Made rude suggestions to a number of ladies." Hank shook his brush-cut gray head sadly. "Last place we traced him to was the Fisherman's Rest, where he turned up around ten-thirty or eleven. Had three drinks real fast and offered insult to

Portagees, Swedes, Finns, Native Americans, and hippies among others."

"Holy shit!" said Mendenhall. "What I can't understand, why didn't they find pieces of him all over the parking lot on Sunday morning?"

"Probably because two bartenders showed him out the door just ahead of snapping teeth."

"Does anyone know," asked Johnny Hebert, "precisely what his big deal *was*?"

"The MacAllister ranch," replied Gutierrez.

"Huh?" said Mendenhall, the only outlander in the room.

"It's south of town, a big sheep ranch with a chunk of coastal ridge as its western boundary. The owners . . ." Gutierrez looked at Svoboda, who scowled as he took up the narrative.

"Jake and Marjorie MacAllister. I happen to know they were setting up a land trust with the ranch, and then Jake died. Seems this Boylan kept after Marjorie some way or other, and she wound up selling the ranch to his company."

"Well, no question what happened to the poor bastard," said Mendenhall. "Bunch of no-growthniks grabbed him, took him out to Mendocino Headlands park and threw him off." He looked at Gutierrez's expressionless face and shrugged. "Sorry, Chief."

"Good. What I want you to do, Duane, is get back to the SandDollar, and to the bars where Boylan was seen, and do it all over again for the third or fourth time. Pick two people to work with you, whoever you can break loose; check it out with Hanson. Johnny?"

"Chief?" Hebert straightened his comfortably curved spine, lifted his chin from his chest, and reached for his notebook. Val thought he looked like a bullfrog who'd just heard a fly buzz close.

"I want you to go to Santa Rosa and look over Boylan's company. See who he's worked with recently, see how the money has come in and where it's gone. We know he hasn't used his charge cards or his regular bank accounts in the last week; maybe he's got access to cash somewhere else. And check on Boylan's contractor's license and any complaints against it."

"Right."

"And keep your ears open around the office there," Gutierrez added, before turning his attention to the next item. "Val."

Val, who'd been thinking himself an onlooker here, snapped to attention and said, "Chief!"

"I need you on this. You know the county better than anybody except maybe Hank; and we've got four officers, one sergeant, and Lieutenant Markham out with flu. I've talked to the doctor, and he's agreed to release you for a temporary assignment to the detective division; and I've asked the sheriff's people to call you as soon as they have anything on Gardner. If there's a connection between Gardner and Boylan, we need to find it."

"Yessir," said Val. Yesterday he'd have been happy as a bird dog who'd just seen his owner pick up a shotgun. Today he'd rather stay around Finn Lane and keep an eye on Charlotte, make sure Martin Lindberg didn't turn up again.

Gutierrez swiveled his chair to look at his closest subordinate and good friend. "Hank," he said to Svoboda, "I'd like you to drop in on Marjorie MacAllister; over a cup of tea with an old friend, she might think of something to add to her original statement. And I'm going to call Mrs. Boylan, before she calls me."

This was a kind of dismissal. Mendenhall stood up, fished a cigarette from his shirt pocket and headed out at a near-trot. Svoboda stretched, said "Well, back to the salt mines," and ambled toward the door; Johnny and Val followed.

"Val, Johnny. A minute." Gutierrez got to his feet and closed the door. "We have a couple of new things on Rip, maybe."

"Ah," said Johnny.

"A lawyer from Southern California, up here trying to put together a land parcel around Finn Park, had his tires slashed Friday night and a Rip flyer was left in the car. And," he went on before either of the others could comment, "a watchman out at Harker's Knob, where an outfit called Tri-Star is laying out a resort and golf course, let fly with a load of bird shot at some people he found 'messing around' on the site Friday afternoon."

"That site was on a Rip flyer several months ago," Johnny remarked.

"And they just moved some equipment . . ." began Gutierrez, but Val interrupted.

"Hey!" he barked. "When did the county start issuing hunting permits to rent-a-cops? Was anybody hurt?"

"Apparently not. Tri-Star put a watchman on only two days earlier, because they'd brought in these earthmovers. The sheriff's people had a long talk with him; he says he stumbled across this bunch of big guys in ski masks and feared for his life. The watchman says he looked the scene over afterward and there was no evidence of a hit." Gutierrez dropped back into his chair with a force that sent it rolling.

"Ski masks yet," said Johnny. "Chief, this weird idea crossed my mind recently, and I can't get rid of it. Do you suppose the Rip people might be behind Boylan's disappearance?"

"Jesus, environmental murders?" said Val.

"You see that as a dumb idea? Me, too—I think." Gutierrez made a sour face. "Kuisma, do you know anybody you can say for sure is involved with Rip?"

Val met his chief's gaze squarely and lifted both hands, open-palmed. "No, sir, I do not. But I guess I've kind of avoided thinking hard about it. Till now, anyway. Do *you*?"

Gutierrez shook his head glumly. "It's damned near a conspiracy. Whoever you might be talking to, you sneak in a question about these folks and you get the wide eyes, the dropped jaw: Who, me? No no, great respect for their aims but absolutely deplore their actions. Bullshit."

"Yessir."

"I have some ideas," said Johnny Hebert. "And some data. But nothing I'd be happy to call evidence."

"Right," said Gutierrez. "Hebert, it turns out Kuisma is in a useful position right now; he's living on Finn Lane, the newest development area to be targeted by Rip. Before you leave for Santa Rosa, I want you to go over your files with him."

He fixed Johnny and then Val with a hard gaze. "Now understand me. Nobody is to hear anything about this. I don't want to piss off the environmentalists, I don't want to stir up any lurking redneck sentiment, and I don't want to have to field any complaints of harassment. Got that?"

"Yessir," they said in unison, and Gutierrez nodded.

"Come along," said Johnny to Val, "and let me introduce you to my computer."

Petey Birdsong pedaled his old no-gear school bike sedately along, at ease with the world. After more than an hour of hard swimming, he could almost look forward to sitting in classes. "Looks like you're getting to be a real good diver," he remarked to his companion. "I heard coach say you might go to the state finals next year."

"I guess I could." Beneath the cutoff sweatshirt sleeve she had pulled on to control her wet hair, Hannah Wilhelm's face was mutinous, lower lip well out. "But diving is boring, I like racing."

Petey tossed a sideways look at his friend, who was not quite five feet tall and probably wouldn't get much taller. "Diving is dangerous," he said, "and lots of girls wouldn't have the nerve to . . ."

"*Women* have as much nerve as men," she snapped. "And I'm perfectly happy being a woman, I'd just like to be a *bigger* woman."

"So go out for the bike team, you've got the strongest legs in eighth grade."

"Yeah, maybe I will. Race you!" she challenged, and took off. Petey chased her hard but knew he wouldn't catch her, not on a hill.

Up the hill, around a corner, and up a gentler climb and then Hannah stopped at the open gate in a chain-link fence and grinned at him. "Hey, you want to go to the computer room?"

He looked at his watch; they were earlier than usual, had forty-five minutes before their first class. "Uh, I don't think so. I think I'll go to the cafeteria."

"My mom says if she was Catholic she'd light a candle every day for thanks, that she's feeding girls instead of boys."

"I beg your pardon?" said an unfamiliar male voice.

Startled, the two of them turned to face a man who was just emerging from the shadow of the building's entryway. Bareheaded and pale of face, he wore a blue nylon windbreaker over a tweed jacket and rumpled gray pants.

"Peter," the man said, and stretched out a hand in greeting. "Don't you recognize me?"

"Uh, well." Petey straightened and squared his shoulders. "Yeah, I guess I do."

"Petey?" Hannah, city-bred and wary, kept her bike between herself and the stranger.

"I think it's Martin. Martin Lindberg."

"Your father, boy. I'm Peter's father," he said to Hannah with a toothy smile.

"His biological father."

"What?"

"You're never around, so you're not a nurturing father. More like a sperm donor."

"Don't talk dirty, little girl!" Martin snapped, his face reddening. "Peter, I'd appreciate a word with you, alone."

"It's okay, Petey, I'll see you in algebra." Hannah took time for a good up and down look at Martin before turning to wheel her bike away.

"I have to go to school," said Petey.

"They told me in the office that your class doesn't start until nine," said Martin. "Come on, let me buy you some breakfast. I spotted a promising-looking doughnut shop on my way here."

Hunger battled discretion and won, aided by a nudge of curiosity. Petey Birdsong had seen this man very seldom in his life, the last time when he was . . . he thought back as he propped his bike in the rack. When he was ten years old, just a little kid. His father was pretty old, Petey noted as he walked beside the man toward the curb and a tan Chevrolet Citation. And he was pretty short, too, shorter than Petey.

Martin kept up a flow of words as he drove, comments on the weather and the town, on how much warmer and more interesting it was in Los Angeles. He talked with his hands in a way that made Petey want to take hold of the steering wheel just in case. They pulled up in front of Fluffo Doughnuts on Cedar a block above Main; Martin backed into a big parking space, scraped his rear tires, and managed to bump the car in front. Charlotte was sure a better driver. Charlotte would never let a Fluffo doughnut into her house.

Petey turned down the offer of a milkshake, asked for a big glass of milk instead, and chose a chocolate frosted, a cinnamon, and a glazed twist. Martin got a decaf latte and poured a lot of sugar into it, stirring gently with the long-handled spoon.

"I stopped in to see your mother last night," Martin said; he lifted the latte glass to his mouth but kept his eyes on Petey's face as he sipped. "Did she tell you about that?"

"No." Petey sank his teeth into the chocolate frosted and wished for a moment he had ordered two of this kind, or maybe even three. Charlotte hardly ever spoke of Martin. What she usually said, when Petey asked, was that she and his father had been in love for a little while and then they weren't.

"Your mother is a wonderful woman, Pete . . . is that what they call you, Pete? Wonderful woman, don't let anyone tell you otherwise. I certainly never blamed her for deciding not to share my life; unless he's incredibly lucky, a serious actor leads a pretty hand-to-mouth existence." Martin tipped his head to one side, stretching his mouth in a kind of sad-clown smile as he pulled a cigarette from a shirt-pocket pack and lit it quickly with a flat silver-colored lighter. The fingers around the cigarette were bony, Petey noted, with nails kind of long for a man; veins lay like bluish ropes over the back of the hand.

"But of course I've always missed her. We had some wonderful times together, your mother and I . . . or you wouldn't be here now, would you?"

Broad grin showing all those teeth, eyes squinting against the smoke. Petey felt his ears and the back of his neck go hot and was suddenly furious with Charlotte for letting this skinny little old man do *that* to her.

"Well, anyway, one of the things that brought me to town was your birthday, the big fourteen coming up. I decided this time I'd ask you what you'd like for a present. It's pretty hard to buy things for a fellow you never get to see."

"Yeah."

"So maybe a nice bike, with lots of gears? To replace that old thing you were riding, women don't understand how guys feel about bikes and cars."

Petey licked cinnamon off his fingers, looked at the glazed twist and felt a little bit sick but decided he shouldn't let it go to waste. He toyed for a moment with the idea of getting another bike, and then he could sell it, why not? Charlotte was why not, she'd be really upset and he'd never manage it without her knowing. Maybe he should just ask for money.

"So what do you say? A bike?"

Had Charlotte ever asked this guy for money? He bet not. "Thank you," he said, and coughed and waved a hand at the cigarette smoke. "I have a good bike, that my mom gave me for Christmas. I don't need anything."

"Well. The other thing I came here for was to see the old house. I grew up in that house, you know, the house where you and your mother live now. Seeing it again last night brought back memories."

Petey put the end of the twist back on the paper plate and sat very still. "My house, you mean."

"The family house, Peter . . . the Lindberg house."

"Names don't mean anything. You can choose any name you want and it's legal. That house is my house."

Martin's eyes narrowed, and then he brushed away smoke, too. "Well. Of course it's yours, that's the way your grandmother wanted it. But houses are like names; they don't go on forever. I hope you won't be too upset when yours has to be sold."

"It's not going to be sold."

"You'll be sorry, of course. We all will. I understand that there are several owners who would prefer not to sell."

"Joe James, he's my friend. And Buck and Billy, they'll *never* sell."

"Everybody needs money, son. Your friends do. Your mother does; I'm sure a person of her talent hates being reduced to giving music lessons."

"Hey, she likes it!"

"And look at me." Martin gestured at his worn clothing. "I got this ugly nylon rag at Goodwill, can you imagine that? And all that talk about a bicycle? I couldn't buy you a bike, even one like that piece of junk you were riding this morning." He sighed and sat back against the bench, shoulders slumped.

"I never sent you anything, because I never could afford anything worth sending, Pete. And you probably can't understand this, at your age. But it's a sad circumstance, a sad and demeaning circumstance, when a man can't afford to give his own son a real present."

The doughnuts were a churning, expanding mass somewhere between his throat and his gut, and his head was spinning, probably from the smoke. "I gotta go," he said, and slid out of the booth, holding onto the end of the table briefly to make sure his feet and legs would work. "I'll be late for school."

"Wait, I'll drive you." Martin got to his feet and trailed behind Petey to the door.

"No, I can get there faster on foot. I'll run, I run lots of times. Thanks for the doughnuts." Petey set off down the street at a trot; he heard an engine start up in a matter of seconds, and expected the Citation to appear beside him, but it did not. It wasn't until he was in sight of the school, breathing hard and sweating but with his head clear, that it occurred to him he hadn't seen Martin pay the people at the doughnut shop.

■

Chapter

Ten

■

"Absolutely no doubt. The Lindbergs raised their son in
decent fashion and supported him through six years of
college. The house was Mrs. Lindberg's to give, and she did it
in legal fashion; her attorney drew a perfectly good will."

"Thank you, Wim. I knew that, but I just needed to be reas-
sured." Wim for William Birnbaum, Charlotte's oldest friend
and personal attorney, was a hardworking man who could be
counted on to be in his San Diego office by 8 A.M. Also, Charlotte
suspected, he found sanctuary there, respite from his loved and
loving but raucous family.

"And if he should find an attorney who'll try to make a case
for him, we will present a bill for thirteen years of child support. No, the only potential problem I see here, apart from
that of your personal safety, which you seem determined to
ignore . . ."

"Wim, I will be careful. And if he threatens me again in any
way I will have him arrested, I promise. What problem?"

"Custody. Martin could get the money, or control of it, by
getting the boy. Proving himself the father, which wouldn't be
difficult, and convincing Petey to choose to live with him."

"Petey wouldn't."

"Charlotte, you say he's basically a sensible kid and I believe
you. But boys that age are incredibly vulnerable; I've got two
of them and I know. Besides, that piece of dreck certainly fooled
you fifteen years ago."

"I was all alone; Petey isn't. Besides, Martin has . . . what's the phrase they use about athletes? Martin has definitely lost a step in the charm department."

Words from the receiver came fast and a little high; Wim was troubled. "Why don't you send him down here? The twins' very expensive school shuts down next week so that everybody can go to Aspen or Kitzbühel for skiing. A visit from Petey would console Jeremy and Jacob for their family's lack of a mountain condo."

"Thanks, Wim, but he wouldn't come. As I told you, what he's interested in right now is his house and preserving it. And on that subject, I have a favor to ask of you." There was a grunt of assent from the telephone. "Can you tell me anything about a lawyer . . ."

"Attorney, Charlotte, I keep telling you."

"Yes, sir. An *attorney* named Hal Michaelson? He's supposed to be from San Diego."

"You sure you don't mean Howie? Howard Michaelson is an old fire-eater, used to be the best-known and highest-priced litigator in town. But he had a stroke or something, and I haven't heard anything of him recently."

"I'm fairly sure this one is Hal, and his firm name had two Michaelsons in it, I remember that. He's young, smooth, and nasty, and he is, or says he is, the representative of the major owner in her effort to buy the rest of us out."

"I seem to recall that Howie has a son. I'm not big in local associations or at temple, Charlotte, I'm too busy just working. I hardly even read the newspaper. But I'll see what I can find out."

"And perhaps about the owner, a Mrs. Cynthia Leino?" There followed a silence in which Charlotte could almost see her old friend wince. "There's just something strange about this, Wim. It all happened too fast, and the lawyer is pushing too hard, as if something were chasing him. I would like to know who Mrs. Leino is, where she comes from, what she's up to."

"Charlotte, what good would you expect this to do?"

"I can't tell you until I find out, can I? If this is too much like gossipy snooping, you could ask Shirley to help."

The groan was audible this time. Wim's wife Shirley was a human tornado, both joy and embarrassment to her quiet husband. Shirley was a lot easier to start than to stop. "I'll think about it, Charlotte," he said finally.

"Thank you, Wim. Please have her call me as soon as she finds out anything. And I'll tell Petey about your invitation."

"Do that. Come yourself if you can; it's been too long. And, Charlotte, please take care and be well."

"I will, dear. I promise."

To be well, she needed groceries and music. On her way to town, Charlotte found the highway blocked by a disabled truck and several police cars and made a short detour through the south-of-town neighborhood: a few quiet streets of small houses, mostly wooden, mostly old, and many looking it. It was north town that was the good end, with big old Victorians built originally for merchants and lumber barons and now spruced up to serve university faculty. But their little green house, Petey's house, would fit right in here on Elm Street. Too bad, she thought sourly, that those old Finns chose to build their commune on such a fancy piece of real estate.

Along South Main, too, Port Silva was simply a hundred-year-old workingman's town that might never have heard of yuppies or universities. The commercial buildings here were wooden, none of them higher than two stories except for the occasional false front. Even those more recently built or modernized looked weathered, because they were; the Pacific Ocean, separated from the street by a meadowlike sweep of grass and wildflowers atop a high bluff, made a rough neighbor.

If she'd had Petey along, they'd have stopped at the Home Port for a breakfast of bacon, eggs, hash browns, and buttermilk biscuits as good as any she could make. Breakfast specials started at 5 A.M., for men going to work on the boats or in the woods. Plaid shirts and billed caps, cigarette smoke and a steady rumble of male voices: Petey loved it.

Too late for breakfast and she wasn't hungry, anyway. She drove past the restaurant and in the next block pulled to the curb on the open side of the street, where wooden stairs led down to a strip of rocky, driftwood-strewn beach. Under a low sky of dirty gray, the tide was in and high, strong winds whipping the water to a surly froth that looked yellow rather than white. Not a good day for a walk down there, cold and nasty and probably dangerous. She shivered, buttoned her jacket higher and cast a quick look around. She'd had this funny feeling ever since leaving her house that there was someone behind her.

Charlotte hunched her shoulders against the wind and ran up a flight of outside stairs to the dusty haven of Bacigalupi's Music Store. She let the door close softly on her heels and began to pick her way along the rows of bin-topped tables crammed with music. This was a place to spend a quiet half hour, and she wasn't likely to run across any of her neighbors here. Or Martin either, she thought suddenly. It would be just like Martin to sneak along after her and try to unnerve her, but she didn't think he'd follow her inside where his harassment could be observed.

"Ah," said a voice from behind her, and she spun around, clutching a yellow volume defensively to her breasts. "Good morning, Ms. Birdsong. Finding what you want?" Mr. Bacigalupi was tall, with a neat narrow head from each side of which his curled and waxed mustache protruded a quivery inch or so. "I'm embarrassed to tell you that I haven't yet received my shipment of the Bastien Course books. I'll certainly call you the minute they arrive."

"Oh, fine, that's fine, no hurry. I'll just take this," she said, giving him the volume in her hands, the *Schumann Album for the Young*. "And the Schubert Impromptus, Opus 142, all four. And Chopin ballades; someone told me Wiener Urtext was bringing out a Chopin edition?"

"If so, I don't have it, and I don't know of it. But I'd be happy to make inquiries for you."

"Thank you, I'd appreciate it. Oh, and these, please," she added, and set two tapes on the counter. She'd give the Gould

Goldberg Variations to Petey, who had worn his out; and the tape of Parkening playing Bach to Val.

"I believe you live on Finn Lane, Ms. Birdsong," Mr. Bacigalupi said as she was signing the credit slip.

"Yes, I do." She had absolutely no idea where Mr. Bacigalupi lived; maybe here in the shop?

"Tell me, please, is it true, the story in this morning's *Sentinel*? That a developer plans to turn the homes and the park into a resort?"

"I . . . there is a tentative plan, and I believe offers are to be made."

He slid her purchases into a paper bag. "That is a wonderful old neighborhood, Ms. Birdsong. I would hate to see it vandalized by people with no sense of history, merely to turn a profit. Here's your music; please enjoy it."

His eyes actually *flashed*, Charlotte thought as she descended the stairs. She'd heard the phrase often, but had never witnessed the event. Maybe only Italians could make their eyes flash.

There was no one lurking around her car, no one in the backseat; and so far as she could tell, no one followed her the two blocks to Silveiras' Emporium. There, low ceilings and an uneven floor gave the place a homely, rural feeling, and the bulletin board just inside the door restated that theme. Trucks, boats, dogs, horses, goats, llamas, and geese were among the items for sale, and housing was needed. Charlotte did a quick survey of the three-by-five cards pinned to the board, and found that more than half were pleas for affordable houses or apartments to rent, or affordable houses with land to buy.

The door opened on a gust of wind, to admit the silver-haired patriarch of the Silveira clan pushing a row of empty shopping carts. "Looking for a tenant, Mrs. Birdsong?" he inquired.

"No, I was just . . . noticing how many people need a place to live."

"Yes, ma'am, it's a sad situation. I lost a good clerk just last month, divorced lady with two little girls, had to move back to

Santa Rosa because she couldn't find a place to live here. And I pay a decent wage." Mr. Silveira's head tipped back, and he looked down his long straight nose at her from narrowed eyes. "This developer who wants to eat up those nice little Finn Lane houses—I believe I heard you don't want to go along with that?"

Port Silva, with a population of about twenty-five thousand including the university community, was the smallest town Charlotte had lived in during her adult life; and even after four years she could be startled by how much everyone knew about everyone, and how quickly. "My personal preference would be to see the Lane stay as it is," she said carefully.

"This kind of thing is bad, very bad," he said with a shake of his head. "Tourism and second-home resorts are like parasites, you know. Too many of them, and a healthy organism starts to fail. Well, have a good day, anyway."

Depressed, Charlotte decided she might as well go home, while she still had a home, and do something useful like cooking. She hurried along, collecting staples and three half-gallons of milk, then two chickens and some nice short ribs from the butcher. Now, a few vegetables and some apples, Granny Smiths pretty but expensive, squinchy little pippins would do nicely for a pie that would perfume her whole house on this gray day. Reaching for a plastic bag, she felt a hand on her shoulder and turned to find Lucy Duarte blinking against the bright lights of the produce department.

"My, Charlotte, you do set a pace." Lucy was a thin, narrow-shouldered woman who always reminded Charlotte of a harried bird, one of those shore birds that run so fast their straight little legs blur. Today Lucy's blond hair was lank, her blue eyes dark-circled in her pale face. Pale puffy face, Charlotte noted, and inspected her neighbor's raincoat-clad body covertly; Lucy must be pregnant again.

"I'll keep you just the teeniest minute. I told Harry that now we'd found you he could keep the boys in hand, he's better at that. And I'd do the talking."

Charlotte followed Lucy's nod and saw Harry Duarte some twenty feet away. He stood with his feet planted wide, curly head lowered, a bull ready to charge but anchored by a small boy on either side. A stocky man no more than five feet eight, he had a permanent air of barely suppressed violence that Charlotte had always read as mostly bluff. Last night's experience with Martin, however, had undermined her faith in her own judgment.

"I'd be happy to talk to you, Lucy," Charlotte lied, "but I'd like to get home before the rain begins. Why don't you call me later?" She moved the cart to swing it into a turn, but Lucy's hand gripped the front edge and held it.

"I just wanted, I *needed*, to tell you how important this is to us. I know you're a kind person, I told Harry that. Harry thinks women are silly and selfish, but I told him that women can understand about love thy neighbor, after all we're Christians just like they are."

Charlotte examined this spate of words for logic and found none. "Actually, I am not a Christian."

"I beg your pardon?"

"My mother was an agnostic and my father was a Jew. Exactly what was it you wanted, Lucy?"

"To ask you to go along with the rest of us and sell your house," Lucy said in a rush. "Mr. Michaelson needs agreement from everyone by Thursday afternoon; he's leaving that night."

"Why is there such a rush?"

"Well, the university's plans, I suppose. And he says the owner is eager to, um, clear her decks is the way he put it." Lucy drew a deep breath. "Charlotte, this is our chance to turn our life around. I'll be able to have a decent modern house and a nice dependable car. And Harry—Harry will have a little breathing space from debts, be able to relax and not be so angry all the time. And be happy about the new baby." She put a splayed hand on the curve of her belly, and a pleading look on her face.

"Lucy, I'm sorry," Charlotte said, and meant it. She couldn't think how to explain that the house and the decision were Petey's, that her son's well-being was vitally involved here. In an evasion she knew for cowardice, she said, "I can't possibly make a decision of this magnitude in two or three days."

Lucy's eyes filled with tears, and she made no effort to keep them from spilling down her cheeks. "It's just not fair. You're just a mean, hard woman who won't even let your poor little boy see his own father. And you have plenty of money, you don't have to worry and work like the rest of us. It's not fair!"

Charlotte was speechless before this litany of her failings. Had Petey made any of these complaints, to a woman he hardly knew?

Some small sound, a clearing throat or shuffling feet, made both of them aware that several people stood nearby watching with interest. Lucy, flushed face reddening further, sniffed and wiped her eyes and hurried off toward her family. Charlotte dealt a polite smile all round to the watchers and took herself and her groceries to checkout.

She watched Mr. Silveira swoop her purchases over the electronic price reader, and made polite replies to his friendly banter, but her mind was busy elsewhere. One thing Petey would never have said, to Lucy or anyone else, was that his mother had plenty of money and need not work. It was Martin who pretended to believe that she was rich, who kept trying to weasel "a small personal loan" from the money she'd had left after finishing school and selling her father's house. Tucked tightly away, that money was Charlotte's emergency fund, to be touched rarely and then only for specific needs, like a new bike for a growing boy, or the cost of shipping a grand piano. Something she hadn't done for a long time now, she reminded herself with a faint sigh.

"Thank you, Mr. Silveira," she murmured, as he put her groceries in the cart and reached for her check.

"You're welcome, my dear. And remember, you're not alone; this is a community where people help each other."

"That's good to know," said Charlotte, her mind still inward.

If Martin was patrolling the Finn Lane community, talking to people like Lucy Duarte, he'd surely, eventually, come across Petey. She had brushed off Wim's suggestion that Petey might be wooed away, but Martin was a clever man when he wanted something, deeply experienced at seduction; while she was just old unglamorous Mom, always whining about vegetables and bicycle helmets.

By midday the county sheriff's people had informed Officer Val Kuisma that the dead Ronald Gardner was born in Garberville, graduated from high school there and married a classmate before leaving for the army and Vietnam. Came back physically sound, got a job and fathered two children, divorced; his ex-wife, remarried, still lived in their hometown. At age forty, Gardner had for ten years been working construction jobs from Eureka to Fort Bragg.

"Ol' Ron could do a fairly good job wherever they put him—framing, sheetrocking, roofing." Bert Canlis, assistant manager of NorCal Builders' Supply, ran a hand over his curly brown hair and shed sawdust like dandruff. "And he was honest, never any funny business with money or with materials. But he was a sorta distant guy, you know?"

"So I've been hearing." Val took a long deep breath, to enjoy the one thing this visit was likely to give him: the good smell of a place where wood was worked. The brief list of Gardner's local friends and acquaintances compiled by the sheriff's office was turning out to consist totally of acquaintances.

"See, what he really liked was poker, poker and booze."

"And that's what he was doing Friday night, playing poker?"

"Right, there was five of us played out at Al's trailer. That's Al Meechum."

"Right," said Val, who had already talked to Al Meechum and the other two cardplayers. "I understand Ron finished winner?"

"Yeah, I swear he took two pots out of every three, the lucky s.o.b." He paused as if hearing the echo of his own words, and winced.

"And you and Ron left the trailer together?"

"Yeah, and it was pretty early . . . Hey, Kuisma, you gettin' at something? Because we are by God in the county here, and I already talked to the sheriff's people."

"I just thought Ron might have said something to you about where he was going."

"Oh, okay." Canlis's long frame settled back into its easy slouch. "We quit earlier than usual, like I told you. I said something like, not eleven yet, any luck I'll get home and my wife will still be awake. And Ron says yeah, what he really likes after a good run of cards is to get his ashes hauled."

"Did he have a girlfriend?"

"Not that I know of."

"So what did he have in mind, do you think?"

"Well, he got talking about that one time." Canlis's voice took on a confidential pitch. "What he'd do, he'd go by himself to some little beer joint, sit there awhile. Generally some woman would turn up, maybe her old man is out of work or something, anyway she's interested in making a few bucks. He'd take her out to his truck and pay her maybe twenty for a blow job."

Ron Gardner, a man who preferred to stay distant even with sex. "Did he ever mention any favorite beer joints?"

"Nope. We weren't close friends, I don't know why he even told me that stuff."

"And he left the game that night with a lot of money."

"Three days' pay plus his winnings. Maybe six, seven hundred dollars."

Dumb jerk, thought Val wearily. There had been no wallet, no identification of any kind, on Ron Gardner's body or in his truck. And no money at all.

"That what they think happened?" Canlis's face wore a skeptical look. "He picked up a woman and she rolled him and killed him? She'd of had to be some strong woman; Ron was what they call wiry, you know? Not much meat but lots of muscle."

"With surprise and a sharp knife, a woman could have done

it. Or she could have had help." Gardner's killer had wielded a very sharp knife with a five- or six-inch blade, thrusting it up from below the man's sternum to reach his heart. He had probably been killed in his truck; the initial examination of the cabin had revealed a blur of recently made footprints on the dusty floor, but no blood.

"But I don't know much. The sheriff's department is working this one; I'm just checking on a possible tie-in with another case." Val pulled a photograph from his shirt pocket. "Have you ever seen this man in the company of Ron Gardner? Or anywhere?"

Canlis took the picture, frowned, shook his head. "Nope, not that I recall. But you didn't hardly see Ron with nobody, except at work. Hey, wasn't this picture in the paper a few days back?"

Val nodded and reclaimed the photo. "He's Edward Boylan, a man from Santa Rosa who disappeared from Port Silva the night after Ron did. The coincidence has got everybody upset, especially Boylan's wife."

"Used to be," said Canlis glumly, "that living up here on the north coast was real safe, except if you worked on the boats or in the woods."

"Right, it used to be." Val had finished with the list of Ron Gardner's acquaintances. The other list, that of the Friday-night patrons of the Rainbow Tavern . . . those the proprietor could or chose to remember . . . was longer, and there was no connector, no name that appeared on both. Whatley, the tavern owner, insisted that he had no memory of serving quiet, unremarkable Ron; Whatley also claimed that he'd never seen the much more noticeable Boylan. So it was time to leave Gardner to the sheriff's people, get out of their way before they got irritated.

"Haven't seen much of you since we sold you that portable mill," said Canlis, happy to have police talk finished.

"I've hardly used it, been too busy."

"Well, here's something," Canlis said with a grin. "Old Arnie Burkett, out by Salmon Creek, is selling out to move to a retirement home. He's got this little bitty old orchard, pear and apple.

You go talk to him in the next couple weeks, I bet he'd let you take a log or two. Might be some good stuff there."

"I'll sure do that. Thanks a lot, Bert." Although he wouldn't have admitted it to some of his friends or most of his relatives, Val found wood hunting even more exciting than deer hunting. "And thanks for your time. If you think of anything else about Gardner . . ."

They both jumped as the beeper in his pocket went off. "And I better get back to work. Can I use your phone?"

"Hey, Valentine! They send you out to supervise?" Officer Alma Linhares grinned at Val, then moved several steps to her left, crouched, and took another flash shot of the dark gray Ford Taurus that had been rented by Edward Boylan nearly two weeks ago. "Or maybe even to learn something?"

"Always ready to learn," Val told her. Hands in his vest pockets, he propped his backside against Alma's black and white Dodge and watched her take three more pictures. "No body, I guess."

"Right, and thanks to the blessed Virgin for that." Alma nodded in the direction of the Taurus's open trunk. "I mean I opened that sucker with my heart in my mouth. Just smelled kinda sour from outside, not putrid, but you never know, plastic bags and all that."

He straightened and peered past her into the trunk. A small duffel bag, its zipper pulled open, was tucked against the left side of the space; and a traveling garment bag, one of the kind meant to double over for carrying, lay flat. A lightish blue, its upper end bore several dark stains and a big, lighter-colored splotch with a grainy residue. Val wrinkled his nose. "What do you think?"

She tucked the camera away in its case and put the case in her own trunk. "I think somebody was lying on that bag. I think he bled some but not a whole lot, at least not in there. I think he vomited, a lot. And I think wherever he is now, he doesn't have his clean underwear or his razor."

"What about the rest of the car?"

She shook her head. "No obvious blood, no vomit, no obvious signs of unusual activity. I haven't printed the inside yet; I'll do that in the garage downtown, with better lights. Just looks like a nice boring empty rental car."

The two-door sedan, its surface streaked and dusty, sat in the garage of an oceanfront cottage that was usually occupied in the summer, often empty in the winter. A local real estate company handled the renting of the property for the owner, who lived in Fresno. The agent, doing an every-week-or-so check of his vacant properties, had called the police to have this free-loading car towed.

The cottage and its grounds were well maintained, Val noted. Solid concrete driveway, any tire prints probably gone in all the rain. Concrete floor in the garage, too, and it was pretty clean, not much oil or grease. No obvious footprints. "What about the house?" he asked.

Alma shook her head and rolled her dark eyes. "First thing the real estate guy did, naturally, was go inside and look around. Nobody there now; he doesn't think anybody got in and I don't, either. Looks to me like somebody brought somebody else, probably Boylan, here in the trunk of the Taurus, transferred him into something else, drove him away. But we're getting a team out here, give the whole area a good going-over.

"Oh, hey. Are you part of the team? And I thought maybe you were here for my bod instead of Boylan's." She raked back midnight-blue hair and grinned at him.

"Lady, you'd break me in half, especially in my damaged state." He grinned back at a handsome young woman who was within three inches of his height and probably twenty pounds of his weight.

"Well, shit, that's what they all say."

"Sure," said Val, who knew better. "What the chief asked me to do was have a look, then start the neighborhood canvass; and Chang should be here any minute to help. Although the population is pretty sparse this time of year," he added, surveying the empty street.

"Let's hope somebody noticed something useful," she said, serious now. "I saw Mrs. Boylan downtown this morning, looking real shaky. This setup, the blood and all, is likely to send her right over the edge."

Chapter
Eleven

■

Monday afternoon's piano students trooped up Charlotte's front steps in relentless progression from two o'clock on. And they should all get their money back, she thought as she ushered the last one out into nearly full dark. She was about to close the door when a U-turning vehicle swept her with its headlights, and she recognized the Jeep.

"Val?" she called as soon as the engine had died.

"Hi, Charlotte." He came around the vehicle, a tall shadowy figure back-lighted faintly from the park. "Feel like company?"

"Oh yes." She held on to the doorpost while he came up the stairs, then shifted her grip to his arm and pulled him inside.

"Hey, what's up?" His face hardened as he looked past her into the house. "Did that son of a bitch come back?"

"No, but I think he's been around the neighborhood, talking to people. Val, I'm afraid he might take Petey."

"Grab him physically, you mean? I don't think so. The kid is skinny, but he's strong; I doubt that Lindberg could handle him." Val closed the door, then put an arm across her shoulders, turning her toward the back of the house. "Come on, I need a drink. Got a glass of wine for a tired cop?"

In the kitchen he sat down in the rocker and watched Charlotte move around the room. "I guess Pete's not home yet."

"No, he's not." She set a glass of wine beside him, then sighed and ran a hand distractedly through her curls. "There must be something to munch on in the fridge."

He reached out to catch her other hand. "Forget it. Sit down, Charlotte. Is there a set time he's supposed to be home?"

"Not exactly. But when he's going to be out after dark or in bad weather, he always calls. Well, I guess seven-thirty is the deadline; that's suppertime."

"Forty-five minutes. Let's give him that before we call out the troops."

"I wasn't thinking that Martin would kidnap him," she said, settling onto the edge of the wicker chair. "More that he might—talk him into leaving."

"Well. If your son *should* decide to pull an adolescent rebellion here," Val said slowly, "and announce that he wants to go home with his daddy, a court would probably let him. Charlotte, haven't you ever talked to the kid about his old man? Charlotte?"

"Oh, sorry. Recently, I seem to have spent every waking moment and quite a few sleeping ones worrying about Petey. Then just now, for one beat or maybe two, I had a vision of peace: no house, no hulking bad-tempered child-man, no ties. And I should be ashamed of myself," she added, pausing for a sip of wine. "What I've said, when the subject came up, is that Martin and I had a brief love affair, but he was not interested in being a father."

"Um, yes, but don't you think . . . ?"

"That I should have told Petey he was fathered by a mean-spirited, grasping man who never loved anyone but himself? I guess I didn't think I should."

"Maybe what you should do, to be safe, is buy the kid a ticket to San Diego, send him to stay with your lawyer friend."

"He wouldn't go. And if you're going to tell me to join the Marines and get tough with my son, you might as well save your breath because I can't do it."

"I know that. I wouldn't . . ." Val bent his head, as a flush swept his face and colored even his ears.

"Yes, you would. But that's all right; I don't mind." A toucher by nature, Charlotte wanted to reach over and lay a hand on his shoulder but restrained the impulse. Hands off Petey, hands off Val lest she send the wrong signal or worse, the right one. Maybe she should get a cat.

Maybe she should just have some more wine. By the time she had refilled the glasses and settled back into her chair, Val had regained his balance. "I'm just a bossy guy," he admitted. "Let me know when it gets to you, okay?"

"Okay."

"Good. Oh, listen, I'm back on duty, detective instead of patrol," he told her with a grin of pure satisfaction. "I'll be working mainly on the Boylan disappearance, but I spent a couple of really interesting hours this morning with Johnny Hebert, the cop who's been following Rip."

"Who? Oh, the people with the tombstone." Charlotte clasped twitchy fingers around the stem of her glass and prepared to take her turn at being a good listener. R.I.P., John Hebert had learned, was a group with no dues, no headquarters, no bylaws and no official membership list. Many people Hebert questioned, from college professors and students to farmers and fishermen, confessed to sympathy with the group's apparent aims, protecting small towns and the countryside from "playground" development; but none was a "member" or knew anyone who was.

"Here's the way it seems to work," said Val, leaning back in the rocker. "Somebody is keeping careful track of property deals in Port Silva and the county nearby. Whenever anything unusual changes hands—a ranch, a piece of coastal property, maybe a group of houses in one area—a notice turns up in public places stating what the new owner proposes to do and what the implications of his action might be."

"That seems reasonable."

"Oh, right. And there'll be follow-up notices, and then ordinary citizens will attend county supervisors' meetings or city council meetings or permit board meetings, to protest or request changes."

"Ordinary?"

"Plain people, not just obvious eco-freaks. Your doctor, your pharmacist, your kid's history teacher. And sometimes they get what they came for; six months ago the council put together a measure to go on the ballot to further restrict both the amount of lot a house can cover and the square footage that can be added to an existing residence.

"But sometimes," Val went on, leaning forward, "people don't act, or whatever is being proposed turns out to be legal and not subject to public intervention. Then come the flyers with a more militant edge, and they're everywhere. Out in the woods, where there's no electricity or telephones? At this or that crossroads, there's a community bulletin board. School meeting, save the whales meeting, stop the oil drilling meeting. Tombstone flyer there, gotta stop this blank-blank development planned for Albany Ridge."

"Or Finn Lane."

"Yes, ma'am, I saw one out at Five-Mile Y today. It was a copy of the flyer you got, with 'Finn Lane' scrawled across the top. Anyway, it's after that a survey gets trashed, or a road chopped up, or a new foundation flooded. Heavy equipment damaged or on one occasion driven off a cliff. Or new wells blown up, that happened last spring."

"Not by Petey's history teacher!"

"Probably not," Val agreed. "But you have to suspect that he and others like him are carefully looking the other way when it happens."

Charlotte sipped wine and ran several ordinary people past her mind's eye in a kind of identity parade: Mr. Bacigalupi. Mr. Silveira. At least two of the musicians with whom she made up a biweekly quintet. And Joe, Joe James. "I think there are quite a few Port Silvans who want to keep the town real. I wonder who does the flyers?"

"So do we. But half the world does desk-top publishing with a computer; it's easy enough to put together a flyer. Easy enough to make a few hundred copies on your laser printer. Or at the corner copy shop, for that matter."

"And you've never caught anybody involved in the vandalism?"

He shook his head. "There have been thirteen incidents in the past two years. Pulled off with incredible luck or incredible timing and information." And he was talking too much, he realized. Johnny had an idea that the real perpetrators of the acts of vandalism might be different each time; a university community, after all, had a nice pool of strong idealistic young recruits. But there was an organizer somewhere, a single mind or small group of minds running things.

"Uh, we do have some ideas," he finished lamely. "But not much evidence."

Charlotte started and spilled a little wine on her jeans as the clock whirred in preparation for striking. Seven o'clock. If Martin had picked Petey up right from school, they could be in San Francisco by now. "Perhaps Rip will demonstrate or something, here on Finn Lane." And the developer would lose interest and her neighbors would not be able to blame her. What a lovely idea.

Val frowned and shook his head. "Revolutionaries aren't that predictable, Charlotte. Not even when you agree, or think you do, with their aims. I don't want to see Port Silva turned into a fog-belt Carmel, but I have trouble with the idea of destroying property."

"Oh. Yes."

"And people operating in the dark and in a hurry sometimes make mistakes, misjudge targets."

"If you're trying to frighten me, you're succeeding."

"Sorry, Charlotte, I . . ."

She made a weary, warding-off gesture with one hand. Benign or dangerous, rescuers were too random an element to be figured into any equation. "Val, do you know anyone connected with the university administration?"

"I beg your pardon?"

"Mr. Michaelson says the university has plans for this land, and would of course pay a lot less for it than a commercial developer. I'd like to know whether or not that's true."

Val thoughtfully stroked the right side of his beard, which

had a tendency to grow up rather than neatly down. "My aunt Flora is administrative assistant to the chancellor, how's that?"

"That is absolutely wonderful. Could you ask her to find out, please?"

Before he could reply, feet came thumping up the back stairs. Then the door swung open with a bang and Petey slunk in, shoulders slumped but chin and lower lip out, looking for trouble. He stopped in his tracks as he saw the two of them looking at him. "So what's the big deal? It's not late."

"It's dark, Petey," Charlotte said quietly. "And rain is coming. Usually you call me if you're going somewhere."

"Hey, I was just across the street. With my friends."

"But I didn't know that."

"Yeah, well. I didn't know my father came here last night, either. How come you didn't tell me that?"

"I haven't seen you."

"Yeah, well," he said again. "Shit, you probably wouldn't have told me anyway."

Val leaned back in the rocker. "Don't be any more of an asshole than you have to," he advised. "What your father did here last night was throw a bottle of booze at your mother. When I came to help, she was half drowned in bourbon and bleeding from a cut on her head."

Petey slumped against the doorjamb, and Val took a moment's mean pleasure in watching the boy's face drain of color.

"It turned out to be a small cut, and she's okay now. But I think she needs a rest from cooking," he added, "so I'm taking her out to dinner. Okay, Charlotte? I'll go get a clean shirt, and be back in fifteen minutes."

"Mom?" said Petey hoarsely after Val was gone.

"I'm fine, Petey. And fifteen minutes should be time enough for you to tell me all about seeing Martin."

"I saw your mother leave with that guy that drives the Jeep," said Annie as she slipped through the back door Petey had unlocked at her knock.

"They're going out to dinner." He felt he should have been asked along. He wouldn't have wanted to go, he'd have refused, but they should have asked him.

"Is that her boyfriend?"

"No way! My mom doesn't have boyfriends. That's Val, he rents our basement apartment."

"If I ever have a house, I'll make sure to have cute tenants that take me to dinner." She grinned at him. "Did you get in trouble?"

He shook his head. "Not exactly. She was upset because she didn't know where I was."

"What did you tell her?"

"I said I was in the park with friends." Petey was fairly sure it wasn't a good idea to have Annie come in here right now. Besides, he'd got yelled at by Hannah when he phoned to say he couldn't come over tonight, and he was pretty tired of women at the moment. Why would Annie bother with a kid like him, anyhow? "Uh, did you want something? I promised I'd stay here and not go out."

"That's okay by me." She ruffled his hair as she brushed past him into the kitchen. "It was cold in the tent, we forgot to get another fuel bottle for the heater. And I thought you might have something interesting to eat. I'm hungry."

Now he felt really dumb, and selfish as well. "There's green chile pork. I'm zapping some in the microwave."

"Super!" She pushed her hands into the pockets of her jeans and leaned against the sink to watch as he filled a handled white bowl with something dark and chunky-looking, then laid a paper towel on top.

"So I guess the peanuts worked," she remarked. "That's a useful thing to know, about chewing peanuts to cover up the smell of beer."

"I guess it worked, because nobody said anything." The oven's beeper sounded; he took a bowl out, handed it to her, put the second one in. "There's a fork in the drawer there. You want some bread? A glass of milk?"

She shook her head, scooped a large forkful into her mouth and then sucked quick gusts of air around the hot mass. "Great stuff, your mom is some cook," she said after a moment. "Did you have a good time with Jesse and Bo this afternoon?"

Petey shrugged. "Sure, it was okay. Bo didn't say much, but Jesse talked a lot, about a bunch of awesome stuff he used to do."

"Jesse has good stories," Annie said. She took another bite of pork and wandered out of the kitchen, carrying the bowl by its handle. "Boy, I really like this house; you are a lucky guy, Peter Birdsong." She paused in the entrance to the living room, found the light switch and flipped it. Petey glanced quickly at the street, then at the clock; Charlotte and Val wouldn't be back for a while yet. He hoped.

"And here's that lineup I noticed the other day. Peter, and Mom, and that must be the monster dog you used to have, and . . . who is this, your dad? No, too old-fashioned," she said at once. The photo in her hand was of a straight-backed, somber-faced man in a shirt, tie, and vest.

"That's my grandfather Vogel, my mom's father; he was born in Germany, and I look like him. And that's my grandmother Vogel in the picture with the piano. Both of them died before I was born."

"Where's your dad?"

Petey shrugged again, a quick sharp movement. "He wasn't around much. But that's his mother, my grandmother Lindberg that left me this house; I knew her a little bit. My great-grandfather, my grandfather Lindberg's father, is the one that built it. He and a bunch of other Finnish people lived here in a commune, like a big family."

"Lindberg doesn't sound like a Finnish name."

"Well it is! Finland is a small country," he added in less-heated tones, "and it like belonged to Sweden for a long time. So some Finns wound up with Swedish names. My great-grand-father came here on a boat from Finland and worked in the woods, cutting down trees and making shingles and stuff."

"For a kid, you sure know a lot." Annie set down the photo

she was holding and took a bite from her bowl. "Who's that other woman in the picture with your Finnish grandmother?"

"Another Finnish lady, Mrs. Leino. She lived next door, in number fourteen, and they were friends when they were young. Then Mrs. Leino got crazy, drank all the time and got real fat and never came outside. She died, too."

"Number fourteen looks a lot like this house, like the same person built them."

"People worked together on them, I think; that's what a commune was about. Dr. Scully, he rents number fourteen, says it's in pretty bad shape. He says Mrs. Leino didn't keep her house up the way my grandmother did. There's my supper," he added as the oven sounded its four measured bleats.

Annie followed him to the kitchen and sat down at the table, to finish her food as he began his. "Jesse's taken a liking to you, which is pretty unusual," she remarked. "And don't get me wrong, okay? He's not such a bad guy. But he and Bo can get kind of rough after they've had a few beers or something. Probably they'd be a bad experience for a lady like your mother. So if you've got a key hidden around here, under the back doormat or something . . ."

Petey, who had been staring at her, now cast an involuntary glance at the back door.

"Sure, that's where everybody puts it. If I were you, I'd put it someplace safer, like at the bottom of the steps, maybe under a flowerpot or a brick. And I wouldn't tell Jesse where it is, if he should ask. Which he probably won't."

"Okay, thanks. Thanks a lot."

"You're welcome." She cocked her head and surveyed him from narrowed green eyes. "Did you know I'm a seer?"

"A what?"

"A fortune-teller, sweetie, a lady with second sight." She slid her chair around the table until it was close beside his. "Here, give me your hand and I'll pay for my supper."

"Hey, look, I don't believe in that stuff."

"Let Madam Zosa reveal your future," she crooned, hooking

her left arm through his right and cradling his right hand in her palm. "Look there, that's the life line. You're going to live practically forever." She ran a long-nailed forefinger along his palm; he shivered and she hugged his arm closer. "Don't be frightened, I come from a long line of gypsy women and we *know*. I see that you're going to be tall, over six feet, and handsome; and women are going to be crazy about you, Peter Birdsong, just look at that heart line!"

That was Annie's breast lying right there on his arm, heavy and warm, soft but springy like something alive of itself. The voice at his ear was not words, just sounds swelling and fading; Petey shivered again as sweat made cold tracks down the sides of his hot face and down his ribs. If he slid his arm back, if she'd let him, maybe he could get that heavy roundness in his hand.

Her voice paused and he felt her draw a breath. He held his own breath, and into the thick silence came the clear two-note call of the foghorn from the nearby cove, E-flat to C registering in his head like words on a screen. Then, close, the sound of an engine, and the mind-screen flashed "Charlotte."

"And then when you're about thirty, and rich and famous, you'll marry a really good and beautiful woman and have lots of children, all boys. And you're going to travel . . ."

His face was flaming hot, and he could smell himself from the same clothes he'd had on since this morning, about a million hours ago. "Boy, that's bullshit," he croaked, and pulled free of her grip. "I told you, I don't believe that stuff. And I'm not going traveling any more *ever*, I'm staying right here."

She shrugged and got to her feet. "You didn't let me finish. I was going to say that wherever you travel, you'll always have this house to come home to. What do you think of that?"

"Uh, I think my mother might be coming home pretty soon."

Chapter
Twelve

■

"**G**ood morning," croaked Charlotte, a terrible falsehood that she uttered almost every day.

"Unh," replied her son, who was standing before the open refrigerator door. He picked up a carton of milk, pulled its spout open with a forefinger, held the carton high and poured a pale stream directly into his mouth. Spilled not a drop, how very impressive; clearly this forbidden skill had been practiced. Charlotte turned to the stove, set a high flame under the teakettle, readied mug, filter, filter paper, and the fine dark Colombian coffee. Could do this in her sleep, *was* doing it in her sleep.

Could get the mug back to her bedroom without its sloshing over, too. And onto the bedside table, and herself back into bed and propped against the headboard, down comforter drawn up nearly to her chin to make a safe, warm cave. She felt hungover, eyes and mind blurry after uneasy stretches of light sleep mixed with jagged dreams of Martin. Martin grinning a toothy, feral grin over a baby-sized, blanket-wrapped form he cradled against his chest. Martin and Petey driving away from her in an open-topped car, neither looking back. Martin staring coldly at her and brandishing an enormous bloody knife.

That last was Val's fault, she thought and lifted the coffee mug to inhale its aromatic, head-clearing fumes. No, her own. She had asked him, belatedly, what had kept him out so late Sunday night, music night; and he had told her about Sunday and then about Monday, too, the abandoned car and bloodstained suitcase. Ugh.

Beyond the six-feet-high, four-feet-wide expanse that was her bedroom's sole window, the black of night had frayed to dull gray morning. She closed her gritty eyes and focused her ears instead, but could hear no sound of rain; just another heavy, threatening, ugly day. Maybe she'd simply spend it right here.

She started and nearly spilled coffee at the rap on her door. At five after eight by her bedside clock, Petey should be on his way down the back steps. "Mom?" he called softly, and opened the door.

He'd been asleep when she returned home last night, or at least firmly shut up in his bedroom. But he didn't look as if he'd had a restful night; in fact, he looked miserable, soft pale hair rumpled and hazel eyes red-rimmed.

"Mom, I don't know why I'm being such an asshole but I'm sorry and I hate it when you're mad at me."

"I hate it, too." She wanted to pull him down beside her and wrap both arms around him; instead, she gestured to the little rocker next to the bed and said, "Can you sit with me a minute?"

He settled with a gusty sigh, shoulders slumped. She held the mug out and said, "Want a taste?"

He took his usual tiny sip, made his usual grimace. "I liked it better when you used to put milk and sugar in."

"Mm. Petey, aren't you going to miss Hannah?"

"I already told her I don't want to do any first-period stuff today. Martin might be waiting there again, and I don't know whether I should pretend I don't see him or maybe punch him out."

"Oh, my, don't do that!"

"Somebody ought to."

"It's too late, and he's too old. If you really hurt him, you'd feel terrible."

"Maybe." He didn't sound convinced.

"If you don't want to talk to him, just tell him to leave you alone, and walk away. If you do talk to him, I hope you'll be . . . cautious. The sad fact is that Martin Lindberg has no real interest in anything but himself. In my opinion," she added in a belated attempt to be fair.

"It's a good thing *you're* a good person, or I might turn out to be a criminal or something."

Charlotte inspected his face for irony and was dismayed to see none at all, only misery. "Well, I'm irritable in the morning. I'm absent-minded and forgetful. And often impatient. But I work hard," she noted. "I respect my fellow man, and woman. I'm kind to animals. I *try* to maintain a sense of humor. So I guess I am a good person. Petey, don't you think you should get ready for school?"

"Now you're embarrassed," he said with an ear-to-ear grin. "You should see how red your face is."

"Go put your bike in the car," she ordered. "And I'll get dressed and drive you to school."

If music was engrossing, putting the real world out of mind, cooking was soothing in a down-to-earth way, Charlotte decided later that morning as she peeled an onion, scraped carrots, washed celery ribs and leaves. She had just pulled a pan of browned short ribs and beef shanks from the oven when someone rang her front doorbell; she moved quickly to answer and found Joe James on the porch, a big Tupperware bowl in his hands. The old man's shoulders were square today, his head high and the pale eyes alert.

"Joe, I'm glad to see you. Come in out of the cold."

"Thank you, ma'am. Here's your bowl, and them folks at the Hall asked me to say their thanks for the fine pea soup."

Last Tuesday, which seemed now like months ago, she'd been making pea soup for the Bluejay, had glanced out her window to see several skinny children sitting on the steps of the Hall, and had immediately doubled the recipe. "I'm glad they liked it. I should send them something more frequently. Joe, can I give you a cup of coffee?"

"I'll take a rain check on that, Charlotte. I got me a job of work to do, helping out in the kitchen over at the Hall, so I'll need to be getting back. The grocer down the corner, that Chinese fella, he's gave the folks some chickens, eight or ten I think there is. We're going to cut them up and cook them for dinner."

"It's good of you to help out."

"Gives me something to do besides feeling old and useless," said Joe. "What I wondered, Charlotte, could you loan us a big pan, like a roaster, and maybe a sharp knife?"

"I'm just finishing with my big roaster. Let me deglaze it, then I'll wash it out for you."

"You know, this has turned into a mean, hard country," he said in ruminative tones as he sat on the tall stool to watch her work. "When I was a young fellow riding the freights, folks didn't act like I was some kind of shit because I didn't have a home. And ordinary people would help out, find you a little job you could do to earn a meal. But somewhere along the line, things went to hell."

Charlotte, nudging crusty brown bits loose with a wooden spoon, looked up and waited.

"Me, after that, I was just like everybody else, had my house and my pension and my health insurance and acted like folks that didn't, it was because they was lazy or dumb or something. But while I was sitting in the sun congratulating myself, the U.S. of A. got to be no good for anybody except pissant lawyers and money men."

"I think this place is better than most." She spoke over her shoulder as she emptied the last of the pan's contents into the stockpot.

"Maybe it was, but it ain't no more. Now folks like them across the street has got to beg for a place to sleep, while rich sonsabitches from Ell-Aay that already got two, three houses can come up here and buy more. I say that's wrong, and I say we got a right to do whatever it takes to stop it."

Like blowing things up? "I . . . don't know, Joe." Charlotte wrapped a boning knife and a pair of poultry shears in a dish towel, put them in the quickly washed roaster, set the lid on top and handed the lot to the old man.

"Well, I do. Thank you kindly, Charlotte; I'll see you get this back."

Today the sky was lighter, as if the clouds might lift and let a little sun through; and beyond the Hall, the sea's rumpled gray was showing a very faint hint of blue. Charlotte watched out her front window as Joe trudged up the path to Finn Hall and disappeared inside. Three children squirted out the front door almost at once, as if the Hall were so full as to require exchange: one large body in and three small ones out. Eight women were living there now, and five men, Val had said, and eleven children. Every one of them must be blessing the slight improvement in the weather.

The three who had come out were really very young children, she noted, not warmly dressed, and there was no supervising adult in sight. The Lane was having more traffic than usual today, probably as a result of the development story in the paper; and the mail van would be along any minute, Danny the postal person not the most careful driver . . . No, her box was slightly ajar, mail here already.

At the foot of her steps, eyeing the children once again, Charlotte opened her mailbox, reached inside, and put her hand on something cold, hairy, and slightly yielding.

Her scream hurt her own ears. She wiped her hand desperately on her jeans and heard feet pounding close as she stared at an enormous dead rat, its lips drawn back in a sharp-toothed snarl above a cut and bloody throat.

"Here, Charlotte, *God* don't make that sound again." Billy Kaplan pulled her back, nearly lifting her clear of the ground. His muscular right arm clamped her close as he peered into the box.

"Aagh! That miserable, brain-dead asshole."

"I'd have thought . . ." She shuddered, and Billy tightened his grip just this side of pain. "I'd have expected an attorney to be more subtle."

"Michaelson didn't do this. Can you imagine him taking the chance of getting rat blood on his Guccis?" Billy released her and stood back a little, watchful. "You okay now?"

"Who, then?"

"Who's solid teak from ear to ear, suddenly thinks he's won the lottery except for you and me, has easy access to wharf rats?"

"Harry Duarte."

"Abso-fuckin-lutely. Here, I'll take the thing and throw it over his back fence." He reached into the box and pulled the rat out by its tail.

"No, Billy! The little boys might find it."

"What I've seen of those two, they'd consider it a treat." But he marched across the street instead, to one of the big covered trash cans that served the park, Charlotte on his heels.

"There," he said, dropping the metal lid back in place. "And you leave it alone, hear?" he snapped at the children who had gathered to stare. "Scat!" he added, and they fled.

"Here you go, Charlotte, wash it off," he ordered, turning on the spring-loaded faucet near the base of the park's drinking fountain. She bent and scrubbed her hands together under the cold stream; then she held the tap for Billy.

"Christ, ain't humanity wonderful," he muttered. "Just wave a few dollars, and a block of ordinary people turns into a cage of pit bulls. I'll have a word with Harry for you."

"Thank you, but I'll do it myself." Charlotte saw the rat again, in her mind's eye: an outrage, it was also a pathetic effort on the part of poor stupid Harry Duarte to get what he thought he was entitled to.

Billy noted her expression and misinterpreted it. "Listen, here's what you do; you set your boarder on him. Handy for a lady to have a cop on the premises, particularly a nice tall young one with a cute ass." He gave her an exaggerated leer. "I'd offer him a room myself, except it's clear he's more your kind of guy than mine."

"Yes, I believe he is," she said, and smiled at him. Billy Kaplan was bad-tempered, foul-mouthed, and utterly devoted to Buck Watson. "How is Buck? I haven't seen him since Sunday."

Billy's ruddy face darkened, and he cast a look down the street in the direction of his own house. "He's in bed, probably crying. Charlotte, have you got a few minutes? Let's walk down to the creek mouth, get some fresh air that doesn't stink of two-legged *or* four-legged rats."

Pomo Creek met the Pacific just below the headland that was

Finn Park. Here the land curved briefly inward, making a little pocket beach. "I don't see how they could put a marina here," she said as they tramped side by side along the packed wet sand. "Not without dredging and building a large breakwater; there isn't enough protection from the north."

"A few more years with Republican governors, they'll build breakwaters at ten-mile intervals and rip-rap the whole coast." Billy shoved his hands deeper into the pockets of his down vest and tipped his head back to breathe deeply. Charlotte did the same, and tasted the salt-iodine tang of the sea. It was a flavor she would miss when she moved away from the coast.

Move. Not yet she wouldn't. "Billy, what's wrong with Buck?"

"Michaelson is putting the heat on us. Our place is vital, he says, because of its location at the end of the lane."

"What is Michaelson using for fuel?"

Billy's face was suffused with blood, so dark that Charlotte feared he might have a stroke right there on the beach, and how on earth would she get him back up the path? "Billy, if you don't want to talk about it . . ."

"Buck has a criminal record, for sex with a minor."

It took Charlotte's breath away, leaving her unable to speak. Petey! she thought, Petey did yard work for them all summer.

Billy was watching her steadily, no expression on his face, and she felt her own face grow hot. "I'm sorry," she said, the words coming in a near-whisper.

"It's okay, Charlotte. I understand." He blew a long breath through pursed lips. "He was twenty-three years old, not dumb but naive. He got seduced by this guy who said he was twenty but was only sixteen; the kid blackmailed him until he was broke and then reported him."

Charlotte thought of that tall, frail, kind man, not much more than a boy himself and scared to death.

"It was a setup; he really thought the guy was older. Buck doesn't go for little boys, didn't then and doesn't now. Of course, I'd believe that anyway, wouldn't I, because I love him." Billy hunched his shoulders in a painful shrug. "But I know it's true.

"Anyway. Michaelson came by last night to offer us more money, and mentioned that he'd come across this interesting old story."

"And what did you do to him?"

"I ushered him out the door of the café, where he unfortunately tripped over the curb and got his goddamned Burberry all muddy."

"So you're not going to sell."

"No, ma'am! Buck served his time, it was almost twenty years ago and he hasn't so much as jaywalked since. We're good citizens running a useful business here. Any fuss that prick raises will blow over. At least, that's what I told Buck, about seventeen times."

Charlotte was cold. "Let's go home before we freeze." She tucked her arm through Billy's and he didn't pull away as she'd feared he might. "I've got stock simmering; I think I'll make minestrone with it, and I'll bring some to Buck when it's ready. And I have to go to the hardware store and buy a new mailbox. Then I have to present the bill for it to Harry Duarte."

Chapter
Thirteen

■

"Hey! Walt, over here!"

Deputy Sheriff Walter Miranda paused at the top of the broad granite steps of the courthouse in Ukiah, then grinned and came trotting down to the Jeep parked at the curb. A black-browed, mustached man in his early thirties, he was nearly the same height as his cousin Val Kuisma, and half again as broad.

"Shit, but it's *cold* over here today!" he said, zipping his sheepskin jacket high as he climbed into the Jeep. "So, Valentine, what brings you to our venerable county seat? I mean, beside the fact it's your turn to buy lunch?"

"Follow-up interviews with three of the people who were at the Fisherman's Rest bar the night Ed Boylan disappeared. Are you finished here?" Val asked, as he pulled out into mild noontime traffic.

"I'm through, gave my evidence and I wish to hell they could lock the bastard up for the rest of his unnatural life." Walt sank lower in his seat with a snort of disgust. "Guy was burglarizing rooms in this resort, eighteen-year-old maid walked in on him and he damned near beat her to death. Where're we headed?"

"South on 101. Two of the people on my list were a wash. The third one is a waitress at that brewery pub in Hopland, comes on at twelve-thirty. We can get there, order lunch, be on the scene when she arrives."

"Now that is a fine idea. Those folks make an ale that just

might wash the bad taste out of my mouth. How come we're in this business, anyway, couple of nice guys like us?"

"We're making a useful contribution to society," said Val, who believed that most of the time. "How are Linda and the kids?"

Walt swung into a cheerful monologue featuring his beautiful wife (a sister of Val's fellow officer, Alma Linhares), his two-year-old son and his infant daughter. He was still talking fifteen miles later as Val pulled into the little highway town of Hopland.

"Married life is the way to go, cousin. You ought to try it. Ah, there's the pub. Pull a U and park on the other side; a man could get killed trying to cross this road on foot. Alma says you're still doing your older-woman number, got a nice new apartment with landlady privileges."

"Alma spends too much of her time with horny old cops."

Walt shot a quick look at his cousin and smoothed the grin from his own face. "Yeah, probably she does at that."

When the waitress had taken their orders, and Walt had downed half a mug of Red Tail Ale, Val wrapped his hands around his own mug and said, "Okay. Let's hear what you guys have turned up on the Gardner case."

"No arrests yet, but we're making progress."

"Hey, Cousin Walter, remember who you're talking to here? A fellow officer? Who was also along on that hunting trip last year, when you and the lady ranger . . ."

"Yeah, yeah. Cooperation between forces, name of the game. We have not yet found anybody who will admit he saw Gardner that Friday night, not at the Rainbow or at any other of the nearby beer joints. But shit, we've only been on it two days. A day and a half. Okay?"

"Okay. What about the cabin?"

"Somebody's been using it. Semen stains all over that mattress, some of 'em fresh. Not much in the way of readable prints; kind of people use a place like that in this weather, probably they don't put their hands on anything but their zippers."

The waitress set plates before them, steak sandwiches and home fries. Eyeing the girl's trim, denim-clad bottom as she moved away, Walt said, "Pour us some more ale, buddy."

"You haven't earned it yet."

Walt sighed loudly. "Under that handsome Portagee hide, you are sure as hell all Finn. The maybe interesting part is, we found a guy who got rolled at the Rainbow the weekend *before*, on Saturday night. Didn't tell anybody but a couple of close buddies, but one of them has a brother who's a reserve with the department. The guy, his name's Bud Hawks, was embarrassed, besides being afraid his wife would find out."

Walt went on talking as he refilled both mugs. "This Hawks was very, very drunk, so he doesn't remember much. He'd been drinking a lot, dancing some, went outside for some air and here was this woman sitting on the steps smoking a joint. Which she was willing to share. Tells him she's from Port Silva, came out with her boyfriend and they had a fight and he left. Pretty soon ol' Bud's sitting real close, gets an arm around her, she lets him reach up under her shirt and grab a handful. Then she says hey, she knows how to get into this old cabin, they should go have a good time.

"So the pair of them stagger out there, things get real fuzzy, and Hawks wakes up a couple hours later with his money, maybe ninety-five bucks, gone from his wallet and his watch missing." Walt picked up his sandwich and took a big bite.

"Walt, what . . . ?"

"Just a minute." Walt chewed for several seconds, then propped both elbows on the table and resumed his story. "He doesn't remember much about her. Ordinary face or anyway not ugly. She was shorter than him by quite a bit, but he's six feet one. She had very large boobs. He says she was definitely a blonde; he doesn't know whether he got the job done but he did get far enough that he remembers real white legs and this light-colored bush. And he has a faint memory of thinking there was somebody else in the room."

"Was he hurt?"

"He says there was a bump on his head, but it might have happened from falling. And that's all I know, except that we're talking to other jurisdictions, looking for similar complaints."

"From what we know of our guy, this Boylan, if he ran into a setup like that he'd put up a fight."

"And maybe get killed like poor old Ron Gardner. You haven't turned up anything on Boylan?"

"Just the car," said Val, and explained.

"That has kind of a different feel from Gardner or Hawks."

"Right, it does. And we haven't been able to place Boylan at the Rainbow, either. Okay, Walt, I just saw a new waitress come in, and she fits Mendenhall's description. She was jumpy when he talked to her, but he thought it was probably because she and her boyfriend were out for sex instead of the movies." Val got to his feet. "You sit here, make some muscles and smile pretty, I'll go coax her over."

"I have to go to work," the girl was saying as Val ushered her to their corner table.

"It's okay, I talked to your boss. Sally, this is Deputy Walt Miranda."

"Hi. Look, I don't know anything. I told the other guy that, the fat one." Sally, a chesty little blonde of perhaps eighteen, sat down on the edge of a chair and creased her smooth round face into a frown. "We went to an early movie, then to dinner down there on the wharf, at The Dock. It was really good. After dinner we went and sat in the truck, that we'd parked in the breakwater lot, listened to some tapes and watched the waves. Then Tommy wanted to go to that place, that bar up on the bluff, because he knew they wouldn't card him. I didn't have anything, I don't drink. And then we came home," she said quickly.

"Here, to Ukiah?" At her nod, Val asked, "Who drove?"

"Well, uh, me. I did."

"Because Tommy was drunk?"

Another nod.

"How did Tommy get home? He lives in Port Silva," Val said to Walt, "and fishes with the Bouchards."

"He . . . I don't know."

Walt bent forward to look into her face. "You didn't put him up at your house?"

She shook her head hard. "My folks don't drink. They don't even like me working where there's booze served, except they know the owners here."

"Sweetie," said Walt sadly, "are you telling me that you let him drive all the way back by himself? On that narrow winding road, middle of the night and the boy still drunk?"

She took a deep breath, blinked back tears, and said, "Yes. I mean, no."

"I just didn't think you'd do that." Walt patted her hand. "Now wouldn't you like to tell us all about it?"

It was sometime around eleven when Tommy insisted on taking her into the Fisherman's Rest—to show her off, she thought. The place was full of rough, loud men she was careful not to look at as she and Tommy went through the bar to the back room where his friends were . . . friends who bought him beers, lots of beers that he drank real fast. When they left he still seemed all right to her, voice a little slurred maybe but he took her hand and they walked together back down to the parking lot by the breakwater.

"And that man was there," she said. "The one in the picture, at least I think so. He was leaning against his car, right next to our truck. He said something I didn't hear, and I stopped and he put his hand on me." She put her own hand protectively on her right breast.

"So Tommy hit him, hard, and then again, and the man fell down behind his car. Then Tommy fell down, and I didn't know what to do, there wasn't anybody around." She paused for a gulp of breath that was half-sob. "So I got Tommy in the truck, and I know the man was alive because he was snoring. I took Tommy to the boat, that he fishes from, and helped him get on. Then I went home. I don't know what happened to that man after, and Tommy doesn't, either."

"We'll have to talk to Tommy," Val told her.

She nodded, sniffling as she wiped her eyes with a paper napkin.

"And we'll need a formal statement from you. Will you come to Port Silva, to the police station, tomorrow morning?"

"Yes, sir."

"And Sally?" Walt waited for her to meet his eyes. "Don't call Tommy."

Sally nodded again and stood up; the two men rose as well, and watched her make her way to the back of the room, where she disappeared through the door marked "Rest Rooms." Then Walt downed his last few mouthfuls of ale while Val paid the check.

"She's probably not as young and simple as she looks," remarked Walt as they walked to the Jeep. "And she sure is blond. But I'd bet my salary and my two kids that Sally doesn't spend her weekends fucking drunks at the Rainbow Tavern."

The shop called Gaia occupied the right half of a one-story, flat-roofed building on Pine Street a block east of Main. In its single window were displayed books, posters, crystals, maps, a set of crossed hiking staffs with bear bells. The blue and green and white Gaia poster was taped to the center of the window-pane, and just beneath it was a strip of white paper, words lettered in black ink: GAIA = EARTH. OUR MOTHER, OURSELVES.

The computer club met in a room at the rear of the building. This afternoon, the touch-panel combination lock on the back door clicked open at Petey's manipulation but the door held firm. "Shit, I guess it's bolted," he said to Hannah. "We'll have to go in the front."

In the dimly lighted shop itself, where potpourri prickled the nose and a Bach partita played on the tape deck, the two of them stayed back in the aisles among geodes and dinosaur mobiles while Sarah Stonemountain's younger daughter put a rolled-up California wildflowers poster and a mountain-lion tee-shirt into a paper bag for a woman customer. Elaine was tall and broad-shouldered, like her mother and sister, but she looked softer. Her wide mouth drooped in a kind of pout, and she kept shooting glances around as if she expected someone to creep up on her.

Her lower lip pushed further out as she corrected an error in the change she'd given. When the customer had finally left, Elaine turned to glare at Hannah and Petey. "As I have already told about eight kids today," she said, "Sarah's away on business and the club room stays shut until she comes back. I'm trying to run the shop and to study, too. I don't have time to baby-sit. So if you two don't want to buy something, you can just go bother somebody else."

"Boy, what a bitch," muttered Hannah once they were safely beyond earshot. Outside, they paused to glance into the adjoining shop; Elaine's brother Rob was busy demonstrating a laptop computer to two people while a third stood watching a printer spew out pages.

"Maybe we should just forget it, Petey. Sarah said . . ."

"All Sarah said was we better not get into trouble. And we won't. We don't need the club anyway; you've got the program at home, don't you?"

"Yeah."

"And your dad won't be there till late?"

"He has the well-baby clinic at the hospital Tuesdays, until seven."

"So we can use his printer. Come on, Hannah, I *need* to do this."

"Well, okay," said Hannah, unlocking her bike from the rack on the street. "But let's hurry. I've got my lesson at five."

"Oh, right. So we'll let Eddie do the last part; he can always get out at night."

By four forty-five they were on their way to Finn Lane, Petey in the lead and wondering why he felt vaguely uneasy. Except that she was a girl, Hannah would be his best friend; maybe she was anyway. She'd gone along with his plan today; and in spite of her quick tongue and intense curiosity, had asked no questions about Martin and as far as he could tell had said nothing to anybody else about Martin's visit yesterday.

Although the sky was blue and white rather than gray, with bursts of sunshine beaming here and there like spotlights, the gusty wind was still February-bitter, making it hard to talk and ride at the same time. Petey tucked his chin into his jacket collar and pedaled hard. It wasn't until he swung from Frontage Road onto Finn Lane that he remembered, and braked so hard he nearly shot over the handlebars.

"Hey!" yelped Hannah, swinging sharply left to miss him. "What are you . . . oh, right, I forgot about all those little kids. Boy, somebody ought to tell them not to play in the street."

"Yeah," said Petey, tossing a sideways look at the north end of the park as they passed. The tent was still there, but its front was closed except for a narrow gap along one edge. Annie was not in sight; he had a feeling she was in the tent, even thought maybe he'd caught a flash of her green eyes at that gap.

Hannah wanted to go across to the Hall and see how things were working out there; but Petey hurried her around to the back of his house, making promises about food. It seemed very important that he get Hannah inside before Annie chose to appear. Hannah would remember the scene in the woods, probably even say something, a possibility too awful to risk. "I smell . . . oh, boy, killer brownies!" he cried as he led the way up the back stairs.

Hannah and Charlotte liked each other a lot, he reminded himself as he opened the door. And it was nearly time for Hannah's piano lesson, which she didn't like him to hear and with good reason. With any luck, he'd be able to grab a couple of brownies, hang around for a polite minute or two, and then go to the park.

Halfway across the park, he paused to observe his new neighbors; the homeless people. Although they'd been in the Hall for about two weeks, this was the first day of anything like standing-around-outside weather. Two skinny women, one maybe black and one white, watched three little kids of various shades of brown. A tall, bearded man with a little boy on one shoulder was guiding a woman across the wet grass toward the Hall, a woman so pregnant that Petey thought a fall would split her belly like a watermelon. Be careful, lady.

He counted five more scrambling and shouting kids, none old enough for school, and several more adults standing on or near the Hall's porch. Then he headed for the tent.

"Hey, Annie?" he called while still a few feet away.

"Hey, Pete? Come on in."

He reached the doorway and then stepped back, as big Bo and then little short Tiffany came out. Bo, head down, paid him no attention; Tif bumped into him, jumped back and said "Eeh!" in a kind of squeak, and blinked slowly as if she was having trouble getting him in focus.

"Sorry," he said. She had red circles painted on her cheeks, and wore jeans and a top that reminded him of Hannah's swimsuit, except that Tif bulged way out of hers. What he noticed mainly was her smell, smoke and pot so heavy it made his stomach tilt.

The tent was almost hot inside, partly from the little stove, partly from the last of the afternoon sun against the west side of the tent. Annie, wearing a pair of black jeans and a plain white tee-shirt, gave him a quick hug as he entered.

"Let's open the flap, let a little air in here," she said, tossing an irritated glance behind her.

"Hi, kid." Jesse was stretched out on an open sleeping bag, smoking. "You see what's happening out there? First ray of sunshine, every blade of grass has got a kid or a nigger standing on it."

"One little kid actually came right in the door a while ago," said Annie.

"Left in a hurry, though." Jesse rolled to his feet, pinched out his joint and set it in the torn-off bottom half of a Coors can. "Time for us to haul ass out of here, is what I say. What Bo and Tif say, too; we're all sick of this dumb little town."

"What I'm sick of is Bo and Tif," said Annie, who was still

fanning the tent flap. "Tif has completely fried whatever brains she had, and Bo didn't have any to start with."

"Come on, babe, don't be that way." Jesse moved up behind her, put his arms around her and rubbed his cheek against the top of her head. "We'll head south, look for jobs. It'll be better when we've all got a little more space."

"Like what, two tents? I told you. I want to stay right here."

"No, you don't, you want to come with the old man." Jesse moved his right hand up, long fingers making a obscene spider-shape over Annie's breast, and Petey, hot-faced, began to back toward the door.

"Stop that!" she snapped. Breaking Jesse's grip with a lifting back-thrust of both elbows, she stepped away from him and turned, chin out and eyes narrowed. "I'm getting pretty sick of you, too. As far as I'm concerned you can just fuck off!"

"Listen here, cunt!" Jesse's right arm bent and swung, in a backhand blow to the face that sent her staggering. Make him stop that! Petey commanded himself, but his body refused to obey, arms hanging limp and feet glued to the ground. He had his mouth open for a giant yell when the taller of the two rigid faced-off figures slumped and turned. "Ah, go to hell," Jesse said, and he pushed the tent flap aside and stumbled out.

"Sorry 'bout that, Pete," said Annie with a shrug. "Get yourself a drink out of the cooler there, and sit down."

Petey obeyed, choosing a Coke to drink and the stool to sit on. He was tempted to roll the cold metal can against his hot face; instead he popped the top and took a slow drink, cool guy. He wondered if this was something you started running into a lot when you got to be his age: men hitting women, like it was just something men did. His stomach hurt, maybe the Coke would help. "Uh, Jesse. I guess you were really right that he's got a bad temper."

"I guess." Annie popped her own can, a Coors, and settled cross-legged on the open sleeping bag. She tipped her head and used the sleeve of her tee-shirt to dab at her right eye, which was watering and already starting to swell.

"Are you married to him?"

"No way! Oh, Jesse's not the worst guy I've ever been with. But I think I'm getting tired of him."

"I figured all four of you had been together a long time, maybe grew up together or something."

She shook her head, then winced and dabbed her eye again. "The three of them did, someplace in Washington, I think it was. When I met Jesse in Eureka, he was on his own. Then he lost his job, Bo and Tif turned up, Bo wrecked his truck, and here we all are."

She took several long swallows of beer, as if to wash away the taste of Bo and Tif. Beer cans littered the tent, Petey noted, and Jesse's leftover joint was one of several in the makeshift ashtray. "Uh, Annie. Nobody's supposed to have booze here in Finn Park, or . . . um, anything else."

"Big deal. And besides, who can see us in here?"

"The thing is, Finn Hall was built as a temperance hall. That means the Finns didn't want anybody drinking there, or in the park either. Val told me about that, he's Finnish."

"Your tenant?"

"Yeah. And he's a cop, too." This was simply the truth, not disloyalty to Val.

"Terrific." Annie looked around the tent. "Remind me to tell Jesse."

Petey, squinting in the dimness, couldn't believe the speed with which her eye was puffing. And there was blood, too, from a mean-looking scratch high on her cheekbone. Jesse must have a ring. What if he came back still mad?

"You better let my mom look at your eye," he said. "It should have something put on it, maybe ice."

"I've got ice here."

"And you can have supper, too. Like I told you, Charlotte really likes to feed people. Of course, tonight's just fish," he added.

She took a long drink from her beer can, looking at him with no change of expression; then she gave one quick nod and got to her knees.

"Okay. I like fish." She drained the beer can, tossed it aside, and began to rummage around in an open duffel bag. "Here, the best I can do. This be okay for dinner with your mom?"

"Sure."

"Good." She peeled off her tee-shirt, dropped it on the ground, and shrugged on a man's blue work shirt.

Chapter

Fourteen

S ally's boyfriend Tommy Larson was a hulking young man with white-blond hair, a heavy jaw, and fair skin roughened rather than tanned by exposure to weather. Advised of his rights, he had insisted he didn't need a lawyer; now with head-down doggedness he was telling the same story for the third time.

"I was real drunk. Sally didn't know how drunk because nobody in her family drinks, her folks won't even have booze in the house. But it was the kind of drunk where you have to squint your eyes to get 'em to focus, and then what you see is in little bursts, like with spotlights.

"So we're walking all the way down that road, I'm sort of feeling for the ground with my feet, you know? And Sally has hold of my hand. I'm looking straight ahead, I hear somebody say something, I manage to get my head turned and there's this guy's grabbed Sally by the boob. And she says 'Tommy?' in this squeaky little voice."

"And what did you do?" asked Mendenhall.

"Well, what do you think? I hit him."

"How many times?"

"Maybe twice." Larson made a fist of his right hand and inspected the knuckles. "Bruises are about gone now, but it was pretty sore for a while. Like I said before, I hit him once in the face, jaw or maybe nose and cheek. Hurt my hand, and knocked him back against his car; I lost him for a minute, then he kind of bobbed back up. So I hit him again, somewhere lower down. And that was it, I think."

"You think?" said Val.

"It seems to me I kind of swung on through after that punch, that he didn't hit me but I just fell down. Anyway, I lost track of things there. After a while I came to with Sally patting me and crying, dripping tears on my face."

"And what was the condition of the other man, Edward Boylan?"

"I keep telling you, I'm not even sure it *was* Boylan. I know, I know, there's bright lights down there, but I was just too drunk. Sally said he was breathing and snoring and anyway, I didn't give a shit about him, I wanted to go be sick and lie down. Sally's the one said it was Boylan, days later when she saw his picture in the paper."

Sally, he told them, had gotten him to his feet and into the cab of his Toyota pickup. Sally had driven him out of the parking lot, past the possible Edward Boylan, who was lying there snoring half under the back end of his own car which was, yes, a Ford, Tommy could see that little oval nameplate in his head, and possibly gray but he wasn't sure. He, Tommy, had managed somehow to get onto the boat, and then remembered nothing until the next morning when he woke up there under a tarp, half-frozen.

"I didn't touch the guy after he was down, and Sally didn't either. I sure as hell didn't go back later to toss him in the harbor or whatever. I guess the worst that could have happened," he said, and swallowed, "is he was lying there and somebody else ran over him by accident and then got rid of the body I suppose that would be part my fault."

Mendenhall snorted; Val finished the note he was making and asked, "Did anybody else come into the breakwater parking lot while this was going on?"

Larson shook his head. "Nope, or Sally would've asked for help. And I'd have noticed. I think."

"What about people around as you were being driven to the boat?"

Larson put his head in his hands, fingers pressing his closed eyelids. "Nobody by the boats. There may have been people at The Dock, I'm pretty sure it was still open."

"Were there any cars in the breakwater lot besides yours and the Ford?"

Larson thought three or maybe four other cars had been there, but he had not paid them any attention. Sally might remember more, although he doubted it because she was really upset and didn't know much about cars anyway.

"Well, he's consistent," said Val minutes later as he pulled the door of the interrogation room shut. "And it's a believable story. The body didn't go into the water there, or it would have been found."

"They could have taken it someplace else."

"Only with Tommy on his feet and sober. And the guys at the Fisherman's Rest back up his story that he was just barely able to navigate."

Mendenhall's grunt was reluctant assent. "But I think we'll hold the guy overnight. And after you get his statement typed up and signed, you and . . . who's available, Boatwright? or maybe Alma. You can go make another pass at the restaurants and bars along the harbor."

"And get some supper while I'm at it," said Val, with a glance at his watch.

"Why not? Meanwhile, I'm gonna go tell the chief about this. And you and I will both keep our mouths shut until *he* decides who else to tell."

Perfect, absolutely perfect, *molto perfecto!* Petey whistled a whole-tone scale slow and mellow-tremolo up, then down in a fast swoop. All his women had behaved better than he could have hoped. Charlotte had cheerfully set an extra place at the table, no surprise there. Hannah had met Annie politely without a flicker of recognition and had then gone quietly home, truly incredible. And Annie had kept her language clean and her clothes on. Maybe he'd turn out to have some kind of magic touch with women, be famous for it in later life.

Don't be a jerk, Birdsong, he advised himself silently as he stacked another plate in the dish drainer. Hannah Wilhelm was a lot smarter than he was, absolutely nothing got past her. He'd bet she was working up a list of questions right now, probably on her Mac. Where did he find Annie this time, who was she really, did she turn him on and how did it feel and what was he going to do about it?

He held a soapy handful of knives and forks under the faucet before sticking them in the holder. He was pretty sick of doing dishes and wished Charlotte would actually buy the dishwasher she kept promising and then forgetting about. Sure Annie turned him on, and he halfway suspected she was doing it on purpose but maybe not, maybe she was just a really friendly, casual person.

What he was absolutely clear on was that she shouldn't be living in a crummy tent with a guy that hit her. At dinner tonight she ate a lot, but neatly and slowly. Talked with Charlotte like one ordinary grown-up to another, about stuff that was sort of personal but not very, like she was almost twenty-three, she'd been a waitress her last job, she was going to go back to college next year, and Jesse was a welder by trade but he and Bo had been working construction before the weather got so bad.

Staring at his own wet and soapy hands, Petey tried to imagine Annie sitting in a classroom and raising her hand to ask a question. Or standing by a table in a black skirt and white blouse maybe, writing down orders. The halibut is very good tonight, pasta for you, sir? Would anybody like a cocktail before dinner? The pictures refused to take shape.

Petey aimed the hose at the drainer, blasted the dishes with a spray of hot water, then closed his eyes and leaned his sweaty forehead against the edge of a cupboard. The notes of a Chopin nocturne drifted in from the music room, where Charlotte was playing and Annie was drinking coffee and listening. His mother had enough trouble with stuff like his father hitting her and asshole Harry Duarte putting dead rats in her mailbox. What if Annie was playing some kind of game here? And what was he going to do if Jesse came looking for her?

The sound of the doorbell jolted him like electricity; he actually yelped, and then skidded on the wet floor as he turned. "Never mind, Mom, I'll get it."

Martin Lindberg slid past Petey's outstretched arm and stepped into the entryway and then into the music room. "Please, Charlotte," he said, in his from-the-diaphragm actor's voice, "may I come in for just a moment? Long enough to apologize for the way I behaved the other night, and to give you these."

"These" were roses, their elegant yellow heads and glossy green leaves set off by Martin's snowy shirtfront. Freshly barbered and shaved, he wore a well-cut blue blazer and a pair of gray flannel trousers with a knife-edge crease. For a moment Charlotte shared in his obvious pleasure; good clothes and a proper appearance were vital to Martin's sense of self and he must have hated the cheap, tired garments he'd worn Sunday night.

Her next thought was that she'd be quite safe from assault this visit; Martin wouldn't behave like a hoodlum unless dressed like one. Where, she wondered wearily, did he get the money, for the clothing and for the roses—yellow roses in February?

"Thank you, Martin," she said, as she rose from the piano bench and turned on the overhead light. "For the roses—Petey, would you take them and find a vase, please?—and for the apology."

"You get out of here." Petey, feet braced wide and hands clenched, made no move to take the roses. "We don't want anything from a man who hits women."

There was a smothered sound—a gasp, or perhaps a giggle— from the armchair in the corner. Martin turned and stared in surprise at Annie, who sat with her feet drawn up. Her red-gold hair gleamed, and hung forward enough to partly obscure the right side of her face.

"I beg your pardon," Martin began, and Charlotte sighed. "Annie, this is Martin Lindberg. Our friend, Miss Annie Lee."

"Ah," said Martin. He laid the roses down on a side table and gave a little bow. "Annabel Lee."

"No, it's Annie!" the girl snapped.

"The poem, my dear, surely you know Poe's little verse. 'It was many and many a year ago, In a kingdom by the sea,' " he declaimed, " 'That a maiden there lived whom you may know, By the name of Annabel Lee.' I'm happy to meet you, Annie. I think I must have seen you before."

"I don't think so." She shook her hair back and looked directly at him, her broad grin combining with her swollen eye to make her face that of a gargoyle.

"Martin . . ."

"Charlotte, I beg you." He stepped back and spread his hands in a pose of pleading. Anyone else, Charlotte thought grimly, would be embarrassed to pursue personal matters before a stranger; to Martin, Annie just made a bigger audience.

"You see, I'm trying to understand it myself. Pete, I am not a violent man. Tell him, Charlotte, please, that I never struck you before, even when you—even when we quarreled."

"That's true, you didn't."

"I just suddenly lost control. I think perhaps it was the liquor. I've never been a heavy user of alcohol."

"That's true," said Charlotte again.

"But I am sorry, I do apologize, and I want to assure you nothing like that will ever happen again."

"Good." She was tempted to point out the inappropriateness of the word "happen" in an apology, but didn't want to prolong this situation. Annie was sitting neat and still, her undamaged eye bright with interest; and Petey was looking flushed and confused.

"All I want to say, in my own behalf, is . . ."

"Please don't."

"Is this," he went on. "I am an aging man making one final attempt to connect with my family. You can't know, Charlotte, how lonely I have been since you left me."

"Martin you have had two wives since *you* . . ." left me?

dumped me? disillusioned me was probably the appropriate phrase, thought Charlotte. "Since then," she finished.

"One of them a rebound, my dear, and the other more of a business arrangement." He put a hand out as if to touch her shoulder; she drew her breath in with a hiss and he thought better of the gesture.

Petey shuffled his feet. "Uh, Mom? Maybe . . ."

"I admit that I'm not strong and independent like you. I'm miserable without a woman in my life. But you were the best, Charlotte, the only woman I ever really loved. I honestly believe that if we both tried, we could . . ."

There was a screech of chair legs against wooden floor as Annie stood up. "Thanks for supper and music, Charlotte. I'm going to get out of here before the bullshit gets too deep to wade through."

"I beg your pardon!" snapped Martin at Annie's back.

"You're welcome, Annie," Charlotte called after the girl, whose forthright rudeness had sliced through the net Martin was trying to cast, a sticky web of self-doubt, remembered lust, and just plain history. "I'm sorry, Martin, but you're still not a very good actor. I hope you didn't spend your last dollar on the clothes and flowers."

"Listen, you impossible woman . . ."

"I'm asking you for the last time to leave. Or I'll call my policeman tenant for help again."

"Tenant, you call him, that furry-faced adolescent. Does he actually pay rent, or do you just take it out in fucking?"

"Petey, let it go!" Charlotte hooked strong fingers over the back waistband of her son's jeans and stopped him short. "Martin, out! Now!"

"Sorry, son," said Martin from the door. "Words spoken in disappointment, not the sort of language I usually employ."

Door-slam, bringing a faint jangle from the piano; then clattering feet on the wooden steps, diminuendo. Charlotte looked at her son, who looked back.

"Boy, he really is a dickhead, isn't he?"

"I would probably choose a different word, but I can't argue with the sentiment."

"I'm sorry," he said, the words meant to cover a world of miseries.

"Me, too. Go to bed, Petey. I'm going to turn the lights off and play for a while."

"Okay, good. But I better lock the doors first."

Chapter
Fifteen

No prior conditions and no pressure, that's what Harold Michaelson, Esquire, had promised. He'd be happy to come to her, he had continued in the same oleaginous tones, but was expecting several important telephone calls over the course of the morning, and would be most appreciative if she could find time to take coffee with him in his cottage at Tidepools Lodge—10 A.M.

Charlotte had quelled her initial impulse, to hang up on the man. Probably he was not the first blackmailer to style himself "Esquire," and on the personal level she could safely leave Billy Kaplan to defend himself and Buck. And even though she had this very morning promised Petey that she would refuse Michaelson's offer, she might learn something if she went to talk to the man.

Besides, she was weary of sitting around in her house, her millstone, taking lesson cancellations and wondering whether it was time to resort to her fall-back income source, working for a tax-preparing service. Now she checked her watch and then rapped on the door of cottage number twelve, Anemone Cottage according to the little sign beside the doorstep.

"Ms. Birdsong. Thank you for coming." Michaelson wore dark gray slacks so fitted to the body that they had to be Italian, a bulky, furry sweater in black and white, and a pair of silver-gray Western boots that had probably been made for him. Martin would positively drool, thought Charlotte as she handed the lawyer her L. L. Bean pea coat and pulled off her own rubber boots. The cottage was set up as a home away from home for busy executives, plushy luxury topped off by computer, printer, and other objects clearly electronic.

When she refused coffee, he settled her in one of several easy chairs, pulled another close for himself, and gave her a sincere-but-worried smile. "Dear lady, I *am* sorry we seem to be at cross-purposes in this matter. As two intelligent people, we can surely find some common ground."

Charlotte smiled politely and ducked her head. In jeans and flannel shirt, her stockinged feet set neatly together before her chair, she was sure she looked like the little beggar girl, or at least like a small, docile woman.

"First, let me say I understand your wish to accommodate your young son. My client has sons, too, and she has always tried to act in their best interests."

The words "my client" set off little bells in Charlotte's head. She smiled gently and fluttered her eyelashes and hoped she wasn't overdoing her role.

"Ms. Birdsong, I want you to know that Cynthia Leino is a fine woman. I had no mother of my own, and from the time I was very young, Cynthia was always there for me. So I know what bad luck she's had, what hard choices she's made. For instance, she stayed married to a man who was a hopeless alcoholic. John Leino, her husband, finally drank himself to death."

Michaelson leaned forward, intense. "John didn't work during his last years, and Cynthia is left with only the house in Rancho Santa Fe and the Finn Lane property. She wants to realize as much from these as she possibly can, as *soon* as she can, and leave San Diego . . . to make a new life for herself. And I'm doing my best to help her."

"I see," murmured Charlotte. Another reading on Cynthia Leino would be interesting; she hoped that her friend Wim Birnbaum had acted on her suggestion and put his wife Shirley on Cynthia's trail. Shirley Birnbaum would be astonished that anyone should wish to flee luxurious Rancho Santa Fe.

"I was sure you would, Ms. Birdsong. You strike me as a kindhearted person."

She hoped kindhearted was the right term. Not wishy-washy. "And because I know you are also an intelligent person I'll explain something else about the situation here. Money, Ms. Birdsong, is forceful stuff and doesn't care at all for feelings. What's happening on Finn Lane is called gentrification. You and your neighbors own something that has become attractive to people who have a lot more money than you do, and this pretty much means you can no longer afford to keep it. But you will all come away with a very nice return on your original investment."

In a minute he would pat her on the head. And she would bite his hand. "Mr. Michaelson, it seems to me that if the Finn Lane property is attractive to your selected gentry today, it will be even more attractive to others in the future. Unless we're expecting a sudden shortage of rich people in this country?"

Michaelson looked at her as if she had, in fact, sunk her teeth in his flesh.

"So what you're asking is that I give up a house my son and I enjoy, a house that is also an appreciating asset, just to suit your client's convenience."

"Ah." He sat back in his chair, and his face relaxed into a half-smile. "Nearly everyone else is eager to sell, as I'm sure you know."

"Yes." What had she said to change his mood?

"Ms. Birdsong, my final offer for the Finn Lane properties will be very respectable. But I can see that we're a pair of realists, you and I; we both recognize that you're in a favorable position." On his feet now, he moved to the desk, reached into the center drawer and retrieved a silver money clip holding a fat wad of green.

A bribe, how interesting! Watching him lay hundred-dollar bills on the coffee table one by one, Charlotte discovered that real money was of itself oddly fascinating, making her fingers itch in a way no check would have. And hundreds, something you didn't deal with every day.

"This is just between you and me, of course," he intoned as he added the tenth and apparently final bill to the neat green fan. "And it is *not* part of the purchase price. Call it a ten percent advance and I'll get the rest of your bonus for you in cash as well, no need to mention it to anyone. You can buy something exciting for your son, or perhaps take a trip."

Martin. That was what had been nibbling at the edge of her mind; Michaelson was just like Martin, not only the manipulative technique but the delivery, that actorish delivery. She became aware of silence, and looked up to find the lawyer's eyes on her. "Oh, I don't think so, thank you. No. That is, I haven't yet decided about selling. Mr. Michaelson, were you ever active in amateur theater in San Diego?"

"Why, yes I was," he admitted, positively beaming. "Some time ago, before my practice became so time-consuming, I worked with the Bay Repertory Group, and also with the Old Town Players. Perhaps you saw me in *The Importance of Being Earnest?*"

"Perhaps I did." No doubt Martin had; he'd been involved off and on with both those groups.

As she pulled on her boots, he moved to retrieve her jacket and hold it for her. "I'll call you tomorrow, Ms. Birdsong. I want to give you time to think about what's really best for yourself and your son. And for your neighbors; civilization after all consists of caring about others as well as about ourselves." He bowed her to the door.

"And let me give you one more bit of information, if you won't be offended. Whatever you may have been led to believe, no one but you and your son has any legal claim to your house, or to the proceeds from its sale."

Outside the cottage, she set off for the stairs to the beach, taking big breaths of clean, sea-tinged air as she strode along. Smarmy was the word for Michaelson. He had set Martin on her, she'd bet on that, had funded his appeals and was now undercutting the older man. Poor frantic Martin. Did he know he'd been abandoned? What would he do when he found out?

At the bottom of the stairs, hard-packed, rippled sand was

broken intermittently by outcroppings of rock, jumbled masses capturing the sea in the pools for which the lodge was named. Pushed along by a wet and gusty wind, Charlotte focused on a whole different world: a hedgehog-like cluster of barnacles on the steep southern side of a tall rock, an enormous starfish spread out along the rock's base, a tiny crab that scuttled into a crevice at her approach. Anemones carpeted lower rocks in a vast relief design of doughnut-shapes seemingly sculpted in sand; only the few submerged in pools waved delicate green tentacles in a display of hunger and life. What ate anemones? she wondered. And what ate lawyers? Something should.

A wave washed over her boots and sent her scurrying toward another set of stairs, those leading to the roadside parking lot where she had left her car. At the top she stepped over a chain that hadn't been there earlier, and paused to read the sign it supported. Danger. High Tides and Rogue Waves. Use the Beach at Your Own Risk.

As Charlotte opened her back door she was greeted by the ringing telephone, a summons no mother dare ignore. Or any self-employed person either. A machine, she reminded herself once again, you need a machine to take care of this machine. Bah.

"Charlotte? Charlotte, it's Shirley."

Sheer energy surged through the receiver and bounced around the kitchen. "Just a minute, Shirley," Charlotte said, and went to the fridge to pour herself a glass of wine. Dealing with Shirley Birnbaum required fortification.

"Are you sitting down?" Shirley demanded when Charlotte said hello again. "Because I'm getting lots of wonderful information, Wim was absolutely astonished."

Charlotte had not seen Wim astonished ever in her life. Bemused, puzzled; at most taken aback. Shirley had once remarked that had she not come along, Charlotte and Wim might have married and blanded each other right out.

"What I'm doing is calling in chits everywhere—Wim's Edith,

who calls herself the world's oldest legal secretary; my newspaper buddies, the gals in the real estate office. It's fun. *God*, volunteer work is boring, I'm a rotten docent."

"I can imagine." The thought of Shirley leading a museum tour brought to Charlotte's mind a television special she had seen on sheep-dog trials.

"First of all, Howie Michaelson, you remember him? Wim told you about him?"

"A well-known attorney. Presumably the father of Hal, who is here tormenting us."

"Correct. Howie set up in practice in San Diego right after World War II and did very well. Was a big man with the ladies, too, finally married some girl a lot younger than he was and she died in childbirth a few years later. I didn't know anyone did that any more."

Hal Michaelson must be thirty at least. "Thirty years ago they probably still did, Shirley."

"I suppose. At any rate . . ." Shirley paused, and after a moment Charlotte heard a pleased exhalation; clearly Wim had not yet managed to persuade his wife to give up cigarettes. "At any rate, next player is a young partner in Howie's firm, did a lot of pro bono civil rights stuff in the sixties, went on to become a powerhouse criminal lawyer. He—John Leino—was a big handsome guy, deep voice, the kind of charm that worked with grandmothers as well as dollies. John fell into a bottle sometime in the seventies; somebody told me alcoholism ran in his family."

"But his wife stayed married to him," Charlotte recalled.

"In name, sweetie. The word is that her bod has been Howie's for years. He hired her as a legal assistant, paid her lavishly, helped her buy a house near his in Rancho Santa Fe; she added his little kid to her own three and raised the lot." Shirley paused for a drag on her cigarette. "Then two years ago, Howie had a stroke. Hasn't been seen in public since; some people suggest he's a vegetable, others that he's only mildly disabled but kept at home by vanity."

"And John Leino?"

"He'd been staying home for a long time. Then one night last December he apparently ordered in a few bottles of Remy Martin, drank one or two, went into the garage and turned his car engine on. And died. You must have read about it; every newspaper in the state did a 'sad end for hero of the sixties' feature.

"The interesting thing," Shirley went on, "is that there was actually a police investigation of Cynthia Leino's movements that night. There are people who think she might have helped John on his way, probably so she could have a chance at Howie's money."

Charlotte felt a pang of sympathy for Cynthia, who had found herself in mid-life with the equivalent of *two* invalid husbands. "Maybe she just got tired."

"Charlotte, you have the most incredibly basic mind. Anyway, no charges have been brought, yet. At the moment she's keeping a low profile and trying to sell her Rancho Santa Fe house."

"And trying to sell the Leinos' Port Silva property to developers," said Charlotte. "Through Hal Michaelson."

"It is *possible* that she thinks the police might eventually charge her in her husband's death," said Shirley. "In which case she might want to get as liquid as possible. And Howie's Hal is reported to be devoted to her. So that's it, Charlotte, end of report. Did I do good or not?"

"You did. Thank you."

"I've got a few more things to follow up; I'll get back to you in a day or too. I think I might have a real talent for this stuff, Charlotte. I wonder what you have to do to get a private investigator's license?"

Her household and business accounts were going to require some creative bookkeeping, Charlotte decided half an hour later. And H. Michaelson, Esquire's ten-thousand-dollar bribe was looking more appealing by the minute. She shoved the books aside, got up to put the kettle on, and realized that she was hearing noise from the street. Raised voices, in fact.

Two police cars were pulled up on the grass in the park, where a cluster of people, the Hall's residents she thought, were milling around under the watchful eyes of a pair of uniformed policemen. Val was there, too, coming from the north end of the park toward the action. From her doorstep Charlotte watched as another uniformed officer, a dark-haired woman, moved into the crowd, which fell back, leaving her in charge of a skinny young woman holding a small child.

The policewoman ushered woman and child to one of the police cars. The two male officers moved slowly after her, clearly on the watch against any sudden move from the crowd; but none came, and they got into the second car.

Val was now talking with a tall, gray-haired man Charlotte knew to be from the Hall. As he turned to glance after the departing cars, Val caught sight of Charlotte and lifted a hand in her direction; stay there I'll be right with you, said the gesture. She waved in return and moved slowly down the steps.

"Charlotte, I was coming to talk to you when all this started. Hey, you look cold. Come down to the Bluejay, I'll buy you a cup of coffee."

"The Bluejay is closed for a few days," she said, and told him of Michaelson's semithreat against Buck Watson. "But come in and I'll make coffee."

"I think Billy's right, they should tough it out and wait for the fuss to blow over. Although I guess that's an easier attitude for Billy than for Buck. Oh!" he said suddenly, and stopped halfway up the front steps.

"What's the matter?" she asked, alarmed.

"Nothing, just something I left in the apartment. You go on, Charlotte, get the coffee started. I'll be up in a couple minutes."

Charlotte was pouring a final bit of water into once-drained filters as footsteps sounded on the back stairs. "It's open, Val," she said, and went on with her task. When she turned with a full mug in her outstretched hand, she gasped and nearly lost her grip.

"Charlotte, I'd like you to meet George," Val said as he rescued the mug.

"George," she said faintly. The dog, shoulder nearly level with Val's knee, cocked his head, wagged his long plumy tail and gave her a pink-tongued grin. "Sit, George," Val ordered. The dog tipped his head again, thinking it over, and then dropped his rump to the floor in a spraddle-legged pose that made Charlotte think of a bear.

"Sit down, Charlotte," Val went on, and she obeyed much more quickly, she thought.

"If he's for us, I have to tell you that I'm not really a dog person, Val. And Petey says he doesn't want another dog."

Val shook his head, his face somber. "George is for you, not Petey. The search for Edward Boylan—you know, the missing developer—is heating up, so I won't be around much. Then this turned up in mailboxes and on doorsteps this morning; did you get one?"

"This" was another flyer. "SAVE HISTORIC FINN PARK!" screamed capital letters across the top of the page. Below the words was a drawing of a street, two little boxlike houses and a bigger box labeled "Hall" and two more houses, sunshine beaming down and ocean waves behind. Then on the lower half of the page, "Zap Development!" as a lightning bolt flew from the finger of a detached giant hand toward a tractor and the stick figure atop it. The tombstone leaned in the bottom-left corner: R.I.P.

"Good heavens," said Charlotte. "No, I didn't. This is much more—elaborate. Drawn by a cartoonist?" She had not received this one, but she was fairly sure she'd seen it somewhere.

"By a computer." Val sat down in the rocker, or rather on its edge. "Yeah, elaborate and specific. Asking for trouble right here, seems to me."

It seemed so to her, too, and the fact was a lot less appealing up close than it had been a few days ago from a safe distance. "Val, what was going on outside just now?"

"Yeah, that's the third thing. The young woman you saw with

Alma, Officer Linhares? She's a supposedly reformed crack cocaine user who's been living with her kid in the Hall, and she obviously found a local supplier. Mr. Cooney, the gray-haired guy I was talking to, is more or less the leader of the group of homeless in the Hall, and he called us in; he was worried they'd all get kicked out."

"Was anyone else involved?"

"Cooney thought the people in the tent might be dealing; but I talked to the three that were there, and searched the tent. Didn't turn up anything but half a dozen cans of beer in a cooler. Illegal in the park, but not very."

"One of them, a girl named Annie, is a friend of Petey's," Charlotte told him. "She doesn't look like a drug-user to me."

"Annie's the good-looking one, long reddish hair? She wasn't there today, but I've seen her. Dopers don't always look different from you and me, Charlotte. Anyway, all of a sudden there's trouble every way I look, and I'd be really happy if you'd humor me on this and keep the dog. Besides, George needs a friend. You're his last chance; from here he goes to the pound."

"That's blackmail," Charlotte protested, and took a sip of coffee, lovely almost-black stuff and stronger than she'd intended. As Val set the rocker into nervous motion, George got up, padded across the room on feet that reminded Charlotte of furry snowshoes, and flopped beside her chair with a sigh.

"Val . . ."

"See, my uncle Art, that raises Labs? Last year one of his young bitches came in heat, my cousin Susie let her out by accident and was scared to tell him. So the bitch had four pups, and Uncle Art kept one for her to raise so she wouldn't grieve."

What happened to the other three? wondered Charlotte and decided not to ask. "Who, or I guess I mean what, was the father?" she inquired instead. She knew what Labradors were, big grinny shiny-black dogs with broad heads and thick tails.

"Um. Well, there's this neighbor out there, a weekender, owns a big white standard poodle."

"Oh." Poodle and labrador seemed an exotic mix. George, she

found as she looked down, resembled neither. He had long gray-with-black hair falling to either side of his spine; and the hair on his head might have been brushed sideways from a center part, away from round brown eyes. His face reminded her of pictures of Carl Sandburg.

Rocking harder, Val rattled off the dog's sins: he wouldn't retrieve, he chose not to swim, he positively disliked guns, he was adept at opening doors and gates to let the other pups out to play with him. "Real problem is, George is a clown and Uncle Art's got no sense of humor. But you'll like him, Charlotte, I promise. Okay?"

"I will keep him," Charlotte said, "on trial. He has to be useful and agreeable, not just one more male creature for me to feed and clean up after."

"Well. Sure."

"And Petey is entitled to an opinion about this; he lives here, too."

"Hey. That reminds me." He brought the rocker to an abrupt stop. "I ran into Pete as he was leaving for school this morning. I said hi, and he said hi back, normal grin. Then he stopped and *looked* at me, you'd have thought I was sprouting fur and fangs right there. Kept his eyes on me so long he almost fell over his feet. What's up?"

Charlotte thought for a moment, remembered, and sighed. "Martin. He was here for a few minutes last night. He said some unpleasant things."

"I see." Val's voice was flat, neutral. "The man is a whore at heart, Charlotte, and wouldn't recognize affection or even good honest lust if he fell over it."

"Yes, I know."

"And some day you might want to run your own life."

"Some day I intend to."

"Sure," he said, and stood up. "I have to go back to work. Keep George with you, okay?"

"All right. Thank you. Val, who do you think is behind Rip?"

"Probably Sarah Stonemountain or . . ." He closed his mouth with a snap and turned to stare at her. "Charlotte, do you do that on purpose, or does your mind just fast-forward all by itself? Why do you need to know?"

No fast-forward now, just the name Stonemountain thumping a slow dah-duh-duh, dah-duh-duh like a mean little song. "I'm sorry. It's just that I'm worried about Rip."

"Let us worry. And keep that name to yourself, please."

"Yes, I will," she said to his departing back. As the door closed, George got to his feet, licked Charlotte's ear and lurched up to drape the front half of his body over her lap. "Oh, my, useful already," she whispered. "Somebody to hug."

Chapter

Sixteen

"Like I told you on the phone, I just didn't think of Chuck when you were here yesterday," said Vern Swigart, whose father had built The Dock seafood restaurant forty years earlier. "He's not my regular, just fills in now and then when he needs the money or I need help. And he'd been out of town, out of mind you might say. But when my sis mentioned this morning that he'd just got back, I had a word with him." Swigart had a clipboard in his hand, full of flimsy sheets he was checking against stacked boxes. Now he hooked his pen over the board's clip and edged his considerable bulk past the boxes. "Come on, he's setting up the bar for lunch."

Chuck Sears, Vern Swigart's nephew and occasional bartender, was a sandy-haired, broad-shouldered kid with a sunburned face and a walking cast on his left ankle. "I left a week ago Monday, real early," he told Val, "for two weeks on the slopes. Stayed with a friend in Johnsville, no radio and no newspaper. Skied all day every day, and I'd still be there if I hadn't got caught in a whiteout and come down a hill wrong."

"So you were on the bar a week ago Saturday."

"Right. The guy, same guy in the picture Uncle Vern showed me, he came into the bar about, oh, ten o'clock. Ordered a shot of Jose Cuervo and lime, and wanted a table. I told him no way, we were booked full clear through, several parties as well as just the usual people having dinner. He acted kind of pissed off, but he didn't get noisy about it, just finished his drink and left.

The bar was about three deep right then; chances are nobody noticed him."

"But he came back?"

"Right. We'd stayed open later than usual because of the parties, but we weren't serving any more dinners; it must have been midnight or later. He was just there at the bar all of a sudden, grabbed my arm, wanted a drink. And I said no. I got him out real fast; he was a fairly big guy but not as big as me and not in any kind of shape. Besides, he was practically falling-down drunk."

And that, thought Val, filled in the empty slots in Boylan's Saturday night. The Dock, then up the hill to the Fisherman's Rest, finally got tossed out of there, staggered back down here where the same thing happened. Made it to his car, and maybe he'd seen Sally in the Rest earlier, that would partly explain his grab for her when she appeared in the parking lot. And then . . . who? what?

Chuck focused on his lineup of bottles for a moment, head down. "Thing is, I should have called somebody. Guy was in no condition to walk, let alone drive. But just as I got him out, Jill came to the bar with an order for eight Irish coffees, so I locked the door and forgot about him. For all I know, he fell in the harbor and the tide took him out."

"The Coast Guard guys don't think so, or the body would have been found," Val told him. "How soon after he left Saturday night did you close?"

Chuck shrugged. "Half an hour, forty-five minutes maybe."

"Okay. What I'll need, Mr. Swigart, is a list of who was here that evening, particularly who was still here when Boylan left."

Swigart was shaking his head slowly, not in refusal but in doubt. "We have forty-eight tables, Kuisma. We serve dinner starting at 5 P.M. and on Saturday nights we serve until 11. For some reason, as I remember it that was a real busy night. And I didn't stay to close; I went home around 10."

"What about your list of reservations?"

"Nope, don't keep 'em."

"Mayor Bondurant was here late," offered Chuck. "He'd brought his folks in for their anniversary. And one of my professors, Dr. Mancuso, with his girl and a bunch of his students; they were celebrating something, drank lots of wine and a bunch of Irish coffees."

Val nodded thanks as he scribbled in his notebook. "Mr. Swigart, I'll ask you to please get out your copies of credit card receipts for February third. And the waitresses and anybody else who worked that night? if we could get them all together here, with you and Chuck?"

Swigart and Chuck conferred briefly over names. Val had a cup of coffee and chatted with Chuck about Plumas County skiing while Swigart made phone calls. When Val left the restaurant fifteen minutes later, it was with the understanding that he would return at four that afternoon to help the gathered employees probe their memories.

Wednesday's lunch deal in the school cafeteria was something called tamale pie, which looked to Petey to be mostly cornmeal with red grease leaking through. It certainly made him wish he hadn't woken up hungry at 3 A.M. and eaten the intended-for-his-lunch chicken legs.

Hannah, he noted glumly, had for some reason settled herself in the middle of a group of girls; and Eddie was working the serving line dishing up salad. Petey fingered the five-dollar bill Charlotte had given him. For once it wasn't raining; and he had his good bike. If he didn't waste any time, he could get to the Burger Shack down on the wharf for a bacon burger and make it back in time for fifth period.

He hurried away before anyone could notice. It was not strictly against the rules to go off the school grounds for lunch, but the principal discouraged such moves and right now Petey didn't feel like standing around arguing with some teacher.

He scanned the streets as he rode but didn't come upon Martin's car. Saw a Jeep like Val's at an intersection but it wasn't Val behind the wheel and anyway he didn't want to talk to Val, either. He turned onto Main Street and wondered if maybe he should go home for lunch, see how Charlotte was doing and check that Martin hadn't turned up there. He was still giving thought to that when Wharf Street came up and his body made the decision for him, leaning and turning right to tuck tight and zip down the steep twisty little street. A guy who wasn't good at this could wind up right in the harbor with the oily garbage and the gulls.

Down here was a whole different kind of place: wet, windy, and smelling of saltwater, mud, and fish. All the men, and it was mostly men here, which was one of the things he liked about it—all of them wore black rubber boots and serious working clothes.

He pedaled slowly and happily along the familiar bumpy road, checking that things were normal. Big icehouse, ships' chandlery where he'd bought his rain suit, fish processing company; guys in rubber suits moving boxes of spiny sea urchins around. Fish stores, fish restaurants a bunch, big and little. Ratty old motel and another slightly newer and fancier; Petey figured fishermen stayed in those motels and ate at the Burger Shack when they wanted a change from boats and fish.

He rode past the big, nearly empty parking lot, waving to a couple of guys who had nets spread out for mending. The eighty-two-foot Coast Guard patrol boat was lined up neatly against the dock; but he noted that the forty-four-foot motor lifeboat was not in the harbor. The water was peaceful here, boats rocking gently in their slips, but out beyond the breakwater the sea was rough and mean-looking under heavy winds. Lots of boats had stayed home today, not just the salmon boats, which didn't go out this time of year, but some of the bottom-fishers, too.

"Hey, kid!"

A guy in a peacoat and a watch cap stood on the deck of a fishing boat, the *Portagee Princess*, waving. Petey looked around, saw nobody else nearby. He stopped his bike and stood astride it.

"Listen, kid, I want you to tell your old lady that nobody likes a spoiler." The man clambered forward to the bow of the boat, and Petey recognized Harry Duarte. Eddie Duarte said his uncle Harry was crazy; Petey thought he was for sure somebody you wanted to keep clear of.

"You're the man of the family, right? Isn't that right?"

"Uh, yeah, I guess," Petey called in reply.

"Then you better act like a man and get that mother of yours in line."

"Hey, she's not . . ."

"You heard me. Get her in line, or somebody else will do it for you." Harry Duarte punctuated his remarks with a skyward thrust of his clenched left fist as he turned to make his way to the rear of the boat.

"How, by putting rats in her mailbox?" Petey asked, but not very loud. Charlotte didn't seem to be scared of Harry Duarte; but Charlotte knew a lot more about music than she did about people, or men at least.

Someone gripped his shoulders from behind, then arms clamped around and hands covered his eyes. In a panic, he flung his own arms out hard and broke the grip before the soft "Guess who?" registered.

"Hey, touchy, touchy!" Annie backed away, hands up.

"I'm sorry," he said, aware that his face must be red. "You just surprised me."

"So I sure won't do that again. What are you doing down here, skipping school?"

"No."

"No, I can see that. Skipping school is supposed to be fun, and you don't look all that happy."

"What I don't understand," he said in a voice he had to struggle to control, "I thought a house was someplace where you keep warm and eat and sleep and . . . live. How come one day it's your home and the next day it's just money?"

"Kid, you are talking to the wrong person. I live in a tent and I never have understood money. So what *are* you doing here?" she asked again as he stepped clear of his bike and turned it around.

"School lunch looked really gross, so I came down here for something to eat. What are you?" He set off down the road, wheeling the bike, and she walked beside him.

"Just trying to pick up a little money. Got any spare change, mister?" she whined, tilting her head to give him a sad-eyed, pleading look that was quickly followed by a grin.

"You shouldn't do that!" he said sharply, without thinking.

"Shut up!" She slapped his shoulder, hard. "I do what I want."

"Sure. Sorry."

"All right. Where were you going to eat?"

"The Burger Shack."

"I'll come along. What's the matter," she said when he hesitated, "are you embarrassed to be seen with somebody like me?"

His face felt hot again as he shook his head. "It's not as cheap as McDonald's, and I've only got five dollars."

"You're a nice guy, Peter Birdsong, you know that? Tell you what, we'll make up the difference from my money . . . just remember not to tell Jesse, okay?"

"Okay, sure."

"Wait till I get my coat." A dark wool jacket was draped over the bumper-high log barrier in front of the nearer motel; she retrieved it and shrugged it on over the tee-shirt she wore with her tight black jeans. Petey thought she must have been pretty cold standing around like that. It crossed his mind that Annie might be making money down here in other ways besides panhandling, but he pushed the notion quickly aside.

In the Burger Shack they sat at the counter and ate bacon burgers with Cokes and shared an order of fries, all of which came to more than ten dollars. "I just won't tell Jesse," said Annie again. Then she tossed her long shining hair over her shoulders and said, "What the hell, who cares? After all, it's his fault my take is down today. People see this"—she touched her right eye, darkly bruised and still slightly puffy—"and instead of feeling sorry for me, they get turned off and just slide past like I wasn't there."

"That's weird," said Petey.

"Not really. That's people. What about your nice house?" she asked suddenly. "Is your mother going to sell it to that lawyer, what's his name, Michaels?"

"Michaelson. No!" He remembered Harry Duarte and his clenched fist. "I don't think so, anyway."

"Well, with the big bucks I hear he's waving around you can buy a very nice, very big house."

"Not one that was built by my own great-grandfather. No, if I can't stay in my house, I think I'll . . . join the Coast Guard."

"Dumb move, too many bosses. Tell you what, you might hit the road with us."

He stared at her for several seconds before realizing his mouth was open. "Could I? That's awesome! You think I could?"

She shrugged. "Oh, I don't know. Maybe. But we're not going anywhere for a while."

She was backing off, from an offer she probably hadn't meant to make. He released held-in breath and wondered whether he felt sorry or relieved. Reaching for one of the two remaining fries, he caught sight of the clock on the wall and groaned. "Shit, I better get going or I'll be late for English."

"English is boring, very boring," Annie said as she swallowed the last of her Coke and rose to follow him to the door. "Why don't you just take the rest of the day off? Enjoy nature," she added, waving an arm to take in the harbor, the boat slips, the sky.

"Well, I . . ."

"Come on, let's go down and watch for boats to come in." She set off at a trot, toward the paved parking lot before the stone breakwater. Petey followed, until she reached the end of the lot, scrambled down a slope and headed for the long breakwater itself. The gray sea beyond was wind-lashed and white-capped, slapping at the breakwater and at the rocky headland on the other side of the inlet.

"Wait, don't go out there. See the signs?" He pointed at a warning on a metal post: "DANGER. Hazardous Wave Conditions exist even on Calm Days. Waves can wash over structure and sweep people into the ocean." A light flashed on a pole at the far end of the stone pile, and an electric horn sounded at thirty-second intervals.

"Bullshit," said Annie. "Doesn't look dangerous to me." She stepped lightly on, and Petey followed more slowly, glancing over his shoulder.

"Annie, this is winter and the waves get really big. It's high tide, and there's supposed to be a storm coming, they say fifteen-to twenty-foot waves."

Annie glanced out to sea, looking skeptical. "I'd like to see a storm from out here, a real one. I love storms. Come on, don't be chicken."

She held her right hand out toward him. He moved forward to take it, and she danced back a step, then another and a third. "Come on," she said again. A stray wave slapped the breakwater and sent water sheeting high across her legs; she gasped and then threw back her head in a shout of laughter.

"God *God* that's cold! Come on!" she commanded.

She stood with long legs braced wide, hand still outstretched. Petey stared at her, saw a gust of wind whip the bright hair across her face, watched her fling it back. He took a deep breath and then a voice bellowed from behind him: "Hey, you! You dummies better come in off there!"

"I have to go to school," he said to Annie, and hunched his shoulders as he turned away. She caught up with him as he was unlocking his bike.

"When's the next high tide?" she asked through chattering teeth.

"Twelve, thirteen, hours, I guess. There's a tides table in the paper."

"And there wouldn't be anybody around then to stick their nose in," she remarked. "Well, you better get on to English class, right? And I have to find some dry clothes. Maybe I'll see you later."

■

Chapter

Seventeen

■

S omeone had once told Charlotte that the worst thing about being a piano teacher was hearing "Für Elise" played badly, or even well, a hundred times a year. Not so, she decided as she watched the handsome ten-year-old pull his anorak over his head. The worst thing was having a student of nearly boundless potential who had heard the word "talent" too many times and the word "work" too seldom.

"Don't forget your music, Jon," she said as he started empty-handed for the door. "And please have your mother call me."

She closed the door behind him and headed for the kitchen, and the aspirin bottle, wondering vaguely what tranquilizers did for you and whether she might benefit from some. Something—her house-and-son worries, the unsettling presence of the poor and unlucky people staying in the Hall, even the endless gray weather—something had reduced to near zero her tolerance for pampered middle-class children. Not a good attitude for a music teacher and she certainly hoped it was temporary.

George, who had enjoyed the afternoon's comings and goings, followed her now to the kitchen, drank noisily from the metal bowl she had set out earlier, then turned the bowl over with a clatter.

"What . . . ? Oh, it's empty," she said, and filled the bowl from the tap. "And you'll need something to eat." After poor Fenris was killed, she had put his gear, including dishes and food, in the basement. But the open bag of kibble began to attract rats, so she threw it away.

Well, she'd just send Petey . . . no, he'd said coach was taking a group of them to the high school wrestling match after school today. Thinking unkind thoughts about dogs and men, Charlotte washed two aspirin tablets down, snatched her jacket from the its hook by the back door, hurried down the hall toward her bedroom and purse, and stopped short.

The door to Petey's room was half-open. Except to drop off clean clothes and sheets and collect soiled ones, she rarely went in there, on the principle that a person of any age beyond six or seven years was entitled to his own private place. However, today . . .

Dah-duh-duh dah-duh-duh was thumping around in her head again. Stonemountain, that compelling and intimidating woman. Shop owner, computer club sponsor or in some views dictator, probable . . . what was the term Val had used earlier? Eco-freak. Val's choice suspect as leader of R.I.P. And Sarah Stonemountain and her son, Rob, out of the pure blue sky and the goodness of their hearts, had loaned Petey a computer for his very own use. She was reaching to push the door wider when George beat her to it; he shouldered his way into the room and stood looking around him like a tourist.

Petey was neat for a boy; the comforter on his bed had been pulled into place, and the only dirty clothes in view were a sweatshirt and a pair of jeans dangling from the open hamper. And he was orderly: the wall shelves displayed, like a history of his childhood, what seemed to be every toy he'd ever owned, stuffed baby things on the top shelf down through trucks and Lego blocks to Star Wars figures and the green turtle-people. And books the same, lined up from *Goodnight Moon* through *The Monkeywrench Gang*, which must have migrated from her own shelves, and J. E. Lovelock's *Gaia*; had he actually read that?

Posters on the walls were of whales, otters, redwood trees. Mount Shasta, Half Dome in Yosemite, a blue-and-green planet earth called Gaia. Shouldn't there be some rock-star posters? Movie or TV sweeties in those lady-jockstrap swimsuits? Nothing like that on his bulletin board, either, just a snap of her, one of the dog Fenris, a photo of Glenn Gould cut from a newspaper. And the flyers. Save Our Sheep was there, and No Castles. But he didn't have, or at least had not yet displayed, Zap Developers, even though she was fairly sure she'd seen a copy of it yesterday when Hannah pulled her piano music from her backpack.

Petey couldn't have made the flyer, because the computer that squatted there on his desk had no printer. At least, she reminded herself, he couldn't have made it here. But at Hannah's house?

Behind her, the dog gave a cheerful little yip. She turned and watched him paw something out from under the bottom shelf and take it in his mouth.

"George, what are you doing? Give me that."

He sat down and let her take it from him: two flat strips of wood perhaps an inch and a half wide, with . . . No, it was one piece broken in two and folded back on itself, a bright orange, ribbonlike piece of plastic trailing from one end. Something she'd seen on open pieces of ground or building lots: a stake, a surveyor's stake.

She stared down at the thing without seeing it. One of the R.I.P. tactics involved moving surveyors' stakes, Val had said. Doing that would require neither skill nor knowledge, just energy, something any thirteen-year-old had plenty of. And anger.

Val had also talked of fences cut, machines damaged. She bent to pull out the last book on the shelf, a paperback titled *Ecodefense. A Field Guide to Monkeywrenching* was its subtitle, and the table of contents listed a variety of disruptive acts one could commit in defense of the natural landscape. Clear straightforward language inside, with drawings and diagrams, useful and probably sufficient given again the energy and anger and a good clear mind. Petey was not only very bright, he was logical and good at understanding how things worked, things like her car.

Each of Petey's big posters had been stamped in a lower corner with the word Gaia; the same stamp appeared on the back of the book she held. "All right," Charlotte said softly to herself. She put the book back in its place, was about to do the same with the surveyor's stake and then changed her mind. Better to put it out of view somewhere, top shelf of her own closet perhaps. "Would you like to come for a ride?" she asked George. "We need to buy you some food. And then I think we'll go by the Gaia shop to find out what Ms. Stonemountain might have to say about computers and maybe about surveyors' stakes, too."

On her way down the steps she pondered how she might tell her son she had been snooping among his belongings. It wasn't until she had recovered Fenris's old leash from the basement and was snapping it onto George's collar that something went "click" in her head, too, and events and possibilities rearranged themselves into a nasty picture. If a thirteen-year-old boy committed crimes, his parent, his mother, might be declared incompetent. Might lose her son to the authorities or perhaps even to his other parent.

"Four P.M. is when everybody could make it," Val said to Captain Hank Svoboda. They were in Svoboda's small office with the door closed, avoiding the reporters who haunted the station these days. "I figured this was the kind of situation where talking to the whole bunch together would be an advantage; they'll prime each other's memories."

"Probably will." Svoboda, in a tipped-back chair with his boots on his desk, tugged thoughtfully at an ear lobe. "What you do, you get back to me soon as you finish."

"Yessir." Val started for the door, then hesitated. "Excuse me, but I haven't heard. Did you find anything out from Mrs. MacAllister?" Marjorie MacAllister, the source of the "big deal" developer Ed Boylan was celebrating the night he disappeared, had been Svoboda's assignment a long two days ago.

"About Boylan? Not much," Svoboda admitted. "Marjorie was happy to discuss just about anything else—the weather, or her recipe for blackberry brandy, or some new kind of sheep she was thinking of trying. What it is, she's embarrassed that she let that outlander sweet-talk her into doing something she really didn't want to do, that made her neighbors mad at her. And she's mad at them, her friends and neighbors, for being mad.

"And of course," Svoboda went on, "she's maddest of all at 'that s.o.b. Ed Boylan.' But she swears she hasn't seen the fella since the Wednesday before he disappeared, and we got no evidence or testimony to the contrary. Or any real suspicion, come to that."

"What about the sale?"

"She says it's off. Says she's got a new lawyer working on it, and he expects to prove she was coerced into selling while her mind was troubled by grief. Something else interesting, though. In her time of trouble, with like I said her and her neighbors not on speaking terms, she's real grateful to this new friend been helping her out some, lady named Sarah Stonemountain."

"Hey! I read Johnny's files, and he thinks she's . . ."

"I read 'em, too, and his thinking's real interesting. You ever meet the lady?"

"I guess I'd know her to see her, but I've never talked to her." According to Johnny Hebert's files, Sarah Stonemountain, original name Harriet Sarah Muller, was a sixties activist who married another, a David Steinberg. He finally converted to real life and the family business; she kept his name, translated it to plain English, and stayed out there as journalist, social worker, day-care teacher, and mother. She had settled in Port Silva with her three teen-aged children nearly four years ago.

Svoboda's homely face creased in a frown. "I've run into her more or less officially a few times, last time at one of the big anti-logging demonstrations. She's quiet, and moves slow, but she's a big strong lady even if she is past fifty. Thick black hair without much gray in it, eyes yellow as a goat's. Real serious-seeming person, kind of like her name."

For some minutes Val had been half-aware of a peculiar sound, a faint wail like a far-off police siren but in an unusual key. Now the sound grew louder, and there was shuffling and bumping in the hall, and low voices.

Svoboda swung his feet down and sat up straight as Val opened the door; and they both watched Chief Gutierrez move past, Bob Englund and Lieutenant Hanson trailing just behind with watchful expressions. Gutierrez had his arm across the shoulders of a short, skinny woman whose reddish hair looked like a fright-wig around her haggard face. The woman's wail had dissolved into harsh sobs; she shuffled along in Gutierrez's grip like a just-ambulatory patient being guided by a nurse. She had a big black purse and a newspaper clutched to her chest.

"Mrs. Boylan," Svoboda said quietly. Val, in the doorway, saw Gutierrez reach the end of the hall and hand his patient over to a gray-haired man in a suit and tie.

"I guess the story in the *Sentinel* upset her." Val thought he would enjoy stuffing that particular edition down the throat of the young reporter who had provided not only a very detailed description of the stab wounds that had killed Ron Gardner, complete with anatomical diagram, but a sidebar interview with a Pentecostal preacher who suggested that drinkers and fornicators were after all breaking God's laws, and He might well have decided to make an example of one or two such sinners.

"Looks like it. It sure as hell would have upset *me*," said Svoboda. "Poor woman's got four kids, and Boylan kept her on this piddly little housekeeping bank account he put money into every now and then. She's used up all of hers, can't get any of his, can't get insurance or anything at all until somebody finds him or his body.

"Same thing with the business," he went on. "He's the boss, every damn thing has to have his signature, nobody has power of attorney. I get the feeling the fellow's employees, at least, would as soon we find 'em a body as a walking-around man."

Svoboda stood up, bent to dust off his boots, then took his jacket from its wall hook. "In fact, I think we ought to get busy on this, young Val. I believe I'll come along to The Dock with you."

"Yes, sir," said Val, and stepped back to let the older man precede him. He was following Svoboda down the hall toward the back door when a tall figure unfolded from the bench along the wall.

"Officer? Officer Kuisma, is it?"

Memory check, thought Val, and then said, "Ah. Mr. Cooney. Hasn't someone taken your statement?"

"No, sir, not this time." He stood with shoulders rounded forward, watch cap held in his two hands; his lantern jaw was set. Frightened, but determined, Val decided.

"This time. What's up, sir? More drugs?"

"Nope, not yet anyhow. What it is, this lawyer fella come by the Hall about an hour ago and told us to get ready to move right away, because he was fixing to evict us. So I'm here to ask you, can he do that?"

"I . . . don't know, Mr. Cooney. What you'd better do is talk to Chief Gutierrez. Come on, his office is this way."

Port Silva's streets were awash from a wild cloudburst an hour earlier, but the wind had abated now and the rain slacked off to a gentle, steady fall. Val took the Jeep carefully through flooded patches, to avoid drowning smaller vehicles in the wash from his big tires.

"Dr. Mancuso, a professor of computer science at the university, says he and his party were the last to leave The Dock that night," he told Svoboda as he turned from Main Street onto the steep, narrow road that led to the wharf area. At the bottom of the hill, the Verde River curved past to the left, to the boat anchorage, while the road bent around to the right, lined on both sides with fish and marine businesses and several restaurants.

"They were there until almost one," Val went on, "he and his lady with four grad students; they'd just finished a big project and were celebrating. He didn't pay much attention to the other diners: he saw the mayor, and another professor. And a student, a Robert Steinberg, who stopped by the table to say hello."

"Well say, now. This Steinberg could be Ms. Stonemountain's son," said Svoboda. "The girls call themselves Stonemountain;

the boy stuck with the original name. Mancuso see anything when he left the place?"

Val pulled into the parking lot of the last, and largest, of the restaurants. "He says there were half a dozen vehicles up here, probably the workers. Has an idea the lot down by the breakwater was empty, but he's not sure. He said we should call and talk to his fiancée, Cat Smith; she was designated driver that night and the only person in the crew, I guess, who was sober. Maybe I'll go see her after we finish here."

In summer The Dock was open all day, breakfast through dinner; in the wintertime it opened at eleven-thirty for lunch, shut down at two-thirty and opened again for dinner at five-thirty. At four in the afternoon the place was almost hushed, table settings in place, chairs neatly squared up. Vern Swigart met the two policemen at the door, took their dripping slickers and ushered them into the bar, where nine women, most of them middle-aged or older, were seated around a long table smoking cigarettes and sifting through slips of paper.

"Got an early start on you," Swigart told Val. "Howdy, Hank. What we've got is our copy of each order slip, and of course receipts for anybody that paid with plastic. The girls look at what was ordered, what table, and they pretty often come up with names. I'd say we had three hundred people here that night; probably we'll get you half of those, maybe more."

"They all work on till the end that night?" asked Svoboda.

"Nope. Virgie and Helen and Edie went home early. The cooks left at eleven or so, but the two busboys were here until pretty late. And dishwashers, but they stay in the kitchen."

"Val, why don't you start out with the fellows in the kitchen," Svoboda said, "while I give the girls here a hand."

When they left the restaurant just before five-thirty, Val and Svoboda had a long list that could be handled by telephone the next day; and a short list. Five groups had come in fairly late and had definitely stayed until midnight or beyond: Mayor Bondurant and eight members of his family; Dr. Joe Mancuso and his party; one local young couple (in love); one out-of-town trio of businessmen (drinkers, from San Francisco according to the credit card slip); and Sarah Stonemountain, her son Rob, her daughter Elaine, her daughter Julie, and Julie's boyfriend, name not known to Grace, who had served them. Nice boy, though, Grace thought.

"Nothing from the people in the kitchen," Val said to Svoboda as they climbed back into the Jeep. "Except that one of the dishwashers went out for a cigarette and saw Chuck, the bartender, hustle some drunk out. Time was right for it to have been Boylan. The guy finished his cigarette and went back inside, didn't see where the drunk headed."

"Well." Svoboda's deep voice had a ring of satisfaction. "I believe we've had a real useful afternoon. Let's cap it off by paying a call on Ms. Stonemountain."

The Stonemountain house was some miles out Bacheller Road, an old farmhouse set at the end of a long driveway lined with high, anonymous bushes. A yellow Labrador ambled out into the rain for a friendly inspection, then led them with easy paces and slowly swinging tail to the front door.

"Ms. Stonemountain," said Svoboda to the woman who opened the door to their knock. "Glad to find you at home."

Val had seen her around town but not close up. Nearly as tall as his five-eleven-and-a-bit, she looked calm but not placid, a forceful person who knew how to contain herself. Goat's eyes, as Svoboda had said, or witch's eyes. Intelligent eyes.

"And what may I do for you, Captain Svoboda?"

"Officer Kuisma and I," he said, with a nod at Val, "would like to talk to you about Saturday night, February third, the night you and your family had a late dinner at The Dock."

"And you are talking to everyone else who was there?"

"Yes, ma'am, everyone who was there late."

"I see." She stood back to let them enter, waited for them to put their slickers on a coat tree, then led them into a living room furnished with chairs and a couch that did not match but were good to look at and nice to sit on. The rug on the floor was patterned, with fringed edges; the pictures on the walls were

not posters and probably not prints, thought Val. There were
tables around, a half-empty cup in its saucer on one of them.
And the place smelled good. Sarah Stonemountain was probably
a lady who offered tea or wine and homemade something to
visitors who were invited.

"And am I first on your list?" she asked as she sat down.
"Never mind, it doesn't matter. What is it you want to know?"

"You've probably heard about this developer from Santa Rosa,
man named Edward Boylan, who went missing here? Turns out
he was at The Dock that night, the night he disappeared, late
and drunk. We've got one person saw him, and we're trying to
go on from there."

"I don't know Mr. Boylan."

"No, ma'am, but his picture's been in the paper plenty since
then. Which is how the bartender remembered him."

"Yes, I've seen the picture."

"Did you see the man?" The country-easy tone of Svoboda's
voice sharpened; but it didn't matter, thought Val. Nobody was
going to fool this lady.

"Not that I recall. We were talking and enjoying each other's
company in the restaurant, and frankly, drinking more wine
than usual."

"Who was with you, ma'am?"

"My son, my daughters, and another young man."

"Your son is a junior at UC-Port Silva, your daughter Elaine
is a freshman there, and your other daughter . . . ?"

She shrugged. "Julie is our free spirit. She's a sometime student at Humboldt State."

"And the young man?"

"Julie's friend. He also goes to Humboldt."

"Did you all go to the restaurant together? In one vehicle?"

The woman was wearying of this; Val half expected her to
stand up and tell them to leave. But she sighed and said, "No.
Rob took Elaine and me in his small pickup. Julie and Bill? or
Bruce? I'm afraid I don't remember his name. At any rate, they
met us there, driving her Volkswagen beetle.

"Could you tell me, ma'am, where you parked?"

"I suppose I could, but why should I?"

"Just to be a good, helpful citizen?"

"I am a good citizen, Captain Svoboda. Of Port Silva, of California, of the world. Of the universe, I hope. We parked in the breakwater lot, because the other lot was full."

"Did you and your family all leave the restaurant together?"

"We did."

"And at what time was that?"

"I don't wear a watch. I believe it was sometime after midnight."

"And did you see anyone, Mr. Boylan or anyone else, when you returned to your vehicles?"

"No."

"Were there any vehicles besides yours remaining in the breakwater lot?"

"I don't remember." Now she did stand up, and Svoboda and Kuisma followed suit.

"What I'd like to ask, ma'am, is that you let us look over your vehicles."

"You'll have to ask my son about his truck. And Julie's little VW is here, but Julie is not; she's away on a ski trip."

"And where did she go to ski, Ms. Stonemountain?"

"I have no idea." She turned and moved toward the door, clearly meaning them to follow. "I am a busy woman, gentlemen. If you want to inspect my cars, or my home, or my person, you'll have to come with warrants."

"Ms. Stonemountain, I wouldn't attempt to deny you your rights," said Svoboda. "I sure do hope you feel the same about other folks' rights."

"Mrs. Boylan's, for instance." Val was remembering the tearstained, frantic woman he'd seen just hours ago. "She needs to find her husband. She has four kids, no husband, no money."

"Mrs. Boylan's plight is sad, but not interesting," said Sarah Stonemountain. "Women all over the country work and raise children on their own; I certainly did."

. . .

Val drove the Jeep on past the house to the end of the drive-way, where he let its headlights shine into the open shed that was the only outbuilding and clearly served as garage. There was room inside for two vehicles or perhaps three very carefully parked; a bright yellow Volkswagen beetle was alone there now.

"That Steinberg, that she was married to? I'll bet she didn't divorce him," said Val when they were back on the road. "I'll bet she ate him."

"Kuisma, I'm surprised at you," said Svoboda.

"Me, too. I didn't mean that. Actually, she's a sexy lady and I'll bet she's had as many men as she wanted."

"Ate 'em all, do you think?"

"Maybe." Val was trying to understand his reaction to Sarah Stonemountain. He didn't think he was intimidated by big strong women; his mother, whom he liked as well as loved, was big and strong and noisy. So were three of his sisters.

"She's one of those people who know the way, absolutely," he said. "She'll be so sure she's right that she'll bend the rules, and other people, too, for whatever matters to her. I think."

"Probably you're right," said Svoboda.

"I've seen her son's truck, little Japanese number with no shell or anything," Val went on. "If they were there with that truck and a VW bug, and decided to pick up Boylan . . . well, that would make sense of why his car was used."

"It would at that."

"And after that . . . I didn't see any car out there except the bug. I wonder what Ms. Stonemountain Senior usually drives?"

"I believe I've seen her around town in a white Toyota van, looked like a four by four," said Svoboda.

"Maybe that went skiing with Julie," suggested Val.

"Might've done. And we should probably put out a watch for it, in ski areas and other places. For now, though, let's you and me go down to Johnny Wing's for some supper. And after that we'll call on the mayor and on Joe Mancuso's lady."

. . .

"Oh yes, you will. You will feed him and walk him if I ask you to, and help me take care of him just as I helped you take care of Fenris for years."

Charlotte had spent an unsettling afternoon. At the Gaia shop she had found only Sarah Stonemountain's not very friendly daughter, who would not say when her mother would return to the store nor reveal Sarah's unlisted telephone number. And later, when she took a pan of lasagne to Annie's tent, tall, ugly Jesse had thoroughly intimidated her. She was not now in any mood to bend to the whims of a thirteen-year-old boy.

Petey blinked and closed his mouth. "Well. Sure, I just didn't think *you* wanted another dog. I didn't think you liked dogs."

"I like this dog."

"Well. That's okay then." He hung his jacket and slicker on their hooks, turned and was surprised to find his mother still right there, arms folded, looking at him in this funny way. Measuring and weighing him with her eyes. "Mom, is something the matter?"

"Petey, do you know anything about the group calling itself Rip?"

He gulped a quick breath and shook his head. "Just what everybody knows."

"And what is that?"

"That they don't want developers here, like on Finn Lane. They do stuff to stop them."

"What kind of 'stuff'?"

"I don't know. Mess up their machinery, I guess."

"Monkeywrenching."

"Yeah."

"Have you yourself ever done any monkeywrenching?"

"No."

Her heart gave a sick lurch as she decided he was lying, was managing only with great effort to keep his chin still and his eyes meeting hers. "Is Sarah Stonemountain connected with Rip?" she asked and knew at once that she shouldn't have, that one lie would have to be followed by another.

"I don't know."

"I see." Perhaps it wasn't a lie. She'd had a look at the club room today, after telling a lie of her own to the Stonemountain girl, and had seen nothing sinister there. Nevertheless. "All right, Petey, I'm going to give you some information and an order; please pay attention to both. First, if you do something destructive, I'll be the one held responsible both legally and financially."

"Boy, that's really dumb!"

"Perhaps, but it's also true. And the order: you are not to go to the Gaia shop again, not for the computer club nor for any other reason."

"Well, shit, Mom! I already paid my dues for the month and everything."

"If that's an issue, Petey, I will refund you your money. But the order stands."

"Well. No, it's not that much, I just . . . Hey, where are you going?" he asked as she reached past him for her jacket. "It's dark out. And it's raining."

"I'm going to the Bluejay. Billy has called another neighborhood meeting."

"Wait, I better come with you."

"No. I won't be long. There's lasagne in the oven." She touched his shoulder lightly as she moved to the door; he stood and listened to her rapid steps descending the stairs.

She was late, partly because she'd been waiting for Petey but also because she wanted to make her statement without delay. The café was warm, crowded, smelling of coffee and wet wool; she nodded at Billy and moved quietly to the back of the room, where she remained standing.

Except for Buck, it was much the same crowd that had been here Friday. Jennifer, looking hot and depressed, had not brought Cybelle with her tonight, and Mrs. Lee had apparently stayed home. Chris the poet was here, drops of rain glistening in his curly blond hair as he bent to talk to his girlfriend, and the two young women renters, looking grim. Joe James sat erect, watchful.

A newcomer sat at the front near the door, a solidly built

young woman in jeans, eyes bright behind gold-rimmed glasses, a notebook in her lap. Reporter, local no doubt, thought Charlotte. Her own eyes met those of Harry Duarte, who was on his feet talking. He flushed an ugly red, looked quickly away but lost his train of thought, or at least his words, for a moment. Harry had blustered and snorted and denied responsibility for the dead rat, but had finally agreed to pay for Charlotte's new mailbox.

" . . . and I mean to tell you, it took a lot of talking to get him to that point." Harry had found his theme again.

"Big fuckin' deal!" snapped Billy. "Two hundred fifty is the figure I predicted two days ago, you can ask Buck. And it's contingent upon all of us selling, isn't that right?"

"Hell, yes, that's right. Stands to reason the man's gotta have the whole parcel."

"Well, the man is just outta luck. I like it here, and I'm staying. Sorry, folks," he said to the room at large, "but it's still a free country."

"Not so free that people with kids have to share their neighborhood with a child molester." Harry Duarte's eyes glowed red, and Charlotte thought again that the man resembled an angry bull.

"You're disgusting, Harry Duarte." Jennifer Mardian rose to set her coffee mug on the counter. "And I've just switched teams; I can handle living on Spanish rice for a few more years."

"By God, you can't do this to me!" Harry missed with his grab for Jennifer's arm as she passed him, and was stopped from pursuing her out the door by Billy Kaplan, planted before him like a rock.

"Get out of my way, you fuckin' faggot."

Billy grinned and stood where he was. "Make me. Sweetie," he added, and lifted and then dropped his shoulders as he flexed his hands.

"Excuse me," said Charlotte loudly. All eyes turned to her, all voices dwindled to silence, and she took a deep breath. "Mr. Michaelson has been putting pressure on me in a way I consider unethical. He has also lied to all of us about the university's immediate interest in Finn Lane and the park; the chancellor's office tells me there is no such interest. For these and other reasons, I called him a short while ago and told him that I do not intend to sell my property at this time. I apologize to those of you whose plans I have upset."

"That's that, then," said Billy, brushing his hands together.

Charlotte was out the door before anyone else had moved. The rain still fell, surprise. The pole lights in the park were out for some reason. No one seemed to be running after her, that was good. Lights from her house fell on empty pavement where Val usually parked his Jeep and that was not good; she felt a need for affectionate, approving company. In her mind's eye she was seeing not Harry Duarte but Lucy. Mrs. Lee. Jennifer and Cybelle. It was possible that she was acting not on her son's behalf alone, but out of stubbornness and spite, taking mean revenge on Martin and disrupting other lives in the process. This possibility, this view of herself and her motives, made her acutely uncomfortable.

Chapter
Eighteen

P etey Birdsong rolled free of sticky sheets and sat up on the
edge of the bed to peer at his clock. Shit, almost midnight!
And he'd been lying here since ten, his attempts to get to sleep
defeated by ghosts and half-dreams: his grandmother shaking a
warning finger at him, or Annie at the breakwater, grinning as
she took off her clothes.

Without turning on a light, he padded into the bathroom where
he tried for once to pee quietly so as not to wake Charlotte, whose
room was right next door. Another image that had kept flashing
against the inside of his closed eyelids, every time he almost got
to sleep, was his mother's face when she was questioning him
tonight. Probably he should have got mad when he could tell she
didn't believe him. Probably he should have told her that a big
fourteen-year-old guy didn't like getting "orders" from his mom.

No, he shouldn't. Because she knew that already, just like she
knew he was lying to her but didn't actually call him on it. And
because what she really meant was that at fourteen he was old
enough to know the difference between video games and messing around in stuff that could get you in real trouble and maybe
get somebody hurt besides.

In the kitchen he filled a glass with water and stood staring
out the back window as he drank. After a moment he noticed
that the rain had stopped, for a while at least, and the clouds
had broken enough to let moonlight flicker through. No storm
tonight, so probably Annie would forget about going down to
the harbor at high tide.

What he'd really like to do, to get the itch out from between his shoulder blades and the twitch out of his leg muscles, he'd really like to go out for a walk. Sure, at midnight. If his mother found out she'd have a fit, and he was uneasy about doing something else to upset her. Guys he knew, like Eddie, thought it was a pain in the ass to have two parents because they always ganged up on you. He thought, himself, that it was extremely, weirdly scary to have just one.

A light click-click-click nearby made the hair prickle on the back of his neck, and then he looked down to see a black shape, gleam of eyes. "I forgot about you, you dumb mutt," he whispered to George. "Hey. I bet you'd like to go out. You *need* to go out, right? And I promised I'd help take care of you."

Petey threw off his pajamas and scrambled into jeans, sweatshirt, heavy socks, his jacket. Picked up his boots, looked around for a moment before remembering that the dog's leash hung beside the back door. Crept along the hall to listen at Charlotte's doorway to her quiet, even breathing.

He turned again to the back door, then recalled hearing Val come home about an hour ago. He might be still awake down there, better go out the front. "Come on, George," he whispered, and when the dog hesitated, Petey patted his head, pulled his ears, and clipped the leash on. "Now. Come."

On the sidewalk in front of his house he stood still and drew several long, deep breaths. The air was cold and sharp, smelling clean. Not even very wet, probably because of a breeze that blew in from the sea, whipping the high moonlit clouds along.

His house his house his house. He turned and looked up at it, at the gentle slope of its roof, at the protective mantel over its doorway, at the three-sided bay window giving different wavery reflections of the moon. Nice long flight of steps saying come on up. He wished he could draw, like Hannah could, and he'd make a picture of it. What he should do was make a song, in a major key, rich swooping melody in the lower treble, good solid thumping bass. "No sale, bastards," he whispered.

His eyes had by now adjusted to the darkness, on a street where no light shone in any house or in the park, either, except for a small dim glow from Annie's tent. He saw a shadow-figure inside, silhouetted as it passed between the light and the canvas wall. Then another figure, tall; he watched for a little while longer and decided that there were at least three people in there. And Jesse's van, which must be working now, was parked at the curb. Annie was at home, not out on the breakwater.

He should tell her that his house was safe for now anyway, that Charlotte had called the lawyer and absolutely rejected the deal. Petey crossed the street, then hesitated at the park's grassy edge. Charlotte had told him . . . no, Charlotte had asked him. She'd asked him not to go over there, not actually go into the tent. Annie and her friends were rough with each other, Charlotte said. She didn't want him to get caught in the middle. He should bring Annie home for dinner again, if he wanted.

With a gusty sigh Petey turned his back on the shadow-drama, shoved his hands into his pockets and set off toward the north end of the Lane, head down. Rough didn't sound so bad to him right now. Do something stupid and you take one upside the head, that's it, no big deal about hurting somebody's feelings. You could say shit if you wanted, scratch or fart when you felt like it. He bet big old mean Jesse didn't say "Excuse me" when he farted.

"Excuse me. Oh puhleeeze excuuuse *me!*" he said aloud, but softly, and did a little jump-shuffle.

The dog, who had been trailing along quietly, responded with a bark, just a single "Yip" that sounded like a gunshot in the quiet night.

"Hey, dummy! You want to wake up the neighborhood?"

The leash had pulled loose from Petey's inattentive hand and now George took off, racing madly across the wet grass, soaring over a log barrier like a furry black antelope, leaping high and twisting in mid-air to snap at a drooping treelimb.

"George!" Petey wanted to shout but dared only a whispery croak. "Come back here!"

George spun around, crouched, and flung himself forward, four long strides and then a final upward push from his hind legs to carom off Petey's defensively braced body and land and leap again, for another shoulder-to-rib-cage rebound.

"You crazy . . ." Petey grabbed and missed, served as a backboard once again, grabbed and got the dog around the barrel of his chest and the two of them fell to the grass and rolled.

"You're crazy." Petey lay back in the grass, arms and legs flung wide; the dog planted his front paws on Petey's chest, licked his face once, then flopped in his turn.

"Loony mutt. Loony tunes." Petey squinted up at a piece of the moon, said "loony tunes" once more, and giggled. "Val Kuisma gave my mother a craaazy dog."

The grass was long and really wet, he could feel it under his head, and soon the damp began to penetrate his jeans. Petey rolled over and pushed himself to his knees and then his feet. An enormous yawn threatened to crack his jaws, and he was suddenly so tired he thought he could go to sleep standing right there. "Come on," he whispered to George, and paused to yawn again. "Let's go home and go to bed."

He crossed the street to the sidewalk. Drawing abreast of the tent, he cast a guilty look sideways in hope of one last interesting silhouette, and saw that the light was out. Thought maybe he heard a voice, a man's. Then nothing, everybody in the world except him was in bed.

He reached his own front steps, paused to dig in his jeans pockets where he'd better have a key or he was in deep shit . . .

From the corner of his eye he caught a bit of light down at the end of the Lane and stepped quickly into the shadow of the stairs. Might be a car, if it came this way it would pin him like a bug in its headlights.

No car, or at least it wasn't moving. Just a faint glow, not bright enough for headlights. Petey decided positively and with mounting worry that his jeans pockets were empty except for a couple of coins. Jacket pockets; he yanked at Velcro flaps and explored depths with cold fingers, finally found the key, and noted through his relief that the glow down there had flickered a bit. Maybe behind Jennifer's house, or the Bluejay, and this was a really strange time for anybody to have a bonfire.

Feeling easy now that he knew he could get back in the house, he moved without really meaning to in the direction of that funny light. There was a piece of beach down there below the bluff, past the Bluejay; maybe somebody was having a late beach party.

George gave a low growl and Petey heard it, too—somebody running. He tightened his grip on the leash and hurried forward as a figure darted across the street, any distinction of shape or size lost at once against the shrubs and trees of the park. Petey said "Hey!" in reflex, but the runner was past and gone, out of sight and quickly out of hearing, and the glow just ahead now was brighter, definitely flickering.

"Oh, shit," he said loudly, and dropped the leash and set off at a dead run. He dashed between Jennifer's place and the Bluejay, swerved into the long backyard of the restaurant, and saw a low bank of flames against the building's rear wall.

"Help!" Petey screamed. "Help, fire!" He saw somebody tall against the glass door of the restaurant, inside, sliding the door open and leaning out for a look. A sudden great whoosh, like a gigantic indrawn breath, stopped Petey in his tracks. Then came a thunderous clap of sound, and a stick-figure lurched through a billowing wall of fire and fell flaming to the ground.

Chapter
Nineteen

"**H**elp! Somebody! HELP!" Petey skidded on wet grass and steadied himself by grabbing the low brick wall that separated patio from garden. The big hose should be . . . there it was, neatly rolled. Buck, long and skinny it had to be Buck, a flaming shrieking branch blown clear of the big blaze. The night was orange and yellow and stank of burned meat.

Hose cold and slick against his palm *there* the pistol grip, yank and make it unroll, rough circular faucet handle under his left hand push and turn. Sizzle and another shriek, oh, shit! He twisted the nozzle and hard stream eased to soft spray. Please stop making that noise, he begged silently.

"Fire department's on the way!" From somewhere a woman's voice, Jennifer? and from farther away a faint rising and falling wail of sirens. Here with him the hiss of the spray, Buck's screams now fallen to a kind of sobbing howl, the crackle of flame from the building and its bright heat pounding at him, crisping his hair and searing the back of his neck. Where was anybody?

His hand was frozen around the hose grip, still aiming the spray at the legs where the burning had mostly been, black sticks now, Buck all burned out, burned up? "Oh, God, I'm sorry," whispered Petey. Should he turn the water off? "Somebody, please?"

Footsteps and muttered words came as if in response, and Billy Kaplan's lunging body brushed Petey and knocked him sideways. "Sons of bitches, I'll *kill* the sons of bitches! Hush now, you hush, babe, they're coming, they'll be here in a minute."

Petey picked up the hose he had dropped, and stood flatfooted and limp to watch Billy fall to his knees beside Buck, then sit to cradle the injured man's head and shoulders in his arms.

"Sssh, hush now, you're going to be all right, the doctor's gonna give you a shot and take care of you. Petey," he said, without lifting his head or changing his position, "maybe you could turn the water on his legs again, just easy."

He lifted the nozzle, realizing belatedly that he had drenched his own jeans and boots. "I'm sorry. I didn't know what else to do."

"You did fine."

The yard was suddenly full of people, or maybe he had just noticed. Round white faces, hunched shoulders under bathrobes or coats, hushed voices and occasionally a loud question. Two firemen pounded around the corner of the house carrying a big hose, someone called out, "Medic! stretcher!"

Several more uniformed men appeared, to surround Buck and Billy. Petey turned the faucet off and got the garden hose and himself back out of the way. He scanned the crowd for his mother but did not find her. Joe James was there, and Jennifer, Lucy Duarte. People he didn't recognize, renters maybe or just people who'd been passing. Jesse, and Annie, her eyes glittery wide.

Just as he remembered George, he spotted the dog sitting as if on watch at the far edge, the bluff edge, of the lot. Petey stepped wearily over the low patio wall and trudged toward the waiting animal, nobody paying either of them any attention. He had to hurry, get home before he fell down or started to cry.

As he passed the corner of the building, he glanced back into the glare and saw something wink at him from the grass where it was untrimmed close to the foundation. He stepped back, bent to look, reached down and picked the object up gingerly. It was a flat silver-colored rectangle with a flip-back top, a big old-fashioned cigarette lighter. Petey dropped it into his jacket pocket and snapped his fingers at George, who came at a trot.

At the front of the building he paused, astonished by bright lights, two fire engines, snaking hoses, people yelling. So many people, where had they all come from? And where was . . . he saw his mother's white and terrified face, and threw himself into a headlong run, to fling his arms around her. "It's bad, Mom, really bad. Let's go home."

Charlotte pushed the curtain aside, peered out, and opened the door quickly.

"Are you all right?" Val asked as he came in.

"I'm fine, we're both fine. Oh, and George too," she added.

"It was a while before I realized you were practically the only neighborhood person not out there watching."

"I'm frightened of fires," Charlotte told him, leading the way into the kitchen. "We saw one when I was very little, my parents and I; I was on my father's shoulders to watch, I think. I had dreams about it for a long time."

"Hi, Pete," said Val as he dropped into the rocker and stretched his legs out. "Jennifer Mardian tells me you were the hero of the night."

Petey, slumped in the wicker chair, looked up from his cup of cocoa and stretched his mouth in what he probably meant as a smile. He wore flannel pajamas, a too-small plaid wool robe, and big hairy slippers that imitated bears' feet. His hair stood up in wet spikes above his pale face.

"Tea, Val? Or brandy?" asked Charlotte.

"Ah. Maybe both?" Watching Charlotte fill a cup, he wrinkled his nose and sniffed. "What's the funny smell?"

"Me," said Petey. "I rinsed my hair with vinegar, to get the smoke out. Boy, I'm never gonna smoke cigarettes, that's for sure."

"How is Buck, have you heard?" Charlotte handed Val his cup, then went to perch on the tall stool beside the worktable.

"He has second-degree burns on both legs, some third-degree on his left. So he's in serious pain, but it doesn't look as if his life is in danger. Pete must have come on the scene just as the whole thing blew and he turned the hose on Buck right away." The gaze Val directed at Petey was both admiring and speculative.

"I do yardwork for Buck and Billy, so I knew where things were," said Petey with an attempt at a shrug.

"Pretty lucky for them you happened to be outside at midnight," Val remarked. Charlotte straightened and frowned at his tone, then turned to look at her son.

"I got up to go to the bathroom, and George acted like he needed to go out," Petey said quickly. "What happened, anyway? There was this funny light, sort of flickering, that's why I went down there. Something was burning along the back of the building, and I think Buck was coming out to see what was happening. Then it was like a bomb went off."

"Somebody took newspapers from the garden shed, stacked them along the back wall, poured gasoline on and lit it. The bomb was a big propane-fueled barbecue parked there by the door; the burning newspapers set off the propane tank."

Charlotte shivered, pulled the belt of her robe tighter, and poured a little brandy into her own teacup. "Were the firemen able to save the building?"

"Pretty much. Everything was so wet from all the rain that the fire was slow taking hold. They'll probably need to replace most of that back wall."

"Did Buck, or Billy, see anyone?" Charlotte asked.

Val shook his head. "They were upstairs, in bed, and the outside eating area in back has a trellis over it, with vines. Anyway, Buck woke up, wanted a tranquilizer and then remembered he'd left them downstairs. Got down there and saw the fire and opened the back door, apparently just as the tank blew."

"It was like he got shot from a cannon or something." Petey slouched lower in his chair and closed his eyes.

"Did you see anyone, Pete?" Val asked. "Near the house, or out on the street?"

"Sort of. Like almost." When no one replied, Petey opened his eyes. "I was home, by the front steps. I saw that light, like I told you, and I wondered what it was. Then I heard somebody running, but he went into the park right away, it was just this dark figure for a minute. I couldn't tell anything about him."

"Harry Duarte?" said Charlotte, and then put her hand over her mouth. "I'm sorry, I have no right to make accusations."

"Lucy said Harry went down to his boat right after supper, hadn't come home yet when the fire started. He turned up about ten minutes ago, said he'd been on the boat the whole time. Nobody down there now, we'll check tomorrow."

"I'm sorry," said Charlotte again. "I can't believe even Harry would do such a rotten, cowardly thing."

Petey shivered and got up to take his cup, still half full, to the microwave oven for warming.

"It's possible the propane bomb was accidental," said Val. "Billy says the barbecue is usually kept right there by the door, and the arsonist may not have realized what it was. Oh, Pete?"

"Yeah?" Petey came back to his chair.

"Were the park lights, the one by the hall and the one near the Bluejay . . . were they on?"

Petey shook his head.

"Have you seen anybody messing around with them the last day or two?"

"No."

"Well. They're broken, both of them. Maybe by kids, maybe by the arsonist. Can you remember when you last noticed them?"

Petey said, "Uh, no."

"I noticed that they weren't on this evening, I mean yesterday evening," Charlotte said, "when I came back from the Bluejay about seven."

"Pete, did you see anybody moving around in the park, by the Hall, when you first went out?"

"No."

"What about the folks in the tent, any action there? Any light?"

Petey merely shook his head again, and Val said, "Do you mean no and no, or you didn't notice?"

"Val!" said Charlotte. "This is hardly the time for a police interrogation."

"It's okay, Mom," her son said quickly. "There was a light in the tent when I went outside, around midnight. There were people moving around in there, three or four, but I couldn't tell who was who. Then the light went out. After that I just fooled around with the dog for a while, and when I came back over here I saw the light, like I said."

"He's my only witness, Charlotte, to a really rotten crime." Val's voice was even. "It's best for me to talk to him while the evening is still fresh in his mind. Okay, Pete. Is there anything else, anything at all, that you saw or noticed, that was unusual, or strange, or suspicious?"

"No."

■

Chapter
Twenty

■

M artin, was what Charlotte thought midmorning Thursday as she huddled inside her slicker and surveyed the Bluejay. A wet, burned-wood smell hung in the air and caught at the back of her throat. The formerly neat front lawn was crisscrossed with deep, muddy wheel ruts, and debris littered the side yard. Buck was responding well to treatment, she had learned upon calling the hospital this morning. And Billy was still there as well, which was a good thing. If she talked to him in person, if he saw her face and met her eyes, he would surely catch her thoughts.

Good thing too that she had yielded to Petey's wishes, that he was now safe in school. From the moment it got really light out, there had been a steady stream of traffic along Finn Lane, some of it official but most consisting of sight-seers. Young men in pickup trucks, occasionally a station wagon with one or two women inside. Now another truck drove by on high wide tires, and she stared at the banner taped to the wall of its bed: Faggots Go Home, lettered by hand on paper that was stretching and sagging in the light rain. As the driver's fist began a slow drumbeat on his door, bam-bam-bam, Charlotte put her head down and set off for her own house.

In spite of Val's recent remarks about inept revolutionaries with a tendency to mistake their targets, she did not believe that the R.I.P. people had set the fire. The Bluejay stood at the very end of the Lane, which it seemed to her made confusion about its identity unlikely; and Buck and Billy's intentions about the sale were widely known. Besides, she doubted that R.I.P. would expect arson at this site to serve as a blow against developers; Michaelson would surely be delighted to see every house on the Lane burn to the ground.

At home she let George out the back door and stood watching him. Could the arsonist have been simply a passing homophobe, fueled by the information about Buck that Michaelson was apparently circulating? Maybe.

George came back and stood patiently to be toweled off. "Harry Duarte?" Charlotte said softly to herself. No word yet from Val as to Harry's alibi, if any. Harry was a jerk and a homophobe. Pretty dumb, too, but surely even Harry would realize that he'd be a prime suspect in any act against Buck and Billy.

She considered, and at once rejected, Michaelson himself. As Billy Kaplan had noted, Michaelson was not the man to soil his own hands.

A shiver swept her, and she went to put the kettle on; there was just time for a cup of coffee before her Thursday morning student arrived. If the brutal, desperate stupidity of the act fit Harry Duarte, it fit Martin just as well. If Martin had set that fire, he was probably now . . . halfway to Los Angeles. Or holed up somewhere in Port Silva quaking in terror and telling himself it wasn't his fault. Or holed up plotting his next assault.

The rhythm Charlotte had been marking with movements of her head and body now moved into the snapping of her fingers, finally the slap of her right foot against the floor. "Right, Karen, that's right! But I'm doing it for you."

"I know, Charlotte, I'm sorry. But it's hard."

"It's difficult indeed, and you almost have it. Begin again, please."

Karen Wu took up the opening phrases of the Chopin ballade, and Charlotte moved with her into the music, eyes on the flying hands but most of her attention in her ears. "Stop, Karen. That's too fast." She stood up and stepped to the girl's left, leaned over and played for a moment in a sweep that took her right hand past Karen almost to the end of the keyboard.

"Like that," she advised. "Or you'll have nowhere to go later. Remember that you need always to keep the whole piece, the shape of it, in your mind and in your ears."

She sat down again, the girl began again. The notes glistened and flew, in a piece of music that was brilliant but not cheerful. Karen had a wonderful right hand, but her left . . . "Watch the left hand, Karen; your thumb is too heavy."

Half an hour later, Karen rose from the piano bench, blotted her dripping forehead against the sleeve of her gray sweatshirt and grinned from ear to ear. "Thank you, Charlotte," she said, and reached out in soloist-to-conductor fashion to shake Charlotte's hand. "By God, I'll knock 'em dead."

"Yes, I believe you will." Port Silva's various service clubs, Lions and Rotary and others, had joined in organizing a benefit concert for the town's small public library, and Karen Wu was to be one of the featured performers.

"Now remember, Friday, March second. You *have* to be there."

"I'll certainly try." She owed the girl, for almost two hours of freedom from her own thoughts. "Oh, are you on your bike? The rain's gotten worse; let me drive you to the university."

"Thanks, but my dad let me have the Subaru today. He didn't know what might be happening down here, after the fire and everything."

"Oh, good," said Charlotte, who didn't want to talk about it.

"It was on the radio this morning while we were having breakfast." Karen caught moods and nuances only in music. "My dad thought maybe Rip was responsible, like for that other fire, but my little sister said no way, Rip didn't hurt people."

"Rip?" Charlotte kept her tone in the mildly curious range.

"They're supposed to be some kind of antigrowth group, I think," Karen said with a shrug.

Charlotte had seen the younger Wu girl several times, and thought she was about Petey's age. "Is your little sister musical, too?"

"Nope, Donna's a jock, and a computer freak."

"Ah. Well, I'll see you next week, Karen."

Someone must have complained about the earlier drivers-by. Charlotte watched from the music room window as Karen edged a squarish little green station wagon past orange traffic cones that were funneling outgoing vehicles onto Frontage Road. A horizontal pole had been set up across the incoming lane, and a slickered policeman stood guard over it.

As the green car faded into the distance, something red came into view and stopped at the barrier. Hal Michaelson's Jaguar, for heaven's sake; and the policeman was moving the barrier to admit him. Michaelson had a right to be here, she supposed; but she was glad, and Michaelson should be, too, that Billy Kaplan was not at home.

She pushed Buck and Billy, Hal Michaelson, and even Martin to the back of her thoughts. Her quick survey of the club room at Gaia yesterday had failed to turn up anything like a membership list; probably it was kept on a disk. But she had her own private list: Petey, Hannah, Eddie Duarte, and probably Phil Johanson, another of Petey's close friends. And maybe Donna Wu.

From the parent of any one of those kids she should be able to get another name or two. And she thought most of the parents would be unhappy to learn that their not-quite-adolescent children were involved in illegal and possibly dangerous activities. Might be involved, she corrected herself. She would make no accusations, simply some innocent inquiries.

Adam Boatwright, rookie police officer and hero-in-training, was getting a little nervous about the activities of Harold Michaelson. Adam's instructions had been to keep unauthorized persons off Finn Lane, and generally to see that no one bothered the residents. Michaelson, who had made a pretty good case for being authorized, was now, under a big black umbrella, doing a slow door-to-door along the Lane.

Whether this could be considered bothering wasn't clear. Nobody at this end of the street had seemed upset; at least nobody had come outside to complain or ask for assistance. But the people in Finn Hall had clearly been bothered as hell, had set up a sudden chorus of angry voices he'd heard from a hundred yards away; and Michaelson had come back through that big double door real fast, as if he'd maybe had some help.

Adam had expected a summons to assist right then, had checked his baton and cuffs and radio and his revolver. But the lawyer just stalked off to ring another doorbell, and nobody from the scraggly bunch living in the Hall came out in pursuit or protest.

A honk jolted him, and he turned to see a white van nosed up against the barrier arm. Adam squared his shoulders and strode to the driver's side of the van, where the window was being rolled down.

"Could I have your name, sir?"

"What the hell's going on here?"

The driver's face was flushed, his eyes baggy and bloodshot. Adam leaned closer to sniff for alcohol. "Are you a resident of Finn Lane, sir?"

"Bet your ass I am, sonny, and you'd better move that stick before I . . ." The man let his shoulders slump, closed his eyes briefly. "My name is William Kaplan, I live in number 26 at the end of the Lane. And I need to get home right now."

"Oh, right. Sorry, sir." Adam hurried to the curb, pulling the swing-arm with him. Kaplan nodded and drove on; Adam squinted into the drizzle and watched the van move slowly down the lane and ease into the turnaround at the end. Looked like the lawyer's red Jag was parked right in front of Kaplan's place, the café; and the driveway there was full of junk from the fire.

An engine howled, tires squealed, and then came a crunch of metal. "Hey, Mr. Kaplan!" Adam yelped. A head popped out from the tent under the trees, someone opened the door of the Hall. "Hey! Be careful!" Adam set off at a run for the end of the street, where Billy Kaplan's white van was backing off from the Jaguar.

Revving engine and another crunch. Michaelson came flying

down the steps of a house four doors up from the café. "Stop that! Get away from my Jaguar!"

"Mr. Kaplan," Adam said loudly, reaching for the door handle of the van.

"Out of my way or you'll get hurt." Billy Kaplan backed the van off, swung it around, aimed it at the side of the red car instead of the bumper.

"You're a policeman, for God's sake! Stop him!" Michaelson howled at Adam, then covered his ears as the van smashed into the Jag's rear fender.

Adam unsnapped the holster of his revolver. "Mr. Kaplan, you've gotta stop that now! I don't want to have to injure you! Please, Mr. Kaplan!"

"You get that gun out, sonny." Billy rolled his window lower to look out as he backed away with a screech of metal. "You get it out, I'll take it and use it on this motherfucker of a . . ."

Michaelson darted past Adam, yanked the Jag's door open, fell inside and in a second had the engine running. Billy's next forward lunge caught the edge of the red car's back bumper; Michaelson gunned his engine and pulled free with another screech, and roared off down Finn Lane.

Petey Birdsong pedaled heavy-footed along Main Street, braked to make the turn onto Frontage Road and gave a little yip of pain; the bike wobbled as he let go of the handlebar and brake lever to flex and then shake his right hand. Really sore, he hoped it wasn't broken. He squinted out from under the helmet, blinking against the rain and a generally foggy feeling inside his head. Hadn't had anything to eat since breakfast, that was what was wrong with him; he was so hungry his stomach actually hurt, knotted and twisted and growled with pain.

First thing he'd do when he got home was eat. No, first he'd call Hannah and tell her thanks for locating Martin. He'd forgotten to do that at school this morning, and she'd been all pissed off and he didn't blame her. And he'd check with Eddie, see if he'd managed to keep the science substitute from noticing Petey's absence.

Something, maybe a cat, streaked through the rain right across his front tire, and his stop was so abrupt he had to put both feet down to keep from falling. Didn't matter about science; he was in deep shit anyway because he'd missed all the other classes after, hadn't been back to school since second period. Couldn't even remember where he *had* been some of the time, just riding around and now he was wet clear through to his underwear with rain and sweat. Wet and cold, there was a mean wind howling around his ears and slapping the rain at him.

And tired, God he was tired. Helmeted head down, he went over the little bridge and through the mud without standing, squinted into blowing rain to mark the beginning of Finn Lane, took the bike into a slow swing right by inclining his body. Too tired to explain anything to anybody, and if Charlotte noticed he was early, he'd just say he didn't feel good and decided to come home, which was more or less true.

His eyes registered something that hadn't been here this morning, a barrier, and traffic cones. Without pausing in his slow progress he leaned left, to slide between the cones and the sidewalk.

"Pete! Pete, watch out!"

Shouted words, he thought Annie's voice, then a pure scream. And engine-sound, whine over deep roar, and the hiss of tires in water. His tired mind said oh shit as he blinked and squinted at the big red shape looming before him. Squeal of brakes, the front end dipping and swinging to his right, and he let go of the handle bars and threw himself up and over, diving left.

The Jaguar caught the bike and jerked it away from him, some piece of it slapping his backside as he flew. He hit head and shoulder, rolled, scraped along on his face and belly and slammed against something, a mailbox post, curled around it and lay still, trying to breathe. Somewhere in this flight he had registered a crunching, the cartoon sound of a monster chewing up a robot, and as his body began to take account of itself, leg here pain there shoulder hurt! his mind classified the noise: death of a bike, his good bike. Son of a bitch. He heard sloshing and feet thumping and loud voices but simply kept his eyes shut and concentrated on getting breath in and out until somebody took hold of him and rolled him gently away from the post.

"Oh my God!" from out in the street, he thought. "I didn't see him! I couldn't help it! My God . . ."

"Shut your fuckin' mouth!" in a fierce whisper so close he could feel breath on his wet cheek. Annie bent over him to wipe his face with the tail of her shirt. "Pete? Are you okay? Don't move, just tell me."

Don't move why, was he dying? Bleeding, bones sticking through? He pulled free of her, rolled onto his belly and came up on his forearms, head hanging. All there. No blood.

Annie was on her knees beside him, hand lightly on his shoulder. "Go slow, Pete."

Feet on the other side of him, pointy boots. "I couldn't help it, he was on the wrong side and in the rain . . . Boy, young man, I'm sorry, we'll get you to the hospital."

He got his hands under himself and pushed back, onto his knees. Everything worked, but under the regular pain, which he'd already noticed, he thought there was more, worse, gathering itself. His helmet had tipped over his eyes; he clawed at the chin strap and tossed the thing away.

"You shouldn't have come around the corner like that, without looking." The lawyer, sounding more the way Petey remembered; and behind that other voices, running feet.

"You lump of dog shit." Annie's voice was low but full of anger. "I saw the whole thing, you were doing about eighty."

"I was being attacked by a madman in a car!"

"You came tearing blind down a private street in that tank! Look at what's left of his bike and think what you almost did to his body!"

Petey gave another push and sat up against his heels, closed his eyes against a spinning world, opened them. Two people above him, head to head: Annie, eyes glittering and teeth bared, long hair plastered to her head and stringing down over her wet shirt. And Michaelson, skin gray like *he'd* been bleeding, water dripping from his hair down his face.

"Who are you? You're not this boy's . . ."

"My bike." Petey was embarrassed to hear the whine in his voice. He lurched to his feet, stumbled and grabbed at the mailbox. "That was my mountain bike." His right knee buckled under his weight and he sat down abruptly.

"Look, boy, I'm sorry, I'll buy you a new bike."

"All right, Michaelson, get away from that kid!" Billy Kaplan's rough city voice, and he appeared out of the misty rain followed by somebody tall in a uniform. Not Val, Petey noted.

"Here, boy." Michaelson's voice fell to a near whisper. "What did it cost? Never mind," he added quickly and took from a pocket a silver clip, hinged, a bulge of green folded in it. Michaelson flipped the hinge, pulled the green wad free and stuffed it into the pocket of Petey's jacket.

"Hey, I don't need your . . ."

"Pete, are you okay?" Billy Kaplan squatted beside him, his face creased as if he might cry. "Kid, that was partly my fault, I'm sorry as hell and I think we ought to get you to a doctor right now."

"Nobody is going anywhere just yet," said the young cop in a young smart-ass voice. Petey noted that Annie had already gone somewhere, but probably that wasn't what this guy meant. He was up for who he could bust. Petey wasn't very interested in that, whose fault it was; he thought he might like to throw up pretty soon. He wondered how come Charlotte wasn't here.

Oh. There she was. "Hey. Mom, I'm okay, I'll get up in a minute. Don't sit in the mud."

"Petey." Even Charlotte had gray skin, must be the weather. She picked up his helmet and turned it over in her hands, rubbing the mud off. "Petey, thank you for wearing your helmet."

Chapter
Twenty-one

Harry Duarte was a less colorful curser than most fishermen; just kept saying "fuck" in its various forms even in Portuguese so far as Val's not-very-bilingual ear could tell.

"I guess the idea is he didn't do it?" Val called out to Officer Ray Chang, who was passing his door.

"Probably he'd be more convincing if he didn't also keep saying he'd like to congratulate whoever did." Chang shook his head wearily. "And if he'd been seen by anybody at the boat anchorage last night. And if he hadn't turned up with a half-empty five-gallon gas can in his truck."

"But that's all you've got?" Harry had just left the station after his second interrogation of the day.

"So far. Incidentally, we found out where Martin Lindberg's been staying."

"Ah," said Val. In his view, that little rat was as good a bet for arsonist as Harry Duarte, and he had said as much here this morning. But from that point on he'd left the matter strictly alone, knowing himself to be far from objective in the matter. Chang was a good thorough cop and would explore all possibilities.

"Unfortunately, it seems Lindberg is gone."

"Gone?"

"He's been staying at the Urbanite Motel, on Chester Street, for the past week. But the manager says he left today. In fact, the guy was unhappy and was thinking about calling us; apparently Lindberg skipped out on some damage. I'm on my way out there."

Chang gave a mock-salute and left; Val rolled his chair well back from the desk, rubbing the back of his neck with one hand and his left ear with the other. Except for a few call-backs to those who were unavailable, he had worked his way through the whole long list of people known to have been at The Dock on the night of Ed Boylan's disappearance. None of them had been any help at all.

Nor had the other people on the short list, those known to have been late-stayers that night. All of which seemed to leave the Stonemountains looking more and more interesting, thought Val. That was Johnny Hebert's view in spades. In two days in Santa Rosa, Johnny had found nothing at all shady or weird about Edward Boylan's business. The man was personally a son of a bitch, but people worked with and for him because he was smart and made money.

"His acquisitions may be high-pressure, but they're not illegal," Johnny had said with a shrug. "His vacation developments screw up perfectly good rural areas, but people from San Francisco and Los Angeles line up to buy them. This makes him a natural enemy of people like Sarah Stonemountain; I can envision that woman squashing Boylan like a bug, if she got the chance."

Natural enemy of me, too, thought Val now. And of a whole bunch of other people here in town. But none of us would kill the guy. I don't think.

And he wasn't convinced Sarah Stonemountain, witchy lady though she might be, would commit murder in defense of her adopted town. He visited the men's room to get rid of the coffee he'd been drinking all day, then collected the file on Boylan and took it to his desk.

The sheriff's department report on the interview with Bud Hawks, the man mugged at the Rainbow a week before Gardner died and Boylan disappeared, didn't reveal anything more on rereading. The woman was pale, blond, much shorter than six feet one, had large breasts. Had access to pot, as who didn't. She and Hawks had not exchanged names, at least not that he remembered; and she hadn't mentioned her boyfriend by name.

One more phone call, thought Val, and he found the man on the second try, at home rather than at work, baby-sitting. With his wife not at home, he didn't mind talking but was sure he had nothing to add.

"Blond, like I said," he told Val. "But long or short, curly or straight—on her head, I mean—I can't say, because she had on this cap, kind of like a watch cap, and there was just little wisps of light-colored hair sticking out. Her eyes were light, I remember that, at least not brown or black."

"And she told you she was from Port Silva?"

"Yeah, but I think she meant she'd come from Port Silva that night. Now I think about it, she might've said something being from up north, but how far up she meant I got no idea."

"Okay, that's interesting. Now is there anything else, anything at all? If you close your eyes and try to see her face?"

"Um. Nope. Well, one thing, I had the thought she might have been knocked around some."

"Bruises?"

"No. Well, maybe, I don't know. Just a feeling I had, probably for no reason. Oh, shit, there's the car. I can't talk with my wife around. And I told you everything I remember." He dropped his receiver with a crash.

Not a lot. Val rose and stretched, walked to the window and back to the door. But more than nothing. Up north, as in northern California? Or maybe Oregon or Washington?

"Hey! Valentine!"

Alma Linhares came down the hall from the back door, bringing with her a gust of wet, cold air. She shed her slicker as she walked, tossed it toward a wall hook, gripped his arm and pulled him into the patrol room.

"Come in here a minute, I've got some news for you. I just talked to Walt, and . . . Hey, no uniform! That's right, I did hear something about you working detective. You get promoted, Kuisma?"

"If they promote me before you, lady, you can bet I'll come to work in full riot gear. I'm on temporary assignment to the detective division. So what's up?"

She sat down at her desk, spinning her wheeled chair around so that her back was to the typewriter. "They've come up with two more guys got rolled recently instead of just laid, which was what they'd had in mind. One was in Del Norte County, near Crescent City, end of December; the other was in Eureka, second weekend in January."

"Dead?"

She shook her head. "Drunk out of their minds and probably knocked out by a blow to the head. One of them got cut a little, defensive cut on his hand. He told the Del Norte County deputy he didn't remember how that happened."

"The same scenario."

"Right. A trucker and a logger, money in their jeans, drinking in out-of-the-way rough bars and thought they'd got real lucky, here's this friendly lady with big boobs willing to give a guy a good time."

Val felt a little strange talking about this with Alma, who was a tough woman and a cop but still somebody he'd known since she had pigtails and gaps in her teeth.

She caught his uneasiness and gave him a shrug and an open-palmed gesture. "Hey, it's a cold lonesome world out there; I don't see anything wrong with trying to get laid, whichever sex you are. It's sure not something you ought to get knifed or beat up for, unless you're being real mean about it, and these guys weren't mean, just horny, or so they say. Anyway, Walt's going north to talk to both of them. He'll let us know if anything useful comes of it."

"Val Kuisma?" Cathy Cardoza, a clerk-dispatcher, put her head in the door. "I thought I heard your voice. You live out on Finn Lane, don't you?"

"Yeah, why?"

"More trouble there, I've sent two cars out in the last ten minutes."

"What kind of trouble?"

"First some guy was bashing another guy's car, and then a car hit a kid on a bike. It was a boy named Birdsong, isn't that the name of the woman you rent from?"

"How bad was he hurt?"

"They weren't sure yet. They were taking him to Good Sam."

"Thanks, Cathy. Oh, Alma?" he said over his shoulder as he headed for the door. "Would you make sure the chief hears about the report from Walt?"

Val parked his Jeep in the hospital's emergency lot, flipped the visor down to show his police status, and ran through the rain to the door. "Birdsong?" he said to the middle-aged nurse behind the counter. "Police business, and I'm a friend of the family."

"Examining room three."

Petey Birdsong sat in his undershorts on the examining table. His face looked like a prizefighter's, with bloody scrapes chin and nose, a reddening lump on one cheekbone and another on his forehead. Pete would be lots of different colors tomorrow, Val thought; but the boy's eyes looked clear and he held them steady against the probing of the doctor's small flashlight.

"And you're sure you didn't lose consciousness, even for a moment?"

"Yeah, I'm sure. I hurt, and I was sick to my stomach, but I didn't pass out."

Val spoke Charlotte's name very softly; she started, looked up, and managed a smile that was mostly a narrowing of her eyes. He crouched beside the straight chair she sat in, taking her hand and touching her lightly with his shoulder.

"Thank you for coming, Val. He's . . . he's not broken anywhere, just bent and scraped."

"Hiya, Kuisma," said the doctor. Erik Brodhaus, a local man

a few years older than Val, had dated Val's sister, Rosie, in high school. "What kind of story should my patient here tell his girl, maybe that he just went five rounds with a bigger guy?"

Face flushing, Petey jerked away from the doctor's hands and then yelped.

"Sorry, Pete," said Brodhaus. "This is the other bad spot, this knee; I bet it got caught in your bike?"

"I guess," Petey said sullenly, his eyes on his extended right leg. The shin was scraped, the knee looked puffy.

"Now what we'll do, we'll have you put ice on this at home in thirty-minute intervals for the rest of the day, and then tomorrow we'll go with an elastic bandage, maybe a pair of crutches for a day or so."

As Petey digested this, Val asked softly, "Just what happened?" and Charlotte told him.

"I didn't see any of it, of course, but that's the way the policeman told it, and Billy. Michaelson didn't say anything, except to repeat that it was an accident. But Billy felt terrible; he kept saying it was partly his fault."

"I'd say he was right." Val looked at his watch, and then got to his feet. "I'd better call the shop and tell them I'm taking the rest of the day off."

"No, don't do that."

"Don't you want some company?"

She shook her head. "I just want to get Petey home and into bed, and quiet. And to stay there with him."

"Well. Did you come here in an ambulance?"

"No, I drove."

"Are you okay to drive back?"

She held both hands out before her, palms down; they trembled for a moment, then were steady. "I'm fine. A little light-headed from relief, but I'll be careful."

"Okay. I'll call the officer on duty on Finn Lane, let him know you'll be coming. He'll make sure nobody bothers you. And I'll see you tonight, unless I'm too late."

"Please. I'm sure I'll be up."

∎ ∎ ∎

"Mom?"

Charlotte, who'd been mindlessly playing at a Chopin waltz, rose from the piano bench and hurried to the door of her son's room. Propped against the headboard with his right leg extended and cradled in a pillow, he was pointing the remote control at the television set.

"There's nothing on TV," he said, a dark frown making his face fearsome. Channels flipped past, and then he hit the off button.

"I'm sorry."

"Is there anything to eat?"

"Besides the last pork chop?" He'd eaten three for supper, and two baked potatoes and about half a pound of broccoli. "Just a minute."

In the kitchen she punched down the bowl of bread dough and tweaked off a piece to carry in to her sullen and hurting son. "I have to go make the loaves now; if you're still awake at, let's see, about eleven, you can have some of this baked."

He popped the dough into his mouth and said, around it, "Mom? You did ask Annie to come over?"

"I did. I went to the tent and thanked her, for me and for you, and asked her to come to see you. That was about six o'clock, and it's eight now. She said she'd come."

"Okay." He pushed himself higher against his pillows and gave a neatening tug to his blue-and-white striped pajama top. It was too short, Charlotte noted with a sigh. "Thanks, Mom."

"You're welcome, dear." She aimed herself back at the kitchen, where she greased pans and shaped, not very well, two loaves of bread. "I'd love to take you for a walk," she said to George, who licked and nosed around and finally rejected a piece of dough. "But the rain is getting worse. I'm afraid you'll have to settle for a quick trip to your bush."

As she was letting him back in, the doorbell rang. The two of them went to the front of the house and found Annie standing on the lighted porch, the tall figure of Jesse looming behind her with an umbrella.

"Thank you for coming," Charlotte said. "Petey's been asking for you, Annie; he's in bed but awake."

"How's he feeling?" Annie unzipped her down vest and flipped her hair free of its collar.

"He hurts, and he's bored."

"I bet." She headed for the hall, and when Jesse followed on her heels, she turned and waved him back. "Cool it, Jess. I can go see my boyfriend by myself."

Jesse scowled darkly but stayed where he was, hands in his jacket pockets, following her with his one good eye. He really was very tall, several inches over six feet, and quite skinny; probably it was the eye patch that made him look so fierce. She should offer him . . . what? The leftover pork chop? a piece of bread dough? Her kitchen was unusually empty at the moment. "Would you like a cup of tea?" she asked.

"You got a beer?"

"I think so." While he stood there as if rooted, Charlotte went to the kitchen, found to her relief that there was a Sierra Nevada in the fridge, glanced down the hall and was pleased to see that Petey's bedroom door was open. That would definitely be a rule, she decided, old-fashioned as it might seem. Girl in the room, door open.

"Annie says you play the piano," Jesse said as she put the bottle in his hand.

What a nice solution to the problem of making conversation with this grim young man. "Yes. Come and listen." She stopped just short of asking whether he liked Chopin.

For perhaps twenty minutes she played, giving him (and George, who seemed to be a musical dog) an impromptu, a nocturne, a prelude, and another nocturne. She wasn't playing well; her fingers felt stiff and she was trying to listen, too, not to the music but for Petey. Jesse sat on the edge of a straight chair, sipping morosely at his beer, gaze fixed on the hall down which Annie had gone. Charlotte glanced at him frequently, and thought he was gradually relaxing.

When Annie came back, Jesse stood up slowly, drained the beer bottle, stretched. "So, babe. How's the kid?"

"Bored, like Charlotte said."

"Me, too, let's go. Better zip up, it's cold out and raining like hell. Thank you, ma'am," he said, nodding to Charlotte without quite looking at her.

Annie's eyes narrowed in irritation either feigned or real, Charlotte wasn't sure. "Thank you for coming," she said to the girl. "Thank you for being there today."

"I'm just glad I was. He's a really neat kid."

"Come on, babe." Jesse's big right hand stroked Annie's hair and then settled on the back of her neck. "Let's go."

The knock at her front door brought a little yip from George, and brought Charlotte to earth as well. As she stood up wearily, she realized that a real storm was raging now, heavy rain hard-driven by wind.

"Hello, Val. Come in."

"I've been standing out here, listening." He shook off his slicker and carried it to the back hall. "Charlotte, that's the saddest piece of music I ever heard. Are you okay? Is Pete?"

"We both are, I think. Thank you." She turned to look at her piano. "Schubert, that's what it was. The slow movement of the B-flat sonata. I guess it is sad."

"I won't keep you, I just wanted to let you know I'm home."

"I'm glad you are. Oh, the bread," she said as the clock struck ten. She hurried to the kitchen, to uncover two cloth-draped loaves that sat on the griddle, and to turn the oven on. "What . . ." She paused to yawn. "What's happening? Have they charged Harry Duarte?"

"Harry?" Val had spent the afternoon and evening with the chief and Svoboda and Johnny Hebert, going over the Boylan case and trying to decide what to do with what they had, what if anything to release to the press. Johnny did not believe that the Stonemountains did not know where Julie was, and he wanted to put an arrest warrant out for her instead of the present request to be notified should she be seen; but the chief had refused to do that. Val hadn't given a thought to Finn Lane and fires in many hours, he realized now with some chagrin.

"I don't really know," he said as he unzipped his jacket. "I know he's been questioned and sent home twice. Oh, one thing I do know. Your ... Lindberg has left town, or at least has left his motel."

Before the fire, or after? Hugging her arms close against a sudden chill, she inspected Val's face and saw no sign there of anything being held back. "Do you know when?" she asked.

"When did he leave? This morning, I think. I've been on the Boylan case since I left you at the hospital, and I haven't had a chance to talk to Ray Chang, the main guy who's working the fire. I'll call him now, if you want me to."

Ten o'clock already, and she was too tired to care, really, where Martin might be. Keep the doors locked and depend on George. "No, never mind."

"Charlotte, you have had one hell of a day." He opened his arms to her and she walked into them, leaned against him. It was nice and warm inside his jacket, against his chest. And he had that wonderful smell of light, healthy male sweat. After a moment he tipped her head up and kissed her, and kept kissing her.

She was transfixed by the pure sensuous pleasure of it. His beard was surprisingly soft, slightly damp and smelling of rain. His mouth against hers was gentle but not hesitant, lips cool and then warming. She inhaled his faintly minty breath, felt the steady thump of his heart and felt her own settle to the same rhythm. "You're too tall. Standing up anyway," she murmured against his mouth.

Catching the implication of her words as she heard them, she put her palms lightly against his chest and stepped back. "I'm sorry, that was misleading."

He let his arm drop and stood there looking at her, no expression at all on his face.

"I'm sorry, Val. I'm not a prude, but I'm very bad at casual sex."

"I failed that course myself, Charlotte. Sex One-B, the friendly fuck. I'd have thought you'd know that about me."

"Oh, Val, of course I do. I just . . ."

"Mom?" came a plaintive voice from down the hall. "Mom, is somebody here."

"Nope," said Val, "nobody at all." Hand on the back door, he paused and turned, with a faint smile and a shrug. "Forget it, Charlotte. Last thing in the world I want to do is make your life more difficult."

Chapter
Twenty-two

■

"I apologize for the earliness of the hour, but I heard you moving around." Behind Val was a brightening eastern sky at last blown free of clouds. Charlotte pulled the door wider and he came inside, but only as far as the hall. "We need, Chang needs, to talk to Martin Lindberg, and we thought you might have his address."

What a silly thought. She ran both hands through her tangled curls, trying to get her sleep-deprived mind to function; Petey's restlessness and the howling rainstorm had combined to keep her up for most of the night. "No, I haven't. I think he said something about Long Beach. Why?"

"Do you have any idea how we might get in touch with him?"

"Just a minute, Val." Charlotte left him standing there and went into the kitchen to retrieve her half-finished mug of coffee. "What address did he give at the motel?" she called over her shoulder.

"This one."

Ever consistent, Martin, dressing up intent and naming it reality. "Why do you want him?"

"Well. Harry Duarte is still a heavy suspect in the arson at the Bluejay, but we haven't got any solid evidence against him yet. And Michaelson has an airtight alibi."

No doubt, thought Charlotte.

"So Chang wants to question several other people, and one of them is Lindberg."

"Your best bet would be to contact his agent; I'd be really surprised if he's changed agents in the last ten years. Anton Marovich, in Los Angeles."

"Thanks, Charlotte." Val scribbled the name in his notebook.

"Val, when he checked out of the motel, didn't he say anything about where he was going?" Like, my agent just called with this fabulous contract, watch for me on prime time: that was Martin's usual style.

Val, whose face had worn a faintly distant politeness when she opened the door, now shoved his hands into his pockets and looked thoughtfully over her shoulder. In a moment he'd be shuffling his feet. "Uh, he didn't check out, exactly."

"What did he do, exactly?" Charlotte set her empty coffee mug on the washing machine, crossed her arms over her breasts and propped her left shoulder against the wall.

"Okay, it's sort of strange. He had breakfast in the coffee shop around nine, stopped by the office to tell them he'd be staying a few more days. The maid was doing the rooms around eleven, and heard noises from his, like things being thrown around. She told the manager, he went to knock on the door; and somebody, he thinks Martin, said sorry, he'd been having bad dreams." Val's fingers smoothed the right side of his beard in short, absent strokes.

"Then a couple of hours later the manager happened to walk by, the door to the room was open and Martin was gone, along with his belongings and his car. But the room was a mess, like there'd been a fight. Picture knocked off the wall, lamp broken, bottle of booze spilled on the bed: the manager is pissed. Charlotte," he said, meeting her eyes for the first time in his recitation, "did you call the Urbanite Motel yesterday morning and ask whether Martin Lindberg was staying there?"

"No."

"Somebody did, a woman. Does Martin have any local connections?"

"I have no idea." Except of course for his old lover and his old son. Who, the son, was behaving as if something more than simple pain were bothering him. What had Petey done?

"Charlotte, I don't think you should worry yet; there's probably . . ."

"Worry. About Martin? Don't be silly." She straightened and turned her head, as if to listen. "Val, if you'll excuse me, I think Petey is ready for breakfast."

Petey was first of all ready for a shower, but didn't want any help with it, would manage to get there on his crutches. Charlotte, sneaking sidelong glances at his lopsided and discolored face, was secretly relieved that she didn't have to view the bruises that must cover the rest of him.

"And don't come in unless I call you," he instructed, "not even if you hear me fall down."

"How will I know you haven't drowned? Oh, for heaven's sake, all right! How many eggs do you want?"

"Three. No, four."

In the kitchen Charlotte put some Canadian bacon in a skillet, noting absently that the house was warming up now that the wind had dropped, the day outside her window promising sunny and fair as if in apology for the wildness of last night. These environmental matters out of the way, her mathematician's-daughter's mind left eggs and orange juice to her fingers while working out facts. However unsettling, they were still facts and not to be ignored.

"How do you feel?" she asked when Petey clomped into the kitchen on his crutches.

"Okay. Sore," he added, maneuvering into a chair and stretching his right leg out. She saw that he had managed to wrap the elastic bandage around his injured knee. Not well, but well enough.

"Have you talked to Hannah?"

"Not this morning. I did last night."

Charlotte set his orange juice before him and went to the stove to turn his eggs. Her son's voice had not yet changed completely, was still reedy and inclined to slide; but no one would mistake it for a woman's voice. Hannah, however, Petey's best friend or near it, had a light and distinctly feminine voice.

Charlotte dished up eggs and bacon, put two slices of buttered toast on the plate and carried plate to table.

Oh poor baby! was her visceral response to seeing his face in the brightening light from the windows. Evasive baby, however, she reminded herself. Perhaps untruthful baby. She sipped strong coffee until he had eaten more than half his food, and then said, quietly. "Petey, did you go to school yesterday?"

"Huh? Sure I did."

"And did you stay there? Because your last class usually doesn't end until, what is it, three-ten? And it was not quite two-thirty when the car hit you yesterday."

It really wasn't fair and she should turn her eyes away; but she didn't. Instead she watched thoughts and feelings display themselves in eyes, mouth, chin angle, and line of shoulders, reading them as clearly as she would an announcement across the bottom of a television screen. Defensiveness: leave me alone I don't want to talk about it. Evasiveness: I got sick and came home early, yesterday was a minimum day, the school flooded. And finally, relief.

"I did go to school, but then I left and went to see him, Martin."

"Oh, Petey. Why?"

"Mom, he set the fire."

"How do you know?" she asked, her voice husky.

"I didn't lie that night! Not much, anyway, because I didn't see him. I couldn't tell who it was that ran away."

"Then what?"

"I found his cigarette lighter, the same one he used the day he took me to the doughnut shop. It was in the grass beside Buck and Billy's house."

She set aside several questions beginning "why!" and asked, instead, "What did Martin say?"

"He said he didn't do it. He said he'd missed his lighter that day at the doughnut shop, and I must have taken it and started the fire. He said no one would take a kid's word against a man's. Then he tried to get the lighter away from me."

"And that's when the motel room got torn up."

He folded his arms on his chest and nodded. "But he didn't get it. Mom, I'm stronger than him, lots stronger." His voice broke slightly on the last words, and she thought he looked both proud and confused. Perhaps this was a signpost, a male rite of passage: the day you can defeat your father in hand-to-hand combat. Charlotte tried to think of a female equivalent, but none came to mind.

"Except he did get in a couple of punches that hurt. Anyway, I told him he'd better not ever bother us anymore."

"Or you'd what? Beat him up?"

Petey shook his head.

"Turn the lighter over to the police?"

"Nope. I said I'd take it to Billy Kaplan and tell him who it belonged to and where I found it."

"Oh, my." Charlotte remembered what Billy Kaplan had tried yesterday to do to Michaelson, whom not even *he* could have believed to be the actual fire-setter. No wonder Martin had hit the road—if that's what he had in fact done. And now what?

"Now what?" she said aloud, softly.

"Now nothing. He's gone, and I bet he won't come back." He was watching her face closely, apparently doing some thought-reading of his own. "Mom. Don't tell the police, don't tell Val. Please."

Bad enough to have no father at all, or an inconsequential, lying father. But a father who set fires? "What if the police charge somebody else with arson? Harry Duarte maybe?"

He squeezed his eyes shut briefly, and moisture glistened on his lashes. "If that happens, we can tell." He sat straighter, repositioned his outstretched leg and looked down at his plate. "Could I have some more toast?"

Val, who had spent the morning catching up on paperwork, decided it was time for lunch. There had been no sighting yet of Julie Stonemountain; the weather was bad everywhere and especially in the mountains, probably keeping the highway patrol very busy.

Nothing from the sheriff's department on the recently discovered mugging victims, either. According to the Fort Bragg office, Deputy Walt Miranda had waited out the storm before leaving very early this morning for the northern tip of the state; Port Silva could expect information when any became available.

Hebert, a frequent lunch companion, didn't seem to be around. Val wandered into the patrol room looking for Chang, always hungry and right now a possible source of information. Next to locating Ed Boylan, what Val wanted most was to be able to go home to Finn Lane and tell Charlotte that Lindberg had turned up, owned a total and perfect alibi for Wednesday night, and was on his way to Southern California after promising never again to come north of the Tehachapis.

The clerk answered his question with a shake of her head. "Haven't seen him all morning. I know he got a Long Beach telephone number for Lindberg, but no one answered there."

Val thanked her and set off down the hall, toward the back door and the parking lot.

"Officer Kuisma?" Gerry Beale, Chief Gutierrez's secretary, caught him at the door. "The chief needs to see you, right now."

"Yes, ma'am."

Gutierrez, not a large or heavy man, was pacing his office with a tread that should have shaken the building. Svoboda was already there, and so was Johnny Hebert.

"Harold Michaelson, the lawyer from San Diego who's been trying to put together a deal on Finn Lane, is missing," Gutierrez said to the room at large. "He had an appointment in San Diego at ten this morning with his principal client, Mrs. Leino, who is also his personal friend. His secretary called Tidepools Lodge, where he'd been staying, when he failed to arrive; she says he would never under any circumstances have failed to call *her* if he knew something was going to delay him."

"Had travel arrangments all set up," said Svoboda. "A charter flight from here at 5 A.M. to connect in San Francisco with a 7 A.M. flight to San Diego. Didn't make the first; we haven't checked with S.F., but his secretary says he sure didn't get off the other end."

"What do they say at Tidepools Lodge?" asked Val.

"He had paid his bill and arranged to have somebody from the lodge pick up his Jaguar at the airport this morning, take it to a garage downtown for some bodywork. The guy couldn't locate the Jag when he went to get it; and when they checked Michaelson's room, his bags were still there, packed and ready to go." Gutierrez pounded fist into palm.

His talk with the sheriff's department fresh in his mind, Val said, "Maybe he went out looking for sex last night and ran into trouble."

"Or maybe he's just another disappeared developer," offered Johnny Hebert. "Did you see the last Rip flyer? Hand of God or whoever delivering a thunderbolt?"

"More likely he got caught in that God-awful storm last night and either flooded out or got washed off a road somewhere," offered Svoboda. "Highway patrol and the sheriff's department are keeping an eye out."

Gutierrez's hand sliced the air in a gesture of impatience. "Kuisma, you and Hebert go to Tidepools and talk to the manager, give the room a good look. No sirens, low profile; we'll get a lab crew out later if necessary. I'll expect to hear from you within the hour. And keep your interesting hypotheses to yourselves."

"Why don't you drive?" suggested Johnny as the two of them reached the back door.

"Fine," said Val, and veered left toward the Jeep. Johnny Hebert drove a maiden-aunt Volvo that probably hadn't been pushed to thirty-five in years.

"You know, it *is* interesting. A developer, and a lawyer representing developers. And you might add Lindberg, a man pushing for sale to developers; I hear he's gone missing, too. A real haul, I wonder if she could have managed it?"

"Jesus, Johnny! If you mean who I think, I've met the lady,

and she's tough. But a mass murderer? What have you got against Ms. Stonemountain?"

Val was on Main by now, moving south at just a bit over the limit, tapping the Jeep's horn lightly to signal his approach to a light. Johnny braced his feet and fastened his seat belt. "It's not personal. To me the most dangerous person in the world is the burning-eyed charismatic leader, especially the one who believes absolutely in his, or her, cause. Fundamentalists of whatever stripe, Christians or Moslems or Sikhs or Jews. Maybe deep ecologists. All those guys who charm us into turning our minds off and dying for their cause."

He took a deep breath and shook his head. "Sorry, end of diatribe. Anyway, it would be neat, Val. Bizarre, I'll grant you, but not illogical."

"Just hang on to that 'would be,' " Val muttered. "And there's Tidepools." A burst of speed, a quick right turn, and then he slowed along a driveway bordered by cleverly manicured cypress trees, to stop at a blue chalet bearing a discreet wooden sign: Tidepools Office. Inside, on a refectory table masquerading as a registration counter, a smaller wooden sign said, "Charles Clifton, Manager."

Clifton took them literally in hand, one arm each, and hurried them into his office. The guy was Stanford or Ivy League, Val guessed. And seriously worried.

"I have questioned all my employees thoroughly," he said as he retreated behind his desk after pointing them at chairs. "They'll be available to you, of course; but please, be discreet. We have some guests to whom privacy is a major concern."

Val ignored that line and said, "Tell us what you know of Mr. Michaelson's movements yesterday evening."

"He came onto the grounds around 5 P.M. One of our attendants noticed that his car had been damaged, and mentioned it to me. Mr. Michaelson came in here just before six, to make arrangements for his departure tomorrow, that is, today, early. I asked about his car, and he said it had been attacked by a deranged man. His manner was abrupt, and I didn't inquire further."

Clifton brushed a hand over close-cut blond hair, then tugged at the knot of his tie before continuing. "The evening bartender tells me that Mr. Michaelson came in for a Stoli martini just after seven o'clock, drank that quickly and had a second. He appeared to be upset and angry. He ordered dinner from the restaurant, I believe a house salad and poached salmon and . . ."

"Keep that information for later," suggested Johnny. "In the event of a postmortem."

"Ugh. Well, he ordered dinner and asked that it be brought to his room. It was delivered there at eight promptly. When the busboy came to pick up the dishes at eleven, the room was dark."

"Is there an attendant at your entrance at night?" asked Val.

"There is a small gate house set back in the shrubbery, with a security man on through the night, but his function is to prevent unauthorized persons from coming *in*. Last night, in the storm, he didn't see Mr. Michaelson leave." Clifton shook his head unhappily and tugged at his tie again.

"Then this morning, as I told Chief Gutierrez, the man who was to collect the Jaguar from the airport called to say he couldn't find it. So I went to Anemone, that's the cottage Mr. Michaelson had occupied, and knocked, and then went in."

"Was it locked?"

"Oh yes, I used my passkey. The room was orderly, the bed still made but dented, as if someone had had a nap. Closets and drawers were empty; Mr. Michaelson's bags, all three of them, were packed and locked and set near the door. And that's all I know. Oh, except that Mr. Michaelson's secretary telephoned from San Diego at about 11 A.M. to ask where he was. That's when I called Chief Gutierrez."

Val stood up, and Johnny followed suit. "What we'll do now, Mr. Clifton, is have a look at the room."

"I would imagine that Mr. Michaelson simply got surprised by the violence of last night's storm, took refuge somewhere and will turn up any minute," said Clifton in a rush. "I would imagine he'll be upset that we're making this fuss. But I just couldn't risk waiting. I mean, this may be another unexplained disappearance, some kind of serial crime happening to men! A terrible thing for Port Silva!"

"You should probably keep that kind of speculation to yourself," Val suggested, "until we've done some investigating. Unless you want a flock of reporters at your door."

Chapter
Twenty-three

J agged was the way life felt today; she couldn't get the tempo
right nor hold the shape-defining notes in her ear. By noon
three students had canceled or rather their mothers had, reluctant to deliver their darlings into the perils of Finn Lane. It
was bright and sunny out there now, childish shouts in the park
being made by actual children; but who knew what next? Not
Charlotte.

The policeman was gone, young Officer Boatwright packing
up his gear about nine last night after telling her that his supe-
riors felt the storm would keep arsonists and other villains
safely at home. And so it apparently had.

But Billy Kaplan was at home; she had met him to her dismay
while she was walking George. Billy embarrassed, feeling guilty
about Petey's accident; Charlotte accepting his apologies without being able to offer any of her own, her promise to Petey in
the way together with the knowledge that Martin had no money,
no insurance, could provide no reparation for the damage he'd
apparently done except by going to jail. Dishonesty was a pain
she was not inured to and she was not handling it well.

Petey was up again after a morning nap, sweating and breathing hard and wincing with each step as he clumped up and down
the hall in crutch practice. "Billy says Buck is feeling better
and would like us to visit him," she told him. "Tomorrow."

He flung his head up abruptly, like a startled horse, and
nearly lost his balance. "I don't want to. I can't, I'm sick."

"Yes, you can, and so can I." The ring of the telephone rescued her from his pleading gaze.

"Charlotte? Charlotte, it's Shirley."

Shirley who? Charlotte shifted mental gears and bit the words back just in time. "Ah. Shirley, how are you?"

"I'm fine, just fine. Did you get the pictures?"

"Pictures."

"Charlotte, listen." Two sharp sounds. "That was my fingers snapping. Now are you with me?"

"Yes. You've sent some pictures, which I have not yet received. Of what, Shirley?"

"Whom, Charlotte. Have you forgotten the Leinos?"

She very nearly had; at the moment Cynthia Leino's motives didn't interest her much. "No, of course not," she lied to her helpful friend.

"That's good, because I have been busting my tushie all over San Diego on your behalf. One thing I've learned is that Howie's boy Hal is not only Cynthia Leino's attorney, but her good friend and her best kid. Devoted to her welfare."

So Hal had been truthful in this, at least. "What about Cynthia's own children?"

"The oldest, John Junior, is an attorney, twenty-nine years old. Junior is said to be a prematurely middle-aged fellow with a boring, rich young wife and one boring child. His mother has never liked him much."

Preferring smarmy Hal, her lover's child. Poor Junior, thought Charlotte.

"Then there's Brad for Bradford, Cynthia's maiden name," Shirley went on. "According to Corazón Villereal . . . Corazón has been housemaid for the Leinos for three years . . ."

Charlotte broke in. "How on earth did you get to the maid?"

"Chica, you forget my roots."

"Oh," said Charlotte. Mexican-born to a family of Sephardic Jews, Shirley spoke excellent Spanish.

"I dolled myself up in flowing clothes and lots of jewelry, like a true real estate lady, and went to look over this piece of lovely

Rancho Santa Fe property, for a client who wishes to remain anonymous. This was when the madam was away, of course, and only Corazón at home. She's from El Salvador.

"According to her, Brad is a jerk; got a college degree but has never had a real job, just plays guitar in no-talent groups and runs around in hiking boots defending trees and owls. Lives off his mama. Corazón says Brad has no *cojones*, Cynthia has no morals. Corazón was fond of John Senior, who apparently retained his charm even when drunk."

Charm should be something you could get vaccinated against, like measles, Charlotte thought, and remembered a bit of information from Shirley's earlier report. "You said three: Cynthia's own three kids."

"There was a daughter, a lot younger than the boys. She was killed in an automobile accident years ago."

"Oh, I'm sorry. Shirley, are the Leino boys in San Diego now?"

"I think Junior is; at least he was at some soirée Wednesday night, the kind that gets newspaper coverage. Corazón said she hasn't seen Brad since his father's funeral, and that was two months ago."

"I wonder if he might be up here, making trouble?" Wouldn't it be lovely if Petey were mistaken about Martin, if Brad Leino had set the fire.

"That's why the pictures, Charlotte. I thought you should get a handle on all the possible players."

"How . . . ? Oh, the newspapers."

"Nope. There were photographs all over the house, pinned to walls or stuck in mirrors, and I appropriated two. One is a shot of Junior and Brad, the other is Cynthia with Hal. Corazón identified them for me."

"Does Wim know about all this?"

"Are you crazy? Anyway, I sent them express mail yesterday; they should be there any minute. Listen, one more really interesting thing. After John Leino's death, Cynthia got some mean anonymous phone calls and letters; John was a popular guy, like I said. Corazón said old tough Cynthia didn't turn a hair until one letter about a week after the funeral. All Corazón knows is it came in a hand-addressed envelope from someplace in California. Cynthia got very pale and quiet, and it was right after that she put the house on the market."

"Hm. I don't suppose . . ."

"Sorry, but it's ashes, sweetie, beyond even my sticky fingers. Corazón saw her burn it. Say, how are you and Petey doing?"

"We're—we're okay, Shirley. I'll write you a long letter someday soon."

"I'll look forward to that. Now I've gotta go, my guys haven't had a from-scratch meal in three days. Love you, Charlotte."

"Thank you. I love you too, Shirley."

"Goody. I'll use you for a reference when I apply for my license."

The doorbell rang as she was replacing the receiver. And as if by magic, she thought, signing her name on the clipboard and accepting the red-white-and-blue envelope. Shirley says it, it's done.

In the top photo of two, a younger Hal Michaelson stood trim and flat-bellied in very brief swim trunks on the deck of a large blue pool. The woman in the canvas chair beside him was also trim; she had a skirted white suit, shapely legs, a cap of dark hair. Nice features, clear-cut just missing sharp. She was looking up at Michaelson with an affectionate smile. Charlotte turned the photo over to find a note in Shirley's scrawl: Prince Hal and the Queen.

The second picture, its color a bit faded, showed two young men in shorts and tee-shirts squinting into the sun. One was dark and stocky, with features very like those of the woman except that hers were somehow lively and his were not. He gripped a tennis racket with both hands. Shirley's note here was in the upper margin: John Junior above the stocky fellow, Brad above his companion.

Brad was much the taller, his long fair hair wildly curly where his brother's was straight. Light eyes. Clear features, high forehead, broad cheekbones with slight hollows beneath.

Hell-with-it smile. He looked familiar, she decided, but she couldn't pin down where she might have seen him.

"Petey? Take a look at this. Is there anyone in either of these pictures that you recognize?"

He leaned on his crutches in worldly fashion and looked. "Sure, there's that asshole that tried to kill me. Michaelson."

"What about the two young men? Is either of them familiar?"

He frowned at the faces, then shook his head. "Nope."

Charlotte's visual memory was not good, and she didn't think her son's was much better; she should show the photo to other, more perceptive people. "I have to go to town," she said, "for a few groceries, and then to Miss T." Miss Tolmachoff, a retired schoolteacher, was reliving her youth in piano lessons; since Miss T. was wheelchair bound, Charlotte took the lessons to her.

"Okay." He made an awkward turn, gathered himself up and marched back.

"There's food in the fridge. Please don't try the outside stairs by yourself."

"Hey, Mom, I'm getting really good with these things. And I might want to go outdoors, it's the first sunshine I've seen in about a year. I promise not to do anything dumb, okay?"

"Well. All right then, I'll be back in less than two hours. If George should need to go out, just open the back door and wait there for him."

It is not happy out here, Charlotte thought as she surveyed a street where the sun was intensifying the burned-wood smell, where the children in the park were ill-dressed and scrawny. But it's not dangerous right now, either. Martin will not come here in broad daylight; Harry Duarte wouldn't dare make any trouble. Val will be home this evening. Well, maybe he won't.

As she fired up her Toyota, she tried without much success to put Val Kuisma out of her mind. At the moment she had nothing to offer him, not sex, not honesty. She had even, last night, given his last beer away, to Annie's Jesse.

■ ■ ■

Petey still hurt, but the pain was something he was used to now, he could handle it. And he had the crutches pretty much under control, had even made it all the way down and up the back stairs. Didn't want to launch off from back there, because it was still seriously muddy; but he could go out front when he was ready, steps to sidewalk to street.

Early, just after breakfast, he'd looked out the front window and seen Annie's tent looking lopsided and abandoned; he'd meant to go find out what was up, or ask Charlotte if she would, but then he suddenly felt real sore and sleepy and went back to bed instead. Now he could tell somebody was there, because the tent frame was back in line and the rain fly off. He figured he could manage the stairs, stand up pretty straight once he was on level ground and not look too much like a jerky kid. Could go see Annie.

"Hey!" he yelped, as his mother's dog nudged him in the butt and nearly knocked him over. Old gooser George needed to pee; and then so did he, kind of a tricky act on crutches. He washed his hands, brushed his teeth and combed his hair. Let his eyes focus, only briefly, on the image in the mirror; yuk, not much he could do about his face. He struggled into clean jeans, his oldest, softest ones, and found a clean plaid flannel shirt that didn't have holes in the elbows. Then he took a deep breath and a hard grip on his crutches and opened the front door.

There were fourteen steps, and he stopped to rest several times, and to look at what was going on over by the tent. The door flap was open, and all the side flaps he could see. Somebody had strung a couple of lines in the trees, to hang clothes and blankets and stuff on; and two sleeping bags lay open across a nearby picnic table.

Petey moved across the pavement with relative ease, then began to pick his way across the soggy grass. What must have happened, that big storm last night probably swamped the tent, maybe blew it down. The van was gone but he could see somebody moving around inside the tent. A bent figure, in jeans, backed out the door pulling something, then stood up and he saw the bright hair swing and shine in the sun. "Hey, Annie," he called.

She turned with a jerky motion; and the breath he was drawing caught in his throat. He was in front of the mirror again, seeing his beat-up face and trying to look away except he couldn't and the bruises were different and even uglier, the eyes green . . . Petey squeezed his eyes shut, dizzy.

"Hey, Pete, what's the matter?" Annie's hands were flat against the front of his shoulders, arms braced straight to keep him from toppling. He stiffened his spine and shook his head, looked down at his crutches and moved them carefully closer, right one and then left.

"No, I'm okay. It's muddy, see? They're sinking in."

"Crutches are a bitch."

Oh, God. Jesse had really done a number on her this time, split her lower lip and blacked her right eye so bad it was just a slit of green in the swollen flesh. "Somebody ought to kill the son of a bitch," he mumbled.

"Hey hey, lighten up, Peter Birdsong." She gave him a lop-sided grin, then turned and bent awkwardly to pick up the object she had dropped, a sodden strip of carpet. "Take a week to get that dry," she remarked, and carried it to the closest garbage can.

He licked his dry lips and settled for Annie's game of what's-real. "Looks like you practically drowned last night."

"We would have, but the people in the Hall took us in. Not cheerfully, you understand, more like with gritted teeth."

"Are you going to stay there?"

She gave a bark of laughter. "That wasn't included in the contract."

"Well, maybe the weather will stay nice."

"In February? Actually, we're all pretty tired of tent living. Jesse is getting antsy, wants to hit the road. And Bo got himself a little truck, so everybody's real flexible."

Head down, Petey hobbled across four or five feet of muddy grass to the picnic table and lowered himself carefully to sit.

He'd gotten used to seeing her here, to thinking about her and wondering what she was doing, whether she was okay. "It's not right, you shouldn't stay with him."

"And you shouldn't mess around in things you can't possibly understand." Moving from tent to garbage can again, she paused to reach out and ruffle his hair.

A band tightened around his chest, making a new and different pain. Something bright, some kind of high promise, was pulling away from him, leaving him here in ordinary gray time. He'd felt like he had a share in Annie, he'd found her and so she was his in some weird way. "You said . . ." He paused to clear his throat, and looked up at her. "You said maybe I could come with you. When you went."

"I was just kidding." She turned away to toss a pair of jeans over the line.

"But why couldn't I? I'm big and strong, I could work. Get a job. Why not?"

"You stupid baby!" She spun around and glared at him. "Do you know what kind of job you'd get, a baby like you? The kind where you drop your pants for fat old men. Get out of here, Peter Birdsong! Go away, go home go home go home!"

Chapter
Twenty-four

"No, sir," said Val. He stood before Chief Gutierrez's desk, heels together and spine straight and shoulders squared. He knew Johnny Hebert was standing to his right, but peripheral vision registered only another perpendicular, no bulge of belly or forward roll of shoulder; even Johnny had tucked it all tight.

"Everything at the lodge, everything in his room was consistent with Mr. Michaelson's intention to leave this morning. He'd cleared out the desk, arranged to have the computer and printer and the FAX machine collected today. The room showed no signs of disturbance. The suitcases were carefully packed. He'd picked up money and papers from the safety deposit box in the office, and the contents of the smallest case would appear to include that material." Val paused for breath, and Gutierrez simply sat there looking at him.

"There was an expense sheet, and some credit card slips and a stack of receipts. And six thousand four hundred and seventy-five dollars in cash, in that small case with a lock your grandmother could open with a hairpin. Another reason I don't think anybody messed with the room."

"His secretary says he always had at least a thousand dollars in his pocket. Jackass," added Gutierrez.

"Yes, sir. We have the computer printout of Michaelson's outgoing calls, but it doesn't look interesting, mostly to his office or Cynthia Leino. Incoming calls are direct, messages go to an voice-mail system with a password, cleared by the recipient. No nice handwritten notes by a clerk with a good memory," said Val with a shrug. "Techs are out there now, collecting prints and looking for anything odd; but I don't think they'll find it. I think he went out somewhere last night and ran into trouble. Or went to meet somebody who turned out to be trouble."

"There's been no sighting yet of his Jaguar?"

"No, sir," said Johnny.

"I talked with the Coast Guard," said Val; this was an automatic action when anyone went missing in a coastal town. "They're busy looking for three overdue boats between Point Arena and Cape Mendocino. And close in, everything's a big mud puddle right now, rivers dumping silt from the rain. But if they hear anything, they'll let us know."

"In the meantime," said Gutierrez, "we've had nothing new on Boylan. And this Lindberg hasn't turned up, although Chang thinks he skipped to avoid connection with the arson on Finn Lane. Okay, you two hustle back out to Tidepools and start interviewing the staff. Not that anyone's likely to have seen anything during that storm," he added glumly.

"If I may, Chief," said Johnny "I'd like to check on the Stonemountains, too, where they all were last night and whether they've heard from Julie."

"*After* you finish at Tidepools." Gutierrez looked at his watch, and then at the window. "It's after five, not much daylight left this time of year. Disappearance Capital of California, that's what they'll be calling this town. Get moving, both of you."

There was a tap on the door; it opened and Gerry Beale stepped in, looking harried. "Chief, I'm about to leave, but you should know that we're suddenly buried in press people out here. Somehow they've heard about the new disappearances, and they want information. And I'm not the one who talked . . ."

"Gerry, you don't have to tell me that."

"And I don't know who did."

"Shit. Go home, Gerry. I'll send somebody out to deal with them."

The door closed softly. "I have an appointment with the mayor," said Gutierrez grimly, "and then an even more important one for dinner with my wife. Last time I called home, she said 'Vince who?' Hebert, go get started at the lodge. Kuisma will join you later, after he's talked to the press."

"Uh, well," said Val as Johnny left. "What do you want me to tell them?"

"As little as you can get away with and nothing important. All coated with charm. Oh, if Officer Linhares is still here, get her to help. Better backup you'll never find. And Kuisma?"

"Sir?"

"Let's avoid saying anyone has been 'disappeared.' Please."

"No." Charlotte underlined the word with a shake of her head.

"Ms. Birdsong, I merely want to talk to your son. You will be free to stay in the room; in fact, I will insist on it."

"Officer Chang, you're not insisting on anything here. This is my home, my son is ill and I will not permit you to bother him."

"Perhaps if you were to have your attorney present?"

"My attorney is in San Diego. Why would we need an attorney?"

"Your husband . . ." Charlotte could feel her face go rigid, and the policeman stopped short. "Martin Lindberg is missing, or at any rate we haven't been able to find him."

"I don't know where he is, and I don't believe Petey does."

Officer Ray Chang was tall, lean but strong-looking; his thick black hair, longer than she'd have expected to see on a policeman, slanted across his forehead from a side part. His uniform was fitted and unwrinkled; his face, uncreased as his clothing when he arrived, had acquired a line between the eyes and another to each side of his mouth. Now he drew a deep breath.

"We need to question Martin Lindberg in connection with the arson here on Finn Lane. We have been unable to locate him. But one of the maids at the Urbanite Motel has described a boy or young man she saw near Mr. Lindberg's room on Thursday.

He left on a bicycle; and his appearance sounds very similar to the description I've had of your son."

"Do you suspect my son of having spirited Martin Lindberg away on his bicycle?"

"No, of course not." His face colored slightly. "But he may know where Mr. Lindberg went. He may know . . . something."

Charlotte shook her head again. The two of them stood in her living room; she had not sat down nor invited him to do so. "I'm sorry, but no. Perhaps tomorrow."

"But . . ."

"My son was hurt in an accident yesterday, knocked off his bicycle by a car. He slept poorly last night. I had to go out this morning, and when I returned I found him back in bed, in pain and depressed." Depressed was a strange word to apply to a child, but it was the only term that seemed to fit Petey's state. Go away, he'd said to her, and rolled himself over with some difficulty so that all she could see of him was his broad, hunched back. Leave me alone, stop bothering me.

"What I'm afraid of is that he may have some injuries that weren't apparent yesterday; his doctor is coming to see him." Charlotte felt as if something had knocked *her* down; her shoulders ached, and the back of her neck, and her jaw.

"Ms. Birdsong, perhaps your son said something to you about his father? About going to see him?"

"Petey is almost fourteen. When you were fourteen years old, did you tell your mother everything that was going on in your life?"

"Well, I suppose not."

Charlotte was good at saying nothing, or at telling the truth. She could not lie convincingly and was determined not to try. "Officer Chang, please go away."

For a moment she thought she'd won, that he was going to leave before she collapsed into exhausted tears. Then he straightened his slumping shoulders, brushed back the wing of hair. "I could wait, outside if you like, until after the doctor has seen him."

"Leave her alone!" The hoarse voice came from the hallway, where Petey was propped green-faced and sweating against the wall. "It was me. I told my father to go away and quit bothering us, I said he'd better not hit my mother again ever. We had a fight in the motel. So if you want to take me to jail," he said, with a sweeping gesture of his left arm that nearly carried him off his feet, "that's okay, I don't care. But first I'm gonna be sick."

He didn't send her away this time, but let her hold his head while he gagged and retched over the toilet, let her bring him a glass of water and then sponge his sweating face. She did all this silently, in amazement at the mixture of truth, bravado, and misdirection he had just displayed, this gangling baby. Martin the actor's son he was after all, and better at it than his father.

"Mom," he said in a hoarse whisper after she had helped him to his feet, "if I go to jail . . ."

"Petey, you're not going to jail."

"Jesse beat Annie up again, Mom, really bad. Could you try to help her?"

"I'll . . . see what I can do." The doorbell rang, and after a moment Officer Chang came diffidently to the doorway, another figure behind him.

"Ms. Birdsong, the doctor's here."

"That was a big fat waste of an evening," said Alma Linhares, who had helped out with the questioning at Tidepools.

"Well, you could say it was useful in a negative way; we eliminated a number of possibilities." Val poured rich brown ale slowly from bottle to glass, then took a sip and sighed. Perhaps his facial muscles weren't frozen, after all.

"Jesus, *negative.* Kuisma, do you suppose your good Portuguese mama had any idea what she was doing when she took up with a northern Protestant?" Alma took more than a sip from her scotch and water.

"We found out that Michaelson drank but not heavily. That he was usually in his cottage with the lights out by eleven. That he wasn't friendly but tipped fairly well. That there was never any indication a woman had been in his bed. That he did not ask either of the bartenders to get him drugs or a woman."

"So they say, Kuisma."

Val shrugged and took a good big swallow of ale. "I thought they were telling the truth. We found out that the only woman who visited him alone was Charlotte Birdsong."

"I still say someone could have come up those stairs from the beach at night without being noticed."

"Maybe. But not during the storm Thursday night." Lifting his glass again, he found himself staring at a mirror, at the upper half of a door reflected there, its glass pane scroll-edged and gilded, the word BAR reversed in its center. Nice simple name. Then door and word faded back and in the space was framed John Hebert, who like the two of them had left Tidepools about half an hour ago. Big Johnny looked as irritated as Val had ever seen him.

"Hey hey!" chortled Alma. "I can have another drink and catch a ride home with Mr. Sober." She patted the stool beside her with one hand, snapped her fingers at the bartender with the other.

"Only if you promise not to smoke in the Volvo. Ginger ale, please," he said to the bartender.

"I guess you didn't bring anybody in," said Val after the bartender had left.

"Julie has not been heard from, Mama presumes she is either still skiing or snowed in somewhere. No worry apparent. Rob is twenty-one years old, does not live at home, does not check in with his mother every day and how should she know where he and his truck might be? She herself was at home last night with Elaine, they can vouch for each other. Probably they were playing whist. That damned woman is—irritating."

"Who?" asked Alma.

"Sarah Stonemountain," replied Johnny.

Alma crossed herself. "My grandmother says Sarah has the evil eye," she said, only half in jest.

"Two evil eyes," said Johnny morosely. "I forgot to ask, how was the press conference?"

Val winced. "Don't remind me. They knew Lindberg and Michaelson had disappeared, they knew about the other guy that got mugged at the Rainbow. One guy said maybe Port Silva was a flip-side Green River, vengeful prostitutes doing in johns."

Hebert made a grimace of distaste. "I don't know what the Lindberg guy's resources were. But somebody in H. Michaelson's income bracket wouldn't need to go looking for sex in cheap bars."

"Um, John . . ." began Val.

"John-boy, your auntie Alma has some things to tell you," said Alma. "In fact, show you, if you'd like to drive with me by, say, the Hinky-Dink. It ain't just Chevy pickups picking up there, it's sometimes big old Mercedeses."

Val drained his glass and tipped in the last few inches of ale from the bottle. "The thing is, nobody with any sense could have expected street whores to be working in that kind of storm."

"True," said Johnny.

"So what else would have been important enough to take a careful, city-boy lawyer out into the wind and the rain?"

Johnny shook his head, and Alma shrugged. "Beats me. Well, early days tomorrow; anybody want to go get something to eat?"

"Sure," said Johnny.

"I think I'll just head for home," said Val. "See you both tomorrow, or sooner."

The broken bulbs in the park lights had been replaced, and flimsy cones of light shone down now. Lights in the Hall, too; but it was only nine o'clock, not as late as it felt. Val parked before the Birdsong house and was wondering whether Charlotte would welcome his presence when he heard a "Mr. Kuisma? Officer?" from the park.

The figure came with the light behind him, but Val recognized the anxious angle of the tall body. "Mr. Cooney, how are you?"

"I'm well, sir, thank you. Got something I thought I might

mention to you?" As Val simply waited, Cooney clasped his hands before his chest and shook his head.

"See, them folks in the tent? Well, their tent took a lot of damage in the storm last night, and one of 'em come asking could they maybe sleep in the Hall what was left of the night. I knew we were as many as permitted, and I hope that lawyer don't find out; but I and one of the women that was awake thought we should make room. So we did."

"I don't think anyone will hold that against you, Mr. Cooney."

"Well, but here's the problem. One of those young women, the one with red hair? This big fella she's with, looks to me like he beats her up, sir. Don't suppose there's anything we could do about that?"

"Well, probably not, Mr. Cooney. Not unless she asks us to."

"Yeah, that's what I thought. Same thing happened to my daughter, and she wouldn't do nothing about it neither," he said with a sad shrug."I guess whatever it is makes women loving, some of 'em got too much of it. Well, I just thought I'd call your attention to this."

"Thanks, Mr. Cooney. I'll watch, maybe have a word with her if I can." Val said good night to the older man and set off for his own apartment, weariness now further weighted by sadness. He reached the door, unlocked it, and stopped with his hand on the doorknob. Cold in there, and lonely.

Go formal, to the front door, he told himself, and went around the house to climb the steps and ring the bell. The porch light came on, the door's curtain was pulled to one side, and Charlotte peered out. He saw apprehension in her face, then relief, and then something he couldn't read. He shouldn't be bothering her; he'd simply make sure she was okay and then go down to bed.

Charlotte, looking past the curtain, felt her heart give a little flutter of pure selfish pleasure. Affectionate concern was what she saw before her, no demands for help or information or even understanding. She might just fling herself into his arms and demand that he take her away from all this. She pulled the door open and said, instead, "Val, come in."

"I'm on my way home, just wanted to make sure you were okay," he said, lowering his voice on the last words as she cast a quick look toward the back of the house.

"I'm okay, except that I'm not very good at fire-building," she said softly. "Can I trade a glass of wine for your help?"

"Not wine, I guess. I might have to go out again." He dropped his jacket on the bench and turned to the living room, to the fireplace. George the dog left Charlotte's side and came to watch.

"Cocoa, then? There's some already made."

When he had poked the fire into productive shape, and settled himself into a low cushioned chair before the hearth, Charlotte brought him a mug of cocoa and a piece of apple pie. "Chaos swirls around me, and I cook," she said half apologetically as she curled up in the matching chair with a glass of wine.

"Doesn't look to me like you've been eating much," he said, surveying her. There was a sharpness to the line of her collarbone under the spread collar of her shirt, and tonight he would not call her face round.

"I haven't been very hungry. But I always, now and any other time, have about ten pounds I can spare. Val, what is it you might have to go back for tonight?"

"Nothing on Martin," he remarked, keeping his voice carefully low. He had learned from Chang of Petey's visit to his father's motel, had declared the circumstance none of his business and meant to keep it that way. "Haven't you had the news on tonight?"

"Oh, dear. No," she said, and took a quick sip of wine.

"The lawyer, Michaelson, has disappeared," he said, and told her briefly of the circumstances.

"Open season on disagreeable men," she remarked. "Oh, I'm sorry I said that, and I didn't mean it. But it certainly is strange."

"At least. John Hebert, he's big on mind-games, Johnny has this theory that somebody out there is picking off developers."

"Somebody like who?" she said, and her eyes widened. "You mean somebody like Rip?"

"I guess."

"Do you believe this?"

"No, and I shouldn't be talking about it anyway. And I don't think for a minute that you should worry about Martin, that he'd be a target for such a group."

"I am *not* ..." she lowered her voice to near-whisper. "The only worry I have about Martin is that he might come back."

"Oh. Good." A piercing electronic noise invaded the quiet room, and Val slapped at his pocket.

"Sorry, that's my beeper," he said as he pulled his long body together and upright. "Okay if I use your phone?"

Charlotte sat and stared at the fire, hearing Val's low voice but purposely not listening to his words. When he returned to the room moments later, he was pulling on his jacket.

"They've found Michaelson's car. No body, but quite a bit of blood, and the interior banged up as if there'd been a fight. I'm going to go help."

"I'm sorry," she whispered. "Where was it?"

"Down at the wharf, in that trailer park. There's a little separate area where the trailer people park any extra vehicles, and the Jag was there, tucked in between a couple other sedans, covered with what looks like its own cover."

He picked up his plate for the last bite of pie. "The newspapers are going to love this. It looks after all like Michaelson went out looking for a whore, and found a bad one. Maybe even the one *we've* been looking for." He saw Charlotte shaking her head.

"That's a known local place for a quickie, Charlotte. There are two handy and fairly low-class motels, and if the manager of the Sunset doesn't actually procure women for his guests ... and I think he sometimes does ... he sure doesn't discourage the ladies from working the street out front."

It didn't feel right to her, Hal Michaelson and a street whore. Not that she had ever seen a street whore up close; but she'd bet Michaelson hadn't, either. If Hal Michaelson had wanted to buy sex, he'd have spoken discreetly to the manager or whoever was the appropriate factotum at Tidepools Lodge and asked to have the best delivered discreetly to his door. Unless he was one of those people who had a need to debase themselves. Charlotte considered that notion for a moment and discarded it.

Val was on his way to the door. "Thanks again for food and company. I hope the beeper or my phone call didn't wake Pete; I haven't even asked how he is."

"Oh, he's not here, he's in the hospital. He was depressed and shaky this afternoon, and Dr. Brodhaus decided to take him in for a few more tests. He called later to say he's sure there's nothing to worry about, but he thought it would be a good idea to keep him off his injured knee for a day or so." The fact that it would also keep him out of trouble and safe from police questioning had won Charlotte to the suggestion.

"I see. Charlotte, if Pete's not here, who were we keeping quiet for?"

"Annie."

He took a deep breath and stared at her. "Annie. The girl from the tent? That Mr. Cooney says gets beat up by her boyfriend."

"She's Petey's friend. She saw the accident coming yesterday, and if it hadn't been for her screaming at him, he'd probably have been hurt much more seriously. He asked me to help her."

"And she has been knocked around?"

"Oh my, yes." Spared the sight of her son's bruises by his modesty, Charlotte had had no such reprieve with Annie, who was as casual about nudity as any three-year-old. "She's been hit with fists, I think, all over her upper body as well as her face. She wouldn't see the doctor, but she doesn't think she has any broken bones. So I let her soak in a hot bath, and then gave her some of the pain medicine Dr. Brodhaus left for Petey. And she's been asleep for an hour."

"Charlotte, suppose the guy turns up here, and I'm not around? Intervening in a domestic situation is like stepping into a war zone, even for people trained to it. I can't go off and leave you . . ."

"Val. I'm not silly, or careless. I'll lock my doors, and take the telephone into my bedroom. And without Petey to worry about, I can get out of the way in a hurry if things get nasty. I promise."

"Well, shit!" He looked at his watch, then looked around for his jacket. "I have to go. Charlotte, there's a revolver in my closet, in a metal box, and the key's in the drawer of . . ."

"Don't be ridiculous!" she snapped.

"No. All right. Call downtown if there's any trouble; and I'll see you in the morning." He bent to give her a distracted kiss, then hurried out.

Chapter
Twenty-five

■

T wo policemen this morning: the baby who had manned the barrier the day after the fire, Boatwright, and an Officer Englund, very tall with white-blond hair and eyes like chips of gray ice. She thought of Officer Chang from yesterday and wished him back, a more civil man altogether.

". . . whole neighborhood, ma'am. And we'd like to talk to your son, too, if you please."

"My son is in the hospital."

"Well, maybe we'll go see him there, later. With your permission, of course," Englund added quickly.

Not likely, she said silently and could tell from his face that he had read hers. As she led the two of them to the kitchen and motioned them to chairs, she sent an unspoken but fervent request down the hall to the room where Annie slept: stay there, stay quiet, *please* don't come to join the fight.

"What we're mainly interested in, ma'am," said Englund, "are the events of Thursday night."

"I wasn't noticing much on Thursday night," she told him, and registered a sloshing sound from the back hall. "Oh, excuse me for a minute and I'll finish loading my washer."

Englund remained in Val's rocker, Boatwright perched on the stool as Charlotte tossed a last pair of wool socks into the machine and picked up Petey's jacket, muddy from his accident. Ripped as well, but not too badly; she could mend it with tape. "Thursday was the day my son was hit by a car," she said over her shoulder. She turned the pockets out automatically, putting three quarters and a handful of rubber bands and several rocks on the shelf above the washer. A big lump of something . . . She stared at the bills that unfolded in her hand. Hundreds, a lot of them. Where had they come from?

"What time was that accident, Mrs. Birdsong?"

"What? Oh. At, um, two-thirty in the afternoon, about." Her bribe? But she hadn't taken it. Had Petey, somehow? As she heard a chair move in the kitchen, she opened her hand and let the bills fall into the churning, sudsy water. Dropped the jacket in. Closed the lid.

"You were here," she remarked sharply to Boatwright as she returned to the kitchen. "Didn't you record the time?"

"Yes, ma'am. Two twenty-seven."

"Well then." Charlotte sat down in the wicker chair, folded her hands, answered their questions. No she had not actually seen the accident yes she had met Michaelson yes she had turned down his offer to buy her house. No she had not known him before this last week. Yes she had visited him just once in his cottage at Tidepools Lodge (with an inner quiver as she thought of those now-very-wet hundred-dollar bills).

"No, of course he didn't hit Petey on purpose; I didn't think that then and I don't now. He was trying to get away from Mr. Kaplan."

"But you were angry."

"No, I was terrified."

"What about your son? Wasn't he angry? I hear the boy has a real temper on him, and Michaelson's car had just crunched his bike."

"Mostly he was frightened, and in pain."

Englund's long, rather sour face did not change expression. "Mrs. Birdsong, does your son drive?"

"Of course not; he's thirteen years old . . . well, nearly fourteen."

"But does he know how to drive an automobile? Do you ever let him take the wheel, drive into the garage, like that?"

Oh. "He has driven my car, in the ways you mention."

"So why couldn't he have driven your car on Thursday night?"

Charlotte took a deep breath and pushed her clenched hands into her pockets, out of sight. Things to do and besides there was contraband or something in her washing machine. "That is a remarkably silly question. He was in serious pain and could walk only with crutches. There was a raging storm blowing down trees and flooding streets. My car was in my garage Friday morning, dry and undamaged."

"I see." Englund wasn't convinced, but wasn't going to push it. "Now, about your neighbors."

There followed a barrage of questions about Joe James, Jennifer, Harry Duarte. Billy Kaplan, Mr. Cooney from the Hall. Annie and Jesse and the other two people in the tent, the latter apparently gone now from the Lane and from town. Charlotte explained that she was busy, not very curious, and knew little about her neighbors beyond the surfaces they presented to the world. After that, she simply kept shaking her head.

"Mrs. Birdsong, we're dealing with a serious matter here, a disappearance that looks like turning into a murder." Exasperation narrowed Englund's pale eyes.

"I'm sorry, but I know nothing about Mr. Michaelson's disappearance, and if any of my neighbors is involved, he or she has said nothing to me about it." My but she sounded like a Victorian schoolmarm or some such; words were not her medium. Come, Officers, let me play a sonata to show you what kind of person I am. "I wish Mr. Michaelson well, truly."

Moments later she ushered the two of them out the front door. Yes yes, on your way and out of mine, she thought. She then moved quietly into the hall and to the door of Petey's room, which was slightly ajar. She pushed it wider, peered in and saw that the extra bed was empty, covers pulled up neatly. Somehow Annie had gotten out without being heard. And without breakfast, which was a shame.

In the back hall she took clothes from the washer, tossing

socks and jeans into a basket and putting Petey's jacket in the dryer. And the money, might as well dry that. She felt around the inside of the tub to make sure she hadn't missed a bill, and something small and hard rolled away from her exploring fingers.

In room 204 at Good Samaritan Hospital, Petey was playing chess with Hannah on a portable set they'd laid out on the bedside table. Today he looked less pale, less bony, more like himself. Charlotte hated to spoil his mood.

He caught sound or movement and lifted his head. "Hi, Mom. Hey, did you bring me something to eat?"

Normalcy here for a moment, like a comfortable cloak. "Apple pie. Cheese. Ginger ale, tomato juice." She set two paper bags on his bed. "And your Walkman, and some tapes. How are you?"

"Okay. I'm sore all over, especially my knee, but I went down for physical therapy once already."

"Hello, Hannah."

Hannah nodded, watchful. "Hi, Charlotte."

"Petey, I need to ask you . . ."

"Mom, did you talk to Annie?"

"I brought her home last night. She didn't want to get involved with the police, but she had a long soak in the bathtub, and something to eat, and a good night's sleep. So she's all right for the moment," Charlotte said, trying to put conviction into her tone. "And she asked me to say hi for her."

"She thinks I'm just a kid."

"And so you are. Big, strong, and very smart, but you have a few years of kidhood left yet. You and Hannah both."

Hannah, her wary look deepening, got up from her chair. "I should probably go now. We can finish the game tomorrow."

"Please stay, Hannah," Charlotte said. "I want to talk to both of you. Petey, I found these in the pocket of your jacket. Where did they come from?"

The bills in their plastic bag were clean, and had emerged from the dryer nice and smooth. Very new-looking.

Petey shook his head, his face blank. "My pocket? No way."

"Not from Martin?" knowing the idea was ridiculous. "What about Sarah Stonemountain?"

Hannah gave a snort of derision and then clearly wished she'd kept quiet. "Um," she said, as Charlotte gave her a long, silent look, "um, well, the thing is, it's really hard to imagine Sarah giving anybody anything."

"Wait," said Petey. "That has to be the money Mr. Michaelson shoved in my pocket right after he hit me, and I never even looked at it. Honest, Mom, things were so crazy I just forgot."

"All right, I'll accept that. But what about these?" She pulled her hand from her own pocket and turned it over, to show two tiny metal pellets rolling around in her cupped palm. "These were in the washer after I washed your jacket . . . which has among its holes two that these just fit. Petey?"

"Oh, shit," he said, and slid lower in the bed.

"It appears someone shot at you. Were you hit, except for your jacket?"

"No."

"Was anyone else?" Charlotte looked at Hannah, who shook her head. "And was this shooting involved in some way with Rip, or Sarah Stonemountain?"

The silence lengthened, and Charlotte put the shot back in her pocket. "I see. Tell me, do you take an oath of secrecy? Sign your name in blood?"

Petey kept his mouth shut. Hannah's face flushed as she said, "That sounds pretty silly."

"Do you want to know what's silly? People as smart as you two playing seven-year-old games."

"Mom, we can't talk about this. Sarah would be mad."

"You have a choice, Peter Birdsong. You may displease Sarah Stonemountain, or you may displease your mother."

"You know that's not really a choice." Petey pushed himself straighter against the headboard, all blue-and-white-striped dignity. "And maybe the club business is silly, secrecy and war games and like that, but Rip isn't. They—we—just think the land should be let to rest in peace. That place where the watchman shot at us, they're taking out native trees to build big fancy houses with lawns and pools and stuff, and a *golf* course. When they put in wells for all that, it'll drop the water table that's already real low and siphon off water from Deer Creek that the salmon need."

"Peregrine falcons are nesting out there," said Hannah. "They got along all right with the dairy cows and sheep; they won't like golf carts and lots of cars. And the place will need a big new entry road and parking lots; road-building really screws up the watershed."

"It will be a road along the bottom of a ridge," Petey added. "Rocks and dirt and stuff will fall on it every rainy season, and then have to be pushed off into the creek."

"And grazing cattle can pack land into virtual concrete, and I believe produce methane gas as well," said Charlotte, who each year wrote larger checks than she could readily afford to a number of conservation groups. "And the purest of motives can still get you shot at. What have you and your friends been doing for Ms. Stonemountain?"

"It's not exactly for Sarah," said Hannah. "We hardly ever talk to her. What we do, we print Rip flyers, and take them around; that last one we did all on our own. And we're spies for Rip."

"And just how do you do this spying?"

"We ride around on our bikes and keep an eye on the neighborhoods, and the land out in the county when we can. We report if it looks like something is for sale, or if a project is starting up, or whether there's a way in to a work site."

"Or if a place has a watchman," added Petey. "That's what happened Friday. This project out by Harker's Knob didn't have a guard before, but this time it did, and he had a shotgun."

"See," said Hannah, "the idea is that nobody pays any attention to kids on bikes. But after Friday we sort of decided Petey shouldn't do this stuff anymore, because he's too big."

"Wonderful." Charlotte shivered, and felt a chilly dampness at her temples and along her spine. "How do you get your instructions?"

"We have a network," Petey told her. "On the computers. We can access it down at the club or from home, the kids who've got their own computer and a modem."

"But, Charlotte," Hannah said earnestly, "the message always says to not do damage, not talk to anybody, to be careful and not make anybody mad."

Charlotte's clenched teeth were making her jaw ache. Don't don't don't, out there where older people would and did. And no doubt some of the thirteen-year-olds did, too; how could they resist?

"Did you do any damage?" she asked her son.

He sat straighter. "I pulled up a bunch of surveyors' stakes one time. I can't talk about the other kids."

"Really? How heroic, expecially since you will be equally responsible, or I will, and Hannah's parents, for whatever damage was done."

Hannah gave a little squeak of misery, and Petey hunched his shoulders. "Well, Phil Johanson—we—messed up a bulldozer one time, Phil knew how because he runs his dad's tractors."

"A bulldozer. How badly . . . never mind, I don't want to know just yet. If ever." She took a deep breath, damage to a bulldozer fading to insignificance next to the possibility that had been setting off little starbursts of fear in her brain ever since Val's remarks last night. "Petey, was there ever anything on your Rip network about Edward Boylan?"

"Who?" said Petey.

"The guy in the paper, who's missing? No, why?" from Hannah.

Wide hazel eyes, wide gray eyes, and if those faces were hiding lies she'd never trust anyone again. "Never mind. Now, I would like to see these instructions. Petey, can you bring them up on your computer?"

He shook his head. "There haven't been any since I got it. And we're not supposed to store the instructions, just read them."

"Bullshit," said Hannah, and flushed as the other two looked at her. "Well, *I* saved them. On a floppy."

"Ah. I will drive you home, Hannah," said Charlotte. "And

you will print them, at least some of them, for me, I believe you can do that?"

"Yes, ma'am."

"Petey, Mr. Michaelson has disappeared," Charlotte said. "The police came this morning to ask me where you and I were on Thursday night. I believe I convinced them of the truth, that we were at home. If they should come here, do *not* talk to them; just call me."

"If you don't move that out of my way I'll smash it."

Charlotte looked sadly at her nice little Toyota, which she had parked at an angle right across the back bumper of a much larger Toyota van. "I suppose you could," she said to the furious woman looming over her. "But I don't think that would get you out of the garage."

"Ms. Birdsong, please. My daughter went to the police station some time ago, and I can't get anyone there to tell me what's going on. If they've arrested her, she's going to need some clothes and her medicine."

"Arrested her for what?" asked Charlotte.

"Kidnapping, murder, *I* don't know. It's utterly ridiculous, she—we—are savers, not killers!"

Can't always tell dopers, Val said. Even harder to tell killers, to know at what point devotion becomes fanaticism and stretches morality out of recognizable shape. Would whatever lay behind that strained, hot-eyed face be capable of murder? or of planning murder and encouraging others to accomplish it?

As Charlotte didn't move or speak, Sarah Stonemountain glared anew. "What's the matter with you, woman? You have a child of your own, suppose he were . . ." The narrowed eyes widened, and she stepped back. "Oh."

"I certainly have. He's the one who got shot while playing your game."

"I have no idea what you're talking about. But if you insist on blocking my van, I'll simply call a cab."

"From the company owned by James Watterson, father of

Jonas?" Charlotte opened the letter-sized manila folder she carried. "Who is a friend of Kimmie Silveria, who is a friend of Derek Mazzini, who is a friend of Jamie Armino, and so on."

"Ms. Birdsong . . ."

"These children have parents, too. I've spent a lot of time on the telephone recently," Charlotte said, choosing her words with care, "and it appears that local parents are not eager to provide troops for a new Children's Crusade." She had in fact said nothing specific to the other parents about her suspicions, on the principle that a riot would do no one any good.

With a toss of her head that sent the heavy hair swinging, Sarah took another step back and crossed her arms over her chest. "I think all those names you mentioned belong to the computer club that meets in my shop. It's a convenience to the children, and a way to increase computer literacy; I personally have very little to do with it."

"Then who is it that puts the Rip instructions on the network?"

"Ms. Birdsong, someone has been feeding you a story, a fantasy." Sarah turned on her heel and set off for her house.

"But the instructions have been saved, as have replies. On a floppy disk. On a machine with a clock and a calendar."

Sarah paused, then turned and shook her head. "Doesn't matter. There'd be no way to prove where a message originated."

"I'm not sure that's true. But what I do know is that there's a positive correlation between the dates on the disk and those of flyer distributions and various disruptions, most of which were not legal."

"This is all just the kind of fantasy a bunch of preadolescents would dream up. Their own version of dungeons and dragons."

"A bunch of preadolescents who spend most of their free time in a back room of your shop, a place with a coded lock, its combination known only to the children and to you and your family."

"What the hell are you implying?"

"Oh, don't be stupid," said Charlotte wearily. She tossed the folder through the window of her car and then shrugged herself more deeply into her jacket. "You'll have no difficulty imagining the conclusions the press and the public would draw from the facts as I've stated them."

"You think I'm a monster, don't you?" Sarah settled back on her heels and shoved her hands into the pockets of her jeans. "Maybe I am, maybe a fire-breathing dragon is what's needed. The earth has rights, to exist and breathe and keep itself healthy. People who live carefully and respect their mother earth have rights, too, and they'd better learn how to defend them. If they—we—don't, we'll all live in city slums or on wasteland edges, while rich people build mansions and golf courses and health resorts in the good places. All with private roads, so we'll have to pay just to drive by and look."

Snake and bird. Charlotte blinked and broke her gaze away from the other's burning yellow eyes; no wonder the children were ready to march and fight. "There are political controls available, laws already in place and more to be made if necessary."

"Not in time, they won't be. Not while oil and timber interests pour big money in against initiatives, and county and state governments are run by real estate people and lawyers. Playing a couple of piano concerts to benefit redwoods is a nice gesture, Charlotte, but gestures don't accomplish much in the real world. Tell me, isn't there a place or an idea you'd go to jail for? Risk your life for?"

"My own, perhaps, but not someone else's. I could never be that sure I'm right." Old wishy-washy again, she thought sadly.

"Your son is sure. Don't you think he should be free to act on his convictions?"

That stiffened her spine properly. "As I said earlier today to a policeman, that's a remarkably silly question. What I have to do is protect Petey from people like you until he's old enough to make his own choices. I insist that you, you and your group whoever they are, leave him and the other children alone, now and from now on. Retroactively, in fact."

Sarah frowned, and blew out a long breath. "Ms. Birdsong, come in and let me make a pot of tea, and we'll talk."

Val parked his Jeep a block away from the station and walked to the back door. Saturday evening coming up, and too bad it wasn't raining like hell; he could see a number of press cars in the lot, and a couple of television vans. He hoped the chief didn't decide to throw him at those guys again, because right now he was too tired to be good-tempered.

Inside, there were loud voices and sounds of movement from the front of the building while the routine back here was pretty normal. The people who'd been on through the night were distinguished by bloodshot eyes, unshaven jowls, sweat-stained clothing; Val felt a little guilty for having gone home for a short nap and a shower.

"Hello, Officer and lady," he said to Alma Linhares. "Anything happening?"

She shook her head vigorously. "Noise. Bullshit. Misery. Mostly from a bunch of snoopy sons of bitches that won't let us get on peacefully with our work."

"Is Johnny here?"

"Oh boy, is he ever. Julie Stonemountain got back to town," said Alma, rolling her eyes so high they were nearly all white. "She is a good kind person who came in because she heard we were interested in her. The fact that we were also interested in her mother's Toyota four-wheeler is really too bad, because see, up there on the snowy ski-country highways they use salt to melt road ice, and it gets thrown up under the vehicles, been known to eat holes in the metal. So she had the van steam-cleaned and scrubbed inside and out the minute she got out of the hills. I mean, it squeaks. It sucks."

"So Johnny's talking to her?"

"Oh yeah."

"She say where she was Thursday night?"

"Thursday? I don't think that's come up yet."

"Well, I think I'll look in for a few minutes." He tapped on the door of the small interrogation room, then opened it and stepped inside.

Julie Stonemountain, rump propped on the edge of the table and long legs stretched out, was a copy of her mother in warmer tones. The long hair, in a thick single braid reaching well down her back, was brown, streaked and edged with gold; the eyes a yellowy hazel. Five-eight or -nine, Val judged, with broad strong shoulders, well-muscled arms, big solid breasts. Her face wore a dusting of freckles and an expression of calm tolerance in which he detected a hint of contempt.

"You don't have to be polite in fighting off rape," she said to Johnny, registering and dismissing Val's presence. "This planet is my home, the only one I've got. I have a right to protect it."

"By subterfuge and disruption," said Johnny, who stood with his feet apart, arms crossed. Officer Adam Boatwright sat in a straight chair against the wall, notebook open on his thigh.

"Sure."

"Or by the destruction of property."

"Here's the proper ascending scale, Officer Hebert. Property rights. Human rights. Earth's rights."

Val shifted his feet uneasily; this struck him as time-wasting and potentially dangerous, however entertaining to Johnny.

"And how far do you go to defend earth's rights, Ms. Stonemountain? Physical violence? Murder?"

Julie's eyes were hot, more yellow than brown. "In principle, one might. In fact, violence is likely to be counterproductive."

Entertainment going both ways here, Val noted. He wished it didn't feel so much like a personal and acrimonious debate, and he wished Julie had a lawyer with her.

"Have you found that out by experience, Ms. Stonemountain? Have you, in fact, killed anyone in defense of your planet?"

"Don't be stupid. And if you're going to ask me things like that, I want my lawyer here."

"Fine, very good idea. Because I'm going to take your fingerprints, Ms. Stonemountain, and in addition ask you for a lock of your hair."

What was this? Johnny looked relaxed but alert, pleased; Boatwright's face showed no surprise. Julie was clearly startled.

There was a rap at the door, and a second later Alma stuck her head in and beckoned to Val. He stepped out and closed the door behind him.

"Coast Guard just called," she told him in a low voice. "They've got a body, could be Michaelson."

He followed her to the break room, where she lit a cigarette and drew deeply on it. "Fisherman spotted it, just above Point Arena. Male, short dark hair, fully dressed in what looked to him like a suit. The fisherman didn't want to try retrieval, so he's standing by and the Coast Guard will do the job. They'll let us know when they get back, maybe a couple of hours. And we get to go down and identify. That'll be fun."

"If it is Michaelson, he's only been in the water a day and a half at most, and the water is cold this time of year. So the body might not be too bad."

"Sure, unless it's been banging around in the rocks turning into hamburger for fish." Alma took another long drag and released the smoke slowly. "Anyway. Nobody's found anybody who saw anything on the wharf late Thursday. The weather was so rotten that the motels had only seven rooms rented between them. Nobody from either place went outside after about nine o'clock. Restaurants and bars all closed early. And we've talked to four women who are known to have worked the street down there. They were all someplace else Thursday night, indoors."

Val, who'd been standing and jittering, rocking heels to toes and back and jingling pocket change, now moved to the door and looked down the hall. "Let's not forget Mr. Boylan. Alma, what was that business with Julie Stonemountain's prints and hair?"

"We got several unidentified prints from the trunk of the Ford Boylan had rented. And there was this little tuft of hair we found. Like maybe from a long braid that swung and caught?"

"And you think it's Julie's?"

"It's just the right color, which we couldn't know for sure until we saw her." Alma grinned and dropped her cigarette butt into an empty Coke can. "But here's the kicker, Valentine. The prints are all on the outside of the trunk lid, okay? could have been left by somebody walking past. The hair was inside the locked trunk, caught in the open zipper of Ed Boylan's duffel bag."

Chapter
Twenty-six

"Bo and Tif took off yesterday, and Jesse was all set to leave today, but the cops won't let him." Annie paced the kitchen like the skinny, frantic coyote Charlotte had seen once in a cage at a desert zoo.

"Mm," Charlotte said. She had taught three lessons this afternoon and could remember nothing about any of them; a fugue state, psychologist Gil Feder would have called it and she certainly preferred the Bach version.

Gil. Oh, my. Last Saturday, after their quintet session, she had for some reason agreed to a piano and violin evening with Gil here, this very night. Just the two of them. Charlotte sighed and tried to look on the bright side. Gil might be, as Petey thought, a dweeb; but he was also a very good cook, and he'd promised to bring dinner.

"He had the tent down and packed, he'd settled up with his . . . with this guy he knows. We were gonna head south. Well, he thought I was coming along, I hadn't told him yet I wasn't. No point in giving Jesse time to think, he's not real good at it." The girl shook her head and took a long pull from the bottle in her hand, just mineral water because Charlotte's refrigerator had proved empty of beer.

"Anyway, now nobody on the Lane here is supposed to leave town, not without checking in with the fuckin' po-leece. *Shit* but I hate it when people try to run your life! Jesse is sleeping in the van, tonight at least, and he knows I hate that, so he won't get mad if I stay here. Can I still do that, Charlotte? That's why I've been hanging around waiting for the little kids to leave, so I could ask you if that's still okay."

"For tonight, yes. Tomorrow I expect Petey will be back."

Annie's brief, sudden grin lit up her bruised face. "Hey, right. Fourteen-year-old kid probably wouldn't sleep real well with a bimbo right there in the next bed, even one that looks like me. Anyway, what I'll do now, if it's okay, I'll leave my stuff here." She gestured toward a zippered duffel perhaps two feet long; not really big enough, Charlotte thought, to hold all one's worldly belongings. "Then I'm going to go hang out with Jesse for a while, probably get something to eat. See you later."

Gil Feder arrived at six-thirty as arranged, but empty-handed: no violin, and worse still, nothing that might contain food. "I ran out of time and energy, Charlotte," he told her as he stepped inside and brushed her cheek with his. "So I thought instead of cooking I'd take you out to dinner, and you could tell me all about what's been going down on Finn Lane. I brought the tape we made of last week's session," he added, "with the idea that we could listen to that after dinner."

Trade-off. She would have to sing for her supper, a song she was weary of; but she would get out of the house, away from sudden small noises and shadowy corners. Sometimes she thought Petey's house was haunted.

"So, what do you say? If you don't like the idea, just say so, and I'll call Mary's and cancel the reservation. Hey!"

"George, stop that! I'm sorry, Gil. This is my new friend George; Petey calls him Gooser George."

"I can certainly see why." Gil brushed at his backside, keeping a wary eye on the dog. "If I'd known you were looking for a pet, Charlotte, I'd have saved one of Sukey's kittens for you. Well, are we on?"

"Just let me get my coat."

■   ■   ■

Chief Gutierrez would be ready to leave for the wharf, he said, in fifteen minutes. Val checked his watch and headed for the break room and a quick cup of coffee.

"Hi, Johnny."

John Hebert slouched on his tailbone on one of the old couches, feet resting on a chair and a can of ginger ale propped on his belly.

"Greetings, Kuisma. Anything new on the body?"

"Not yet, we're going to go have a look. What about Julie Stonemountain; will you hold her?"

"Oh yes. She refuses to say where she was after leaving the restaurant that night, says she just drove around with her boyfriend. Who isn't in town and she doesn't know where he is. That's all. No more from Julie."

"But you got the hair sample."

"Yes, although I thought for a while we were going to have to gag her and cuff her to get it."

Val grimaced, at the idea and at the taste of the coffee. He was surveying the soft-drink machine when someone rapped on the doorjamb, and Cathy Cardoza stuck her head in. "Officer Kuisma? There's somebody here to see you. I think. She asked for 'the cute young cop with the green eyes and the funny name.' "

"Succinct and accurate," noted Hebert as Val set his cup aside and followed Cathy out.

"Sally!" he said as he caught sight of his visitor. Sally Henry from the pub in Hopland; Sally who had been pawed by a drunk Ed Boylan. "I've been trying to get hold of you for three days, but your parents kept saying they didn't know where you were."

"They didn't." Sally lifted her chin. "They were really *mean* about Tommy and what happened that night, and they were going to *ground* me, can you imagine? So I got in my car and went to visit this friend in San Luis. But then I ran out of money, and I knew they'd be real worried, so I came home," she added with a shrug.

"You have some information for us?"

"Yeah, I think so, but could we go someplace besides that stuffy room with no windows where they talked to me last time?"

"Come into the break room," he said, and opened the door for her. "This is Officer Hebert, and he won't bother us."

"See, what happened—oh yes, please, could I have a Diet Pepsi?" she said as he gestured toward the drinks machine. "I did what those other policemen asked me to, I thought about it a lot, about that night, trying to remember something that might help."

"And did you?" asked Val as she paused for a drink.

"I think so. There were other cars down there, like Tommy said. And I don't know much about cars. But then yesterday I saw something at this rest stop on the freeway." She smiled at him.

"You saw . . . one of the cars?"

"No, but one that reminded me. I saw one of those old cute Volkswagens, that they call a beetle? It was painted bright blue with daisy decals on its door." She paused for another sip, and Val held his tongue and his breath.

"I really like those little beetles, that's one of the few cars I would recognize. And I'm sure there was one parked there at the breakwater lot that night, when we were leaving."

"And did you happen to notice its license number."

"Oh. No, I'm sorry."

"What about color?"

"It was yellow, nice and bright there under the lights. I just don't know why it took me so long to remember and I'm real sorry."

"Sally, you are a joy and a delight and have nothing at all to be sorry about."

"Huh?" Sally looked up at John Hebert, towering over her with his blue eyes shooting sparks. "What's he talking about?" she said nervously to Val.

"He means that you just helped us a lot with a timing problem, Sally. Look, bring your Pepsi and come down the hall, so big John here can type while we talk some more. Cathy?" Val called as he ushered the girl out the door, "would you see if the chief can find somebody else to drive him to the wharf?"

Mary's was Port Silva's best Italian restaurant, old and quiet and classy. Fairly expensive, too, but worth it. Charlotte was enjoying the food but finding Gil Feder strange tonight; attentive to her in a hovering way, he was also bouncy and full of suppressed energy, dark eyes blinking rapidly. Gil, it turned out, was an avid reader of true crime, those books that appear after every spectacular or spectacularly sordid crime, particularly crimes involving rich or famous people and their families.

"Somebody will get a book out of this, Charlotte," he said briskly over coffee and brandy. *"The Port Silva Disappearances.* I'd like to try it, but I'm too busy to do the job alone; my course load this semester is a killer. I've tried to get Margaret interested, because she's a good writer and fast, too. But she doesn't like to think about crime, won't even read mystery novels."

All this struck Charlotte as seriously premature. "I don't like to think about crime, either," she told him. "Or talk about it. And I certainly wouldn't be interested in writing about it, so you can just cross me off your list of potential collaborators."

"Woe is me," said Gil, but his foxlike face under its wild mop of silvery curls was cheerful enough. "Probably wouldn't work anyway, just mess up a nice relationship. More coffee?"

Relationship? Charlotte looked at her watch and shook her head. "I'd like to get home in time to call Petey." And to let Annie in before the weather got worse. Mary's sat at the tip of a small rocky point north of town, overlooking the sea; fog that had lain offshore an hour ago was enfolding the building now, beginning to turn to drizzle.

On the drive home she made Hmm? and Um-hmm replies to Gil's chatter, wondering what Val had been up to all day, whether he had found anyone. Or anything. Wondering whether Officer Englund and his young colleague had settled on any neighborhood person as particularly suspicious. Hoping that Billy Kaplan had a firm record of his whereabouts for Thursday night; she could imagine Billy punching an enemy into unconsciousness, but not killing him and hiding his body.

"Hmm?" she said again, and realized they had reached her house. Very quiet on the street, no police cars. No tent, and she didn't see Jesse's van. She got out of the car, digging in her purse for her keys, and found Gil beside her. "The tape? And maybe we can catch a little news," he suggested.

She let the dog out, and phoned Petey, who sounded sleepily peaceful and asked no questions. When she returned to the living room, Gil had built a small fire. "No news until ten," he told her. "Let's sit here on the couch and listen to what good music we made."

Unlike Petey, she wasn't peaceful. She looked out the front window, turned the thermostat lower, made sure the telephone receiver was properly in its cradle. Heard the tape start, and returned to listen.

The music was Schubert's "Trout" Quintet, and Charlotte thought they'd done quite well for a group of amateurs. Gil was critical of his violin, probably simply in search of praise, which she gave. He was more unhappy with the cello, with reason, Charlotte thought. "Ah, here, this is a nice bit," he sighed, and in agreement she closed her eyes to listen.

She hadn't realized how close he was, until suddenly he sat forward, cupped her face to turn it and fastened his mouth on hers, tongue plunging deep. His other hand slid inside the neck of her shirt, pushed her bra down and clasped her bare breast, fingers closing on a nipple that responded with embarrassing promptness.

"For heaven's sake, Gil! What are you doing?" She pushed him away and got quickly to her feet, straightening her clothing.

"I'm trying to make love to you, Charlotte. You seemed different tonight, in some way, and I thought . . . if I've offended, I'm sorry."

"Gil, we are *musical* friends, not lovers. And Margaret would be terribly upset."

"Margaret is controlling, Charlotte. Conventional. She insists that sexual expression is most satisfying in the context of marriage."

"What a wonderfully radical idea." Charlotte felt tears pressing against her eyelids, and perhaps a small scream building in her throat. "You're a good violinist, Gil. But I think you're a disagreeable man, and Margaret could do much better. Thank you for dinner, and please go away."

How much her fault? she wondered as she closed and locked the door. Not much. She was worried and vulnerable, and that could probably be a turn-on. And Gil had made it clear that he found crime exciting. What a nasty combination of circumstances, and if he was doing what she supposed he was, out there in his car, she wished him a painful accident with his zipper.

Voices from outside caught her ear, and George's. They both went to look out the music room window, and saw not Val's Jeep, but Jesse's van. After a moment a slim figure stepped from the open passenger door, long hair catching the faint mist-haloed light from the park. Glad to see you, Annie. Come on in; it's a little weird in here but I think safe.

Annie came through the door in a rush of chill damp air; turned and caught Charlotte in a brief hug, press of cold cheek and thin hard arms and sweet smoky smell in the flying hair. She set a paper bag on the floor and shrugged out of her jacket and saw Charlotte's questioning look.

"Huh? Oh, the smell, don't worry. That's from being in the van while Jesse was smoking, but I don't do any dope at all, not even grass. And I'm not carrying anything either, see? Clean." She spread her arms in display and then looked down at the paper bag. "Except beer, and I lied to you a little bit before; I'm not quite twenty-one, not for like three months. Okay? I mean, I know you're not my mother or anything, but this is your house."

"Okay," said Charlotte.

"Oh, good, I really need this. You want one?" Annie kicked off her boots and set off in stockinged feet for the kitchen.

"No, thanks."

The refrigerator door opened, closed; there was a rattle of cutlery, and then Annie returned, opened bottle in hand. "Ooh, a fire! I love fires, I think every house should have a fireplace." She knelt on the hearth to watch the flames for a moment, then got awkwardly to her feet and went to look out the window.

"It's going to rain again tonight," she said, and Charlotte saw her shiver. She wore old, thin jeans, a chambray work shirt with sleeves rolled over her forearms, a tee-shirt beneath that. Her hair was damp, and she was drinking cold beer. And you're not her mother, Charlotte reminded herself as she turned up the thermostat and went to put another small log on the fire.

"If Jesse's smart, he won't lie out there and smoke dope, not on this street where the cops might turn up any minute. Except he's not smart," Annie said harshly, and tipped the bottle high. "He wanted me to stay out there with him, but I hate that van, it's like being inside a big cold tin can."

This she would not do: she would not offer a bed to Jesse. If Annie got drunk, or sick, or angry, Charlotte thought she could handle it. But not Jesse. "I'm going to make a pot of tea," she said to the girl's back. "Would you like some?"

"No, thanks, I'll just stick with beer. I don't like tea, it makes my teeth feel funny." Annie moved past Charlotte to the fridge, to get another bottle; Red Tail Ale, said the label.

She skittered around the kitchen like a blown leaf while Charlotte made the tea. "I'm not hungry," she said when Charlotte offered to make her a sandwich. "We had hamburgers and fries like an hour ago, I can still taste the onions. Beer is what I need, it makes me feel good and it'll make me sleepy. Sometimes I have trouble getting to sleep." The wind, which had been building for a while, rattled the windows in a sudden gust; Annie shivered again and hurried to the front of the house.

She paced the living room, then into the music room and back, looking out each window she passed. Before the fireplace she nearly stepped on George, who was enjoying the warmth; he sat up quickly at her startled exclamation, and took himself off to a corner.

"Petey showed me these pictures the other day," she said, stopping before the mantel. "He said this was your mother, this little woman? She looks sad."

Charlotte settled into a corner of the couch with her cup of tea. "She wasn't sad. She just wasn't very strong."

"And this is your father. He looks . . . kind of stern, I guess. Did he ever smile?"

"He smiled, but not a lot; he was a quiet man. He carried me around on his shoulders when I was tiny, and he taught me to waltz when I was about five, put my feet on his feet and we danced. He called me his little songbird."

"Oh, that's where you got your name!" Annie drained her bottle of ale, set the bottle on the mantel and picked up a photo album lying there. "Wow, look at all these pictures of a baby, I guess it's Pete? Yeah, here he's a little older. He was really cute. He's still cute, he's a really nice kid and he likes you a lot, Charlotte."

"I like him a lot."

"Yeah, I can tell. I'm going to get another beer, you want anything?"

"No, thank you." Charlotte would have enjoyed a glass of wine, or perhaps a splash of brandy in her tea; but if the crackling tension Annie carried with her should explode, she herself had better be cold sober.

"Mothers like their sons, that's the way it works that I've seen." Annie stood before the fireplace with a fresh bottle in her hand. "And fathers are nice to daughters. If I ever have kids, what I'll do is keep the boys and give the girls away."

She took a deep swallow and sighed. With the light of the fire behind her and her bruised face in shadow, she was just a gracefully skinny kid, like Hannah. "Once, when I thought I might be pregnant and Jesse wanted me to have it, I said I would only if it was a boy.

"What did Jesse say?"

"But it turned out I wasn't . . . Did I say Jesse? I meant Dave, back before Jesse." The sound of an engine in the street swung her around, to the music room and its big window.

"Just a cop, looking for trouble," she called to Charlotte. "Didn't stop, didn't bother Jesse. It's funny, I left home when I was fifteen," she said slowly as she moved back to the living room, to the fireplace. "I hated my family, I wanted to be my own boss. But I never have been, not really. I've always been with some guy. I get fed up with one and dump him, here comes another one and it's like, well okay, might as well. I don't understand it, why that happens; I mean, I don't even like fucking that much.

"But you, you take care of yourself and your kid and you do okay, you both look happy. How do you do that? Is there a secret you can tell me?"

Oh dear lord. "I think," Charlotte said carefully, "that if you are living in a way you don't like, and you really want to change that, you can. With help."

"Right. Like a shrink, or a doctor, or a place, an institution." Annie turned her back and dropped to her knees, before the fire. "This isn't much of a fire, and I'm cold." She reached into the kindling basket and began to pull out handfuls of small branches and pine splinters, to throw them on the flames. Wadded a sheet of newspaper, and another, tossed them in.

"Annie, be careful."

"I'm cold!" She swept today's paper from the coffee table and flung it in, then lifted the kindling basket and emptied its contents onto the now-billowing fire. Orange flames filled the fireplace and rushed up the chimney with a roar.

"Stop it!" Pushing the girl aside, Charlotte hooked the grate with the poker and shook it, then used the poker to knock burning kindling off to either side. "This is an old house, an old chimney! You'll burn the house down and kill both of us!"

Charlotte on her knees, Annie sitting back on her heels, they stared at each other. Annie's face was bloodless under its bruises, her undamaged eye round and white-rimmed.

"No. No, I love this house. I love you, Charlotte, I wouldn't do anything to hurt you. I wouldn't, I'd hurt myself first. See?" Fingers tightly shaped as for a salute or a karate blow, she thrust her right hand into the flames.

"Good morning, Charlotte," said Val with what she felt was unnecessary cheerfulness. "I just wanted to tell you . . . hey. You look terrible. Did Pete have a setback?"

"Thank you. No, I'm picking him up at ten." She peered at her watch. "In an hour."

"Then what is it?"

"Nothing. I'm just tired, I didn't sleep very well." Pain or drama or both had sent Annie careening from intensity to torpor the night before. She'd sat slack-spined and silent as Charlotte bandaged her not-very-badly-burned hand, had then let herself be led to her bed. Charlotte, however, unable even to lie down, had stared pop-eyed at late-night television until she finally dropped off in a corner of the couch about 5 A.M.

Sometime between five and eight-thirty Annie had taken her duffel and departed, leaving a note on the kitchen table: Thank you, Charlotte. I'm sorry. I'm hitting the road on my own.

Charlotte pressed her fingers against her eyelids for a moment, then blinked and looked up into Val's worried face.

"No, I'm all right. Annie was here last night again . . . the girl from the tent?"

"The one whose boyfriend beats her up."

"Yes. But she left sometime early this morning. Val, I'm worried about her."

"The tent is gone, Charlotte. And the big blue Dodge van isn't anywhere on the Lane. Looks like they've split, even though they were told to stay around."

That was probably the explanation. Annie would consider it a matter of principle to defy such an order. "Well. I think I'll go collect my son and then just . . . go back to bed."

"Good idea. The police won't be bothering you again. I told Englund I can testify that neither you nor Pete went anywhere Thursday night."

"You can? How can you?"

"Thursday was a night *I* didn't sleep. That was the night you told me to behave myself, remember?"

Oh yes, that night. A long time ago. She seemed to be doing a lot of telling these days, not her usual pattern at all. In Val's case . . . "I think I was wrong," she said, and yawned.

He grinned. "Well, the alternative would have made an even better alibi." He put both arms around her and pulled her close, in an embrace that was meant to comfort and did. "Now I have to go to work. No cops, like I said; but there may be reporters."

"I'll sic George on them," she muttered, and heard the thump of the dog's tail from behind her.

"If that doesn't do the trick, why don't you just lock up here and go down to my place? From the street nobody would even know it's there." He dropped a kiss on the top of her head and released her.

"Val, what was it you came to tell me?"

Memory darkened his face, narrowed his eyes. "I almost forgot. We found Michaelson, or his body; it will be on the news any minute, and probably in the papers that went to press late."

"Oh. I'm sorry."

"He was in the water; he'd been knifed."

"The way you thought, like the man in the truck?"

"Looks like it."

"I'm sorry," she said again.

■   ■   ■

It wasn't until she was working in Petey's room, pulling used sheets off the twin beds and shaking out fresh clean ones, that the selfish but exhilarating fact struck her: they were free and safe, from arson and probably from development, for the moment at least. From suspicion of having committed crimes. From practically everything except the need to crank up daily income, a familiar circumstance and one that didn't frighten her. "It was seventy-three yesterday in San Diego, clear and sunny," she said to George. "How do you feel about long car trips?"

The telephone rang, from somewhere under a pile of sheets. Reporters again, she thought, wanting to know about Martin. Or it might be Petey. She unearthed the instrument and picked up the receiver.

"Charlotte?"

It was a moment before her ears registered the familiar voice under the carefully low pitch. "Martin. What do you want?"

"I want some safety here, Charlotte. And some recompense for the things you've been saying about me to the press."

"All I said . . ." She tried to remember the few words wrung from her by two reporters. "I said I didn't know where you were, I rarely saw you, we were never married. That's all."

"Read the paper, Charlotte; it implies that I am a womanizer, a nonsupporting father, an arson suspect. And a failed actor! I am completely destitute and I've got to have some money right now. Send it to Lawrence Miller, general delivery in Santa Barbara."

Money. She had that worrying thousand dollars from Petey's pocket; why not send it to poor . . . poor Martin the fire-setter, and here she was about to play puppet once again.

". . . and I want my half of the worth of the house, Charlotte, I'm entitled to that much at least. Or I'll file assault charges against that hulking son of yours."

Petey. She should be at the hospital in twenty minutes, according to the bedside clock. As the angry voice, full-throated now, roared on, she replaced the receiver and bent to pull the cord free of the wall jack. She had just time to finish making the beds. Martin had as usual badly overplayed his role; that seemed to be part of their dance, the part that always kept her from doing something really stupid. The big question now was, should she tell the police that he was in Santa Barbara?

Petey was propped on his crutches in the hospital lobby, the bag containing his belongings slung over one shoulder. Clear-eyed, cheerful; obviously the hospital stay had been good for him.

"Hi, Mom!" he said brightly. "Everything work out okay?"

"Yes, I think so. I'll tell you about it later. Wait," she said as he headed for the front door. "Let's go by room 118 and say hello to Buck."

"Oh, right," he agreed, and reversed directions neatly.

Buck was propped against pillows, blankets tented over his legs by some kind of frame. "Charlotte!" he called as she rapped on the doorjamb. "And Petey, what a treat! Come in. Billy, get chairs for our guests."

"You're looking very healthy," she told him truthfully. His color was good, his eyes bright and his head high. "Hello, Billy."

"Good morning." In contrast to his partner, Billy Kaplan looked worn and edgy.

"Why, thank you, Charlotte," said Buck, and giggled. "I think it's this wonderful pain stuff they give you here. I believe that if I weren't a strong person, I could become an addict of some kind. It's so interesting to just order up a way to feel."

Billy snorted. "Bullshit. See that machine, Charlotte? I.V. drip; want to add drugs to it, all you have to do is push a button. I bet he hasn't touched that once in the last four hours."

"But it's the knowledge that I can if I want to, you see. Total freedom."

Charlotte thought of Annie, whose pursuit of freedom merely took her from cage to cage. "Buck, you are a dear person and a . . . how should one phrase it? A very well-integrated personality."

"Good heavens, what an accolade! And what is happening about that ill-integrated wretch, our persecutor? Oh, dear. I shouldn't be so mean. Is there any news of Mr. Michaelson?"

She had honestly forgotten, pushing the knowledge aside in the busyness of preparing for Petey's homecoming. Now she looked at three curious faces and took a deep breath. Val had said it would be on the news. "He's dead."

Petey, eyes round, said, "Wow!" Buck put both hands over his mouth in a speak-no-evil gesture. Billy looked more weary, more worried.

"Well, I spent an hour at the station yesterday," he said softly. "Today I'll probably get to try for two. They still figure Thursday night?"

"I think so."

He sighed, shoulders sagging. "I was here most of the day and all night. But Buck was usually asleep; he did take his drugs at first. And the hospital people were too busy to pay much attention. They can't swear I didn't leave."

"One thing the police are considering," said Charlotte slowly, hoping she wasn't violating a confidence, "is that this might all be part of a pattern, with the man who was killed and the one who's missing. Michaelson might have picked up a prostitute who tried to rob him, and he resisted."

"A prostitute? A woman?" asked Buck.

"Well . . . Yes, I'm sure that was the idea."

"Well, it's a very silly idea. Hal Michaelson wouldn't have gone looking for a woman. Hal Michaelson was gay as a goose."

Charlotte looked from Buck's flushed and righteous face to Billy, who shrugged and spread his hands. "Can't prove it by me, I never know who's what. Buck says I've got no antennae."

"True," said Buck, "but mine are very good. And although he didn't make a pass at me, I'd bet my share of the Bluejay that Hal Michaelson was gay."

"I'd better call Val," said Charlotte.

The pathologist's preliminary report stated that Harold Michaelson had died as a result of knife wounds to the abdomen, at least one of which had penetrated the heart. For the rest, although the body hadn't suffered much from decay or fish, there had been some battering against coastal rocks; this made it difficult to say whether or to what extent Michaelson had resisted his killer. The pathologist thought that broken bones in the right hand could have been the result of a fight. Given the fact that Michaelson was known to have eaten a meal around eight Thursday evening, the condition of stomach contents indicated that he had died between midnight and 2 A.M.

Chief Vince Gutierrez, his demeanor as pressed and tidy as his uniform, dealt with the press and the mayor and, in several telephone calls, with Cynthia Leino, who was shocked and saddened and unable to decide just when, if at all, she would come to Port Silva. "She may send her son, John," Gutierrez remarked to Val when the younger man came in to restoke his chief's empty coffeepot. "Because Michaelson Senior is in bad shape and she's reluctant to leave him."

"Did she know young Michaelson was gay?"

"She says they'd never discussed it. It was clear to me that she wasn't surprised by the idea; but she says Howard Michaelson has always made a big deal about hating 'queers,' and Hal was terrified of his old man." Gutierrez stretched his neck and gave a two-fingered tug against the knot of his tie. "So what's happening out there? Anybody finding out anything useful?"

"Not that I know of," said Val. Captain Svoboda and Ray Chang were slowly and thoroughly questioning again the people who had been questioned yesterday. "Billy Kaplan says he was at the hospital all night, Harry Duarte says he was on his boat; the old man at the Hall, Cooney, says he slept that night in the downstairs office because the storm was keeping all the kids up. No real witnesses to any of this."

"Right."

"Four people who were camping in Finn Park, couple of rough-looking guys and two young women, had a face-off with Michaelson last week. They've taken off, even though they were told to stay in town. But it turns out they slept in the Hall Thursday night, because the storm wiped out their tent. We're trying to verify exact times."

"What about Martin Lindberg? Chang says Lindberg knew Michaelson, visited him at Tidepools at least once, might have set the fire at Michaelson's instructions."

"We're still looking for Lindberg." The hum of voices and movement outside suddenly swelled to shouts and scuffling. Val and Gutierrez hurried to the door, and saw a melee pitting Johnny Hebert and three uniforms including Alma Linhares against Sarah Stonemountain and her son, Rob Steinberg.

"I demand to see my daughter!" Sarah pulled free of Alma's grip and slammed the heels of her hands against Johnny's chest, rocking him several steps back. Rob, eyes white-rimmed, made only a token effort to push past the uniformed arm braced before him; and Val noted that the other Stonemountain girl was pressing herself tight against the wall, well out of everybody's way.

"Knock it off!" roared Gutierrez. Cops snapped to attention but held their ground; Sarah swung around with her mouth open, and closed it.

"You punch a cop again, Ms. Stonemountain," said Gutierrez through his teeth, "and you'll find yourself in the other holding cell."

"You have no right to keep me from my daughter!"

"Your daughter has been arrested. She'll go to Ukiah tomorrow for arraignment. She has had her lawyer with her while being questioned. She is of legal age, which means you have no special privileges in her connection."

"Have you found a body? Any real evidence that a crime has been committed? I told you yesterday, we'll bring the biggest wrongful arrest suit . . ." Right before their eyes she took her fury in hand and tamed it: lifted her shoulders and let them fall, gulped a deep breath through her mouth and expelled it through her nose, closed her wild yellow eyes in a slow blink. Unclenched her fists and dropped them to her sides.

"Chief Gutierrez, I beg your pardon." She was breathing like a runner, but her tone was polite. "I would appreciate a few minutes of your time; please let me hear what charges you've decided to bring against Julie, and for what reasons."

"Port Silva has people missing, Ms. Stonemountain, and people dead. So I don't have a lot of time to spare. Officer Linhares, will you come along, please?" He waved the two women ahead of him toward his office.

"Holy shit," said Val."

"Yes indeed." Johnny Hebert's face was unusually sober.

"Is Julie still not talking?"

"She's telling us nothing, not her boyfriend's name, not where she went skiing or with whom. Just sits there and smolders, as if she'd kill me and crunch my bones given half a chance. You want to know the truth, I'll be glad to get her out of here."

Morning already, the light was gray and she could hear rain. And the wind was blowing something against the house ...

Charlotte lifted her head and stared blearily at her clock: nine-fifteen? Or a quarter of three? She had ... she had come home with Petey. Had a talk with him about R.I.P. Fed him, of course. Then they both lay down for naps.

So it was afternoon, and raining, and somebody was pounding on the front door. She struggled from prone to sitting, got her feet on the floor and stumbled down the hall. Tall figure beyond the curtain there, bending to peer in. Val? She knew it wasn't as soon his name surfaced in her mind; saw the lock was vertical, she hadn't turned it. Reached to do that but too slowly, and the flung-open door knocked her back.

"Where is she? Goddammit, where's Annie?" Wet yellow hair stringing over his face, mismatched eyes glaring, Jesse grabbed Charlotte's shoulders and shook her so hard her mind went fuzzy.

"I can't find Annie, what did you *do* with Annie?" He tossed her out of the way, to the hall bench hard and slippery and she slid helplessly to the floor. He loomed over her like a giant, raging scarecrow, then swung around and set off at a lope through the music room and toward the kitchen. "Annie? Annieeee!"

George, it was George's barking that was hurting her ears; on her hands and knees now she saw him leap with a snarl and get kicked aside. He gathered himself up and Charlotte did, too, to follow pounding feet and angry shouts through the kitchen, into the hall and Petey's room.

"She's not here, I don't know where . . . Ooof!" A back-sweeping arm knocked Charlotte flat once more as she tried to run past Jesse to reach her son. Petey, up on one elbow and staring, yelled something and rolled to his feet, swinging a crutch that Jesse snatched, brandished, and dropped after a look around the room.

"Hey you son of a . . . !" As Petey found his other crutch, Jesse knocked the dog aside once again, turned and stumbled out of the room.

"Petey, wait!" Charlotte, no breath left for another command, simply grabbed the dog's collar and held on. There was a shred of denim in George's teeth, bloody denim. "He's going, let him go," she gasped, to both of them. She heard her bedroom door, a roar of disappointment, running footsteaps but going away. Then the sound of the front door.

"Mom? He hit you!" Petey's voice squeaked high with fury. "I'll kill that son of a bitch bastard!"

"Hush." Charlotte pushed herself to hands and knees and let her head hang. "He's lost Annie. He's trying to find her." Deep breath, bringing the discovery that her chest hurt. "He didn't hit me, he just . . . pushed me out of the way." Didn't hurt a lot, nothing broken. "I think George bit him."

She heard the dog's tail thump, heard Petey get at least one crutch going, thud scrape thud. She'd get up herself, in a minute.

"Where's my telephone? I'm gonna call Val right now."

"Whoo. No." She rolled back onto her bottom, crossed her legs in front of her and gripped her knees. Tipped her head back.

"Let's not call. He wasn't trying to hurt us. If he's arrested, Annie might hear about it and feel sorry. And come back to him."

Chapter
Twenty-eight

H awks, Gardner, Boylan, Michaelson. Cross off the gay
Michaelson, you still had Hawks Gardner Boylan. Except
that the look on Johnny Hebert's face as he came through the
door suggested that this was not going to be a good Monday
morning for the Stonemountain clan. Who, whatever they might
have done to Boylan, sure as hell hadn't been out rolling and
knifing guys in bars. Hawks, Gardner?

"So what's up, John," asked Val, pushing his doodles aside.
"Aren't you taking Julie to Ukiah today?"

"Not leaving until noon," said Hebert with a shrug. "We're
going in this little caravan, lawyer and Mama determined to
keep a close watch on everybody's civil rights. But we'll go with
a few new bits of interesting information."

Val simply looked at him, waiting.

"Item. We conducted another intensive canvas of the wharf
and the nearby neighborhood, asking people about maybe seeing
a yellow Volks the night of Saturday, February third; and we
got lucky with a man who lives near the top of Wharf Road. He
came out about twelve forty-five that night to look for his cat,
and saw just such a vehicle go by, right on the back bumper of
a small, dark-colored car that could have been a Ford or
Mercury. They came up from the wharf, turned left onto Main.
One person in each vehicle, to the casual glance at least. Each
one large, probably long-haired, couldn't say whether male or
female."

"He's sure it was February third?"

"Absolutely, because he found the cat the next morning; it had been killed by raccoons or something, a circumstance that left a definite marker on his mental calendar. The lights are good there; people who plan to commit crimes shouldn't drive bright yellow cars.

"Item. An elderly woman who lives on the street where Boylan's Taurus was found saw a light-colored van drive by about 1 A.M. that same night. She *thinks* it was a Toyota, because her son-in-law drives one.

"And item. Julie Stonemountain worked last summer in the office of the real estate company that handles a lot of rental properties, including the one where we found the Ford. She filled in there again in January, while the secretary was out of town."

"Whoo-eee!" said Alma Linhares, who had come in at the start of Johnny's recital.

"Good work, Johnny," said Val. He couldn't think what else to say, and decided that he felt a little sad. Even though she was a self-righteous, overbearing woman, he hadn't really believed Sarah Stonemountain would commit murder, or prod her family to commit murder, for her cause. Which was, to his discomfort, his cause as well. "Shit," he muttered.

Alma looked astounded, but Johnny nodded, his face somber. "That's the trouble with the hunt," he said. "After the excitement is over, what you've got is a dead animal."

And a roomful of paper, Val thought, looking at the sheaf Alma had just laid on the desk. Technical data on Michaelson's Jaguar, it looked like.

Alma caught the direction of his glance. "The Jag was a mess. Lots of prints, most of them just smears of blood or mud. We were able to identify some as Michaelson's. Then we got a partial palm and a couple of not too bad individual fingers, might match somebody somewhere, we ever come across that somebody. The blood was A-positive, same as Michaelson's."

And that was about the only positive element in the Michaelson case, so far as Val had heard. Lots of motives and suspects, no solid alibis, no hard evidence. "So what's happening?" he asked. "Did Mrs. Leino decide to come to identify the body?"

"Don't you read your local paper, Kuisma?" Alma tossed him Monday's *Sentinel*. "Right there on page one; survivor of old Port Silva family comes home today in sad circumstances."

Val shook the paper flat and looked at the front page. "The delivery boy missed me today for some reason. Says here that Cynthia Leino arrives in Port Silva at 11 A.M. and plans to stay at Tidepools Lodge. I wish we had more to give her on this. Charlotte says she and Michaelson were close as mother and son. Uh, has anything turned up on Lindberg?"

Alma shook her head. "Chang says he's not in Long Beach, his agent hasn't seen him, his car hasn't been spotted. Oh, the reports on the muggings up north are in that stack, from the sheriff."

This was no longer the business of the Port Silva police department, now that Boylan and Michaelson had been removed from the list of victims. Val decided to give the material a quick scan anyway, and was nearly through the interview with the second mugged man when a familiar voice called, "Kuisma!"

Everybody came upright and alert as Vince Gutierrez stepped into the room.

"Yessir."

"Mrs. Leino is arriving early. Go dust off your Jeep, and pick me up out front in fifteen minutes."

Charlotte pulled up before the school building and waited while Petey maneuvered himself, his backpack, and his crutches out of the car. "See you at three-ten, Mom," he said. "You be careful and keep the doors locked."

"I will." She watched him move with efficient speed along the walk and then up the shallow steps. It was only the chance to show off his new skill, Charlotte thought, that had finally won him back to school. What he'd really wanted to do was stay home to watch over her. Something, Jesse's rampage or maybe something Annie herself had said or done to him, had put distance between Petey and the girl; and he'd transferred his protective impulses to his mother. Poor Petey had somehow managed to inherit all the worrier genes so firmly recessive in herself and Martin.

She drove along the curving driveway and onto the street, wincing at the jolt of the traffic bump there. Getting tossed around by a large angry man had left her miserably sore; perhaps she should work out at a gym or something, get into better condition. Perhaps she should simply make sure nothing like that happened to her again.

The sky above Finn Lane was a tumble of yellowy-gray clouds, a bitter wind moving them smartly along. Charlotte waved to Jennifer Mardian, who had a bag of groceries in one arm and a bundled-up Cybelle at the end of the other. On the way up her front steps she waved also to Joe James, who stood on his porch watching for action. Nice people, good neighbors; not today, please.

The house was warm and too quiet; each time she came into a room she expected to see not Jesse but Annie. If Petey had succeeded in banishing that sad angry young woman from his thoughts, she hadn't, not yet. She put on water for coffee, and just as the kettle boiled the telephone rang. Charlotte knew exactly who it was at the other end: Shirley Birnbaum. She could feel the energy from clear across the room, and thought one minute of it undiluted would zap her stiff and dry, like a bug.

She ignored the telephone, made a thermos of coffee rather than a cup, collected the newspaper and a paperback mystery novel from the coffee table. "Come on," she said to George, also subdued and watchful today. "We'll go down to Val's place."

On the front page of the *Sentinel*, there was a picture of Cynthia Leino flanked by her two sons. The story beneath the picture gave a brief history of the old Finnish commune and mentioned the Leino family's prominence in that era.

Cynthia looked older than in the picture Shirley had sent,

and weary; John was plumper of face, with more forehead showing. Brad looked almost the same: same wild curly hair, same
challenging stare, no grin but you could feel one lurking. That
troublemaker's face had not been recognized by anyone
Charlotte had showed it to, so probably Brad had not been in
Port Silva recently making mischief.

Cynthia Leino, in what must have been a telephone interview,
had given the small-town reporter a plateful of platitudes. Her
husband had always treasured his ethnic heritage, and she
hoped their sons would, too. Plans for development of Finn Lane
and Finn Park had been tentative, and were now indefinitely postponed. She did not hold Port Silva responsible for the death of
her friend and attorney; crime was rampant everywhere these
days.

Cynthia was coming today, to claim the body of Harold
Michaelson. While here she would stay at the Tidepools Lodge.
Perhaps she would pay a sentimental visit to her husband's old
home on Finn Lane.

Don't do that, Cynthia; it will just stir people up. Charlotte
poured another cup of coffee, noted that the wall heater was
warming the place nicely, and curled herself back into Val's big
platform rocker. Under the aroma of coffee, the room smelled
sweetly of wood; there was a kind of rack in one corner, pieces
of wood laid flat with smaller pieces separating them. Drying,
she supposed, in preparation for being worked.

A tapping at the door so startled her that she spilled coffee
on her shirt. After a moment whoever it was moved to peer in
the high window next to the door; not a large or tall person,
certainly not Jesse. Annie? Charlotte considered ignoring the
summons, but realized she was spotlighted here under the reading lamp like a character on a stage.

"Just a minute." She straightened her stiff limbs and went to
open the door, to find that her caller was Bonnie Kuisma, the
youngest and according to Val the brightest of his family.

"Hi, Charlotte." Bonnie shook back a silky fall of straight
dark brown hair and grinned. "Hi, George, you look happy.

Charlotte, Mom made this big pot of Portuguese stew . . . really great stuff, has cinnamon in it . . . and sent some to her baby boy, who loves it."

"Just bring it in and put it in the fridge, Bonnie." Any attempt to explain her presence here would make too much of the matter, Charlotte decided, and retreated to the big rocker and her coffee.

"Then I was going to leave a note for my brother to warn him." The girl closed the refrigerator and turned to face Charlotte, "But maybe I can just tell you. All this 'Port Silva disappearances' stuff has the town full of newspaper people. And one of them is Rosemary O'Rourke, I saw her yesterday."

"Rosemary . . ." It was a name she thought she'd heard, from Val.

"Right, that he lived with for a while last year. She'll probably try to jerk him around again, for a story or just for fun. Would you tell him she's in town? And if she comes while you're here, remind her that Val Kuisma has five crazy sisters ready to tear her to shreds. Okay?"

"Okay."

"Hey, aren't these the people trying to sell Finn Hall?" Bonnie picked up the newspaper from the table beside the rocker.

"Apparently they've postponed the idea."

"That's good. Leino, huh? Well, the big guy at least is a Finn. He looks like me when I had my perm." She patted her smooth, shining hair. "Oops, gotta go, or I'll be late for calculus."

Charlotte's phone rang several times, sounding distant and unimportant from down here. Val's rang, and she nearly answered, then decided that she wasn't here, wasn't responsible, and didn't want to talk to any old girlfriends. Finally George planted himself beside her chair and sat there silently until she looked up to meet his fixed and pleading stare.

"Oh, all right." She let him out into the backyard, then pulled her sweater closer around her shoulders and followed. There would be no sunshine at all today, it seemed. From the middle of the yard she turned to look at her house, Petey's house, which was now safe, and then at the house next door, the original Leino house. Cynthia Leino, if she came here, would find the family home looking very shabby.

Was there a light in the Leino house? Frank, Dr. Frank Scully of the UC-Port Silva English department, was in Berkeley this semester but sometimes came home for a day or two. Unless he'd seen this morning's paper, he wouldn't know that his landlady was in town and might come calling.

Frank's spare key hung on a hook in her back hall along with her own house and apartment spares. If he *wasn't* there, perhaps she should get the key, go in and make sure things were reasonably neat. She climbed rickety back stairs, peered through the glass, saw a light burning toward the front of the house but no one in view. She rapped on the door, pressed down on the old-fashioned handle and found it unlocked.

"Frank? It's Charlotte Birdsong."

"Come on in."

She was inside the door before she registered the voice: not Frank's, a woman's.

"It's okay, Charlotte."

She stepped through the door, squinting at the slim figure lit from behind. "Annie? What are you doing here?"

Annie moved quickly past Charlotte to close the door. "I thought this would be a good place to crash, keep out of Jesse's way."

The house smelled dusty and a bit dank, as if the roof had been leaking for some time and rot was well established. There were plates and several dirty glasses on the old tile sinkboard.

"Annie, you shouldn't . . . Dr. Scully is away, but some people might be coming here, today or tomorrow. People who own this house." On the kitchen table she saw an open milk carton, a box of Ritz crackers, and a jar of peanut butter. A newspaper. And a key on a long leather thong, its identifying tag marked in Charlotte's precise black script.

She put out a hand and found the light switch; Annie blinked but didn't turn away. Still darkly bruised, her face was no longer much misshapen by swelling. Something about the set of the eyes, the cheekbones, jolted Charlotte's memory. The mouth, scabbed-over split lip twisting what would otherwise have been a defiant, go-to-hell . . . And the smooth hair, what had Bonnie Kuisma said about a perm?

"Who *are* you?" Charlotte asked in a whisper.

"I'm Annabel Leino. Or I was, before I got killed."

Chapter
Twenty-nine

C ynthia Leino had a trim, tight thirty-five-year-old body and a face that might have matched it not long ago but now looked at least her age, somewhere around fifty. She moved well, kept her head up and her gaze direct; but her extended hand trembled just slightly, and there was the faintest of flutters in her low voice. Val thought Mrs. Leino was full of sorrow.

"My older son is on the partnership track in his law firm," she said in response to Gutierrez's question. "He finds it difficult to get away. And Brad, the younger, is simply too—sensitive to be useful at a time like this. Hal was always the person I could count on when something troublesome came up; he and I were the tough ones."

At the hospital she was tough. Gutierrez kept a hand at her elbow as she viewed Hal Michaelson's battered face, but she simply looked for a long moment, blinked rapidly and turned away.

At the police station she was clearly on edge. Gutierrez, taking her into his office, signaled Val to come along; and Mrs. Leino listened carefully as the chief explained what little they knew for sure about the death of Harold Michaelson.

"So what you're telling me is that you have no idea who killed him."

"No firm idea as yet."

"And this business in the press about serial crimes against men, is that just to sell papers?"

"Not entirely, but Mr. Michaelson's probable homosexuality seems to take him out of that particular chain."

"Could Hal have picked up a . . . a male prostitute?"

"We've had no reports of male prostitutes working the wharf area where he was apparently killed."

"But he was robbed?"

Gutierrez spread his hands. "His money clip was empty; he still had his Rolex."

She shuddered. "I'm sorry. Hal was such a . . . he could be abrasive, wasn't really good with people. I keep thinking that maybe he dealt high-handedly with someone who turned out to be unbalanced. Like those people in the park, he said they were derelicts. Couldn't he have made one of them angry enough to kill him?"

Gutierrez sat behind his desk, back straight and hands clasped on the blotter. Mrs. Leino, wiping her eyes with care for her makeup, would not have seen his expression sharpen. "Mrs. Leino." His voice was slow, and deeper than usual. "Do you personally know of anyone Harold Michaelson might have made angry enough to want to kill him?"

She jerked back in her chair, dropped her purse and looked up at Val and waited, accepted it from him with a nod and a whispered, "Thank you." Drew a deep breath and looked at Gutierrez and looked away quickly. "Of course not. But I feel I'm responsible. He wanted to help me and so I let him, but he was the wrong person to send up here. It's my fault."

"Mrs. Leino . . ."

"And that's just something I'll have to learn to live with," she said, standing up. "Now, if I could have someone call me a cab?"

Gutierrez, knowing defeat when it stared him right in the eye, came around the desk. "Officer Kuisma will be happy to drive you to Tidepools, or to Finn Lane."

"I'll be staying at River's End; either your local reporter is in the pay of the people at Tidepools Lodge, or he simply wanted to make me appear dramatically sentimental. Thank you, I'd appreciate it."

"We'll be in touch with you there if we have anything to report," Gutierrez intoned.

As Mrs. Leino paused to shake Gutierrez's hand, Val stepped into the hall just in time to see the big outside door at the far end burst open. Adam Boatwright came in at a trot and knocked over a waste bin because he was looking over his shoulder at the shambling, disheveled man being propelled through the door by Bob Englund's firm grip on his arm.

"Hey, everybody!" Boatwright's voice was almost a shout. "Look who we found! Edward Boylan! And he's not dead!"

"I guess it was the light, huh? I needed to read the paper and I didn't think it would show through the curtains. Turn this one off, Charlotte. Please."

Annie—Annabel—wore her usual jeans, tee-shirt, and chambray shirt, with a down vest. Her arms hung at her sides, and dangling from the end of the right one like an extended hand was a gun. Pistol, revolver, Charlotte wasn't sure of the proper term; but it was large and dark, and appeared to be heavy.

Not too heavy, though. Annie sighed and lifted her arm, to level the short barrel at Charlotte. "Come on, Charlotte, I don't want to hurt you. I like you."

Demotion: last night it was love. But the girl had no reason *not* to like her, and didn't look frantic right now, just serious. Charlotte reached slowly to the switch on the wall and pushed it. "What killed you?"

"A car crash, and another girl. Her name was Mady, for Madeleine. Like in that kid's book, she always brought that up. Let's go in the other room, so we can watch out the front." She gestured with the gun, then stood aside to let Charlotte pass. "Turn off the light in there, too; then open the curtains enough so we can see out."

Dusty long curtains on rings; Charlotte reached high and pushed one panel back to about the halfway point. She turned and did the same with the second panel, and saw a police car leaving the Lane, already too far away for the driver to see her even if he should look up. At home this was the music room; here it was still a dining room, with a heavy old carved table and four chairs with threadbare fabric seats. When Annie gave no further instructions, Charlotte slid one of the chairs out from the table and sat down. "What happened to Mady?"

"She went to Mexico with a guy; her sister got a postcard. Half-sister."

"And everybody believed that?"

Annie grinned. "Damn right. Everybody knew Mady was hot for Mex dudes. There was this one on the maintenance crew, she was always sneaking off into the bushes with him. Guy didn't even speak any English, but Mady said he had an 'eloquent dick.' She'd been to some very fancy schools before White Oaks. What's happening outside?"

"The police car that was at the Hall just left. I didn't see anyone in the back seat." White Oaks: she thought that was a very exclusive private school near San Diego, a last resort for rich kids who were on the edge of being declared ungovernable. "So you and Mady were running away from school and had—an accident."

"Mady did," said Annie quickly. "She was a rotten driver. The first time, we were hitching and we got this old couple to stop for us. The guy got out, to open the back door I guess, and we jumped in and pushed the old lady out. Mady got the gears wrong and ran over her."

Charlotte made a small sound, and Annie shook her head hard, her hair flying. "I wanted to stop, but Mady wouldn't. Then two days later she was driving again, and that's when she totaled the car and broke her stupid neck."

Annie had let the gun drop to her side once again; but she was not relaxed, only slightly less intent. And she was young and very quick, while Charlotte was stiff, sore, and slow at the best of times. "What did you do?" she asked.

"I took my Navajo ring, and my belt with the Zuñi buckle, and my watch with the turquoise and silver bracelet band. I really liked that stuff, too. I put it all on Mady, we were exactly the same size and build and we both had perfect teeth, wasn't that lucky? And I set fire to the car. What time is it?"

Charlotte yanked her mind back to the present and tilted her wrist to catch the gray light from the window. "Almost eleven-thirty." Where, she wondered, had Annie obtained the gun? And for what?

"She was supposed to get to Port Silva at eleven. Then she'd talk to the cops, and go look at old Hal. Do you think she'll come here next?"

Oh dear lord. "Who?"

"Don't pretend to be stupid, Charlotte," Annie said in a calm voice that Charlotte found very frightening, a voice for talking to a very small child, or a dog.

"If you mean Mrs. Leino, I don't think she will. I know that's what it said in the *Sentinel*," she said quickly as Annie's head came up, "but I think it was just nice noise for the local folks. Why would she come here?"

"Maybe for her guilty conscience," muttered Annie. "Do you know where Tidepools Lodge is?"

"Yes. But they're very watchful there, Annie." Perhaps, she told herself, the gun was for protection, against Jesse or . . . whoever. "Annie, if you want to see your mother, I could go make arrangements for you. And whatever happened with you and Mady what, five years ago? six? Surely that can be . . ."

"Forgotten? Explained? Sure, Charlotte, probably could. But what about what happened Thursday night, to ol' Hal the Prince of Pricks? How do you suppose we'll explain that? What time is it now?"

"Eleven forty-two." Charlotte, her sore body beginning to stiffen, shifted position and found herself looking at the barrel of the gun again.

"Don't try anything, Charlotte. My mother is a rotten person who hated her own kids and cheated on her husband; she turned him into a drunk and she killed him. Besides, you owe me. Pete wanted to come with us, with Jesse and me and Bo and Tif when we left town. And I told him he couldn't."

"Thank you," said Charlotte in a voice that scratched her throat.

"You're welcome. You ought to watch him better, see he doesn't get mixed up with people like us. Tidepools is on the coast, I guess, with a name like that?"

"Yes."

"Then there must be a way to get to it besides through the front gate. I wonder what room she'll be in. Go call them and ask," she ordered suddenly.

"I think Dr. Scully had the telephone here disconnected."

"Oh. Well, what room did Hal stay in?"

"I don't—in Anemone Cottage, I think it was."

Annie edged past Charlotte and went to look out the window. In the gray light there her face looked stern and dedicated, a warrior's countenance marked with bruises like war paint. Bruises inflicted not by Jesse, but by Hal Michaelson?

"Did your mother . . . was Hal sent here to Port Silva to find you?"

The girl shook her head. "They didn't know I was here; I didn't, like, *plan* to come. I'd only been in this town maybe twice before, when I was really little and we came to visit my grandmother; and I didn't remember that until I saw Finn Hall. No, what happened is, Hal recognized me that afternoon when he ran into Pete; I didn't think he had. That night, when I went down to the wharf to see the storm, he followed me."

"What did he want?"

"He wanted me to leave my mother alone and not write her any more letters." Annie turned so that her back was to the light, her face in shadow. "He'd talked to her, and she told him to offer me ten thousand dollars to go away and never bother them again or they'd turn me in to the cops."

She gave a short laugh and shook her hair back. "I told him that now I'd been here a while, I knew what I really wanted. This house, my grandmother's house. Like Petey."

"Oh my," said Charlotte. She could imagine Hal Michaelson's reaction to this request.

"Yeah. He laughed this snotty laugh he always had, and I hit him. He hit me back, and it went on from there until I got scared; and I had on Jesse's jacket, with his hunting knife in the pocket."

Not a planned outright killing, thought Charlotte; maybe even partly self-defense. "Annie . . ."

Annie had tipped her head back, to look out the window without completely taking her eyes from Charlotte. "It's starting to rain. And there is absolutely nobody out there." She straightened and began to move slowly across the room, gesturing with her head for Charlotte to come along.

"We're going to go get your car, and you'll drive us to Tidepools. We'll find a back way in and then you can show me that cottage; in the rain nobody will notice."

"No, Annie."

"I told you, Charlotte, don't make trouble. I'll let you go afterwards, I promise and I always keep my word. Besides, it won't make any difference to me then. But if you won't take me I'll have to shoot you right here, so you can't call the police or somebody, and then I'll take your car."

Charlotte stood up. Believe it, she instructed her incredulous mind. Believe that she would do it. It would be very painful, and very messy, and then what would happen to Petey?

There was a noise from the back of the house, and then a change in the light, the sound of rain and of toenails on the bare floor as George came prancing in, happy to see his friends, happy to show them he could open doors.

Annie, who had moved past Charlotte quickly, gun-arm extended, shook her head and said, "You dumb mutt, you almost got yourself shot. Come here."

But George skidded to a stop in the doorway, planted his feet and burst into a fusillade of furious barks.

"Stop that! Shut up, you mutt!"

George kept barking, Annie leveled the gun, and Charlotte threw herself on Annie's back. She didn't bring the girl down, but she got her hands around that narrow neck, got her fingers laced hard in front and pulled back with them, trying to press inward with her thumbs and the heels of her hands.

"Stop that! Damn you! Let go!" Annie twisted and thrashed around, tried to hit backward with the gun but Charlotte's head was low between her shoulders. Threw the gun away, reached back to slap, to claw.

Hurt, that hurt. Charlotte dug her head down and in, gulped air, squeezed with her strong hands. Carotid artery there somewhere, she'd learned its location years ago in a first aid class. Flow of blood to brain. With an edge of her attention she knew the dog had stopped barking, was making worried whining noises, no help there.

Annie dug both her hands into thick curly hair and yanked upward; Charlotte's mind blazed white with pain, and she thought her scalp would tear away from her skull. She heard a keening sound, realized it was coming from between her own clenched teeth. Stop it, stop the flow of blood. Stop stop stop stop hang *on*.

Val Kuisma drove as much over the limit as he thought he could get away with, taking a silent Mrs. Leino to River's End Resort. She had registered the name Boylan, had asked a desultory question or two as they set out, then had simply turned to stare out the window.

It definitely was Boylan, Val had seen that much. Longer hair very dirty, face under two weeks' growth of whiskers appearing thinner, even haggard. Where the hell had he been, lost in the woods somewhere? In the rain that had been practically constant since he disappeared?

Val pulled into the resort, a place very similar to Tidepools, and stopped at the office at her request. Unloaded her bags right there, also at her request and very quickly. Said a hurried goodbye, ma'am with a fast polite smile, and went back to the Jeep. Where had Boylan been?

"He was out of town about five miles, on Highway 24." Alma, standing in the back entryway to smoke a cigarette, was clearly dying for information herself. "Englund and Boatwright came by, he was trying to hitch a ride and everybody was whizzing right past him in the rain. Bob said the guy was *not* happy when he found out it was a police car he'd finally got, but he was too worn out to do anything about it."

"Where has he been?"

Alma shook her head. "Wouldn't say a word to the guys, beyond agreeing not real eagerly that he was Edward Boylan. Had on jeans and a wool shirt and a pair of old Redwing hiking boots. And somebody's old down parka. He looked—and smelled—like he hadn't had a bath in about a year. Poor Johnny, I think he wanted to take the guy out quick and shoot him, just to make things come out even. Johnny and the chief are talking to him, Boylan, now, in the chief's office."

It was lunchtime, but Val wasn't willing to leave the station, not until he'd heard the story. He got a candy bar and a bag of peanuts from a machine, a ginger ale from another, and sat at his desk to look over the growing file on Harold Michaelson's death. None of the people questioned and then questioned again had changed his story in any promising or revealing way. Harry Duarte continued to be belligerent and devious; Billy Kaplan was being, for him, cooperative. The people from the tent had not yet been found, and there was still no word on Lindberg.

Val finished his ginger ale, put the file back together, added the information on the Jag. His desk was clear now except for the sheriff's department stuff from the two mugged guys, and he gave these another quick read. Something from one of them had been niggling away in the back of his mind, and he hoped to recognize it when he came across it. That hadn't yet occurred when he heard voices from the chief's end of the hall; and John Hebert came trudging along a moment later.

"Johnny? What's happening?" Alma moved to meet him, looked up into his face and then wrapped her long arms around him in a hug. "Poor baby, there went your case. Now tell us about it."

John Hebert was adroop—eyes, mouth, shoulders, even his

belly. "Edward Boylan has spent the last two weeks in a cabin in the High Sierra. An isolated cabin, in the snow. Kept captive there, naked and shoeless. By large female teenage mutant ninja turtles."

"Bullshit!" said Alma. "Guy's been on a two-week drunk, probably with some bimbo."

"That is certainly what everyone is likely to believe," said Hebert. "In fact, I suspect that in a day or two that's what Mr. Boylan will be saying. May even decide to believe, himself."

"Okay, Johnny." Val stretched out in his chair and crossed his ankles. "Let's hear it all."

Half an hour later Val was still grinning as he climbed into his Jeep. He'd found the nugget of information in the sheriff's report, had made the connection with another nugget stored in his memory, and decided he should ask Charlotte about it. Besides, he could hardly wait to tell her the incredible, unbelievable, fantastic story revealed by Edward Boylan.

"Up north," the woman had said to Bud Hawks, before she or her boyfriend knocked him out. Add to that the Del Norte County guy's contribution: the woman who'd agreed to have sex with him wore an old sweatshirt with a faded insignia: Yakima Junior College Yahoos.

That was what nudged Val's memory. The day they arrested the woman from the Hall for crack, Val had talked to three of the tent people and had given the tent itself a quick search. He hadn't found drugs, but he had turned up a license plate in a holder; all that was left, the man named Bo Zelinski had said, of the truck he'd totaled. It was a Washington state plate, and its holder had read Yakima, home of something-or-other. Junior College Yahoos?

Probably not. Worth checking though, as he'd suggested by phone to the Fort Bragg sheriff's office. Worth running past Charlotte and Petey, who might have heard some reference to Yakima. He'd need to be careful with his questions at first, because they had some regard for the girl named Annie; but this was a longshot. Both the earlier mugging victims had been sure the woman was short, not much more than five feet tall; that pretty much eliminated Annie, who had to be at least five-five. But the other woman, Tiffany Swenson ... Val gained Frontage Road, slowed, swung onto Finn Lane and saw a crowd of people standing out in the rain, in front of the house next door to Charlotte's.

He slewed the Jeep onto the grass, shut the engine off and leaped out. "What's the matter? Where's—let me through, please."

Charlotte sat on the ground, right on the wet grass, in a tight huddle of drawn-up knees, wrapped arms, bent head. Around her but back a small distance from respect or fear or something stood Jennifer Mardian, the Lees, the Cunninghams, several people from the Hall he didn't know by name.

"Charlotte?" He knelt beside her, put an arm across her shoulders.

"That redheaded girl from the tent? She had a gun and was going to shoot Mrs. Birdsong." This from a woman Val didn't know.

Charlotte moved against Val's arm, murmuring something that was obviously protest.

"No. The girl was hiding in Dr. Scully's house," said Jennifer, who had her daughter on her hip. "Charlotte surprised her, and she ... I don't know what she wanted. But Charlotte knocked her out."

"Charlotte did?" He felt a tremor shake her, and tightened his grip.

"She choked the little bitch unconscious," said Joe James. "Sorry, Charlotte. Mr. Kaplan and Eamon Cooney are giving the girl the kiss of life, and I called the paramedics."

"Charlotte, what ... ?" He saw the revolver lying beside her. "Hey, that's my gun."

Charlotte sniffled and then sighed, without looking up. "She saw the keys I keep in the back hall. I guess she got into your apartment. I hate that gun, George hates it."

"Joe," Val said, "would you take my revolver? I'll get it later. Charlotte, please, are you hurt? Are you okay?"

"Oh, I'm okay. My head hurts. My heart hurts."

"What did Annie want from you, Charlotte? Why did she attack you?"

"She didn't attack me. She wanted me to drive her to Tidepools Lodge. She wasn't going to hurt me."

"So what happened?"

"Oh, I attacked her."

"While she had a gun? Jesus, Charlotte! Look, here come the paramedics; they'll be over here taking your pulse and blood pressure if you don't move. Come on, let's get up, let's get in out of the rain. Charlotte?"

She sighed, sniffled, lifted her head. Val stood up and held out a hand; she took it and came stiffly to her feet. Reaching to put an arm around her, he brushed her hair and she yelped in pain.

"What . . . wait, medics?" he called.

"No, don't! It's nothing, just that Annabel pulled my hair."

"Annabel?"

"Annabel Leino."

"My God. Leino."

"She's Annie, and she's a . . . a renegade, she killed Hal Michaelson but it was in a fight. I couldn't let her kill her mother."

Chapter
Thirty

"She's a renegade," said Cynthia Leino bitterly. "I swear to God she was born that way."

"Mm," said Vince Gutierrez, and glanced at Val as the coffeemaker on the side table gave the spitty sigh that meant it had finished its work. Val rose quietly and poured three mugs full while Mrs. Leino went on.

"Rules have never been anything but a challenge to her, and from the beginning danger attracted her the way sweets do normal children. When she was tiny she climbed everything in sight: trellises, balcony railings, the ladder to the high board over the pool. In school she stole from other children, things she didn't need or even want once she had them. When she was ten we learned that she'd been breaking, or at least sneaking, into our neighbors' houses. No, just black, thank you," she said to Val.

"By the time she was thirteen she was involved with sex and with drugs. She was fourteen when she was picked up *selling* drugs. That's when we, or rather I, took her out of her latest private school and put her into White Oaks: very secure, very expensive, and recommended by the court. It was that or a facility run by the juvenile justice department."

"That's the school she ran away from?" asked Gutierrez.

"Which just shows how good the experts are!" she said viciously, and then let her shoulders slump. "Two people died as a result of that escape. We believed the body in the burned-out car was Annabel, because it had on the melted remains of all that authentic and very expensive Indian jewelry she loved. You see how clever she could be? She was a slut and a killer then and she still is, men in bars and now poor Hal."

Gutierrez gave Val a look that said, "You're on," and Val cleared his throat. "Mrs. Leino, your daughter has admitted that she killed Harold Michaelson."

"That's Annabel for you," said her mother. " 'Sure I did it, and what do you think you can do about it?' without so much as blinking."

"Apparently it wasn't a premeditated killing," Val told her. "They had a physical struggle, her one hundred ten pounds against his one eighty, and she finally used a knife. But Annabel denies any involvement in the muggings and the earlier murder; and in fact there are warrants out for two others in the group, a Tiffany Swenson and a Bo Zelinski. They've committed similar crimes in another state, and the woman is a good match with survivors' descriptions."

Gutierrez spoke, soft-voiced, before the woman could reply. "Mrs. Leino, when did you learn Annabel was alive?"

She spent a moment sipping coffee. "Last December, after years of trying to kill himself with alcohol, my husband decided to take a shortcut with carbon monoxide. The press gave his death, and his past, a great deal of attention; there were even people who thought I'd killed him. Although why I should have waited so long . . ." She shrugged. "He was a sweet, lost man; nobody could save him and nobody, except John himself, would have killed him."

"But his death brought your daughter back."

"Annabel hated me, always. She adored her father, who could no more resist charming any nearby female than he could resist taking a drink. After news of his death appeared in the papers, she wrote me a letter. I was a whore, I was the reason her father drank, I had killed him for his money so I could live with my lover." Mrs. Leino gave a bitter little chuckle. "I'd be hearing from her again."

"And what did you do?"

"Do you know what I decided *not* to do, Chief Gutierrez?" She leaned forward and fixed unblinking eyes on him. "I decided not to spend what was left of my assets either paying Annabel off or paying for whatever crimes she had committed. I decided to sell everything I owned and move with Howard Michaelson to a place he has in Mexico."

"And you asked Hal Michaelson to help you."

"I could hardly involve my own sons, Annabel's brothers." Cynthia Leino shivered, and her mouth drew back in an involuntary grimace. "I'm responsible for Hal's death. But I'm not responsible for what Annabel is. I don't want to see her, and I will not spend one cent on her defense."

"I went to see her, but I don't know whether or not it mattered to her," said Charlotte. She emptied her glass as if to wash away the memory of Annie in a real cage this time, white-faced and shaking and defiant.

Val tossed a quick glance at her and then signaled the barmaid for another round: scotch and water for Alma, beer for Val, white wine for her and John Hebert. All these nice people were used to seeing people in cages, she supposed, but the visit to the Port Silva jail had been a first for her. One she'd probably have to repeat, since it didn't appear that anyone else was going to. Even Jesse would probably stay clear; he was suspected of having helped Annie dispose of Michaelson's body.

"Her mother won't have anything to do with her," said Val.

"Nor Annie with her mother," Charlotte retorted. Suddenly she remembered Hal Michaelson's wandering thousand dollars and decided to contribute it anonymously to Annie's defense. It was Michaelson, after all, who had pointed out to her that money had no morality.

"There should have been something to do with a kid like that before she went so far off," said Val. "And somebody to do it. Her father couldn't, her mother wouldn't."

"The mother's a bitch but poor dad's just an alcoholic, huh? Bullshit," said Alma.

"Annie was the wrong combination of genes, born the wrong sex into the wrong world," said Charlotte. She could imagine Annie as a boy in some warrior tribe that demanded bravery and stoicism of its youths. Spartans, perhaps, or Plains Indians of two centuries ago. "And probably to the wrong mother, but I can't imagine who would have been the right one."

As the barmaid set fresh drinks around, the other three fell silent. Police training, Charlotte supposed. They were being remarkably free with her, apparently accepting her as Val's good friend and thus a sort of nonsworn member of the group. When she came back to earth from the odd and spacy plane she'd been on since running down the back stairs of the Leino house, she'd probably feel guilty that she couldn't be quite so frank with them, even Val.

"I'll tell you who." John Hebert, said by Val to be a virtual nondrinker, was flushed from the unaccustomed wine, and his blue eyes sparked. "Sarah Stonemountain would have done a fine job. And by God, with that girl and Julie under her command, Sarah could have conquered the world."

"That's interesting," said Charlotte softly. "In fact, it's brilliant. Maybe, if Annie's sentence isn't too long, and if Sarah doesn't go to jail herself . . ."

"Not this time she won't," said Alma, white teeth flashing in a grin. "Though I have to say, she was real worried about Julie there for a while. Probably did her good."

Whatever had happened with Sarah and Julie and Edward Boylan, her three companions were bubbling with it. And she shouldn't ask. Charlotte took a sip of The Bar's chardonnay, which was quite nice, and tried to compose herself. After a moment she looked at Val and found him grinning at her.

"Charlotte Birdsong is the image of the epitome of the soul of discretion," he announced, taking her free hand and wrapping both of his around it. "Even I can't pry information out of her. Go on, John, tell the story; tell what happened to Edward Boylan."

Johnny Hebert glanced around their corner of The Bar, which

was not very busy at 6 P.M. on a Monday evening. "He was brainwashed."

"Kidnapped first," suggested Alma.

"Well, yes. Not that he's using either word. He has a vague memory of being shut up in something he thinks was a car trunk. Then he was transferred into the back of something bigger. This time he was blindfolded, and in restraints of some kind, like a backward coat with the sleeves tied around. Remember, he's still very drunk while this is happening. He has no idea how long it took."

"But he woke up in the wilderness," said Val. "Somewhere high in the Sierra, where there was deep snow on the ground and more falling all the time."

"He was in an isolated cabin," Johnny went on. "Even when it wasn't snowing, he couldn't see another structure from any window. He was mother-naked, nothing but a comforter from the bed that he could wrap around himself when somebody came in. No shoes, just a pair of down booties."

There was a distracting picture: naked goosepimply man, his hairy shanks ending in big puffy down booties. "Who came in?" asked Charlotte.

"People, usually large female people, wearing teenage mutant ninja turtle masks. Came on skis or snowshoes, brought him food and water, wood for his stove. One came to the door with the stuff, the other watched from a distance with a rifle. He said they didn't need the rifle; he tried once to grab the one that came close and got cold-cocked. Some kind of martial arts stuff, he thought."

Johnny paused for a swallow of wine. "The cabin had two rooms, one with a bed and a chemical toilet, the other with a Coleman stove, cupboards, refrigerator, a couch and a table and a couple of chairs. A wood-burning stove kept the place toasty. There was electricity, oddly enough. No radio, no music system, no television, no books or magazines, no paper or pencils. No booze. Just a computer."

"Here's this guy," said Val, "in the forlorn icy wilderness, warm and well fed but with absolutely nothing to do except play computer games. That's what he had, games."

Johnny took over again. "He had a game about designing cities. He had a game about regulating an inhabited planet to mitigate or counteract the damage done by humans. He had a game about designing a planet like earth from scratch, beginning with single-celled organisms. Now I've seen games like these, they're commercially available; but his had been modified. He had to make the environmentally sound choices or everything went blooie, the city or the planet blew up on the screen and the computer turned itself off, no entertainment for at least an hour."

Alma giggled. "Sorry. People shouldn't kidnap people. But God, wouldn't it be neat if something like this could be carried out on a larger scale?"

"The one-at-a-time approach would be inefficient and probably too expensive," said Johnny. "What you'd need would be a big secret facility in the wilderness, so that you could run a lot of people through but keep them mostly separated from one another."

"A training facility; that sounds much nicer than prison," said Charlotte crisply. "Or perhaps you could call it a gulag."

Silence settled over the table, and Charlotte took refuge in her glass of wine. Her ego or soul or something felt more bruised than her head; in running about trying to tell people what to do, she had been instrumental in putting a twenty-year-old girl in jail. Had accumulated secrets she didn't want. Had entered into a conspiracy of silence with Sarah Stonemountain that would keep Petey and his friends from headlines or prosecution, an arrangement for which there was sure to be a price of some sort, some time; Sarah Stonemountain was tough and determined, while she herself was just . . . Birdsong, songbird, lightweight. "So what did they, the turtles, finally do with Boylan?" she asked. "Just let him go?"

Everybody breathed again. "That's where the excitement for them came in," said Johnny. "It's not completely clear from what he says, but I think they left clothes and boots and snowshoes and a map at the cabin door around the middle of last week. Then things kept getting more complicated here in town, the fire and more disappearances and another murder, and Boylan didn't turn up as he was supposed to. Maybe he just decided to be perverse and not do what they obviously intended him to do, or maybe the storm was so bad up there he couldn't get out."

"But by Saturday, the Stonemountains were seriously worried," said Val. "If Boylan somehow, oh, maybe broke a leg in the snow and froze to death, and the evidence connecting Julie with his disappearance held up, they were in deep shit. No wonder Sarah was not cool at the station on Sunday."

"Now one other thing you should know," said Johnny to Charlotte, "is that while Boylan told the chief and me all this voluntarily, he said he would completely deny the story if it ever came out. What actually happened, he spent two weeks shacked up with this woman he'd picked up in a bar. She finally got tired of him and booted him out, he got lost trying to find his way home, and he was too drunk the whole time to remember who she was or where they'd been."

"What do you suppose he'll do now?" asked Charlotte. "I mean, with his business?"

"You mean, will the brainwashing stick?" said Johnny. Alma was shaking her head, Val shrugging. "I think it might. I think he'll be more careful about what kind of developing and building he does. For a while, anyway."

"Speaking of development, what about Finn Lane?" Alma asked Charlotte.

"I'm going to talk to people about getting some kind of historic preservation status for the neighborhood. Nobody except perhaps the O'Malleys bought a house there as an investment; I think quite a few people would agree to forgo windfall profits and keep their homes."

"Make it an ethnic issue," suggested Alma. "Get every stiff-necked Finn in California on the battle line."

And marching in her neighborhood. Charlotte's head was suddenly aching fiercely, and she had to squint to focus her eyes in the smoky dimness of the bar. "I'm sorry," she said, "but I think I need to go home."

Petey didn't want to hear about Annie. "She's a slut," he said flatly. "I bet she went to those motels at the wharf with men that paid her to have sex."

And you wanted her to save herself for you. Charlotte looked at his bony, miserable countenance and considered slapping it. Instead she reached up, took hold of his ears and rocked his head back and forth, not gently. "Stop that, Peter Birdsong," she said, and released him.

As she watched him duck his scarlet face and rub his ears, she wondered whether fierce Annie had ever sold her body. Probably she had, of necessity. Or because it was dangerous? "I don't know whether she did or not," she said to Petey. "But it has nothing to do with you, really. And I think a person might be a prostitute without being a slut."

"I don't see how. And *you* wouldn't, wouldn't let some guy pay you for . . . that."

"Petey, I have money in the bank, a college education, and at least three socially acceptable ways of making a living. I also have a truly terrible headache," she added, and moved with careful steps toward the kitchen cupboard and her aspirin bottle.

"Sure, because Annie pulled your hair and tried to kill you."

"Oh, shut *up!*" she said, but softly; yelling would just make the pain in her head worse. Even the sound of running water was making it worse.

"Well. I don't feel too good, either, but I called Rob Steinberg and told him we'd be bringing the computer back."

The cap of the aspirin bottle was resisting her fingers. "Petey, we will find some other way to try to save the things that need saving, I promise. Something more than just giving money." It wouldn't be nearly as much fun, she was sure, as skulking around playing spy. And getting shot at.

"Yeah. Uh, Mom?"

She turned to squint through her pain at him, and reached out to extinguish the bright overhead light.

"Mom, are you having a sexual relationship with Val?"

That's right; he'd been at the front window a few minutes ago as Val gave her a gentle but thorough kiss, not so much good-bye as see you later.

"Not yet." She tossed three tablets into her mouth and followed them with several swallows of water.

"So you're going to?"

Absolutely. As soon as possible. Maybe as soon as her head stopped hurting. "Probably."

"Oh. Well, at least Val's not a dweeb. But don't you think he's kind of young for you?"

"Not really. Val's a worrier, and worriers age at a much faster rate than other people." The magic of medicine was beginning already; she could open her eyes fully and see her son's knotted brow. "In fact, this should work out very well for you, Petey. If Val worries about me, and he will, then you won't need to. I'm going to go lie down for a while; would you please walk George?"

"Sure. Oh, Mom? Guess what happened?"

"Tell me."

"Harry Duarte blew himself up."

Charlotte moved head, shoulders, and body as a single unit as she turned to face him.

"Joe says he was trying to set fire to his boat, for the insurance. Anyway, it blew him into the water, and he's in the hospital, and the boat burned up. So maybe the cops won't think about Martin any more. I mean, maybe I was wrong and he really didn't set the fire at the Bluejay."

Sensible revision, or wishful thinking? Never mind, it was nice not to have to make another moral decision quite yet. Nice to be a lightweight. "Petey, the most sensible thing for us to do is just wait and see."